HANNAH TATE,

BEYOND REPAIR

HANNAH TATE,
BEYOND REPAIR

LAURA PIPER LEE

UNION
SQUARE
& CO.

NEW YORK

UNION SQUARE & CO.

NEW YORK

ISBN 978-1-4549-4884-1
ISBN 978-1-4549-4885-8 (e-book)

Library of Congress Cataloging-in-Publication Data

Names: Lee, Laura Piper, author.
Title: Hannah Tate, beyond repair / by Laura Piper Lee.
Description: New York : Union Square and Co., 2024. | Summary: "A new mom
 reinvents herself and finds her happily-ever-after in this heart-filled
 romance about family, second chances, and growing into your own skin."—
 Provided by publisher.
Identifiers: LCCN 2022061715 (print) | LCCN 2022061716 (ebook) | ISBN
 9781454948841 (trade paperback) | ISBN 9781454948858 (epub)
Subjects: LCSH: Self-realization in women—Fiction. | BISAC: FICTION /
 Romance / Romantic Comedy | FICTION / Romance / New Adult | LCGFT:
 Romance fiction. | Novels.
Classification: LCC PS3612.E3447 H36 2024 (print) | LCC PS3612.E3447
 (ebook) | DDC 813/.6—dc23/eng/20230519
LC record available at https://lccn.loc.gov/2022061715
LC ebook record available at https://lccn.loc.gov/2022061716

For information about custom editions, special sales, and premium purchases,
please contact specialsales@unionsquareandco.com.

Printed in Canada

2 4 6 8 10 9 7 5 3 1

unionsquareandco.com

Cover design by Jo Obarowski
Interior design by Christine Heun
Emojis: Carboxylase/Shutterstock.com

To Mark,
for helping me build this beautiful life,
and to Leo,
for making it so beautiful

CHAPTER ONE

There's something about new motherhood that makes everything so desperate. Your infant hasn't napped in three hours? Call an ambulance. Daddy brought home the wrong diapers? Get a paternity test. You *lost* your baby's favorite pacifier?! Hope you enjoy the dulcet tones of your shrieking infant, ad infinitum.

Ask me how I know.

I slam onto my knees, then hands, crawling on all fours across the tasteful jute rug in our bedroom. When I decorated with that effortless boho look in mind, I didn't realize how often I'd be crawling across nature's steel wool. One of my heavy, aching breasts pops out of my nursing tank and promptly begins to spritz. Bowie's cries get louder. He's pissed, and my right boob is taking it personally.

"Mommy's coming!" I stuff my boob back in my shirt, but it's like holding back a fire hydrant with an umbrella. Did you know a newborn infant's cries are biologically engineered to increase the mother's cortisol levels by 20,000,000 percent?

The pacifier, the *only* one Bowie tolerates, is nowhere to be found. It's pale blue, has a tiny stuffed hippo attached to it for some fucking reason, and is the bane of my existence. I've bought at least five of them to keep in strategic places around the house, but Bowie has a keen taste for his old spit because no other hippo pacifier will do.

Silly mommy! he seems to bellow as his face turns nearly purple in bassinet. *Don't you know I WILL END YOU?!*

Shit-shit-shit-shit-shit. I should be able to handle this! I'm a disaster comms specialist, for God's sake. I literally handle disasters for a living, and yet losing a pacifier feels worse right now than the time one of my clients got caught using the corporation's charitable children's fund for his own *personal* child support fund.

Bowie's screams intensify. *Did you hear me, woman?*

Lefty joins in now, late to the nipple sprinkler party. I've left a trail of milk splotches across the floor of our bedroom like some kind of weird lactation crime scene. I've tried everything to get Bowie to stop crying this afternoon—diaper change, nap, walk outside, walk inside, a bath—all punctuated with offering one or the other boob every other second, but it's no use. They're like filet mignon the chef can't get right, and Bowie keeps sending 'em back to the kitchen. He only wants Hippo Sucky, which disappeared between night feedings #3 and #4 when Bowie flung it across the room and apparently into another dimension.

The closet door is cracked open a foot, and I army crawl over to it like my life is on the line. Something blue and slimy shimmers within the dark opening of one of Killian's old hiking boots, and I shriek with both disgust *and* joy, a common emotional combo in motherhood. I dump Killian's boot upside down, gagging from the ripe, footy smell. Here's hoping Bowie didn't inherit Daddy's stank-foot.

Bowie's cries turn positively maudlin. He's definitely gonna be a theater kid one day.

Hippo Sucky falls out of the boot in a damp clump. I gaze upon it with dawning horror—the rubber nipple is covered in sock fuzzies and Killian's fungal spores.

I ought to burn it. I ought to sacrifice it to the landfill and apologize to Mother Earth for supporting such a crime against nature. But my child's utter despair makes my shoulders cave.

I can't throw Hippo Sucky out. I'm simply not that strong.

Ooh, the Listerine!

Killian bought a mega bottle for the bathroom, and hey, it kills 99.9 percent of germs, right? Here's hoping that includes fungus, too. I'm about to charge for the door before Bowie does permanent damage to his psyche when I realize something else fell out of the boot, too.

A small, velvet something. A *box* something. Now it's my turn to fling Hippo Sucky across the room as I grab for the box. My heart's beating so hard, I nearly rip the hinges off.

There, nestled in a bed of creamy satin, is an engagement ring. A beautiful, pinkish diamond set in a rose gold band. It's lovely and bespoke—exactly my style. I pluck it out, fingers shaking as I try it on.

It's my size! Well, it *was* my size before my fingers swelled up like those pale mini hot dogs from a can. But when my fingers lose this baby weight, it will *definitely* be my size.

I stare down in disbelief.

Killian's going to propose.

Oh-em-effing-gee, he's *finally going to propose*!

Bowie's still crying, and it yanks me back into the moment. I shove the ring back in the box, return it to the smelly boot, and run for the Listerine.

He's going to propose. He's going to propose. My flustered, sleep-starved brain is stuck on repeat.

After a brief blue dip, Hippo Sucky is offered and accepted, and Bowie finally, *finally* stops crying. I collapse onto the vintage velvet rocker with him in one arm and an emergency bowl of queso in the other. No chips? No problem. I've got a spoon, a frightening intolerance to lactose, and a shaky sense of self-preservation, at best. It's going to be fine.

It's just . . . why would Killian propose *now*?

I shovel a bite of melted cheese into my mouth for thinking purposes. Why wait until *after* we got pregnant by accident, *after* we moved in together, *after* we brought this lovable squish-boy into the world? We're ten weeks into parenthood, and it's not like shit's up to par at the moment. I'm a walking dairy farm, I eat for three, and my pheromones won't be silenced by mere deodorant anymore. My emotions range from intense, passionate joy-sobbing to full-on paranoia and anxiety-Googling. I've never been, shall we say, *competent* at adulting, but motherhood has taken me to a whole new level of chaos. Killian and I haven't even had sex since Bowie was born. My lady parts are all healed up, no thanks to Bowie, aka Mr. 99th Percentile Head Circumference, but sex doesn't even feel like an option on the table.

Bowie's little jaw is working furiously around the pacifier, his brow furrowed over his screwed-shut eyes. I carefully caress the soft skin on his forehead, lightly rubbing where the muscles are still tense.

"That's it, Littleman," I coo as he drifts into sleep. The plump mounds of his cheeks are the pale pink of camellias, and the full, kissable pout of his lips parts a little, grudgingly releasing the pacifier.

God, Bowie's beautiful. Can you be addicted to a face? I feel like I could look at him forever. Despite the harrowing afternoon, I'm awash with all those feelings that make me so grateful I once used this body for sex. Just look at those sumptuous cheeks! Of *course* Killian wants to propose. Bowie has made us a family. How could anyone want anything else in the history of ever?

As I stare at our sweetly sleeping baby in the late-afternoon sunshine whispering through the sheer curtains, all the happiness I should have felt the moment I saw that box starts flowing through my veins. Killian is a total catch, *way* out of my league as some drunker acquaintances have informed me. He's tall-ish, with dark wavy hair, crystalline blue eyes, and a porcelain complexion that somehow never burns. He's basically Prince Eric from *The Little Mermaid*, and I don't want to investigate this too closely, but that *really* does it for me. By day, he's a financial adviser, so basically primo responsible adult, and by night, the guitarist in a local indie rock band that's actually good. I'm not saying that because of the oxytocin pumping through my veins, either. When we met at one of his shows a few years ago . . . wait.

Not a few years ago.

Three years ago. Tomorrow.

I jump in the chair enough that Bowie grumbles and slaps me in the boob. It's our three-year anniversary! *That's* why Killian's proposing now. He wanted to wait until a big relationship milestone to do it, that's all. He doesn't care that we don't have sex or that I look like the former me's long-lost sister who fell down a well and was raised by toads. I sit back with a grin as Bowie finally accepts the filet mignon and sighs happily in his sleep.

Maybe I'm not such a disaster after all.

≋

"Hannah! You guys home?" A deep, masculine voice wakes me from my slumber. A very sexual, sensual voice—the voice of my *future husband*, one Killian James Abbott, to be exact. Amazing how hot long overdue commitment makes a man.

"In here, darling!" I try to whisper, but it comes out like a croak.

Killian walks into the bedroom in his tightly cut suit and gently lowers his leather messenger bag, eyebrows raised in silent question. God bless a man who knows when a hard-won nap is underway. He's only twenty-nine, two years younger than me, but he's looking *all man* right now as he loosens his tie.

I carefully ease Bowie down into his bassinet. For a second, I'm scared I've woken him. His eyes drift open dreamily, and a milk-drunk smile curves across his face. When he sees me, he nuzzles against my palm, and his eyes flutter closed again.

The rush of adoration for Bowie flooding my veins makes me forget Killian even exists for a second. Then he bends over to unlace his shoes, and a stirring down below reminds me. I click on the sound machine.

I tiptoe across the room to Killian, heart thrumming happily, and run my hands across his broad back as he strips off his business attire for the day.

"Hey, you," I try again, and reach up to nip his ear with my mouth.

He startles under my tongue and swats wildly. "What the—oh!" His shoulders relax when he sees my confused face. "Whew. I thought you were a bug." He wipes at his ear.

I blink at him. "Woooow. Wow. That makes me feel—wow."

"Oh, you. Come here." Killian turns and smiles at me, like a magnanimous prince to a hapless scamp, and pulls me into a hug. "You're such a mess, Hannah Tate," he says, which is basically his equivalent of a pet name for me. A pet phrase? A pet sad statement of affairs? His fingers are warm as he brushes my unwashed hair behind my ear. "Got a big night planned, Mama. You free?"

My stomach flips, and I suddenly hope he can't detect any of the queso I just ate. "Tonight? Yeah, absolutely! I can find a sitter."

I most definitely *cannot* find a sitter with this little notice, but I just listened to this podcast on manifesting your dreams, so let's *Make. This. Happen.*

"What did you have in mind for us?" I take his hand and run his fingers slowly over my lips. He used to love this shit. To be fair, I think all guys like to be reminded of the possibility of *Blow Job*. It's their sexual utopia, their Narnia, a nice, wet oasis in the hot, dry desert of life. His fingers taste a bit like car keys, but I try not to make a face.

"Oh, Hannah." The mild interest in his eyes I'd managed to drum up with my unsanitary finger-licking turns to pity. "I have a gig. I was asking whether you're free to watch Bowie on your own tonight."

Aka the one thing every woman wants to hear when she's been stuck at home watching a baby all day. I abruptly drop his hand.

"You didn't say anything about a gig tonight."

He rubs the back of his perfectly coiffed hair and turns away from the shaggy mess that is mine. "It came up last-minute, but it's a great opportunity for the band. We're opening for Fellow Animals at the new Echo Lounge outdoor stage."

"Echo Lounge reopened?" I frown. That place has been closed forever.

"Yeah, six months ago," he says lightly, like it's not weird that my knowledge of Atlanta music venues has evaporated since Bowie was conceived. "I already promised them I'd be there, so . . ."

He trails off, making it clear that this was not a request. More of an FYI, really. When I don't immediately respond, his very essence crumples.

"But . . . I guess I could call and cancel? If you're already busy." He looks like I just asked him to euthanize a baby unicorn. "I guess."

"No, no, don't do that," I say with a sigh. It's not that I don't love being with Bowie. It's more that I don't love being with Bowie in the same house, wearing the same pajamas, moving through the same sequence of feeding-cajoling-napping by myself all day and night. Doesn't Killian understand that? I need to get out of this house.

Out of this *day*.

"Well, I could still try to get a sitter. I'd love to see you play! It's been ages." Though I feel less enthusiastic about it now, I run my hands across his chest. After all, it is my soon-to-be-wifely duty to love him, even when he mistakes me for an insect and treats me like an unpaid nanny. "You know, it's been three years since I first saw you guys play at the Earl . . ."

He tenses beneath my hands. Did I give too much away? Does he know I know something's up? We don't usually celebrate anniversaries. In fact, we've never celebrated our anniversary, come to think of it. I guess it's hard to mark the date in this day and age where relationships meander into existence one casual hookup at a time.

"Three years!" Killian shakes his head and whistles. "Man, what a ride." He pulls off his button-down, and the petty Duchess Downstairs must have a short memory because she's basically hiking up her skirts at the sight of his trim abs and the line of hair running down their middle. "But as much as I'd love to see my favorite groupie out there"—he tweaks my nose—"Bowie has been so fussy lately. Do you really think it's a good idea to leave him with a stranger we don't know? What if they let him cry all night?"

And just like that, I am ready to burn babyhelpers.com to the ground. I don't think he means to do it, but Killian can pull my anxiety out like the winning card, every time. I sink onto the pillow-soft creamy comforter on our bed, which isn't nearly as comforting as I'd like right now.

"You're right." I blow out a breath. "Damn."

He smiles consolingly at me, but it's quickly interrupted when he eyes the bed. "Is that comforter new?"

My cheeks heat on command, like they do every time he questions my decor spending. "*Shh.* I'm nesting."

Killian's eyebrow quirks up. "You've been nesting for a whole year."

I gesture broadly to our now beautiful bedroom with its sophisticated palette of creams and pale terra-cotta, the adorable house beyond that I've freshly painted and styled, and the lush wildflower garden outside I planted last summer. This place is blog-worthy now, and my name's not even on the deed. But what do I get for my efforts at making Killian's house the prettiest on the block? *Tsk-tsks* and pointed remarks about my anemic 401(k). What's even more frustrating is that I do it all on my own dime, but he refuses to acknowledge that.

"What can I say? I want the best nest for our chick." I try to wave his words off like we're joking. The truth is, making our house beautiful is a balm to my soul. Work has been so stressful since, well, forever, and no matter how unattractive I felt when my ankles started to swell and my cheeks inflated, at least I could surround us in beauty. It hurts a little that Killian can't appreciate it.

"Well, it's your life and your money," he says in that dismissive way he always does when he disapproves.

But isn't it our life? And soon, our money?

Killian sighs and heads to the closet—*the closet!!!*—to pull out his hot-guy band uniform. A deep V-neck in a faded navy blue, gold-colored dungarees (he insists they're dungarees, not khakis), and a pair of worn leather boots that magically stay on though he never ties the laces. Not *the boots of stink and commitment!!!* of course, but my deflated heart picks up a little at the sight of him rummaging through his shoes all the same.

So he doesn't get why aesthetics mean so much to me. So what if he's the millennial equivalent of a coupon-cutter? The sexy, responsible father of my child is going to *propose*. Bowie's going to have what I never did—married parents and a stable home. That's worth Killian's nit-picking.

I'm not ready to give up on the idea of a night out so easily, either. Killian clearly wasn't planning on popping the question tonight but seeing the ring box woke something inside of me. Something that's been asleep ever since pregnancy stopped being cute and started being a fucking nuisance. That ring is a shiny reminder that somehow, I haven't completely ruined my chance to be an adult, in an adult relationship, with another adult who I happen to want to do very adult things *to*. The father of my baby, no less.

I hadn't realized until I saw that box that there was still hope for the fairy-tale family life I've always wanted. There were so many times when I thought he'd propose. So many romantic dinners, weekend trips away, hand-holding, looking up at the stars and talking about *our baby*, when Bowie was just a tiny zygote inside of me.

But over time, the fairy tale faded as the stretch marks darkened. Dreamy-eyed wonder was replaced with frantic, fearful research about doulas and breastfeeding and epidurals. Whatever was happening with me and Killian took a back seat to the intensity of new parenthood, and somehow, I forgot about us.

But he *didn't*. Tears mist in my eyes as I watch his fine ass slip into the dungarees, and I'm seized with conviction.

"You know what? Screw it. I'm coming tonight, and so is Bowie. Ten weeks old is a good age to see his first concert, right?" I pace around our bedroom while Killian stares at me like I've lost my mind. "Brody got him those baby headphones for the shower, remember? So we could take him to shows?" I laugh. "I thought that was so stupid at the time. I mean, we needed bottles, but o-*kay*, Brody! But now we can actually put them to use!" I bound over and grab Killian by his V-neck. The soft down of his chest hair peeking out of the top makes me want to rub my face in it.

"Oh, Hannah. I don't know—"

"He should see his daddy up there rocking out." I pull him down for a kiss, a good one, surprising us both. *That's right, baby. There's a sexual goddess beneath this layer of milk and mommy-detritus.* "I'm so proud of you. Bowie will be, too."

In reality, Bowie will be snoozing against my chest, likely with an exposed boob in his mouth. But why ruin the moment with the truth?

Killian's face melts as he thinks it over. "It *would* be pretty cool for Junior to see his old man onstage."

I grin. I knew that'd get him.

"Okay. We go on right at nine." He kisses the top of my head, excited now. "I've got to head out to get our gear loaded up and sound checked. Don't be late!"

He stops by the bassinet where Bowie lies peacefully asleep. With the gentlest touch, he runs his lips over Bowie's forehead with a breath of a kiss. "I love you, Littleman. See you tonight."

Seeing him there, looking at our son like he's the most precious thing in the world, makes my heart more certain than ever. We are a family, and we love each other. It's not just wishful thinking; it's real. We're going to be together forever.

Me, Bowie, Killian, and *that ass*.

CHAPTER TWO

H K M

Tyrannical Infant Support Group

Hannah

I can still be hot. Right?

Kira

What? Of course!!

Mattie

Is this question real?

You're asking two lesbians if you're hot?

Hannah

Absolutely, yes. Could you please speak on behalf of the entire Atlanta gay community? I want to know where I stand.

Mattie

I told you, Kira! Your little bisexual college roomie's trying to swing with us!

Kira

Well, come on! The playground 👏 is 👏 open! We'll raise our babies together, and every day will be brunch day.

Hannah

That . . . sounds really fucking nice. BRB, gonna throw away this engagement ring I found and read some books on poly coupling with your two best friends.

Mattie

I KNEW it!!! Wait. What? A ring?

Hannah

I found an engagement ring hidden in Killian's boot. I think he's going to propose, and I don't want to look like Bowie's drool hag when it happens.

Kira

You WHAT? Whoa!!! That's . . . wow!

Mattie

I believe what Kira's trying to say is,

Fuck that guy. He sucks. But congrats?

Kira

😍 you get me, babe.

Hannah

Excuse me, I came here to get catcalled.
Not dog-lectured.

Mattie

Sorry. You are awesome and beautiful and one THOUSAND
percent better than IRA McPomade deserves.

Hannah

?? You use pomade, Matts!!! I've seen it!!

Mattie

Lies. This Timothée Chalamet with breasts thing I've got going
on is completely natural. And foppish hair aside, Killian is just . . .

Wait. He's just foppish hair.

That's all he's got.

Hannah

Guys. I love him. Could you not?

Kira

. . .

. . .

. . .

Hannah

OMG just spit it out.

Kira

We love you, and we will respectfully stop berating your choice in baby daddies the moment you all make it official. But until then . . . 🐼

Mattie

👻 Don't dooooOOoooOOoo it! 👻

But yeah, you're hot. Smelly, but hot.

Hannah

Sigh.

Kira

Shower if possible and keep us updated. Ooh, and check out these precious pics of June-bug. LOVE YOU!

I scroll through the newest dozen shots of Kira and Mattie's daughter June, who, with her luminous brown skin and hazel eyes, could totally be a baby model, and try not to deflate. Kira is my closest friend. Ever since I walked into my freshman dorm room and found the short Black girl with a pink laptop covered in unicorn stickers singlehandedly rewriting *Pretty Little Liars* one fanfic at a time so that all the Black characters *lived*, thank you very much, we've shared our lives *and* love for salacious TV. Her partner, Mattie, came along later, but quickly earned a spot in my heart all her own. I've tried *so hard* to forge a couples' friendship with us and them, but it always devolves into Killian mansplaining finance to Kira or Mattie cross-examining Killian on his views on women and how they're all wrong. They make each other miserable, which makes *me* miserable.

Staring at my reflection only makes me feel worse. It's way too late in Bowie's nap for me to get a shower in, so I spray my unwashed hair with dry shampoo until it turns a full shade lighter. The old balayage highlights I used to keep in my dark blond hair have long grown out, and I'm not fooling anybody that this is *ombre on purpose* hair. How far I've fallen. I used to melt down my waves with an industrial-grade straightener then artfully curl it back, a process which took *three hours* from shower to finish. I snort, just thinking about having that kind of time again.

Clothes are gonna be more difficult. I haven't worn anything with a waistband since my first trimester. I've dropped most of the baby weight thanks to Bowie's maniacal breastfeeding, which is like having your boobs run a marathon for you every damn day, but that doesn't mean my body's not one hundo percent different. My bones rearranged themselves for Bowie. My rib cage expanded, hips widened, joints loosened, feet flattened—pregnancy was like going Mommy Hulk in slow motion. My body will never go back to the way it was, but I don't feel bad about that. There's a home inside of me, one I built for Bowie all by myself. He's moved out for good, and my abs will one day work again, but this home I created for him will always be there. I hope he feels that every time I hold him close. I know I do.

Ultimately, I yank on my favorite pair of black leggings and grab this giant black shirtdress thing I bought when I still did things like shop for clothes. In theory, it's supposed to drape over you like a hip black shift, if you're skinny. Somehow, the dress knows I'm not, and the effect is not unlike an eight ball.

Still, I can pull out a boob in two seconds flat, so boom. Decision made.

A gurgling noise rises from the ultraexpensive bassinet Bowie barely sleeps in. Then, an angry *meh!* Bowie always wakes up furious, which honestly, most of my generation can relate to.

"Hey, B-B-B-owie! You're awake! Oooh, and you're stinky, too!" I mentally try not to end every single thing I say to Bowie with an exclamation point, but I'm just not there yet. His mouth is pulled down into a comical frown, and he bangs his fists against the mattress as he glares at me, like *And where the fuck were YOU?*

After I change his diaper, we have a few fun minutes of me picking out the hippest baby outfit we have for Bowie's first concert. He's got a lot to live up to with that name, which Killian was dead set on. I can't have him showing up in a onesie with an appliqué dump truck on it; Killian would faint from the sheer lack of cool. I finally settle on a miniature red Adidas tracksuit and a onesie bearing a giant pretzel on it that reads BORN SALTY.

God, dressing babies is fun.

"You look *great*, Bowie! Now, no more poopsies, okay?" I fluff his one lock of hair. It's dark blond and curly, just like mine. It makes me never want to dye mine again.

I strap Bowie into the infant carrier to finish my makeup. We get a bit of a game going. I try to brush powder across my face, he swats it away. By the end, my eyeshadow's streaked across my brows and Bowie's forehead is speckled with blush, so I have to stop and clean up all the red spots so people don't think I'm a very surprised anti-vaxxer. I still manage to do a mean cat eye, though! Bowie smiles at me in the mirror, a big, wet, open-mouthed event, and my heart nearly bursts from my chest. I grab at my phone and try to capture the moment with a selfie, which are the only pictures that ever get taken of me anymore. Alas, not fast enough. Bowie's gummy smile turned into a drooly yawn for posterity, but surprisingly, *I* look pretty good. Hot, even.

I'm weighing whether to post the pic on Instagram since it clearly can't slide in under the culturally accepted guise of *cute baby pic plus see how hot Mommy looks, total coincidence, tee-hee!* when my phone buzzes in my hand. *Fucking Bob* flashes on the screen.

I straight-up hiss. I have two weeks of maternity leave left, but that doesn't matter to my boss, Mr. *Fucking Bob* himself. I let it go to voice mail, like I've been doing for the last two and a half months. *Hannah, answer your phone. This is about that raise you wanted, but you keep ignoring my calls. Guess you don't want it . . .*

The phone promptly starts ringing again. The chance that my sexist boss is actually telling the truth is slim to none. I know this, but I have been passed over for a raise for three years running, and I submitted nothing short of a manifesto to HR on how wrong that is before going out on leave.

"Urghhh!" I snatch up the phone. "Hey, Bob, I'm kind of in the middle of something. It's called maternity leave?" I squeeze the phone between my ear and my shoulder as I try, and fail, to put on mascara. "What's this about my raise?"

Loud static rumbles through the receiver, and I have to yank the phone away from my ear.

"Hannah! Thank GOD you answered, you've been MIA for months! Don't think I haven't noticed." He pauses, presumably so I can feel ashamed for propagating the human species. "We've got a real emergency here. Can you draft up a piece for the ten o'clock news?"

"What? No!"

"Great! Here's the situation," Bob continues, completely unaware I have human agency. "Dorsey Chemical had another *teensy* spill—"

"Oh, God." I cover my eyes with my hand, smudging the new mascara there even more. "Bob, no. NO. I can't work right now! I'm on maternity leave!"

"—only a few dozen injuries or so, really nothing to *fuss* over, but you know the media!" Bob chuckles like the ten o'clock news team is a bunch of puppies and not a pit of cutthroat vipers. You do *not* fuck with Action Tonight at Ten.

"Bob, you've got to find someone else. I can't draft a statement right now. I'm wearing an infant!" Of course, that's not a real excuse, but I'm counting on Bob not to know that. It's already 8:32, and Killian's band is going on soon. "Seriously, Bob. I'm on leave. I only answered because you said this was about my *long* and *painfully overdue* raise. What you're asking me to do is illegal. Did you ask Starla if you could call me?"

Starla is our small PR firm's general counsel. She's paid to sit by Bob and tell him no for eight hours a day. She's unfortunately not on call after five p.m., which is coincidentally when Bob tries his most illegal bullshit.

The line's quiet for just a beat. "Starla's on vacation this week."

Ah. That explains it.

"Besides, disasters happen whether you're making boob juice or not."

Okay, wow.

"And this *is* about your raise. Dorsey Chemical is your client, Hannah, and if they're not around when you finally come back because they fired our firm, you're not going to get a raise because you won't *have a job*! So. When can I expect the statement?"

I breathe deeply through my nose, but it doesn't stop the fury burning through my veins. I cannot believe this is my life. I'd had it all planned out when I was young and perky-breasted. I'd major in interior design, minor in marketing, and after graduation, I'd start my own renovation and interior design business. I'd find a hot contractor to work with, we'd have long, luscious sex on the floors of our remodeling jobs, and basically be the young, hip, liberal versions of Joanna and Chip Gaines from HGTV.

In all of my many fantasies for the future, there were exactly *zero* toxic chemical spills. Yet here I am, and the only thing I get to design is some twisted version of reality where my client is not at fault for spilling cancer-suds everywhere and is in fact a *proud supporter of its local community and committed to ending environmental pollution for all*. This is not what I thought I'd be using my marketing degree for, and every day it gets harder to do.

Being in disaster comms means whitewashing the corporate world's dangerous bullshit again and again and again, until your soul bleeds out of your ears
and you keel over.

Killian says I'm just being dramatic, though.

He insists it's a good job with growth potential, and if I took it more seriously, I could pivot into an *even better* role covering up *even bigger* disasters!
Anything for a 401(k) with employer matching, *amirite?*

Bowie makes a loud, disapproving fart noise, and I couldn't agree more.
But I need this job. As my personal financial adviser, Killian has made that
clear—he does not make enough money to support us all until I can find
a job where my boss doesn't treat me like a toilet seat. For years I've taken
Bob's bullshit, but what else can I do? HGTV hasn't called, and my fledgling
interior design business is just a bunch of ideas jotted out in an abandoned
goal journal I've had since college. I finally hid it under the bed because it
physically pained me to see it.

"Hannah." Bob utters my name like an angry sitcom dad, and something snaps inside of me. Maybe it's the fact I never had a real dad, angry or
otherwise, or maybe it's Bowie's sweet little face, watching me in the mirror,
his worried eyes tracking mine.

I can't let him see me like this.

"I'm not doing it, Bob," I say with a firm, steady voice. "I'll see you in
two weeks when my leave is up."

"You wh-what?!" Bob sputters, and I flinch back instinctively from the
sound of spittle hitting the phone's mouthpiece. "Oh no you won't, missy!
You won't be seeing me or anyone else here because you're . . . *you're fired!*"

The line goes dead, and the arm holding the cell phone dangles to
my side.

Well. *Fuck.*

≈

Anxiety streaks through me, cramps gripping my middle. Now regretting the afternoon's queso most fervently, and yet, wishing for more.

Fuck, fuck, fuck, FUCK.

I force myself to take long, steady breaths in and out and repeat my mantra: *This is not a disaster. This is not a mess. I am not a disaster. I am not a mess.*

I'll call Starla in the morning and tell her what happened, but no, she's on vacation! I'll email her. She'll see it Monday, and she'll fix everything. Bob can't fire me on maternity leave for *taking* maternity leave. It's illegal! I'll be tentatively, theoretically fired for—I mentally count—four days, then she'll make him take it back, and everything will go back to normal.

I collapse onto the bed, trying not to cry.

The thing is, I don't *want* it to go back to normal. Not when normal means I'm stuck in a miserable job doing the devil's work. Fuck! Tears burn in my eyes, but I quickly blink them back and reach for my phone. I start to text Killian, but immediately delete it. It's already 8:45, *shit*. He's about to go on. I can't distract him with my work drama right before his big show. Ugh, we're going to be so late. I've got to pull myself together.

Tyrannical Infant Support Group

Hannah

> Fucking Bob fired me for refusing to work during maternity leave, and I'm freaking out!!!

Kira

> Are you serious?!!

Mattie

On your maternity leave?? I . . .

. . . will murder him.

Kira

That is so illegal! And I'm not even talking about the murder.

Hannah

I know the general counsel will make him rehire me, but I don't know if I want the job back?! Existential crisis!! Occurring! Now!

Mattie

What is your method of choice? Flaying?

Kira

Of course you don't want that job back. It was straight-up abusive, Hannah. And I'm not saying this because I'm an attorney, but you should totally sue his ass!

Mattie

A nice, clean defenestration?

Hannah

Killian's not going to understand. He already thinks I'm an irresponsible train wreck, and now this?! FUCK.

> I also ate way too much queso, 😵 and I do not have time for this!! We're going to be so late!

Mattie

> Hmm. Not so clean for the sidewalk, tho.

Kira

> OK, if Killian is ANYTHING other than supportive, I'm adding him to Mattie's body count. Deep breaths!! Go to the show tonight, have fun. Let's have brunch this weekend and figure this out.

Hannah

> Whew. OK. I love you.

Kira

> Love you, too.

I blow out a gust of air, feeling, if not better exactly, less panicky. I tickle Bowie beneath one of his many chins and even manage a smile. He's so cute curled up against me, like a little snail who forgot its shell, and thankfully oblivious to my internal mayhem. "Ready to see Daddy rock the eff out?"

Bowie gurgles and *blehs!*, which I'm taking as a *hell-effing-yeah, Mom!* Career + queso crisis or no, I'm determined to get out of this damn house and be a loving, supportive girlfriend to Killian tonight. Being cooped up during maternity leave has been the worst part about parenthood so far. Nobody warned me how isolating it is. I heard every other horror story, from blistered nipples to your bladder collapsing on top of your vagina. But the loneliness . . .

I wasn't prepared for that at all. You'd think the fact that I'm never, ever alone would make loneliness impossible, but it doesn't. In the middle of the night when I'm up nursing Bowie for the fourth time, I stare at the dark mass of Killian's sleeping body and try not to cry. Maybe it's unfair, but I wish he could be there *with me*, going through all of Bowie's demands on my body beside me in real time. It'd make it so much less scary when things aren't going well, and so much happier when they are. Bowie's changing every day, but there's nobody to witness these tiny miracles with me. It makes them feel less real, somehow. Like Bowie and I are both missing out on something we need.

So, yeah, I'm going to drag my almost three-month-old infant to a show. I need to feel like Killian and I are living in the same world for one night.

When we finally arrive, no thanks to a cruel 9:15 p.m. traffic jam on I-75 and an epic diaper blowout in the parking lot, the *hell-effing-yeah!* energy has completely disappeared. With Bowie in the infant carrier on my front and his massive diaper bag on my back, I waddle up to buy a ticket like an ornery pack mule. It takes rummaging through one, two, *eight fucking pockets* in the diaper bag to find my wallet while the grumbling line lengthens behind me. Between the July heat and the mortification of being me right now, I am drenched in sweat. Just beyond the ticket desk is the outdoor bar, where taps of beer shimmer before me like a dream. People happily *cheers!* with their cool yellow hefeweizens, laughing and carefree, like a commercial for a life I no longer have.

There! I finally yank my wallet out like it's one of Willy Wonka's Golden Tickets, and the ticket clerk rolls her eyes. I enter the beer line and try to ignore the stares and tittering whispers of younger, childless women who think they know what good parenting is, and that I'm not it.

Killian's voice bounces out of the speakers, and it lures me forward. Thank *God* they're still playing. Maybe he won't notice we're late. It's not hard to get close to the stage. They're the opener, and people are still milling around, waiting for friends, texting furiously, and scoping each other out. Still, a good-sized crowd is paying attention and bobbing their heads along. Killian must be feeling amazing right now, and a little piece of the resentment that lodged in my heart when he told me about the gig crumbles. It really *is* great exposure for them. Fellow Animals is getting big right now, and according to the ticket clerk, I was lucky there were still tickets available.

I position us up front so Killian can see Bowie with his adorably large headphones on, and Bowie can see his daddy. Killian looks so good up there. His dark, wavy hair is mussed and edged with sweat, making it curl softly around his neck and face. The tendons stretch beneath his skin as he sings and strikes the strings of his guitar so passionately that I can't help marveling at him.

This *man*. This beautiful, talented man is mine.

No, I correct myself, as I lift Bowie's little hand and pump it in the air to the music. He's *ours*, and that's even better.

When the song finishes, I wave at Killian like a giddy teenager. Our eyes lock, and the happy, relieved look he always gets when the crowd starts to applaud fades into something else.

Is he . . . annoyed? Or is that disappointment? My stomach clenches again.

But then his eyes land on Bowie, and he lights up like a candle, hotter than ever.

"Hello, Atlanta! We're Jeremiah Was a Nematode, and this is our last song!" The crowd claps and whistles as I try not to visibly wince. Killian's lucky he's fine because that band name is the worst.

"This one goes out to my son, Bowie, love of my life." He points at the baby strapped to my chest with fatherly adoration, and the crowd begins to *awwww!* That is, until they see me, the mommy, a beer in one hand and a boob in the other, trying to get Bowie to latch.

Whew, the judgment! Mommies are always one degree away from becoming total pariahs—one beer, one raised voice, one accidental laugh-pee, and *boom*. Ya judged!

"Alcohol doesn't pass into breast milk," I call out lamely at the horde of hipsters staring. "It's been, uh, proven and stuff."

Killian actually looks pained, but Brody pounds out the opening drum fill of their big rock number, and he turns away to noodle on his guitar opposite the bassist. I always thought that move was so silly, like *Look at me, I know the chords! Doodly doodly doo!*

By the time the song ends, the moon is fully up and shining down on a beautiful, clear Atlanta night. The air's thick and humid like always, but I don't mind. Stepping outside from Atlanta's perpetually over-air-conditioned buildings feels like stepping *into* a greenhouse, where I can finally unfurl and breathe. The beer is cold in my hand, and its bitter bubbles slide down my throat as I trace the skyline's zigzags in the distance. If I ignore the heavy, suspiciously damp weight sleeping on my tit, I can almost pretend I'm having a different life. Young and beautiful—*not* worried about losing a dead-end job working for the forces of evil—just waiting for my exceedingly hot rock star boyfriend who's so responsible, he'll be able to retire by forty-five to come out from backstage and greet me with a kiss. The moment lasts, and lasts, and then my beer's gone and it's *still* lasting.

Where is he? My phone buzzes in my pocket.

Kira

How's the show?

Mattie

Has Hipster-Doodah proposed yet?

I take in a deep breath and type out a quick response:

I bump through a squad of women in ripped black jeans and crop tops. Thanks for bringing *those* back, Forever 21. They're all casually standing around and chatting by the backstage area, stirring their cocktails in plastic cups with tiny straws, or slugging back PBRs in tall, silver cans, but I see them for who they are.

Groupies. Fan girls. Women who, given half the chance, would mount Killian and do some kind of crystal blessing over his forehead before fucking him all night long against their thousand-dollar wicker headboards from Anthropologie.

My eyes narrow.

"Excuse me! Baby mama coming through!" I elbow a little more than I need to, but look, this aggression's gotta go somewhere.

"Killian!" I finally spot him and wave at him again. He's talking to a cluster of college kids, smiling shyly and accepting their praise with an air of bashful humility. One particularly leggy woman is right beside him, long, straight brown hair spilling down her creamy white shoulders and back like a waterfall. She's holding court like she belongs there.

It makes me want to puke.

"Hey, babe!" I rush up and lean around to place a kiss on Killian's cheek, nearly toppling over since bitch-on-the-right won't take a hint and make room. "You guys were so good! Wasn't Daddy so good?" I coo at Bowie, who's looking around like he smells something bad.

"Oh, this must be Bowie!" the woman next to Killian says, reaching a long, thin finger toward Bowie's chin. A flash of white-hot *hell no!* rips through me, and I slap her hand away. She sucks in a tiny gasp, clearly affronted that I don't let strangers caress my baby. So weird, right?

"Sor-ry! He's got a rash." I make my eyes wide. "It's contagious."

The woman laughs a little uncomfortably, then side-eyes Killian. Do they know each other? She can't be older than twenty-five.

"Gotta go, K. Show's about to start. Nice to, um, meet you?" Mystery acquaintance averts her big brown eyes under her lashes, avoiding eye contact with me, then saunters backstage in entirely unpractical platform clogs.

Killian sighs heavily as she leaves.

"Who was that, *K*?" I ask him, more than a little ruffled. He definitely knows her, I can tell. But Killian skips straight over the question, and in fact, me altogether, to kiss Bowie's forehead.

"Did you like your first show, Littleman?" He lifts Bowie out of the carrier without so much as looking at me and tucks him in the crook of his sweaty arm. "Hey, guys! Come meet my son!"

Killian starts for backstage, but I grab his shirt. "Killian, wait. Nobody's smoking back there, right?" He gives me a look, and there it is again—that combination of weariness and disappointment I'd seen onstage. It feels like a shrink ray, as if I'm suddenly three inches high, and my hand falls limply off his arm. "It's bad for the baby," I murmur.

"You almost missed the entire set. I kept looking for you." His voice comes out strained.

"I—" I begin, not sure exactly what I'm going to say. Now is not the right time to come clean about getting fired, but he cuts me off before I can think of anything else.

"I couldn't stop worrying about you two. What if there was an accident? What if you got mugged? What if Bowie was hurt?" He presses his free hand to his temple and squeezes his eyes shut. "It was so distracting, I kept fuck-ing up my parts. This was a big opportunity for me, Hannah, and I spent it freaking out. Why couldn't you be on time for once?"

His words are acid, like it was just Irresponsible Hannah, dawdling around and ruining everything once again, and I step back involuntarily. All my justifications lurch up inside me, and in an instant, I'm back in my grade-school principal's office, trying to *but! but! but!* my way out of detention for chronic tardiness. It wasn't my fault then that I couldn't rouse Mama from bed to take me to school on time, and it's not my fault now that Bob is an asshole and Atlanta traffic is the seventh circle of hell and babies sometimes have exploding shits.

But none of that really matters, does it? Because somehow, I'm always the one who's in trouble.

"I'm—I'm sorry you worried. I tried my best to get here." My eyes sting with tears, and suddenly I feel so stupid. Stupid for trying to have my old life back for one night. Stupid for dressing up only to be smothered by baby gear. Stupid for thinking Killian would want us here at all.

Killian sniffs, clearly mollified that his words hit as intended. "Nobody's smoking back there. I'll just be a minute."

I watch his broad-shouldered back go, holding our baby, without me. For a second, I wonder if that's how he prefers things.

No. I wipe the tears tracking down my cheeks roughly with the back of my hand. *He's going to propose! He loves you. It'll be okay.*

It'll be okay.

CHAPTER THREE

No matter how much sleep I get, the morning always comes too soon. It's such a dick that way. The light filtering in through my gauzy handmade curtains is sunny and cheerful, though, and my tiny hope that Killian will still propose soon makes a small, bleating cry from its deathbed. Tonight is our actual anniversary, but I'm not holding my breath. We didn't talk much last night—just exchanging brief blips of Bowie logistics while we got ready for bed—but he didn't snipe at me anymore, either, so . . . win? I'm going to count that as a win.

I'm the only one awake, which *never* happens, and I grab my cell phone for some quality mindless scrolling before someone changes that. I'm startled to see I've already gotten four texts that morning, all from Mama.

Mama

> Hey hunny! It's your mama! Darryl and I listed the downstairs cabin apartment on Airbnb a month ago, but we don't have any bookings yet. Can you log in for me and see what I did wrong? Love, Mama

3:19 AM

Ahh, that explains it. Mama's a night owl. If she was ever legitimately awake at seven a.m., I'd suspect a hostage situation, or maybe a cult.

Can you check quick, hunny? Maybe I put it on the wrong internet. We need to go to the store, and we won't get our social security checks for another week. Cash money money, y'know what I'm saying? LOL! Love, Mama

3:21 AM

The sigh starts in my toes, building momentum as it groans through me. Is there anything more annoying than having to decipher technology for your elders? I'm barely hanging on myself.

Mama

Come visit!! You can stay in the Airbnb! We got it set up so nice. My login's HotMama69, and my password is BowieIsMyGrandBaby! Love, Mama

P.S. Bring Bowie but leave that boy at home. Got an awful fine neighbor up here. He's a little weird, but it adds to his charm. Love, Mama

3:24 AM

I roll my eyes, but the text still makes me snort. Mama loves Bowie like she made him herself and is so-so about me, but she hates Killian and only ever calls him "that boy." I'm not even surprised she's trying to set me up with her neighbor, but if *she* thinks *he's* weird? Ill tidings for that dude.

The last of Mama's texts is just a picture, which appears to be of a naked man visible through blurry branches. Oh my God, is she spying on the neighbor from the woods?! Squinting, I hurriedly tap on the picture and zoom in. The man's *not* naked, just shirtless, and he seems to be doing . . . yoga, maybe? Not sure, but it's something that involves stretching like a golden god at sunrise on a dock.

Damn, Mama. Thank you for spying on your fine ass neighbor. I hold my phone sideways to get a better view of his arched back.

"What's so interesting?" Killian asks, and I drop the phone on my face in surprise. He's lying on his stomach, his face half buried in the buttery soft linen sheets I got on clearance. He's looking at me cautiously, as if showing me any amount of neutrality might alleviate my shame too soon.

"Just a text from Mama," I rush out, wondering if he saw the picture. "You know how they bought that cabin up in Blue Ridge? They decided to Airbnb out the bottom half for extra cash."

Killian rolls over, bringing the pillow with him. "Seriously? How are they going to manage that? Aren't they total train wrecks?"

I bristle. It's cliché, but only I get to talk that way about my parents. "They're doing just fine. They bought the cabin all by themselves, and it's in a great area for rentals. They need my marketing help with the listing, that's all."

I don't know why I'm defending them, but there's something about the way Killian criticizes my parents that feels like one more strike against me. And that, like blaming me for being late last night, isn't fair.

"Hey. I'm sorry," he says, his voice soft. "I'm sure it's nice."

That surprises me enough to snort again. "I mean, Darryl thinks camouflage is a neutral, so it's probably not *that* nice."

Maybe he's decided to forgive me, or stop being angry at least, because he rolls onto his side and faces me. When he runs his hand down my bare arm, it feels like a truce.

Then, somehow, it feels like *more*.

"About last night, too. I was hype about Bowie being there, like he was going to be my good luck charm. Then when he wasn't, it got in my head, and I couldn't stop worrying about it."

I swallow, the pieces falling together now. Maybe it's something to do with being an investor, but Killian is *deeply* superstitious. He'd never admit it, though. He calls it following his hunch, but he's got a pack of tarot he secretly consults and a pair of lucky underwear with more holes than fabric at this point. It's why it was never a question for him whether we'd keep Bowie and give our relationship a real go. When he gets a sign from the Universe, he doesn't question it. It's cute most of the time, until you break a mirror by accident on the morning of his dentist appointment, and he blames you for needing a root canal. By being late, I'd violated Killian's laws of luck and doomed him, all in one go.

"I get it." I really don't, but I get that this is how he operates, and at least he apologized. "You sounded great, though. Everybody was loving it."

Giving Killian compliments about his band is basically his love language. His fingers trail across my skin, which contracts from the sensation of being touched. The thin fabric of my nursing tank is no match for my ever-erect nursing nipples, but they're so hard from this simple graze, it goes from laughable to obscene. I'm almost nervous to meet his gaze. What if it breaks the spell?

"Brody texted me later—we sold a ton of merch, and our album had about two hundred downloads by midnight."

"Babe, that's great!" I'm only partly talking about the show at this point.

With one finger, he dips under the soft waistband of my sleep shorts, running it along the warm space between the fabric and my lower belly. A fire burns within me, and I finally look at him, willing this not to be an accidental drive-by groping.

He's still lying on his side, but there's a soft flush on his cheeks, and I catch him staring longingly at the press of my full breasts against the struggling rim of my tank top. His eyes drift up to mine, and I suck in a breath.

He's got bedroom eyes, people! This is NOT A DRILL! PREPARE FOR COPULATION!

Killian's hands haven't stopped their campaign tour of caresses, and I keen against his touch. It feels so good. It's been so long. *It. Feels. So. Good.*

"Is—everything okay down there?" he says, and I nearly shush him. If Bowie wakes up right now and ruins this, I'm putting him up for adoption. I'm signing him up for the circus. I'm enlisting him in an army for evil babies. At the very least, I'll be locking myself in the bathroom with my vibrator until I'm able to speak again. I pull Killian's hand down and press it against the aching spot between my legs, which sends heat to his summer-blue eyes and makes me shiver.

"It's very okay. It's so okay," I whisper between gasps because now his mouth has gotten in on it, too, softly biting against my neck. "Oh my GOD, it's so okay!"

This is why I can't dirty talk.

"You're such a mess, Hannah Tate," he says, smiling against the tender divot at my throat and settling against me with a soft groan. When the hard length of him presses into me, it's all I can do not to shove him inside. My hips rise to meet his, and with one hand, he rips off my shorts and the panties beneath. He grabs a condom and rolls it on. No more Bowies for us.

At least, not yet. I smile, my lips parting suddenly when he enters me. With those deft guitarist fingers, he works one hand between us as he pumps, and I come in seconds. *Seconds!* God, I needed this so much. He grins down at me, his eyes hungry, but keeps going. I rise and fall and crash against him.

His chest is warm against my palms, and I can feel the muscles tightening beneath his skin as his climax builds. He gets so hard the instant before he comes, it pushes a gasp out from my lips. I squeeze around him until he cries out, too, and my heart surges.

After, Killian pulls me close to him, my back to his stomach, and folds an arm around me. It's the best I've felt in months, and it's not just the new sheets. I can't remember the last time he's touched me like this. Not the sex, I know the last time we did that down to the date and hour, but held me like this.

The thought brings tears to my eyes, the relief of it overwhelming me. I may be a mess, but he still loves me. We're okay.

Is this what's been missing from our relationship? We just needed to bone to feel like ourselves again? I snuggle into him even more and feel a swell of satisfaction as his dick responds against my ass.

"You want more," he breathes into my ear, cupping my breast and lightly, lightly tweaking my nipple. It's not a question, but I answer anyway.

"I want it all."

≈

Well, we did it approximately one-third times more, because Bowie decided to wake up and demand breakfast just as things were getting moany.

"That's okay, baby," I whisper into his soft cheek as I rock back and forth on my heels, settling him down. "Mommy won't give you to the circus this time."

"Circus?" Killian's brow furrows as he comes out of the shower, his skin supple and fresh from the hot water. "If we're giving Bowie to anybody, it's the Olympic Gymnastics team. Gold medal or bust."

"Ooh, then you can retire to Cirque du Soleil, honey!" I kiss Bowie's little nose. "The *fancy* circus!"

Killian pulls a white undershirt over his head, and I sigh theatrically with disappointment. Objectifying him always makes him smile, but he seems too lost in thought to even notice.

"Listen, this morning got me thinking," he says as he pulls on a pair of slim charcoal pants. "How about dinner tonight, just me and you?"

My eyes widen, and I nearly drop Bowie. "Really?"

Killian strides over to me, buttoning up a crisp blue shirt the color of his eyes as he leans in and gives me a soft kiss on my forehead. Prince Eric, corporate edition. *Dreamy sigh.*

"Really." He runs his hands down my arms and holds me back, taking in the sight of me with Bowie nestled against my chest. His eyes are so tender and wistful, a thick knot forms in my throat. Feeling his eyes on me with no hint of criticism or judgment is like stepping into a pool of warm sunlight. When his gaze slides down to our son curled in my arms, the love pouring from him feels like I could reach out and touch it. It takes my breath away.

"Look at how he looks at you, Hannah. He loves you so much." Killian's eyes crinkle at the corners as he smiles, and he gives Bowie his own tender kiss. "I know the last few months have been tough, but you're a wonderful mommy."

If it was possible to dissolve from words alone, I would no longer be standing here. The ever-present mommy tears well in my eyes. I don't know how Killian knew I needed to hear these things. Needed to hear *him* say these things. But I do, and my heart brims with relief. Let him think I'm bad with money, or aimless, or any other dig on my ability to adult as well as he does. But let him never, ever question the way I love our child, because it's the one thing I'm sure I'm doing right.

"Let me take you out and give you a little break tonight. Sound good?"

I suck in a quick breath, too emotional to form words. But I can nod. I nod so hard, my neck cracks.

"I'll figure out the babysitter," I manage to say, then grin through the tears and happiness filling me up like helium.

I watch him leave, still stunned as his car pulls out of the driveway and heads toward Midtown's shiny skyline.

I've got to lock down a babysitter, stat. Fumbling, I fish out my phone from my pocket.

Tyrannical Infant Support Group

Hannah

Didn't you all say you wanted to have another baby soon?

Kira

Yes! We want dozens of babies! Buckets of babies! As soon as possible!

Mattie

. . .

. . .

Darling, we've been over this. The phrase "buckets of babies" does not come off the way you think.

Hannah

How about one extra baby, and as soon as tonight? If it helps seal the deal, pretty sure Bowie could fit in a bucket.

Kira

OMG, we'd be honored to watch Bowie!!! 😍 Piles of babies!!!

Mattie

Is this so Bobby Patriarchy, Jr., can propose to you?? If so, NO!!

Kira

MATTS, HUSH. The number of times Hannah's babysat June so you could drag me to your sad lady folk shows?? We can do this for her.

Mattie

. . . But June is perfect.

Hannah

June IS perfect, tho.

Kira

As if that was ever in contention! Hannah, you can bring Bowie over anytime after 5. That way, you can shower. 😉

Mattie

NO! If she's clean, he'll def propose!!

Hannah

😍😍😍 you guys!!! Thank you so much!! Be over at 5!!

Mattie

SIGH. Fine. You know where to send the fruit basket. 😬

And it better be HARRY & DAVID'S ROYAL
PEAR COLLECTION!!!!!!

I clasp the phone to my chest and spin around the room with Bowie
in my arms, like it's *Beauty and the Beast* up in here. Though it's quite clear
who's Beast at this moment.

Let the hygiene begin!

CHAPTER FOUR

Feeling pretty chuffed with myself right now. I only cried on the way, during, and after dropping Bowie off with Kira and Mattie, and only violently once I was out of his sight. I've never left him with anyone other than Killian, and even then, it's only to take the occasional shower. It's so hard, even with Kira and Mattie, whom I trust more than anybody. Beyond the logistical nightmare of pumping enough for bottles while you're out, there's also the intoxicating mammalian impulse to snatch your baby back from the arms of your sitter and carry him off by the neck scruff to your hidey-hole where you can lick him in peace.

I did it, though, and with minimal licking. Kira promised to text me every thirty minutes with updates and pictures of Bowie and June as the babies forge the next generation's best friendship. Mattie promised to supervise and, if necessary, put the kibosh on any "piles of babies" Kira attempts. Plus, June is seven months old. That means K&M have *four additional months* of motherhood knowledge on me. Hell, Bowie's probably safer with them!

Or so I tell myself.

Once I get home, the long, hot shower exorcises all the remaining tears I have from leaving Bowie, and also all the untoward hairs. I'm smoother than I've been for the better part of a year, and my new green dress slips over me, cool and silky against my warm skin. I bought it right before I found out I was pregnant, and by a Christmas in July miracle, it still fits. It's tighter around the chest now but not obscenely so, and the skirt cinches high enough to float easily around me. For the first time in ages, I feel light and clean and fresh. Motherhood is fascinating and complex and often, so, so joyful. But it's also kind of swampy.

It's a special occasion, so I've blown out my hair and curled up a few face-framing waves, like old times. Without Bowie strapped to my chest, putting on makeup is a lot easier, if less fun. But now that I'm done and staring at myself in the big rectangular mirror leaning against our bedroom wall, a strange mix of emotions flows through me. I did everything the way I used to—my hair, my makeup, even this dress I bought during that previous era. But I still look different. It's not bad or anything. It just . . . feels like a costume. Like I'm playing at being another person. A beautiful person, I'll admit. My dark blond hair is shining from product and heat, my skin is clear and dewy, and I look alive in a way I don't remember feeling. I just—is it me? I twist and turn in the mirror's reflection, examining what I see from all sides, looking for Hannah.

Killian's footsteps march down the hall before hesitating at our bedroom door.

"Hannah? This is your fifteen-minute warning." He pushes the door open and peeks his head in. "We need to leave in—oh, you're ready!" Killian's surprise is evident, which prickles my skin. I'm not constantly late for fun. It's because I don't have any time to be *on time* with.

"I'll freshen up, then we can go." He stands behind me and leans in for a quick peck against my cheek. "You look amazing." His eyes twinkle with sincerity, and some of my irritation washes away.

Because the world is a deeply unfair place, it takes Killian only five minutes to get ready. He's shed his corporate attire for an expensive pair of dark wash jeans, cuffed tight against his new boots, and a short sleeve button-down that hugs the contours of his shoulders and chest. If he's nervous about tonight, he's not showing it. He looks perfect for a night out in Atlanta, but then again, he always does. Fatherhood hasn't left its mark on Killian. I resent that, a little.

He's all set to step out the door when I realize with a flash of panic that I haven't checked my phone in a while. There may be Bowie updates. I race back to the bedroom and find it on the dresser and am rewarded with a gummy close-up of Bowie and June, June's tiny hand probing Bowie's left ear. My uterus twinges from the cuteness. I'm starting to get Kira's whole "piles of babies" thing. I start to go, but the door of Killian's closet is open. I eye it for a second, and then because I have zero chill, I lean down and dip a hand into his disgusting boot.

The ring box. It's *still there.*

I pull it out, heart beating wildly. What does it mean? Did he forget it?

"Hannah! Hurry up, we don't want to lose our table!"

I crack it open. The ring's inside. What if he proposes, and there's no ring? Worse, what if he *doesn't* propose when he realizes he forgot it? I can't wait for this question anymore. This ring is coming to dinner tonight, even if I have to bring it myself. I shove it in my purse and dash down the hall.

On the way over, I search Killian's profile for any hint of what's to come, but he drums his fingers against the steering wheel of his sensible Honda, seemingly oblivious. I wait for him to tap his pockets, to feel for the shape of the box to make sure it's still there. I know I'd be nervous if I was carting diamonds around, but no, nothing. Unease bubbles inside of me.

No, no. You're just wigging out because you're nervous. I aim the AC vents directly on my overheating face. The proof that he's going to propose is in my purse. The biggest reason why is being babysat by my best friends. How much more evidence do I need to believe in us? This is just my same old bullshit, surfacing again. When I was a kid, Mama and I were always holding our breath until payday, and husband after husband either hurt her, stole from us, or both. Granted, my stepdad Darryl finally broke the pattern. Mama married him after six weeks of dating when I was a freshman in high school, and to everyone's surprise, this time it stuck. But it took her four marriages and then some to get there, and watching her get married and divorced on repeat didn't lay the best foundation for me to trust in love and commitment. It's always felt so implausible. Someone loving me? Messy, anxious, broke *me*? Seems fake.

I draw a deep breath in through my nose, flip back to the newest Bowie pic, and kiss the phone screen for good luck. I even flash Killian a big, sparkly smile as he parks the car.

"Here we are," Killian says, slipping his hand on the base of my back to guide me through an ivy-covered awning. His touch sends a spike of excitement through me.

The place Killian picked is perfect. A small, romantic pop-up restaurant by one of our favorite chefs located in a side garden tucked between storefronts. The strands of Edison bulbs overhead gleam on the young crowd's smiling faces, and the salty, spicy smells of Taiwanese street food wafting from the kitchen make my stomach flutter with desire.

Sweet *Jesus*, I'm starving. I've barely eaten since dropping off Bowie, and I suddenly feel dizzy from lack of calories. Breastfeeding is no joke. There's no skipping meals anymore, or snacks, or second breakfasts, or elevenses, and yes, I realize I have the eating patterns of a hobbit, but I'm also another human's complete and total food source. Bring on the beef noodles!

I'm so busy devouring half the menu I've almost forgotten why we're here. Killian's been telling me all about how cool Fellow Animals is, how amazing their guitarist is, how innovative their songwriting is, and so on and so forth and *beef noooooodles*. Between the sticky pork belly in my gua bao and Kira's never-ending text stream of adorable baby pictures (both babies in June's crib lying side by side, I DIE), Killian could be reading the tax code aloud and I'd still be smiling in bliss.

"Would you like another?" The waiter pauses at our table, gesturing at my empty cocktail glass. Before I can answer, Killian jumps in with a wink. "Make it two, please."

I smile, surprised. Killian is frugal about eating out, and cocktails are a particularly sore spot for him. I mean, I get it. Thirteen bucks for five swallows of gin is a crime, but such a delicious one. The waiter clears our dishes, and I sigh, happily full. The night feels young and alive, and coincidentally, so do I. It feels *good*.

Killian reaches across the table and takes my hand.

Oh shit. SHIT. It's going down! I'm stuffed to the brim with Taiwanese sausages, and it is *going down*. I laugh nervously, and Killian frowns for a second.

"Is . . . something funny?"

"Um, no. Sorry." I struggle to get it under control, but the first cocktail loosened my smile, and I can't keep from grinning like an idiot. "You were about to ask something? I mean, say something?"

"I was?" Killian's eyebrow arches, fully suspicious now.

"I mean, weren't you? The whole future-talk thing?" I clear my throat and blink a few times, as though that will bring things back to normal. Judging by Killian's expression, I'm unsuccessful.

"Well, I guess I was." Killian's grip on my hand tightens. "I've been thinking a lot about us, Hannah, about our little family."

Violins begin playing in my head, my heart lifting. I rest my chin on my one free hand and gaze beatifically at him. "Yes?"

"And this morning was, well." He utters a single laugh, his eyebrows high. "Surprising."

"Surprising?" The violins judder to a stop, and my cheeks flare with heat. It's not like I slipped anything into his ass without asking. "What does *that* mean?"

"We haven't had sex in so long, I thought . . ." He removes his hand from mine to rub the back of his neck, searching for words. "I thought we'd moved past that . . . phase in our relationship."

Phase? Sex is a *phase*? He sounds like my eighty-year-old great-aunt Rhea.

"While it was definitely fun"—Killian's cheeks color—"a *lot* of fun, I think we need to take a step back and consider what the next phase of our relationship should be."

"Which is . . . what exactly?" I say, squinting at him. The waiter brings our cocktails, and I take a big gulp of mine, at least seven dollars' worth, all at once. This could still be a proposal. Right? The sausages in my stomach begin a drum roll.

"Conscious co-parenting," Killian says with one big gust of breath. "We could all still live together under one roof—"

Conscious co-*what*?

"You could move into the other bedroom and pay me rent for your part of the house—"

Um. *What?!*

"I'd be free to see other people. Of course you would be, too," he quickly adds, but the initial omission is glaring.

"And Bowie could grow up in a loving home with both his parents together, but separate," Killian finishes. He breaks into a desperate smile, his eyes pleading with me to understand. "We could all be happy, Hannah, and we'd still be a family."

The sausages turn against me, roiling in my stomach because he's *not* proposing.

He's breaking up with me.

The blood flooding my head suddenly reverses course and plunges into my guts, down my legs, pooling into my too-hot feet. I'm burning up, but feel ice-cold, and the green of the garden swims in the golden glow of the lights. When I finally speak, my tongue feels numb, too heavy in my mouth.

"You're not . . . happy?"

Killian's eyes go tender, and he squeezes my hand, this time in sympathy. "Are you?"

I snatch my hand out of his. "Of course I am!"

How dare he ask me that *now*? What did he expect? That parenting an infant would be all Disney World and ice-cream cones and story time and sweet little *I love yous*? Things have been *hard*, and they'll continue to be *hard*, because we have a fucking *infant*. It's not a sign our relationship is over, it's a sign it's evolving. And yeah, sometimes change isn't comfortable or pretty or regularly shaven, but doesn't he realize that the hard times won't last forever? Can't he give us the benefit of the doubt until then?

I can't speak, I'm so angry. The tears leave hot tracks down my face, and I fumble in my purse for a tissue, but my fingers close around the ring box instead. I throw it on the table, feeling dim satisfaction when it lands in a splatter of chili crisp. The red oil seeps up the velvet, soiling the fantasy that won't come true.

That I know now will *never* come true.

"Then what. The *fuck*. Is this about?" The words barely escape around the knot choking my throat.

Killian's eyes go round as full moons, and he slides back from the table as if the sight of the ring pushed him there. "You—where did you find that?"

"It was in your old boot." The look in his eyes stops me short, and a horrible, churning fear erupts in my stomach. "It's for me, isn't it?"

"Of course it is." Killian squeezes his eyes shut. "Was."

"*Was?* What do you mean, *was?*" My voice is shaking with the effort of remaining calm. I can't yell. I won't repeat the show I saw so many times in my childhood between Mama and the stepdad du jour. God, I'm just like her, aren't I? About to get dumped by the baby daddy and didn't even see it coming. Fury and shame battle inside me.

"I bought that ring when you told me you were pregnant. I thought it was a sign that we, you know, were meant to be together." He pauses, sweat visibly beading on his brow. "I kept bringing the ring with me to propose, on that weekend to Savannah, at your last birthday dinner. But something's held me back each time, Hannah, and I think that's a sign, too. As much as we both want to be together for Bowie, I think we're making ourselves miserable in the process." He takes a deep breath. "We're so different, Hannah. Don't you want better, too?"

"I do want better." My voice has dropped to a choked whisper. "I want *you* to be better. I want you to quit being so selfish and uptight and shitty to me!"

The sympathy in his eyes hardens into indignation. "Me? How am I selfish? How am I shitty to you?"

"Conscious co-parenting?!" I throw my napkin on the table. "You want me to be your live-in nanny that you *charge rent to*! All so you can keep barely parenting and getting away with it? Well, fuck that! I'm tired of supporting your part-time parenthood so you can play shows and go out for happy hours and leave me alone all day and night!"

"I—How can you say that?" Killian's beet-red now. "I help out!"

"Having a baby isn't an after-work hobby for all of us, Killian. I don't know why I put up with it for so long! You've *never* supported me, or my dreams, or even asked me what I want. You'd rather me be miserable in some shitty job for the rest of my life instead of inconveniencing your savings goals!"

"You need that job because you spend all your money buying fancy comforters and—and chunky knit throws!" Killian sputters out.

"You *love* my chunky knit throw!" I toss my waves out of my face so I can glare at him better. "You hog it all the time!"

"That's not the point!" He smacks the table with the heels of his hands. "You can't quit because—"

"Because I already got fired." I fold my arms over my painfully swelling chest. Fighting apparently makes my milk let down. Thanks, biology, you *fucking* asshole.

"*Jesus*, Hannah! You got fired?! You know I can't support both of you on my job alone." The color drains from his face, and for the first time all night, he looks truly upset. That's just like him—more worried about finances than losing me. "How do you get fired when you're on maternity leave?!"

"Illegally, obviously, but sure, blame me! It doesn't matter because I don't want that horrible job anyway, and if you ever cared about me, you wouldn't want me to go back, either!"

Killian rakes his fingers through his hair and palms his eyes. "This is just like you, Hannah. You stumble through life messing everything up and expect others to pick up your slack—"

"You can stop right there." I stand up so fast, my chair crashes behind me. A dozen conversations around us snuff out at once, and all eyes turn toward us.

So much for not making a scene.

If any part of me still longed for Killian to propose, it died right there on the table somewhere between the words "conscious" and "co-parenting." I may not be great at saving money, or investing, or remembering when to file my taxes, but I'm tired of being treated like it makes me less of a person. I level a long finger at his face. "I've been picking up your slack *for months*. Well, no more. Consider this your nanny's resignation."

"*She's* the *nanny*?" somebody whispers.

Before Killian can say another word, I throw back the rest of my cocktail and slam it down in front of him.

"Wouldn't want to waste. Thanks for dinner, asshole."

His car keys cut into my fingers as I snatch them from the table and storm out. Let him dip into his precious Lyft budget tonight.

There's only one person I want to see right now, and he better be hungry.

CHAPTER FIVE

" just mean, *fuck him*! You know?" I make a grabby hand gesture, and Kira passes me the syrup bottle from my right. Mattie forks another piece of challah French toast onto my plate from my left, and I promptly stuff half the slice in my mouth. Kira and Mattie's sun-bright kitchen table is my happy place, especially when it's loaded with brunch. Sitting between my friends, with Bowie napping in June's baby swing a few feet away and June babbling from her high chair, I feel comforted and safe and nourished, and also a little wistful that I never feel this way at home.

At Killian's home, anyway.

"Yes!" Kira says as she saws off a strip of French toast for June and boops her on the nose with it. "Fuck that stingy second-rate Disney prince and leave him on the side of the road!"

"God, I am so relieved." Mattie yawns and runs her hands through her wavy chestnut hair, pre-pomade, and tries to tuck it behind her ears only for it to spring back into her face. "How could you even think about marrying that asshole?"

I take another bite while considering how to respond. As cathartic as it is to sit around and bash Killian with K&M, it's more complicated than that. *He's* more complicated than that. Yes, he's stingy and privileged and selfish, and worst of all, unwilling to recognize it, but he's also creative and talented and pragmatic, and at times generous and thoughtful, too. Like the time he sat down with my neglected 401(k), tax returns, accounts, and loan statements and worked for hours into the night figuring out a way for me to balance paying for debt while putting away some money for the future. I felt so relieved that someone who knew what they were doing finally sat down and helped me. Mama's always been terrible with money, so it's not like I had anyone to teach me how to do these things. But after that night, I could breathe a little for the first time since graduating college.

Killian also introduced me to camping. Admittedly I chalked it up as another not-so-subtle way to be cheap about vacations, but that first night sitting under the stars, wrapped in his sleeping bag around the dying fire, I discovered a side of myself I didn't know existed. Nature Hannah. Hiking Hannah. The Hannah who could build a tent and pee outside without tipping over. It was empowering. I hadn't realized how trapped I felt in Atlanta's concrete arms until I stepped out of the air-conditioning and into an easier way of being.

And the thing is, Killian knew I'd love it before I did. He'd been so sure I would that I half wanted to hate it to prove him wrong, but I couldn't even pretend. That night under the stars felt like a homecoming. It made me feel understood and deeply seen. It was almost like there was a part of me on view, like a third arm that the mirror missed, that *everyone* missed, but he saw. I loved that.

My throat's getting tight, and I wave a hand in front of my face to stop the tears because I prefer anger right now. I don't want to be sad over him anymore. I don't want to feel rejected, or let down, or like I've failed. I'm taking my side for once, and here on Team Hannah, we're *furious.* Because he didn't just reject me. He rejected our family. I know he thinks he didn't with that conscious co-parenting bullshit, but he did. He saw what we had, and it wasn't good enough for him.

And that makes him the biggest idiot in the world. I'd marry a ketchup bottle for Bowie.

I push my hair off my neck and force a smile. "It doesn't matter anymore. What matters is what comes next."

"Hear, hear!" Kira says, lifting her coffee in salute. We all clink our mugs together and take long swigs.

"Not to be the one asking all the annoying questions"—Mattie pauses, her brow furrowed—"but what comes next?"

I set my mug down and heave a sigh. "Well. I stole his car." Judging by the sheer amount of text messages I've gotten from him since last night that I refuse to read, he's taken offense at that. "I guess I'll take it back to the house, pack up my things, and move out." I grimace. "It's a bad week for my car to be in the shop, though."

"We'll follow you over," Kira says quickly. Her big, brown eyes train on me, steadying me like they always do. "We'll help you pack, load up the wagon, and you can come back here and stay with us. June has *loved* hanging out with Bowie—you should have seen how she brought him every toy she owns last night—and we don't get to see you nearly enough."

I glance at Mattie, expecting to see her usual dismay when Kira over-promises, but she just raises her eyebrows at me. "She's not wrong. Ready to go?"

"I love you both, you know that?" The tears are coming now anyway, but these are happy ones. Relieved ones. So what if I didn't get the family I wanted with Killian? I have this family. I wipe my eyes and laugh a little. "I can't live here, though."

"Why not?" Kira places her hand on mine. "You stayed here for weeks taking care of me when I was sick and still recovering from Junie's birth." She squeezes me tighter. "Let us take care of you."

"That was before Bowie, though. You don't have enough room for us both, and I have no idea how long it'll take me to find another job."

I can tell they want to argue, but they really can't. They live in a two-bedroom bungalow in Cabbagetown that's already tight for their family of three. Plus, I'm in my thirties now. I can't sleep on a couch long term. I'll throw my back out or something.

"Well," Kira begins, sounding strangely tentative. I instantly distrust it. She lifts her hands as though to ward off any sudden attacks. "Just brainstorming here, but what about your parents?"

"My *parents*?" It's a good thing for her I wasn't drinking my coffee because I would have done a spit-take on purpose. First of all, I don't have "parents." I have Mama and my stepdad, Darryl. Second, I bail *them* out, not the other way around. It would violate the laws of the Universe. "How could they possibly help?"

"Didn't you say they opened up an Airbnb but can't get anyone to rent it?" Kira prods my shoulder with her finger. "That means they have room for you. And aren't they both retired? They could help with Bowie."

"They don't know anything about babies. The last time they visited when Bowie wouldn't sleep, Mama suggested putting vodka in his bottle."

"She was joking!" Kira exclaims.

"Was she, though?" I squint.

"It would be temporary, Hannah. Not forever. Just until you get on your feet again."

Kira's suggestion swirls through me. Mama. Darryl. A cabin. The mountains. An Airbnb nobody wants to rent. I take a long sip of my coffee, trying not to cringe.

"Come on, it's brilliant!" Kira says, now fully in love with her idea. "They need your help with the Airbnb, and you need a place to stay and help with Bowie. Win-win!"

Kira's right. They probably need my help with lots of things, that's the problem. There are always fires to put out when it comes to Mama and Darryl, and they treat me like their own personal firefighter. Me! I'm clueless when it comes to adulting, but compared to Mama and Darryl, I'm like all five members of *Queer Eye* meets the *Wall Street Journal*. I've tried telling Kira this, but how do you make someone who has parents that actually parent them understand?

Once, Mama asked me to deal with this tower of unopened mail while I was home for Christmas, and I found out she'd been sued, summoned to court, and lost due to failure to show, all in the same stack. Her checks had been garnished for months, and she'd had no clue why and never bothered to find out. But once I opened those letters, she made it *my* problem to solve. I spent the rest of my Christmas vacation getting to the bottom of that lawsuit, only to find out it was justified against my mother, and I couldn't do anything about it by then, anyway.

I was nineteen years old.

I'm so tired of cleaning up other people's disasters. I'm the one who needs help right now, ME. Could Mama and Darryl really step up, for once? I chew the inside of my cheek, mulling it over. They don't know how to change a diaper, but they *are* obsessed with Bowie. They'd say yes, for sure.

Do I want them to? Can I handle all their responsibilities plus my own right now?

Do I have another option?

I squeeze my eyes closed, my spirits collapsing even further, and grumble into my coffee. "That could . . . work. I guess. Temporarily."

"Yay! I'm texting your mom right now." Kira grins and is halfway through the text before I can groan in protest. Kira's loved my mom since we were roommates in college, and to my horror, initiated a group family text chain that refuses to die.

H K M D

FOR HANNAH'S FANNAHS ONLY

Kira

CODE RED EMERGENCY, TRISH!

Mama

Oh, Lord! What's happened? Did Jericha dump our guy on The Bachelorette?? I haven't seen last night's episode yet!!!

Kira

The Disney Prince's done it again!

Darryl

WUT THAT BOY DONE NOW

I audibly moan as the texts flood my phone's screen.

Kira

Long story short: Killian sucks, and Hannah dumped his ass. Also, she got fired.

Mama

Praise Jesus! Hallelujah!

Darryl

I'LL KNOCK HIM FLAT, WHERE HE LIVE?

Though I do not want to, at all, I enter the fray.

Hannah

You will NOT, Darryl, and you know where he lives. It's where I live. Well, used to live.

Mama

Oh, blessed day! You're moving home!
I prayed this day would come!

Hannah

You prayed that my life would explode so magnificently that
I'd need to move me and Bowie in with you? THX, MOM.

Mama

Yes I did! Praise Jesus! The crystals worked!

Hannah

Mama, stop. You're not even religious.

Mama

I am now! HalleLUJAH!

I'll have your room ready by 2 p.m.

≈

Kira's Subaru clambers up the bumpy dirt road, weighed down with its payload of women, children, and my vast personal aesthetic squeezed into the trunk. I'm not happy about moving in with Mama and Darryl, but I *delighted* in liberating my things from Killian's house. It was a rescue mission and a raid all at once, and victory sang through my veins as I ran to the car clutching every last chunky knit throw in the place. I'm done with feeling overlooked and undervalued, taken for granted and casually rejected. *Done.*

By the time we pulled out of the driveway, it looked like a tornado ran through there, and in a way, it did. I tore through my former life and home, upending it all until it no longer felt recognizable, until it didn't feel like home at all. Without me and Bowie and my beautiful things, Killian's house looked lonesome and bare. I hope that's how he feels when he comes home later. I hope he looks around his empty house and feels the absence of the home I created for us.

The home I'm taking with me.

To my parents' cabin. Temporarily. *Not* forever.

"Ooh, there's shotgun dude on his porch!" Mattie shouts like it's a game of bingo and points out the passenger window at the old man dressed in a bathrobe. He's sitting on a dingy-white rocker with a shotgun propped over his knees, right where Darryl's map said he'd be. "This is our turn!"

From my spot wedged between June's and Bowie's infant car seats in the back, I give the man a salute, which he returns with an enthusiastic spit. I think Darryl calls him Sergeant.

"I am digging this map Darryl made," Mattie says, chuckling. "Now keep an eye out for something called '*Snaky Pond—u will know it when u see it.*'"

"Um, snaky? As in snakes? As in the having of lots of venomous snakes?" Kira's voice gets squeakier with each mention of *snake*.

Mattie pats her arm. "I'm sure it's just a coincidence, babe. Probably no snakes in these barely populated mountain forests at all."

"Is that right, Hannah?" Kira's eyes flick to me in the rearview mirror. Kira is terrified of snakes. Once she saw a long worm on a sidewalk and nearly passed out. She hasn't seen Darryl's map herself, though, so I don't mention the horde of squiggly serpentine stick figures emerging from the pond drawing, or their devil horns.

"Yup. Probably just Darryl joking." I have to smile through my life-in-shambles ennui. The map Darryl texted to us since GPS doesn't work on their mountain is pretty special. With misspellings, rude caricatures, and the kind of logic only Darryl would use, it's like a treasure map, but for hillbillies.

It's led us from the asphalt monolith of I-75 to four-lane highways bisected with wildflowers, onto two-lane country roads ringed with rolling mountains until we reached this narrow dirt lane winding up and into the forest.

Kira drives us over the threshold of an old covered bridge. Bands of blue peep out between the crooked red boards overhead, and the sullen teenager mood that's gripped me ever since I realized moving in with Mama was my only option lightens, just a little. Kira, Mattie, and June are staying for the weekend, and Kira's going to help me put together a slam-dunk case against Bob's illegal firing. She'd rubbed her hands together and cackled. I'm no attorney, but I think that's legalese for *Bob's fuckin' doomed.*

More importantly, they'll be here standing beside me when Killian comes up tomorrow. He's bringing my car once it's finally out of the shop, and my beloved velveteen rocker, which is admittedly decent of him. He also wants to spend time with Bowie. Once I read his texts, which ranged from indignation over me taking his car to sad, broken-up pleas to rethink this, to not take Bowie away, I finally responded. I'm furious and hurt and so, so resentful that he's forced me to this, but I would never keep Bowie away from him. They love each other even if we don't, and that is precious.

I let Bowie and June grasp the pinkies of each of my hands and gaze out the window. Everything is lush and green like it just rained. The trees hanging over this dirt road have transformed it into a tunnel of emerald leaves, and the rhythmic buzz of insects is audible through the closed windows.

When Mama and Darryl sold their house in rural Georgia in a cash deal and bought a fixer-upper cabin in the mountains from one of Darryl's cousins, also with cash, my first reaction was to hyperventilate. Mama and Darryl are the kind of people who eat lobster on payday and beans the five days before. They're both retired, but not for any responsible, money-saving reasons. Darryl had to medically retire from working at a gas station after a heart attack, and Mama was forced to retire early from the nursing home or be laid off. Altogether, their social security checks and Mama's miniature pension barely let them scrape by, much less buy a "retirement cabin" in the prettiest mountain town in Appalachia.

But, looking at these ancient green mountains, rounded by time and rain, and how they laze beneath the big, blue summer sky, I question every judgy thought I've had. It doesn't matter what the cabin looks like. This place is heaven.

Okay, heaven plus Shotgun Sergeant. But still!

"Hey, what's that up ahead?"

Kira leans over the steering wheel and squints at the sign. It's covered in kudzu and half toppled over, but the letters still visible state:

_ _S _ _ NA_ _ KY POND

Mattie positively crows with delight, and Kira lets out a timid laugh. "Just a joke, then. No snakes at all."

"No snakes at all, babe." Mattie leans over and gives her thigh a squeeze. "Turn right here. It's two cabins ahead on the right."

I hold my breath as we pull into the narrow parking spot, but the tightness in my chest unravels when I see the woodsy little cabin. Beneath a cheerful red tin roof, dark reddish-brown logs stack neatly together, like the old school Lincoln Logs I played with as a kid. The cabin's built on the gentle slope of the mountain, with a wraparound porch circling it in a hug. It looks out onto the small, shimmering lake below, nestled in the towering trees. My heart dares to soar at the thought of staying here (temporarily, not forever), looking out onto that lake. The summer sun dances on its surface.

My design brain revs its engine, and all the little touches I could add to the exterior for Mama and Darryl burst into my head. Big hanging baskets of red pansies with silvery-green vines spilling over their edges. A stained-glass suncatcher over the kitchen window. A hand-carved birdhouse staked out front. They need curb appeal to impress guests the minute they arrive.

And a *name*. An Airbnb always needs a name. Woodsy Wonderland? Cozy Cub Cabin? A small thrill of excitement pulses through me, against my better judgment.

This could be . . . *fun*?

Down the hill out back is a garden, where a big man is hunched over, weeding. He's wearing a beat-up Braves hat and a shirt proclaiming, "'Murica! Home of the Badass!" that I got him this past Christmas. I'd know him anywhere.

"Hey, Big Dad-day!" I cup a hand around my mouth and holler. Darryl turns around with a start, his face lighting up with a big dopey grin when he sees us. I smile, too. He's the best stepdaddy of the several I've had by a long, long shot.

I scoop Bowie out of his car seat, and he's all drooly smiles. "Look at these *trees*, Bowie!" I coo, spinning slowly around and pointing at the towering giants above us. "We're in the woods! We're visiting G-ma and Big Daddy!" I can't help exclaiming. Everything feels exciting when I present it to his sweet, innocent face.

Darryl ambles up the hill to greet us. "Baby, the girls are here!"

"Women," Mattie corrects automatically as she closes the passenger door. "The women are here." Mattie and Darryl haven't met yet, but she strides up to him and holds out her hand. "Hi, I'm Mattie. You must be Darryl."

Darryl lifts his chin, sizing her up from her brown leather working boots to her plain white T-shirt, sleeves rolled up the way Kira likes. I wonder if he realizes Mattie's doing the exact same thing to him. Kira assured her that Darryl, while 100 percent country, is not a bigot, but I could tell Mattie had lingering doubts. I can't blame her. Being gay in Atlanta is one thing. Being gay in Georgia is quite another.

After a long second, he reaches out his hand and shakes hers. "You with our Kiki?"

"Yep," Mattie replies evenly.

Darryl squints. "Y'all lesbians?"

"Yes."

"Y'all like ham?"

Mattie raises her eyebrows. "Um. Yes?"

Just then, Mama comes through the screen door. "Darryl, what a thing to ask our guests!" Mama rolls her eyes. "Everybody likes ham!"

"Well, then," Darryl says, the dopey grin returning as he opens his arms wide. "Welcome to Bear World!"

"We are *not* calling our cabin that." Mama leans over to hug Kira and kiss June's curly head. "We're so excited to see you all. Welcome, welcome!"

I give Darryl a kiss on his scraggly cheek and watch with amusement as he makes goofy, exaggerated faces at Bowie, who, to Darryl's credit, *also* seems amused. Despite being a dedicated Big and Tall customer for life, Darryl never scares kids. Maybe it's the gap between his front teeth that makes him look so young and mischievous, or that he's in his sixties and still plays with remote control cars, but babies, kids, and all manner of pets love him. It's a testament to his good energy.

"You help Mattie with those bags, I'll take my grandson for a bit." Darryl reaches eagerly for Bowie, but I falter.

"Oh, Darryl—" I don't want to hurt his feelings, but Darryl is a two-pack-a-day smoker. Nicotine passes through skin-to-skin contact, and I don't want Bowie's precious little body sullied like that *or* to hold a baby all night that smells like the Coca-Cola cans Darryl uses for ashtrays. But the moment's interrupted when Mama hustles over and squeals. And *boy*, is she a sight. She's wearing a faded pair of blue jeans and an old Georgia Lotto T-shirt, which is normal enough, but she's added a crocheted shawl over her shoulders like some kind of granny cape and a dangly chain with charms on it attached to her bifocals. Being that she's only sixty-two, it comes off like she's cosplaying Sophia from *Golden Girls*.

"My grandbaby!" Mama reaches for Bowie, and I gratefully hand him to her. She doesn't smoke, and it keeps me from having to explain to Darryl why I don't want him to hold Bowie until he's showered and dipped his hands in Listerine.

She bops an increasingly skeptical Bowie around the porch, cooing all kinds of nonsense at him. *Who's my little beepy-boop! Tee-hee! Who's the littlest littler! You! That's who! Doop!* I seize the opportunity to help Mattie with the bags.

Together, we haul a load down the external stairs to the Airbnb. It occupies the bottom floor of the cabin, like a guest apartment, with its own door to the outside and wraparound porch overlooking the lake, too. This porch is in considerably worse shape, though. The floorboards are beaten and warped, and there's a foot-shaped hole beneath a lone rocking chair abandoned awkwardly in the middle of our path around. I'd bet anything that was Mama's idea. Covering up problems is her specialty.

There's a sound up ahead, the unmistakable *spi-spi-spis* summons of a cat. Then an unfamiliar voice, deep and coaxing, says, "Come on, buddy. You can do it!"

When I round the corner of the porch, I stop dead in my tracks. There is a man there. A *man*. His sizable back faces me as he stretches precariously over the top of a Pack 'n Play travel crib, reaching. A massive tabby cat in a black harness sits next to a shiny red toolbox a few feet away, staring drolly at his grasping hand.

"Like we practiced now. The Phillips-head," the man says, then snaps his fingers, which must be a bridge too far, because the giant cat waddles off in the other direction. "No, Battle-cat! Come back—"

"Hello?"

The man glances up, eyes widening, but the movement disrupts his balance, and he tips forward into the small nylon travel crib with a manly yelp.

"Oh! Are you okay?" I reach out a hand, then pull it back uncertainly as he practically *rockets* out of the Pack 'n Play and onto his feet.

"It's okay! I'm fine." He laughs a little. A lock of hair the color of raw honey slips out of the messy knot he's tied it back in and catches in the dark stubble on his cheek. It's only a shade or two darker than his golden skin, and he shoves it behind his ear and takes a quick breath. He winces as he smiles sheepishly. "Would you believe me if I said I was trying it out?"

A smile spreads across my face. "Nope."

"Damn. There goes my cover story."

I laugh, surprised. This man is . . . *fuck*. How does he know my mama? He's tall and thickly shouldered and completely *gorgeous* in a pair of low-slung jeans and a worn chambray shirt, sleeves rolled up to reveal tanned forearms. They have at least three distinct ripples of muscle each, and I suddenly understand that dude in *Grease* who bites his knuckles at the hot lady. Who *is* he? Did an Urban Outfitters model get lost on a shoot in the sunset wilderness? But that doesn't explain the Pack 'n Play. Cognitive faculties currently experiencing difficulties.

"Is that your cat?" I gesture at the giant tabby stalking across the yard.

"That's my apprentice." The beautiful man frowns. "I think he just quit."

Another surprised laugh bubbles out of my mouth, and his fake frown melts into a satisfied grin.

Mattie mutters something about *heterosexuals* under her breath, which is offensive because I'm bi, then clears her throat. "I'm Mattie. This is Hannah."

"I'm River." He hitches a thumb over his shoulder at the tabby. "That's Battle-cat. Nice to meet you both." He gives us a small salute and leans over to grab the forgotten screwdriver himself. Mama's words come back to me— *the neighbor's weird, charming, fine as hell* . . . The way his shoulders move makes it all click into place.

"You're yoga man!" I blurt out. The insanely hot neighbor, also known as River—*River*, damn, that's a sexy name—furrows his brow, so I hastily add, "My mama watches you in the mornings."

Well. That made things better. Mattie sighs loudly and heads back up for another load.

River *hmms*, and for a second it's quiet as we both contemplate how awkward it is that my mom spies on him. "I've gotta start wearing more clothes out there."

Sorry, Mama.

"She asked me to put this together for your baby before you got here. Added a few improvements, hope you don't mind. These things are so flimsy." He stretches up to standing, and it's like watching a scroll unfurl. Up and up and up, and I want to read every damn word. I blink, and he wipes his hands on his knees. "How's that look?"

The new Pack 'n Play stands before me, perfect and more than a little tricked-out. He's added a crossbeam and slats for comfort and support, he explains, a tiny mount for an infant monitor, and an external rig to hold a diaper caddy. "Oh my God, thank you! This is amazing, but I'm so sorry for my mom putting you out. She shouldn't have asked you to do all this."

River shrugs, and it's like watching water move. There's a triangle of golden skin visible from his throat to his chest, and I force myself to meet his eyes. They're warm and a rich brown, framed by long, dark lashes.

"No trouble at all. Your parents are good people, and I'm always happy to help."

I scrutinize his expression, looking for any evidence that he in fact hates my parents, hates me, and wants to file a nuisance suit against all three of us. But there's nothing. Just that pleasant smile. It feels like the breeze through an open window. He kicks his work boot against the porch, and I realize I've been staring at him for a beat too long while thinking all these horny, poetic thoughts. *Fuck.*

"River Aronson, you sweet boy! You've finally met my baby girl, Hannah!" Mama comes down the stairs with Bowie in her arms and a grin as big as I've ever seen it, Kira and June right behind her. "Now you can meet my grandbaby, too." Bowie's drowsy against her chest, but his navy-blue eyes are open and looking for me. When they find mine, he smiles and gurgles, and the world feels beautiful all over again. I take him from Mama with a burst of pride, and she presents us both to River in a grand Vanna White flourish. "This is our Bowie."

"Hey there, little buddy," River says. He approaches us slowly, reaches up a hand, but asks first, "This okay?" I nod, and he gives his hand to Bowie, who grasps one of River's fingers with all five of his tiny ones.

"Yowza!" River says, then winks at me. "Strong grip."

Yowza? Did this hot guy just say *yowza?*

"Hi-iii, I'm Kira, and this is June. We're gonna scooch inside for a second. This one needs a diaper change." She eyes River, then waggles her eyebrows at me, and I want to punch her, right in front of her baby.

This close, I can smell the scent of River's shirt. Pine needles and cedar and something deeper, something that plucks at the center of my belly.

Jesus! I get laid one and a third times, and I act like I just emerged from the Sahara desperate for sex. I mean water. Desperate for water. *Gah*, I can't even think straight.

River catches me looking at him again, this time at the curve of his stacked shoulders, and now *he* blushes. Oh God, can he tell I'm thinking about sex?! A sweet kiss of pink is just visible beneath his scruffy beard. "It's nice to meet you, Hannah." His voice is soft and low, all the playful goofiness gone, and now I've got a blush to match his. It takes me aback, but I try not to show it. Here I am, exhausted, dumped, and broke, a complete and utter mess, but he's looking at me like I'm a *woman*.

Like I'm not a mess at all.

The moment is magic, the color gold made tangible, even though Mama's standing by watching with her grin jacked to max capacity. I search my brain for something to say, preferably something intelligent, funny, or thoughtful.

But then, from inside the Airbnb, Kira *screams*.

CHAPTER SIX

River's the first to react. His heavy boots thud against the porch, and he's diving inside before I can process that Kira is legit *screaming*. Lung-emptying, no holding back *screaming*. Mama and I bumble inside after him. If there's a serial killer in there, we've just invited ourselves to the party.

"What is it?! What's wrong?!" I ask, which I immediately answer for myself the second I trip through the Airbnb's door.

Everything. The answer is *everything*.

"Aw, *damn*, Mama!" I cover my nose with my forearm. "What's that *smell*?!"

Kira's frozen in front of the fireplace, clutching baby June and the diaper bag like she might turn and run as soon as her brain starts working again. The screaming's stopped, but she's still emitting a strange, squeaky sound from the back of her throat. June's not even upset; she's just staring dumbfounded at her mama. Kind of like how I'm doing to my *own* mama right now.

"What smell?" G-ma meets my gaze a bit guiltily. "I don't smell anything."

River pulls Kira gently back from the mantel.

"It's not alive, right?" she breathes out in a shaky whisper, her eyes locked on the shiny slitted pupils of the rattlesnake draped across the mantel like fucking fear-garland. The snake's jaws are jacked wide open, revealing two curled fangs and a dusty brown mouth bed that would blow away with a strong gust. On its other end, the rattle is poised straight up like an exclamation mark.

To his credit, River gives the ancient taxidermy an honest assessment before leading Kira to the camouflage-print recliners in front of the fireplace, which make me shudder more than the dead snake.

"Pretty sure that one died before we were born. Come, sit down. Take a deep breath."

The recliner leans back with a shriek, and Kira grips June to her chest with wide eyes. I can't blame her. The wildly venomous snake on the mantel isn't the only stuffed animal au naturel in the joint. There are squirrels perched in various positions of nut-gathering all around it, as if saying *Hidey-ho! Snacky time! Don't mind Mr. Hissy Pants!* Hanging above the mantel is a trifecta of heads—two judgy-eyed bucks and a freaking *black bear.* Lining the walls on either side of the fireplace are plaques featuring gaping fish mouths *blurp*ing at us straight on, like we caught a strange, underwater choir mid-aria.

That's when I realize what the smell is. I whirl on Mama, but I can't say anything for fear of vomiting. I just gesture wildly at the reeking fireplace of death and formaldehyde.

G-ma performs an exaggerated shrug of innocence. "Darryl's cousin used this space for his taxidermy shop before he sold it. He left some of his best work behind." When my glare doesn't recede, she sniffs and crosses her arms. "They're for ambiance. People like animal heads."

"No, they don't," Kira and I say in unison.

Just then, the door swings open, and Mattie enters with the bags.

"*Holy* shit." She drops the bags on the floor, her head moving in a perfect clockwise motion as she takes in each of the Airbnb's atrocities. From the fireplace to the industrial sink in the corner, to the one tiny window high up on the wall. Her gaze stops on the stained concrete floor. "Is this where they filmed *Saw?*"

G-ma's face lights up. "I love that movie!"

Not unlike a horror movie, Kira extends a long, trembling finger upward. "The bear is"—she pauses to swallow—"so wrong."

We all turn to face the de facto president of the wall of heads. I press a hand to my mouth, muffling a strange croak. One of the bear's big white marble eyes has drifted inward toward his snout, while the other eye wanders vaguely toward the ceiling, like someone just bopped it over the head. All it needs is a harmonica and some suspenders, and it could be Zeb from the Country Bear Jamboree. I've never been drawn to PETA activism before, but this is a crime against bear-kind. If I were that bear, I'd come back and haunt the hobby taxidermist who did this to me.

Still hunkered by Kira in her recliner, River clears his throat and breaks the tortured silence. "I'm gonna get you a glass of water. Trish?" He eyes the deep metal sink in the makeshift kitchenette in the corner of the big main room, but Mama shakes her head slightly and points at a stack of bottled waters. "I think he used that sink for . . ." She trails off when she sees my horrified face. "Well. Just take one of the bottles."

River hands a water bottle to Kira, who accepts it limply. Mattie pulls Kira to her feet and takes June, who, unlike her mother, is pointing and squealing happily at each animal head in turn. "Why don't you go outside and enjoy that water on the porch?" Mattie says. "I'll change June."

"But the heads . . ." Kira whispers, her dazed eyes still locked on the rattlesnake's.

"I'll change her in the kids' room, where they can't see," Mattie says consolingly. "Then I'll take care of everything in here. Okay, baby?"

Kira nods, and River leads her out of the Hellbnb like he's her very own trauma Sherpa. When he passes me, I duck my head and feel the heat flame through my cheeks once more. I want to dissolve into a puddle and disappear down the large, rusty drain in the middle of this terrible floor.

Oh, *God*. That's for body fluids, isn't it?

Mattie, absolute champion that she is, calmly turns to Mama and hitches a thumb back at the fireplace. "Trish, y'all attached to any of these dead animals?" The way she says it, completely devoid of judgment, makes me love her even more. She's always been the most even-keeled of the three of us, but this takes my respect to a whole new level.

"Not really." G-ma taps a finger against her chin, her expression pensive. "Maybe the squirrels?"

"Mama!"

G-ma rolls her eyes and huffs. "All right, all right. I'll get some trash bags."

"And gloves!" Mattie calls cheerfully after her.

It takes a surprising amount of effort to de-corpse the fireplace. I take a long swipe at my sweaty forehead with the back of my rubber glove, then wrench off another fish plaque. Big Daddy puts up a fuss about taking them down, but I don't care if I have to sneak out in the middle of the night with a shovel, I'm gonna give these animals a proper Christian burial so they don't haunt my ass.

"Sorry, President Bear," I whisper as we gently place him in a bag. His marble eye glares up at me, and I quickly tie the bag shut. So wrong.

G-ma and Big Daddy are upstairs with Kira, who's currently cuddled with our babies on the porch swing. She's talking again, so that's good. Big Daddy feels awful about the snake. He keeps bringing Kira beef jerky and leaving it on a plate in front of her like a strange, meaty peace offering. Meanwhile, Mattie and I have gotten the cabin as habitable as we can. Though I tried to shoo him away, River insisted on helping with the heads and taking the full trash bags away, for which I'm forever grateful. The crunch and crackle that came from within them is nightmare fuel.

With the door open and the cabin aired out, it doesn't smell nearly so murdery in here. We throw a blanket over the scary sink and turn on the tangle of Christmas lights and light-up hot sauce bottles Mama has hanging over the bed. I can hear her explanation already—*for ambiance, baby!*

I stand back and take stock of our hard work. "Think Kira will be able to sleep in here now?"

Mattie cuts her eyes at me and raises one eyebrow. "Sure," she says, diplomatic as ever.

I let out a long sigh. Of *course* Mama and Darryl would try to rent out a taxidermy shop and act surprised when there are no bookings. I knew coming here would mean me solving their problems, but this? I scuff my shoe against the floor, then take a step back when I realize I'm too close to the horror-drain.

This feels impossible.

Mattie pats me on the back, sensing my overwhelm, and brings me in for a side-hug. "You're gonna make this place amazing, Hannah."

I snort. This isn't like Killian's house, which had great bones and just needed some personality. This place needs an exorcism.

"Come on," Mattie says, steering me toward the door. "This lesbian wants some ham."

≈

The July sunset streaks across the sky, and the world is green and blue and pink. All around, the leaves sigh from the tall canopy of green, and the sweet, grassy smell of summer is thick enough to taste. I sway like the yellow wildflowers on the breeze from the porch swing, with Bowie in my arms, sitting next to my two best friends. It's creaking pretty bad underneath our weight, but we're all too tired to care.

The smell of dinner wafts through the open windows.

"Haaaaaaam," Kira moans softly, her eyes rolling back in her head, and June giggles at her from Mattie's lap, so she does it again, louder.

Mattie smiles. "The healing power of ham."

"Dinner's ready, *women!*" Big Daddy announces through the screen door, looking awfully proud of himself for remembering.

Inside, G-ma and Big Daddy's cabin radiates warm golden tones, the long pine boards gleaming happily. Their furniture is nothing fancy, a mish-mash of thrift store finds and family hand-me-downs. But over the years, my surreptitious design help and strategic giving has brought it all together. Vintage Turkish rugs in muted pinks and oranges line the floors, and big potted plants bring bursts of green and pink to the corners. There's the old grandfather clock I bought and refinished for them in a dark, dusty blue, and the green carnival glass globe on its brass chain hangs over Mama's crosswords chair. I think of it as fortune-teller chic—cozy, eclectic, wacky but charming, just like Mama and Darryl themselves. And even though it's my first time stepping inside their new cabin, it already feels like them.

And it is *worlds better* than the horror show downstairs.

Still, Kira nervously checks the mantel over their fireplace. "No snakes in here, right, Big Daddy?"

"Cross my heart, Kiki. And if any of them copperheads show up, I'll get my shotgun and—"

"*What?!*"

"Nothing, he's joking with you, dear." G-ma's bustling around the table with the dishes. Big Daddy's made all my favorites—a big country ham decked with sticky pineapple rings, fluffy buttermilk biscuits, and green beans from G-ma's garden. I don't have to see it to know there's peach cobbler for dessert, keeping warm under a sheet of tinfoil in the oven. The delicious smells wrap around me like a hug and an enthusiastic *welcome home!*

But as good as dinner smells, a little whiteboard hanging on the wall stops me in my tracks. The ingredients for tonight's dinner are scrawled out in G-ma's neat handwriting, along with tallies for the month's grocery expenses.

A . . . *budget?*

In all my years, I've *never* seen Mama or Darryl use a budget. If they ran out of money before payday, or didn't have enough to keep the lights on, I'd hear about it in one of their impromptu calls. They'd mention it in passing as if it was nothing, but guilt would squeeze my middle until I transferred them whatever money I could. They haven't done that in ages, though.

Not since I told them I was pregnant.

A tear slips down my cheek, and I wipe it away quickly when I catch G-ma looking at me.

"It's been a day, hasn't it, baby?" she says, grasping me by the shoulders and giving me a quick peck on the cheek. "You sit down. I'll fix you a plate."

The food is *glorious*, and I, too, feel the healing power of ham. Heads down, Mattie, Kira, and even baby June are going to town on the feast Big Daddy's prepared for us. The table is quiet except for the tap and scrape of forks and knives and Bowie's soft snuffling sounds. After dinner started, I tucked Bowie into his infant carrier sling on my chest, and yeah, there are a few green beans lost in there, but he doesn't seem too concerned.

The delicious food can't stop my head from spinning, though. Ideas for how to fix downstairs stream through my brain, but there are more problems than solutions, the biggest one being money. How can we fix any of it? There's so much to do with so little. Tension grips my shoulders like a set of heavy hands, and the same old irritation and resentment at being the only one trying to be an adult in this family rises like a specter within me. How am I going to get that Airbnb in any decent shape without money? What am I supposed to do—raid my measly savings? Empty another 401(k)? After I finish chewing the last bite of salty, sumptuous ham, I push my plate away and clear my throat.

"It's time to discuss the Airbnb." Each word is slow and deliberate, because this isn't going to go over well. It's a good thing there was a ham dinner between my afternoon and this conversation, because I couldn't do this civilly without an abundance of carbs in my system. "It's a disaster."

"It is not," Big Daddy protests loudly.

G-ma wags her finger at both of us. "It's a work in progress."

"Mama, that fireplace violated the Geneva convention."

Big Daddy huffs. "Who *the hell's* Geneva?"

"Big Daddy!" G-ma admonishes. "No cursing in front of the babies."

Mattie and Kira watch this exchange back and forth as if it's a Williams sisters' tennis match. I take a deep breath, willing my blood pressure to lower, and try again.

"If y'all have any hope of renting that out for income, we have to start over from top to bottom." I hold my hand up and begin rattling off a to-do list. "We need to scrub out that smell, put down new flooring, change the fixtures in the kitchenette and bathroom, get new furniture, fix the holes in the porch, and if possible, put in some extra windows so it doesn't feel like a murder hole."

"Murder hole!" Big Daddy throws his fork down. "Those animals were dead when they got there!"

Kira whimpers a little at that, and Mattie's arm goes around her.

"Sorry, Kiki," he barks out, then rubs his temples. "Hannah, we don't have money for that, and neither do you." His face is pinched, and without his signature grin, he looks old and tired. Bone tired. The kind of exhaustion you feel when you've lived an entire life paycheck to paycheck, and there's never enough, and now you're old enough to know there never will be. It's not like Big Daddy to let the money stress show, though. He's taking this worse than I thought.

"Is something wrong, Darryl? I mean, Big Daddy?" I correct myself before G-ma yips at me.

"No," he snaps. "I'm very happy you're here!" The way he says it, you'd think I'd just scratched his truck. Despite the hefty plate of seconds steaming in front of him, he shoves a stick of gum in his mouth and chews viciously.

"Um . . ." My eyes travel from him to G-ma. "What's going on?"

G-ma places a hand on Big Daddy's arm and gives him an encouraging smile. "Big Daddy quit smoking when we found out y'all would be staying here. He's a little tetchy, that's all."

My eyes go wide, but Big Daddy raises his finger and stares me down. "It's just while my grandbaby is here. I want to hold Bowie without making him smell like the corner booth at Rudy's Rack and Cue. That all right with you?"

I squeal, the tears coming down all over again. "Yes! Oh my God, Big Daddy, that's so sweet! We appreciate it so much, don't we, Bowie-boy?" I tickle Bowie under the chin, and he gives Big Daddy a big, sloppy smile. Big Daddy's taut face softens in an instant.

"Can I hold him now?" he asks sheepishly.

"As long as you don't try to smoke him." I hand Bowie over to Big Daddy, who has turned into a bowl of human pudding. I've been trying to get Darryl to quit smoking since he married Mama. This is huge. It touches me even more than the dinner, and that juicy ham is *touching as hell*. The meal, the budget on the wall, Darryl quitting smoking. My throat tightens, and I wipe a fresh slate of tears away with my napkin. Kira gently takes my hand under the table and squeezes once. Maybe this time they can rise to the occasion. They're really trying.

I can try, too.

"Look, I know we don't have the money, but—"

"Yet." Kira cuts me off, her eyes alight with mischief. "Y'all don't have the money *yet*."

Everyone stops to look at her. Mattie's eyebrows go up as she clocks Kira's infamous *up-to-shit* smile.

"Oh, hell. Who's going down now?" Mattie says as she leans back, folding her arms across her chest.

Kira's smile breaks into a grin, and she flashes her phone to the table. It displays a screenshot of texts, *my* texts, with Mr. Fucking Bob himself.

"The mothereffin' patriarchy," Kira says. "And we're starting with Bob."

CHAPTER SEVEN

The sound of wheels crunching against loose gravel heralds the arrival of my beat-up Corolla and the ex-boyfriend inside. I'm that unique blend of awful made from equal parts anxiety at seeing Killian and exhaustion, having stayed up late into the night going through years of texts and emails from my diabolical former boss with my far more diabolical best friend. By two a.m., Kira felt like we had enough to wipe Bob's personal savings out. By four a.m., she was satisfied with his complete and total annihilation.

We stopped at five a.m.

Kira's sending the initial demand letter like a Monday-morning bomb addressed to Starla, Bob's unfortunate general counsel. I almost feel bad about that, but Starla should know better than to leave Bob unattended with a cell phone for an entire week.

The car door slams out front, and I grudgingly leave my view of the lake from the porch swing. Bowie's just finished nursing, and he's content in my arms. It may be July, but the morning air is pleasantly cool in the mountains, and Bowie's cheeks are rosy. He's spent the last five minutes watching the hummingbirds flit around the bird feeder, eyes wide. I think he likes it here.

I brace myself as we turn the porch's corner but seeing Killian there at the front gate is more of a soft squeeze of pressure around my heart than a slap to the face. His eyes are puffy, and there's a restless, jittery air to his stance I've never seen before. This is new and horrible for him as well.

Too bad, asshole.

"Am I early?" Killian asks but doesn't wait for an answer before holding out his arms eagerly. "Hey, Littleman!" It feels both natural and like a joint coming out of its socket handing our baby to him. Bowie regards him curiously, but if he's noticed it's been longer than their normal time apart, he doesn't show it. I step back, and the pressure builds.

It hurts, knowing all of this didn't have to happen. I don't want Killian and Bowie to be strangers. I wanted us to be a family, a real one for Bowie like the one I never had, with two employed parents and a cozy house where the lights never get turned off. I wanted it more than I've ever wanted anything. Yet here we are, passing our baby over a literal fence.

The tears gather in my eyes. I look away, but not quickly enough. Killian pounces on them like emotional ammunition.

"Hannah, this is ridiculous, and you know it! Come home. If you need help with Bob, I can coach you on what to say to get your job back. We can make this work, I *know* we can!"

The whole time he's talking, I keep my eyes firmly fixed on the forest towering behind his back. The tall, skinny pines sway in the breeze, but when the wind stops, they're still standing.

Now it's my turn to keep standing, too.

"That may work for you, but it won't for me." My words come out scratchy from the feelings whirling inside, but the weight of their truth anchors me. The wind lifts my hair, cooling the skin beneath. I open the gate's latch and let Killian in, and we head toward the cabin. As we walk, he continues spewing more panicky arguments for how dumb this is for my career and how selfish I'm being—*ha!*—to my back.

Now that he's here on our porch, I'm not sure what to do with him. How do parental visits work with an infant? I'm torn between leaving them alone and hovering over his shoulder. For all Killian's love for Bowie, he doesn't know shit about taking care of him. Not by himself. It's clear Killian doesn't know how this is supposed to work, either. He's standing there with Bowie in his arms, jiggling him every few seconds for no good reason. Bowie looks at me nervously from his daddy's embrace, like *you're sticking around, right?*

The screen door swings on its hinges, and G-ma sweeps out onto the porch, granny shawl tucked tight around her shoulders. Maybe I judged the shawl too soon; I could go for a blanket cape right now. She takes one look at Killian, her eyes hard and narrow. She opens her mouth to speak, but it's not to Killian.

"Big Daddy! That boy is here." She says it like a warning. Killian stumbles backward into the porch swing.

"Watch it!" she snaps at him, then holds out her hand to me. "Come on, baby."

Bewildered, I let her lead me inside. Through the screen door she says to Killian, "You can visit with Bowie on the porch, down by the dock, or inside here if he gets too chilly." She checks her watch. "He'll be hungry in about two hours, so you can leave then."

With that, she shuts the heavy wooden door and hands me a fresh cup of coffee with too much sugar and almond milk.

It's delicious, and also, what the *hell* just happened?

"Bravo, G-ma!" Mattie says and does a little flamenco dancer clap before sprawling on the couch in her pajamas. "That guy's a dick."

"Hole in one," Big Daddy agrees. He's holding June in one arm like a football, and they're both watching golf from his massive recliner.

G-ma turns around from the blinds she's peeking through to shoo me away. "I've got my eye on him, Hannah. You go rest."

Speechless, I take my coffee and plop down beside Mattie. Kira obviously couldn't handle sleeping downstairs after the snake incident, so she, Mattie, and June slept up here, and Bowie and I bunked downstairs in the kids' room. I can hear Kira's light snores from the guest room where she's still sleeping, and every now and then Bowie *mehs!* with displeasure from outside. After one startled cry and Killian's cursing, I stand up too fast and slosh coffee on my sweats.

"I better check on them."

"Sit yourself down," G-ma commands from her perch by the window. "You need to stop bailing that boy out. It's time he learned how to be a daddy, and he can't do that if you're rescuing him every time Bowie gives him the business."

Mattie nods, sipping her own confectionary coffee appreciatively. "Listen to your mama, Hannah. She knows what's up."

Listen to your mama. That's a new one. I blink as G-ma opens the door and throws a diaper and a bag of wipes at Killian's head, then shuts the door again.

She catches me staring and smirks. "Honey, don't look so surprised. I'm an expert with deadbeats."

Yeah, that checks out.

With nothing to do and no babies to cuddle, I feel unmoored. I roam around the cabin idly, picking up odds and ends Mama and Darryl have collected over the years, brushing off the dust, and putting them back. A spiral-bound sketchbook peeks out from the china cabinet, and my eyes widen. It's my old ideas book. I grab the sketchbook and flip through the aged yellow pages with a smile. Clothing I wanted to design—a pair of daisy-print overalls and a futuristic jumpsuit that screams *Barbie in Space*. Next is the mock-up of the fairy-tale bedroom I longed for, complete with canopy and netting and carved wooden posts. The smell of colored pencil still lingers on the pages, and it brings me back to the days I spent sketching all the ways I wanted to beautify my small world. I clasp the sketchbook to my chest. My heart brims with a strange mix of pride at the potential little Hannah had, but also pity for her, too, because her dreams still haven't come true.

Yet. *Yet.* It's a magical word, *yet.*

"Hey, Mama? You got a notepad I can use?"

The rest of Killian's visit flies by. There's more cursing from outside, and more crying, too, but G-ma intercedes like a nurturing mercenary on my behalf before permanent psychological damage occurs for either one. I'm banished to G-ma's crosswords chair, a big, cushy thing nestled in the corner between two large windows. The gentle mountain sunshine warms my shoulders as I curl up and sketch vision after vision for the downstairs renovation. I imagine what *I'd* want in a cabin and develop those ideas against the backdrop of what we already have, including my furniture rescued from Killian's. No matter what, though, this dream will cost money. I hope Kira's right about our case against Bob. Otherwise, I'm going to be combing the internet for blood stain removal and ideas for making concrete floors bespoke.

A soft knock at the door wakes me from my daydreams. Killian's sheepish when he hands Bowie over to me, and the look of pained relief on his face is unmistakable. Maybe now he'll realize how little he actually did for Bowie before, and how much more of himself it's going to take to be an equal partner in Bowie's life.

"Hannah, please. Think about what I said." Killian runs both hands down his face, his shoulders slumped in defeat. All from two uninterrupted hours with our son! I shake my head, both in disappointment and response to his request. I won't think about it. There's a big red *X* across Killian's face in my head, and that's how it's going to stay from now on.

A vintage Jeep Wrangler rumbles up the road, its top off to let the sunshine glow against the long, shiny brown hair of its driver. My stomach drops when I recognize the woman behind the hip, round sunglasses that I could never pull off. It's the woman from the show. The one that called Killian *K*. Something clicks audibly, and I realize it's my teeth snapping together.

Killian sees me watching her and rubs the back of his neck. "That's Jamie, the—uh, friend I was telling you about."

"You never told me about her." I'm doing the best I can to squash the jealousy roaring in my ears, but it still shows through my tight, clipped words. *Dammit.*

"Yeah, I did. At dinner? She's the guitarist for Fellow Animals."

Looking back, I do remember him rambling on about some amazing guitarist he'd been jamming with in between Taiwanese sausages numbers 1 through 7 on our dinner "date." I didn't realize it was *her*. His eyes follow the Jeep as it parks alongside the edge of the dirt road on the steep embankment. Don't Jeeps tip over a lot? Maybe that will happen. His morning's frustration dissolves when he looks at her, replaced by clear boyish longing. I want to vomit at the sheer expanse of his crush.

"Geez, *K*." My cheeks heat with embarrassment and anger—at him for bringing her here, at me for caring, and at her for wearing another goddamn crop top. "Really selling this whole *please come home* bullshit."

"Look, I brought your car back, and I needed a ride home. She offered, okay? It's not like that." Killian rolls his eyes, like I'm the one being irrational. Two days ago, I thought he was going to propose, and now he's bringing his new crush to my parents' house? *Fuck* him.

"Yeah, cool, whatever. Let me know when you can handle spending time with your son again." I start to stomp away, but a deliciously petty urge fills me up.

I whirl back around and wave at Jamie, still sitting in her Jeep, like a maniac. "Oh, HEY, Jackie, right?! Great to see you again! Killian and I had sex two days ago, and he just begged me to come home because he can't change a diaper! Guys these days, *amirite*? Also, he once said women guitarists can't rock as hard because their hands are too small!" Victory surges through me when her mouth drops open, then snaps shut in a flat, dismayed line. I leave Killian standing there with a horrified look on his face, then smile over my shoulder at the wreckage.

"Have a *great* ride back!"

With Bowie in my arms, I take the stairs down to the Airbnb with a grin too big for my face. But as the engine revs and the Jeep disappears down the mountain road, so does all the delight from messing up Killian's day. The way he looked at her flashes through my mind—without judgment, without disappointment.

With admiration. *With* respect.

My heart crumples as I reach the bottom step, and I hold Bowie to my chest tightly, willing myself not to sob into his soft cheeks. It's not because I lost my job, boyfriend, and home in the span of one godforsaken day, or because I want any of them back, because I don't. But it still hurts, being unwanted. It hurts being left behind. And because Bowie can't feel it yet and I pray he never will, I feel Killian's rejection for us both.

And it hurts. It hurts.

The tears are coming down thick, and I sink onto the last step and let them claim me. I don't want to see G-ma right now, or Big Daddy, or even Kira and Mattie. They'd tell me Killian's not worth crying over, and I already know that. But my dream of a family is. The one that still hasn't come true, like all the others.

Yet.

Yet. I cling to that magical word, *yet*, but right now, it feels like a lie.

"Hannah? Are you . . . okay?"

I flinch, the rough wooden step digging into my back as I smear the tears away quickly. Goddammit, River's standing on the edge of the porch, a drill dangling from one hand. I didn't even see him there. Before him is the hole, or rather, where it used to be. The rotten wood's been replaced with a clean new plank, making the rest of the beaten gray wood stare in envy.

I think I'm projecting.

The corners of his full mouth are turned down in concern, and worse, pity. *Fuck.* Did he hear all of that? Me yelling at the new girl like a deranged, bitter ex? A single, isolated laugh barks out of my mouth, then resolves into a sob. Not helping my case here but come on. How much humiliation can a person handle in one day?

"No. I'm not okay. I'm thirty-one years old, and I had to move in with my parents because I lost my whole life in one epic stroke this week." My voice breaks, but I shove myself up to standing, hoisting Bowie higher onto my chest. River's standing there stock-still, like a rabbit assessing whether to run from the predator. Well, let him run. Why should I care what the hot neighbor thinks, anyway? Do I really think he'd be interested in *me*? A broke-ass single mom with breasts that fury-leak?

Fuck. Two giant wet blotches on my T-shirt now approximate where my nipples are. Judging by how cold they are, that happened when I was yelling at Jamie and Killian. Another laugh rips out of me, and I gesture at my front like *Exhibit A.* "I am *a disaster.* I am a *mess.* I'm tired, I'm embarrassed, I'm sad, but more than anything, I'm so *incredibly* angry!"

My breath is coming out in pained huffs, and I'm staring at River, like it's his place to defend the world's shitty treatment of me, to explain it away and tell me how much I deserve it. But he just stands there, bearing witness to my meltdown and looking infuriatingly gorgeous while doing it. He's still in his yoga pants, and a long-sleeved T-shirt whose neckhole has been cut away, revealing the elegant dip of his collarbones. I absurdly want to press my tear-swollen face to this stranger's chest, feel his arms wrap around me and Bowie both. The audacity of me wanting such a thing when I can never, ever have it completes the devastation I feel.

"I'm—sorry. I've got to feed my baby now," I mumble, then flee for the Airbnb's door. I shut it against his warm brown eyes, against this morning, against my whole disaster of a life.

CHAPTER EIGHT

"You ready?" Kira places both hands on my shoulders, peering closely into my eyes. Even though Starla frantically scheduled this meeting two weeks ago right after Kira sent the letter, I'm unbelievably nervous. I'm not sure why. I don't work for Bob, and as Kira keeps saying, he can't hurt me anymore. Sure, he single-handedly made my life a pressure cooker of stress, but who's traumatized here?

Okay, me. It's definitely me.

I breathe in for four long counts, and out for longer. Kira is by my side, and she made Atlanta's Top Plaintiff Attorneys list before she cracked thirty. She's a champion for the wronged and discriminated against, a hero of the people.

And she's *my* best friend.

"I can tell you're worrying." Kira boops me on the nose. "Stop. This is gonna be fun." We're standing outside the door to her firm's best conference room, the one with the killer view of Midtown. Her hand shoots to her ear, and her eyes stray from mine for a second. "They're here? Send them in."

"You have a headset on?!" I squeal. I squeal when I'm nervous. Kira holds up a finger to shush me.

"No coffee. Give him a glass of tomato juice but nuke it for ten seconds first. Okay, we'll be in soon." She turns back to me, a devious, closed-lip smile rendering her adorable face into something mischievous and vaguely alarming. I know that face. That's the same face she made as she poured barbecue sauce, vinegar, and mayo into the carton of soy milk she kept in our dorm's communal fridge. We suspected our obnoxious neighbor Shayna

Plunkett was the thief stealing Kira's soy milk, and after Shayna complained loudly about having to room next door to a Black lesbian because of Obama, we decided she had to be destroyed.

And she *was*. The next morning, we watched with glee as Shayna spewed a stolen mouthful of curdled condiment milk all over her laptop screen in the common room, then *bonus!* vomited on the keyboard, ruining her technology on the morning a big paper was due.

She never stole Kira's milk again.

"You don't have any barbecue sauce in there, do you?" I'm joking, but also, not?

Kira tosses her head back and laughs so loud that Starla and Bob definitely hear it through the door. Then she throws the door open and saunters into the conference room like she owns the place, which she kind of does since she's already made partner. I follow behind, trying not to knock anything off the fancy bookshelves, fancy credenza, *or* fancy table as I enter the room. The knickknacks look expensive up in here. Bob and Starla are seated opposite the big window that looks down on Midtown, and my jittery heart drops like a rogue elevator. *I'd* been planning on sitting there. How can I stress-dissociate into the silver tower skyline now?

"Finally!" Bob slams his palms on the table, making the large glass of warm tomato juice in front of him tremble. "We've been waiting half an hour!"

It's been three minutes, tops. Bob's connection to reality has always been tenuous, though.

"Can someone tell me what the hell's going on?" He eyes me first with disgust, then Kira with disdain. She doesn't notice, too busy giving the handsome receptionist a set of instructions before taking her own seat across the table. With his thin lips curled in full glower, Bob spins in his seat and points at the male receptionist. "You. *You* tell me."

"Bob!" Starla snaps, but he ignores her like usual. I know this game. He's trying to bait Kira because it makes so much sense to double down on sexist asshole behavior when you're at a settlement negotiation for sexist asshole behavior. Total Bob logic.

The receptionist, I think his name is Peter, smiles mildly at Bob.

"Gladly, sir. You're about to be annihilated."

With that, Peter's mild smile turns vicious, all mayhem and chaos and bloody battle yells, and a trail of goose bumps fires up both of my arms. I get why Kira likes this guy now. Bob shrinks back into his leather-cushioned conference chair, and for some reason, takes a tentative sip of the skunky tomato juice like that'll appease the raw Viking energy Peter's giving off right now.

Okay. Maybe this *is* going to be fun.

I settle into my seat next to Kira and take the mug of hot, frothy cappuccino Peter sets down for me. Bob looks at my mug, then at his smelly, warm glass of tomato juice, and emits a strange mewling sound.

"Can I get you anything else, Ms. Tate?" Peter's blue eyes twinkle from behind his thick-rimmed glasses as he smiles gently at me. I shake my head, intensely grateful that Kira and her Viking receptionist are on my side.

"Mr. Groashe, Ms. Kumar," Kira begins, her expression and tone even, professional, and yet, utterly dangerous. "Unless you would like to meet me in federal court, you will pay my client two years' of her salary and the monetary value of all her accrued vacation and personal time off."

Silence. Then:

"The *fuck* did you say?!" Bob's entire essence seems to heave forward, splatting all over the table in front of him in an indignant uproar. I'm unable to move, however. Nothing except my eyeballs, which dart so hard to the right to stare at Kira, I almost sprain them. That's . . . that's . . . I'm bad at math, hold on a sec . . .

That's *$130,000*, plus I don't even *know* how much PTO. Bob never let me use those days. They were practically an imaginary number on my paystubs.

"That's for violating my client's FMLA rights." Kira folds her hands, her face placid as ever. "You demanded that she work during her federally protected FMLA leave, then fired her when she refused, as she was legally entitled to do. This is a slam dunk case, and a sweet young mother like my client? A judge could easily tack on another hundred thousand in punitive damages. Do you want to take that risk?"

The mug slips out of my grasp, but Peter swoops in and catches it. Where the hell did he come from? I feel woozy.

The only person who doesn't look surprised is Starla. Her mouth is set in the flat grimace of a woman resigned to a very unpleasant fate.

Bob whirls on her. "You're my lawyer, aren't you? Fight her!"

Starla's nostrils flare slightly. "I advise you to take the deal."

Bob's eyelids practically disappear into his skull. "What the hell am I paying you for?! You're as bad as them!" He jabs a finger at each of us, like all the world's vaginas are uniting against him, which is weird because I'm pretty sure vaginas have as little to do with Bob as possible.

"Take the deal, Bob," Starla says through gritted teeth.

"No!" He turns his sneer on Kira. "You don't have a case against me. You're just another lazy millennial snowflake, looking for an easy ride off someone else's succ—"

"I am happy to share this preview of our case with you, but this meeting is only slated for half an hour. For every fifteen minutes longer that you drag this out, our settlement requirement increases by ten thousand dollars."

Bob nearly spits. "You've got nothing!"

Kira holds up a printout of the email Bob shot off to me at one a.m., just a few hours after he fired me. "Ms. Tate, would you mind reading this aloud for the record?"

I take the paper, willing my hand to stop trembling, and begin to read. It's a typo-ridden manifesto on "what's wrong with entitled mommies today." In it, he blasts me for being lazy for refusing the work, stating he'd fire me a hundred times if he could before going off on some fairly gross fake news about the toxins found in "boob juice."

I'm still shaking when I finish reading, but this time with fury. Not because this email is grossly misogynistic, but because it's not *special*. He's said terrible things to me for years.

And I let him. For a paycheck, I fucking *let* him.

"Bob, *take the deal*." Starla's glaring at him over the printout.

Bob glances nervously at her, then at my reddening face. "No?"

I'm pretty sure he didn't mean that as a question.

Kira laughs politely, then slaps a book down on the table, neatly bound and thicker than one of those mega-bibles with the big print. I realize she never told me exactly what she was going to do with all those emails and texts we went through, or the voice mails we transcribed. The sight of it sends hot fire down my neck. "This is every recorded communication you've had with my client for the last seven years. Do *you* want to venture a guess at how big a damages award my client would receive if she took you to court for the rampant sexual harassment present in these communications?"

Bob stares at the book, his face now paler than his shirt, and scoots his chair back a foot. He *should* be scared. I'm ready to use that book as a weapon.

Kira smiles patiently. "Seen enough?"

"Fine!" Bob crosses his arms, avoiding my searing laser-beam glare. "I'll settle this . . . this . . . little *grudge suit* you're whining about. Twenty thousand, take it or leave it."

Kira raises her eyebrows as I ball my hands into fists. "Time's running out, Mr. Groashe."

"Fifty thousand dollars!" Bob licks his lips. He doesn't look good. The sweat's seeped through the collar of his white dress shirt. "That's more than fair!"

"Your total is now two years' of Ms. Tate's salary, one hundred and thirty thousand dollars; the value of all her unused time off, which I am estimating to be valued at ten thousand; plus an extra ten thousand for your unreasonable delay today."

Bob's gone still, stock-still. Starla leans over and whispers vehemently in his ear. I can't pick out much, but I hear the words *lucky, fucking unreal,* and *goddamn asshole.* She's not really trying to be quiet. After a minute of her diatribe, Bob throws his hands in the air, the pain visibly etched in the folds of his forehead.

"Fine. FINE! Goddammit, fine! But this isn't over!" He points at me. Now *his* hand's shaking.

"Yes, it is." Starla produces a pen and shoves the settlement agreement Kira's already drawn up in front of Bob's face. "Sign."

Bob takes the pen, grumbling. "Fine. I'll sign for now."

Starla rolls her eyes as he slashes his signature on the line.

"Wonderful," Kira says, her wicked smile returning as she eyes me conspiratorially. "I believe my client has something she wants to say before she signs."

Bob looks up, visibly frightened, as I stand and lean over the table.

"Now apologize to me, you *fucking asshole.*"

≈

My head's still reeling as I pull into Killian's driveway. *What just happened?* I must've asked Kira that twenty times before she had Peter escort me to my car for fear I'd wander through the parking garage all day. It's fair. I don't even remember the drive over here.

Bob . . . apologized . . . to *me?*

Bob's going to *pay me $150,000*?? He gets to do it in installments, but *still.* It's like I've slipped into a different dimension where everything *looks* the same, except I'm suddenly not poor. Or a terrible old man's punching bag. In fact, I think he's *my* punching bag now. The weirdness doesn't let up, either, when I enter Killian's house. It feels so familiar and yet completely bizarre without all my things. I see Killian's finally hit up IKEA to replace the furniture I reclaimed. Everything's white, angular, and econo-Swedish. The smell of pressboard and warmed breast milk fills the kitchen, where I find a frazzled Killian bustling about. Somewhere, Bowie's gone full hangry.

Killian doesn't notice me standing in the doorway. I take a full second to absorb the scene. Killian, frantic and disheveled. His perfect princely hair mussed and oily. He probably hasn't had a chance to shower since I dropped Bowie off with him at eight this morning. He finally looks up, and a smile spreads slowly on my face when I see the large streak of spit-up rainbowed across his forehead.

He blinks at me, perhaps sensing the same weird unreality of this role reversal. Here I am, dressed in a pair of crisp black cigarette pants, a white tank with no stains *please clap*, and a cropped gray suit jacket that's been generously tailored to accommodate a breastfeeding mom. I look amazing, but I can't take credit. When I got to her office, Kira dressed me up in her clothes like *Barbie Goes to War Against the Patriarchy*.

"So." I divert my gaze and rock on my heels a bit, a little embarrassed on his behalf. "Where's Bowie?"

Killian glances at the empty activity mat on the floor, and his face erupts in panic. "He was just there!" He takes off in the mad catastrophe sprint all parents know, crying out "BOWIE!" as though our three-month-old son can answer him.

Bowie, it turns out, is perhaps six inches away, just out of sight behind an aggressively large teddy bear. They can barely move at this age, but Killian doesn't seem to realize that.

Both Killian and Bowie look utterly dumbfounded at how he got there, but I clap and squeal. "Bowie baby, you rolled onto your side! You're getting so strong!" I reach down and swoop him up into my arms and speckle his chubby cheeks with kisses. "You'll be rolling all the way over before we know it!" Bowie coos with happiness at my return and not so subtly stares at my chest.

Damn. That starts young.

"Mind if I . . . " I trail off, thumbing at the living room.

"No, no, please *God*, feed him." Killian shoos me toward the living room, which now looks enormous with only a small, cheap two-seater futon couch and a Poäng chair.

I take the Poäng. They *are* comfortable.

Killian shuffles in behind me, exhausted from his three hours of baby-sitting. He plops onto the futon. "So, how did it go?" he asks dryly, his tone implying exactly how he thinks it went. No matter how Bob treated me, it never made an impression on Killian. His perennial take is that all bosses are terrible to their underlings, and it was just my fate to be constantly bulldozed by a maniac with zero boundaries.

As I lift my shirt, I start to tell him everything, just like I would've when we were together, but I stop abruptly. It doesn't feel right. I don't want to share my good news with him, I don't want his commentary, and he doesn't get to see flashes of my boobs anymore. "Excuse me, can you leave?" Killian's brow furrows, confused all over again. "I'm about to feed Bowie, and I need privacy."

Killian's body responds to my tone before his brain comprehends the situation. *Me* setting boundaries with *him*? He straightens and stands. "Um, of course. Sorry. I—I didn't think—"

"I'll let you know when we're finished so you can say goodbye."

"Right, sure." Killian runs a hand through his hair, then pulls it away with a grimace.

I smile. "Go take a shower. You'll feel better." Now *I'm* the magnanimous prince, and *he's* the hapless, filthy scamp.

My oh my, how the *Lack* table has turned.

CHAPTER NINE

The first deposit from Bob hits my bank account at midnight three business days later. I stare at it over my morning coffee, blinking at the big, unreal number on my laptop. Twenty-five thousand dollars. My dinky online bank must think I've become a hitman on the dark web because I've never had that much cash in my account. The craziest part is there's more coming. According to the terms of the structured settlement plan, Bob has to pay me twenty-five thousand dollars for the next five months. Is this life?

For the first time ever, money isn't a concern, and the sudden release of financial stress has thrown me off balance. You'd think a windfall like this would have me celebrating, and I am, but look what it cost me to get here. Years of unhappiness and stress. Of being minimized and dehumanized and never measuring up and being told so every day. First by Bob, but eventually Killian, too. The damage that did to my self-esteem and confidence, to my dreams, to my ability to dream at *all*. Is it any wonder I chased the love and acceptance of a man who didn't respect me? Is it any wonder I lost myself?

I grit my jaw. The era of me taking shit from men is over. I know $150,000 can't provide for Bowie and me long term. But used wisely, this money could change everything. I can pay off my college loans, put a whopping nest egg away for Bowie, max out my IRA, and make an emergency savings account with real money instead of a tarot card representing financial prosperity and three of G-ma's best crystals.

Most immediately, it means I can get the Airbnb renovation going so that G-ma and Big Daddy won't have to worry about money anymore, either. Then, with the Airbnb open for business, I'll finally figure out what I want to do with my life. My old ideas sketchbook stares down at me from G-ma's china cabinet. I knew how to dream once. Maybe I can learn again.

Right. I bring up a fresh browser window and type into the search engine: *River Aronson Blue Ridge Georgia.* A brief blush envelops me, but this is business. Last night, we had a long discussion about who we'd hire to do the renovation. Both Big Daddy and G-ma were adamant—it has to be River. He's the best carpenter around and does contracting, too; he's trustworthy; and he's fine as hell (that was Mama). The thought of seeing him again after he witnessed my meltdown a few weeks ago makes me want to disappear into the mist, but I promised them I'd think about it. I'm putting up the money, after all, and it makes sense to research and get a few quotes first. Right?

So me googling his ass is actually very responsible. Go me!

And . . . there's nothing. No website for his carpentry or contracting businesses, no social media page, no Google reviews. I frown at the screen. Did he go out of business? Now that I've given myself permission to e-stalk him, the disappointment at coming up empty-handed is potent. I try different search terms and click over to the Image results. My cursor hovers over a small thumbnail of a young Chris Hemsworth in a button-down and an off-kilter tie. It's the smile, though, that makes me click through. It leads me to an old business networking profile for *R. Aronson*, located in Atlanta, Georgia. My eyebrows fork into my hairline. It's an old picture, but it's him. His blond hair is short and corporate-looking, and his cheeks are free from the tawny stubble that shadows them now. His face is open and guileless, a baby in discount business attire. The sole entry under Experience is *Digital Associate, Farmers Family Insurance Co.*

Huh. So, Yoga Man has a corporate past. What's the story there?

After looking up the numbers of two other local contractors with decent reviews, I finally close my laptop.

"Hey, G-ma." I prod her slippered foot with my own. She's nodded off in her crosswords chair, reading glasses balanced precariously on the tip of her nose. They slip off when she wakes with a start, but the dangly chain catches them.

"Whuh?" G-ma sits up and blinks. "What is it, baby girl?"

"Can you watch Bowie for a while?" I eye her with earned skepticism. She put Bowie's diaper on backward last night, which I discovered when I found *poop* in his *hair*.

The onesie could not be saved.

"I was thinking of walking over to River's place to talk to him about the contracting job. See if he's interested."

"Of course!" G-ma looks fully awake now, her voice eager. "You go on. Bowie will be fine with us."

I'm trying not to feel discouraged. After my research this morning, the renovation costs ranged from *A Lot* all the way to *Just Buy Your Own Island, Why Don't You*. I've set fifteen thousand dollars aside for this project, but that has to cover everything: the reno, furniture, *and* decor. I could spare more, but G-ma and Big Daddy don't want me to spend a dollar of my own, let alone fifteen thousand of them. They only relented when I agreed they'd pay me back once the Airbnb starts bringing in money.

"I know we leaned on you more than we should have at times, but we've put an end to all that. Just cause you're rich now don't change a thing. You understand me?" Big Daddy had said, sounding strangely fierce.

I'd nodded, too surprised and grateful to speak. Part of me was worried they'd see the settlement as license to turn into their former selves, spending money they don't have and looking to me to make it all better. I felt guilty about that, but angry it was justified, too. Hearing Big Daddy's words felt like an apology and a promise, all at once.

"You've got Bowie to think about first, and yourself, too," G-ma said. "This is your chance to get a leg up, baby. I'm sorry it took Kiki terrifying that asshole boss of yours to get you here, but if there's one thing we know how to do, it's how to make lemonade from lemons. Right, baby?" She'd laughed and wiped the tears from my cheek, and I let her. Just one more thing in this streak of unreal reality. Mama being . . . well.

My *mother*.

So they want to hire their neighbor. The one who saw me at my worst.

I cringe all over again, but the least I can do is check him out.

For the work, I mean. I am *determined* not to undress him with my eyes this time.

"Great. I'll head over now then." I slap my hands against my legs, then look down at my baggy jeans. They're old skinny jeans that are so stretched out I could fit two butts and a foot-long vulva in here. They seemed a good idea when I thought all I'd be doing today is cleaning out the Airbnb, but now . . .

"I'm just gonna go change first."

G-ma nods, her eyebrows raised higher than the rims of her glasses. "Good idea, baby."

"When Bowie wakes up from his nap, he'll be hungry. There's a bottle already made up in the fridge."

She waves her hand at me, and I know I've been dismissed.

Ten minutes later, I'm tromping through the woods in a sundress and my favorite sandals. It's a hot, humid day, so the sundress is very practical. The fact that it makes me look like a whimsical forest sprite with fantastic breasts is a low-key bonus, and I will be taking no questions at this time.

Where *is* it? I've never seen River's cabin from the road. I assumed it was set back in the woods out of sight. His work truck is parked out front, so he's definitely home, but where *is* home? There's a beaten path that cuts through the middle of his property, but it leads from the road down to his dock on the lake. Does he live in a freaking burrow? The noon heat's making me vaguely desperate. Ten more minutes sweating out here, and this sprite will transition to full hag.

"River!" I cup my hands around my mouth and yell, hoping he'll hear me from Narnia or wherever the hell he is. I stop to sniff my underarm and wince.

"Hannah?"

My head jerks up, caught in the act. I don't know what I expected, but a shirtless River hanging out the window of a *treehouse* wasn't it. A completely epic treehouse, at that. He looks amused, and my cheeks flush on command at the curve of his smile.

"Oh, um, hi!" I wave frenetically, as though waving was what I was doing the whole time. "You live in a treehouse!"

Jesus, deliver me from myself.

"You noticed!" His smile grows until his whole face has gotten in on it, and it radiates such good-natured fun, such *friendliness*, my own smile breaks through the crush of humiliation. Is this what acceptance feels like? Whenever I embarrassed myself in front of Killian, he'd shake his head. *You're such a mess, Hannah Tate.* He'd smirk down at me, shrinking me a little more with every affectionate put-down. But even though River's witnessed my petty, pit-sniffing, unhinged waving self, his smile isn't mean or at my expense. It's just . . . nice. Open, welcoming, and *nice*.

It leaves me a bit breathless.

"D'you want to come—?"

"Yes!" The word is out of my mouth before he even finishes the question, and we both laugh. I *do* want to come up. His treehouse is completely magical. The main house is made from a rich honeyed pine, its top disappearing into the green canopy of leaves. The walls are more window than not, and the glass reflects the trees around it. No wonder I didn't see it. The house blends seamlessly into the woods surrounding it, supported by multiple trees growing up, around, and in one case *through* the house itself.

"The ladder's round back."

The *ladder*? I stare down at my sandals. *Don't fail me now, Target clearance rack.*

I step around to where a wooden ladder ascends in a nearly vertical line fifteen feet in the air. River waits at the top for me, Battle-cat *rrrriaow*ing around his feet. He sees me hesitate, then sees the reason why.

"Want me to Tarzan you up here?"

Yes. A *thousand* times yes.

"No! I've got it!" I give him a double thumbs-up, and seriously, what's wrong with me?

It's a sturdy ladder with a handrail on each side and rungs that function more like steps. Just really, really vertical steps. *Come on, Hannah, Battle-cat can do it.* One of my sandals slips a bit, and I swallow my shriek before I show how scared I am. I don't know why I'm doing this. All I know is that if I quit now, it'll feel like I've failed a strange pop quiz, and River will decide something about me that I won't be able to undo.

When I get to the top, angels sing. River extends a hand and helps me through the trapdoor onto the platform. The sight of him up close, dressed only in his loose yoga pants, makes the angels kick it up a notch. His chest is smooth, rounded by natural muscle that moves in harmony beneath his skin with every move. Mesmerizing. With great effort, I rip my eyes upward to meet his gaze.

"Laundry day," River says with a simple shrug. Is he smirking? The punk. A line of clothes hangs from the branches, drip-drying, which I may need to do now, too. He pulls a shirt off the line and slips it on, and thank god honestly because I'm not sure I could carry on coherent thought otherwise.

I step carefully away from the trapdoor and smile feebly. "I wouldn't have worn sandals if I knew you were a hobbit."

River laughs, the amusement opening up his face like a window into sunshine. "Don't hobbits live in the hillsides?"

"You're right," I say, my own smile feeling truer now. "You're more like an elf up here."

"Welcome to Rivendell, milady," he says, gesturing me forward with a genteel half bow. "Can I get you water, or perhaps a nice, frothy grog?"

Now it's my turn to laugh, and he grins. This guy's a total goofball. Come to think about it, a treehouse is pretty on brand for him. I'm intensely grateful for his easy demeanor. After what River witnessed, he'd be justified in maintaining twenty feet of distance from me at all times.

But he's just so . . . *pleasant.*

"Water would be great." I crane my head around, taking in the place. The structure is impressive from the ground, but up close, the details are breathtaking. The platform curves along with the natural line of the trees supporting it. An arbor crisscrosses overhead, with dangling honeysuckle vines climbing happily up from their terra-cotta pots. Beneath their shade are two low wooden chairs angled toward the sun.

And the *view.* I thought nothing could top the view from G-ma and Big Daddy's porch swing, but this . . . it feels like a bird's view must, like it's just you and the sky and the green, green earth.

"Wow," I breathe. River hands me a glass of cold water, and I drink it all in. "Did you build this?"

"Yes ma'am." His smile is small and shy but pleased. I marvel at how someone so talented could be shy about anything. If I built all this, I'd run for president.

"Can I have a tour?"

His rich brown eyes light up, and I wonder how many people he shows this magical place to. I start to ask, but then bite the question off at the quick. It's none of my business who he brings home. I'm here to talk renovation, contracting, money. Head in the game, Hannah!

He leads me into the house through a window wall curled open on a track overhead.

"It's a glass garage door," he explains when he sees me gaping at it. "I keep it open on nice days."

The view it provides is of blue skies streaked with white and the crests and dips of the forested mountains that reach for it. Maybe this is why River seems so happy and zen.

If you wake up entangled in the beauty of an untouched world, free from power lines and highways and corporate expectations, maybe perspective is easier to come by.

Inside is small, but efficient. There's a kitchen area with two burners, a tiny oven, a counter for prep, and a sink. A set of white dishes lies stacked on open wooden shelves, the kind used by people with nothing to hide. A black wood stove is centered against the wall, a well-worn leather armchair happily sagging in front of it. The best part is the shelf that wraps around every wall of the treehouse like an embrace, hovering just below the ceiling. It's stuffed with books. An image of River sitting by the fire in that leather chair reading *The Fellowship of the Ring* while the wind whips through the trees comes unbidden to my mind. I realize with a start that I'm fondling something soft, and I snatch my hand off the back of his chair.

"This place is amazing, River."

"Thank you." The words are simple and earnest. The whole time I've been taking in his home, he's stood quietly by, leaning against a wall and watching me. I meet his eyes, then glance quickly away from the warmth I see there.

I'm glad I climbed the ladder.

I stand on my tiptoes and reach for the first book I see. My finger brushes the chapped paper spine, but I can't quite grab ahold of it. Then warmth radiates across my exposed back, sending a cascade of prickles across my body. River's standing so close behind me that I freeze, every inch of me aware of every inch of him. He reaches over my shoulder for the book, and for an instant I feel deliciously trapped between the heat of his body and the cool, smooth wood of the wall.

God*dammit*, nipples! Can you *not* right now?

He rocks back onto his heels with the book and hands it to me, a well-worn copy of *Uprooted*. I turn around to face him, breath catching when I realize he's still as close as before.

Stay calm. Do not wave!!

I press the book to my chest, hiding the traitorous nipples trying to drill holes through my bra.

"This is one of my *favorites*."

"Me too. Wizards in towers, magical woods, a badass witch." His eyes twinkle as he looks down at me. "Definitely my thing."

I swallow.

There's more, too. Pulpy fantasy novels, novelizations of every *Star Trek* show, *The Hitchhiker's Guide to the Galaxy*. I don't see a TV anywhere, so reading must be how he spends his free time. I hand the book back, hoping he'll reach over me again.

He sets it on the side table beside his chair, and I die, just a little.

I've carefully avoided looking at River's bed in the back corner of the room, preferring instead to sprain my eyeballs to take in what information I can from my peripheral vision. Windows ring around it, but the leaf canopy provides natural privacy. The bed's low to the ground, on a chic wooden platform he probably built himself. The bedding is white, simple, crisp. I'd bet anything it's linen, and I feel a surge of satisfaction.

This guy knows what he's doing. It suddenly strikes me that he has no clue why I'm here; he hasn't even asked. For all he knows, I'm the neighbors' wayward daughter who invited herself over to gawk at his treehouse.

I spin around to face him. "We want you to do the renovation on our Airbnb."

Welp. So much for getting quotes. But in my defense, this place is beautiful. If he makes our Airbnb feel half as special, my parents will be set for life.

I clear my throat and try to recoup some dignity. "Would you be interested? We have a modest budget, but I'd love to see what you could do with it."

River folds his arms, his stance widening. Is this his business look? It's a good look. His face is thoughtful. "I'm guessing you'd want to start right away?"

"As soon as you can. I'm staying with my folks temporarily. I'd like to get them all set up before I go."

His brows connect in something like a frown. "Temporarily? That's too bad."

The weird thing is, I think he means it. A flush of heat sweeps through me.

"It's good timing, actually. I'm about to finish the final book in the Vorkosigan Saga. Have you read them? I've been so obsessed, I haven't taken a job in months."

"You . . . took time off to read a *book series*?" Can people do that? I couldn't take maternity leave without getting fired.

"I work when I want to," River says, like it's that easy. Maybe it is for him. Judging by the five articles of clothing hanging dry and the literal washtub in the corner, it can't cost much to live as simply as he seems to. "I'll check around, see who's available for the crew." He strokes the stubble on his face. "Let's talk fees."

His business tone helps cool the fire rumbling in my belly, and I'm grateful for the reprieve. Being around River has a strange effect on me, like someone flicking the lights in the house on all at once. I'm not sure I like it.

"Yes, fees! Of course." I shake my head quickly, trying to dispel any vibes my pathetic self is putting off. "How does that work?"

"We'll need to cover my crew's daily wages and the price of materials," he muses. His face is thoughtful, like he's trying to decide whether to say more. Perhaps a pointed, *And you'll need to keep it in your pants, Tate.*

After a long pause, he adds, "And I have a special request."

I swallow, my entire body on high alert. Please, let it be an *Indecent Proposal.* "A r-request?"

He takes a step closer, and though there's still plenty of room between us, his presence collides into mine, jarring me with the size of it.

"I'd like to come to Sunday dinners at your place, if that's all right." For an instant, a feeling like loneliness darkens his sun-browned face, but then it's hidden by his sunny smile.

I blink. "You want to spend time with my family? Voluntarily?"

"I like your family. Besides, Darryl and Trish know how to cook." His crooked smile lights up my chest. "Maybe you do, too?"

I shake my head. "Only thing I know how to make is breast milk."

River's eyes flicker downward before he quickly averts his gaze and clears his throat. The birds stop singing, probably because they've fallen dead from contact embarrassment. I eye the platform for a quick getaway. Does he have a fireman's pole? He ought to. My *god*.

"Not even . . . Pop-Tarts?" he ventures, lips twitching.

I can't tell if I'm frowning or smiling or both. I laugh incredulously. "Okay. Breast milk and Pop-Tarts."

"Sounds like breakfast to me." He shrugs, giving me his goofiest grin yet, and I'm laughing *again*. This guy . . . what is the deal with *this guy*? I'm the human equivalent of that phrase *You made it weird*, but no matter how awkward I am, he doesn't seem to mind.

"What about your fees? Can't just be Sunday dinners." I wipe the mirth from my eyes, grasping for some shred of professionalism. I find none, just a swell of stupid, earnest excitement.

He likes my family?

"After all your folks do for me, I'd like to do this for them."

"What on earth do they do for you?" I'm genuinely puzzled.

River lowers the corner of his waistband, revealing the ridge of muscle that starts at his hip bone and dips beneath the rim of his yoga pants. My mouth dries up in response, spit a distant memory. What is happening? Did I miss something? He points at a small, thin scar across his hip, which must be what I'm supposed to be looking at. "Working in carpentry, you get your share of nicks and cuts. Your mama has stitched me up more than once out of the goodness of her heart."

My eyebrows rise. Probably not her *goodness* driving that. River lets his waistband go, and for a brief second, I consider going to nursing school.

Nah, too many body fluids.

"Also, Darryl got me into that show *Treehouse Masters*. He invites me over whenever there's a new season."

I have to shake the lust out of my brain to comprehend what he's saying. "So, my folks perform some first aid and let you watch TV, and you're going to do a renovation for them? For *free*?"

He holds a hand up when I start to protest. "I don't need the money, and we've already established I only work when I want to." He cocks an eyebrow. "And I want to."

My mouth opens, but nothing comes out. This man is a mystery. A weird, hot, anti-capitalist mystery.

"Give me a few days to round everybody up, and then we can put our heads together."

"Great. Um, okay," I say, feeling strangely light-headed. "So . . . see you Sunday?"

"For dinner," he says, his eyes flashing mischievously. "Not breakfast."

≈

I stumble back to the cabin in a state of swimmy wonder, overwhelmed with the urge to tell Kira and Mattie *everything* so I can relive it a second time. But also, completely unsure what there is to say.

The neighbor lives in a freaking treehouse!

I hired him because he has linen sheets!

It was laundry day, so he was half naked!

But when my fingers find our text chain, an ugly surge of shame makes me close the window. Why am I acting like this? There's nothing special to report. I had a human interaction with another human. One who just so happens to have amazing hips, but is that newsworthy? No.

The cabin's weirdly quiet when I enter through the porch door.

"Mama? I mean, G-ma? Big Daddy?" The lights are off, which isn't weird since the afternoon sun is bright, but the TV is off, too, and that *is* weird. It only takes a few seconds to confirm—nobody's home. I peer out the kitchen window, but their truck is parked out front beside my Corolla.

I frown. They aren't outside. I would've seen them as I walked back. Where did they take Bowie? My stomach drops, and I force myself to breathe in deeply as I call G-ma's cell phone. When it rings behind me, I jump, then curse. They left their phones? What the *fuck*, Mama?

I stomp into the guest room, where Bowie and I are staying for the time being, and grab the sneakers I should have worn to River's in the first place. The tension builds in my chest as I make my way down the dirt road, stopping to call for them every few feet. I don't know if it's the hormones, or if it's that the stakes have been irretrievably raised for me forever, but since I had Bowie, my capacity for imagining catastrophe has become *boundless*. The farther I get from the cabin, the more panic edges my vision. The world is bright, defined, almost too sharp to look at.

Where's Bowie?

"Mama! MAMA!" I'm yelling hard enough to damage my vocal cords, but I can't shake the feeling that something terrible's happened. I begin to run. "DARRYL!"

"Hannah! Over here!" Through the trees, I see my mother waving her arms. I barrel down the road, around the bend, running toward them at full speed. There they are, sitting on a porch I don't recognize—Mama, Darryl, and Bowie, but he's sitting in someone else's lap. An old man wearing a bathrobe. My heart judders in my chest at the sight of the long rifle propped up on the porch.

I storm up the steps, a terror in tennis shoes.

"Hannah, what's the matter with you?" Mama laughs a little, standing and blocking my immediate path to Bowie.

"God*dammit*, Mama!" I push past her hard, then dive forward to snatch Bowie from the stranger's surprised hands. Lucky for him, he doesn't try to fight it. "What were you *thinking*?!"

"Now listen here, Hannah," Darryl starts, but I mow him down before he dares try to father me right now.

"Stay out of it, Darryl!"

His face turns to stone, but I don't give a shit because he sure as hell didn't consider my feelings before taking my baby without telling me. I spin back to Mama. The surprise has left her face, replaced with a grim set to her jaw. "You took Bowie, you didn't leave a note, you didn't even take your phones!" The fury in my voice is quickly turning into raw, hoarse sobs. "I couldn't *find you*!"

Mama's mouth opens, but she doesn't try to defend herself, or belittle the panic that's gripped me and won't let go. Her eyes fill with tears.

"Oh, Hannah baby. I'm so sorry! I didn't think you'd be back yet, I didn't know you'd worry." Her voice breaks as I completely lose it in front of her. She holds her arms out for me, but I back away, down and off the porch.

"You let a *stranger* hold my *baby*! No offense, sir," I say to the old man through my wild sobs. "And there are guns *everywhere*!" They're propped on every available surface. It's like a goddam militia up in here.

"I'm sorry, baby! It's just Sarge—he's the neighborhood watch!" Mama's wringing her hands, more upset than I've seen her in years, but it doesn't make this all right. "I don't think they're loaded!"

"Course they are, Trish," Sarge says, then makes it up to his feet. "Though I'd never let anything hurt your baby, miss. I'm awful sorry for scarin' you."

I suck in breath after breath, willing my chest to stop heaving. Bowie's looking at me, his little face pinched with worry, and that hurts my heart more than anything. How young was I when I started seeing my mama like this? Panicked and bawling?

How young was I when I started worrying for her, too?

I can't say anything else.

I turn and flee.

CHAPTER TEN

don't know why I'm so nervous. You'd think I'd be auditioning for HGTV instead of having Sunday dinner with my contractor. I've already changed outfits three times, which feels ridiculous, but I want to strike the right tone. We are in a client-contractor relationship now, and I want him to respect me.

But I also want him to think I'm hot. Respectfully.

The grandfather clock chimes five long peals, and a tiny swell of relief rises in me. Time to wake Bowie from his nap. There's nothing like the *here and now!* of a baby's needs to distract you from everything else.

Our small room is dark and cool, the overhead fan's chain tinkling lightly. I lean over the crib's edge and check on Bowie, still sweetly sleeping. I've started putting him down in those swaddles with the batwing arms. Zonked out on his back with his arms up, he looks like a little cactus. I brush my index finger softly against his warm, silky cheek, and my body floods with happiness hormones. It's these little moments that mean the most to me. The edges to my day when time slows down enough that I can step back and marvel at all that he is.

The fear of him being gone hits me like a reflex, but with some effort, I squash it back down. It's gotten easier to do each day that passes. I know G-ma and Big Daddy didn't mean to scare me, but that's the problem. How did they not realize disappearing with Bowie would fling me into a full-out panic? It's not that something bad almost happened, or that Bowie's life was ever seriously in danger, but it didn't need to be any of those things, either, for my feelings to be justified. Some realities are so terrible that to face the mere possibility of them is damage enough.

I think that's why Mama felt so bad. She knew that fear, once. I think all mothers do. She'd just forgotten it until she saw it take hold of me.

Bowie murmurs in his sleep as I gently lift him to my chest. I settle into the velveteen rocker and pop out a breast, which is probably a lot of dudes' favorite way to wake up. I admire Bowie's ability to groggily nurse.

"I'm good at eating half asleep, too." I boop his nose.

By the time he's finished, I feel almost relaxed. When Mama yells through the door that River's arrived, I don't even panic-change my outfit again. God bless oxytocin.

I nuzzle Bowie for one last hit of bliss, grab my sketchpad, then open the bedroom door. Mama's busy giving River a tour of the menu, taking him from each simmering pot to crackling pan to explain the culinary feats for today's Sunday dinner. Fresh trout caught in the nearby stream, dredged with butter, cornmeal, and cayenne and fried till crispy. With roasted okra, corn on the cob, and a small summer salad with strawberries, we're in for a *treat*. Pretty sure Mama and Darryl are showing off for River and trying to make it up to me at the same time.

I approve of this tactic.

River's eyes flicker up from the kitchen counter, where he's inexplicably holding a long summer squash in each hand, to meet mine. "Hey, Hannah." He waves a squash awkwardly at me. "I'm here for Sunday dinner."

My eyebrows rise as a smile lifts the corners of my mouth.

"You came prepared." I gesture to the squash in his hands, and he looks down, as if he isn't sure how they got there.

"Give me those," Mama fusses. River relinquishes the vegetables and lets Mama push him out of the kitchen, grinning in pleasant bewilderment.

"Hey, Darryl, what's the—"

"There ain't no Darryl in here." He snaps his tongs at me, then flips another fish in the skillet. "Only Big Daddy."

I drag my palm down my face, then wince apologetically at River. "Calling him Big Daddy in front of others always makes me feel like a pervert."

River shrugs, the corners of his mouth twitching. "That's why I only call him Big Daddy in private."

That surprises a laugh out of me, and he flashes that grin again. Mama bustles by, then stops and eyes us both, her hands on her hips. "What are y'all doing in here? Go on outside and visit while Big Daddy finishes up."

"Yeah, stay outta my kitchen!" Darryl hollers, then cackles to himself as he fries up another fillet.

Mama's gaze strays to Bowie in my arms. "Want me to take—"

"Nope, we're good." I avert my eyes before I see the guilt in hers and turn to River. "Wanna go downstairs and check out the space?" I swallow against my own dry tonsils and hold Bowie a little bit closer for strength. "I've got some ideas. Sketches. That I'd like to show you." The words come out squeaky and halting, but I said them, so I get a big gold star anyway.

I've spent the last few days sketching all my ideas for the renovation, and I *think* they're good, but what if they're unrealistic? Or structurally unsound? What if they're completely hack and cliché, and River hates them and has to pretend he doesn't? I pull the hair off my neck and fan myself. There's something so terrifying about trying to do what you love. This thing I've always had, this drive to design, to create—I don't know if it's talent because it's never really been tested. I'm so scared I'm going to try, really *actually* try, and then . . .

Fail. Spectacularly.

The thought alone makes the bottom of my stomach fall out. Believing that there's talent within me I haven't yet explored has gotten me through hard years. That small seed of hope has quietly sustained me, because I've never dared to speak it out loud. Not when Killian scoffed at my projects around his house, not when my secret design Instagram account maxed at eight followers. But if I try now, if I *fail*, what will I have then? It feels safer to hoard the dream than expose it to air.

"Sure." His hair is down today, the gold striped with darker shades of brass, and it sits softly on his exposed collarbone. He's wearing that old chambray shirt again, the one he was wearing the day we met. The top few buttons are undone, and my eyes keep sliding down his throat until the blue cuts off my view of his chest beneath. It hits me like a reset button, and I start all over again from the top with his friendly brown eyes, willing myself *not* to trail down to his full mouth, the hard line of his jaw, the shimmer of stubble on his long, exposed throat, and *dammit*, I'm doing it again. Reset.

As we head down the creaky external stairs, he skims his hand along the banister thoughtfully. "Any plans for the exterior?"

"Yes, starting with these stairs." My pulse picks up. *Don't say anything stupid, Hannah.* "I'd love to replace them with something more functional and less . . ."

"Terrifying?" River suggests. He bounces a little on the bottom step, the board dipping beneath his weight.

"That's the theme of this entire renovation, honestly."

"More functional, less terrifying. Got it. Those your ideas?" His gaze drops to my sketchbook. "Can I see?"

My heartbeat's thumping in my temples. Show River my sketchbook? *The whole thing?* "Umm—"

He holds both hands up. "You don't have to."

"No, here." I thrust the book at him, then take a quick step back before I can snatch it away again. I perch on the edge of an old rocking chair, and he sinks into the other one.

He opens the cover carefully, brow furrowed as he slowly scans each page before flipping to the next. He's so intently focused, he doesn't notice how I'm drinking in his attention to my ideas, analyzing every hitch of his breath, every pause, every thoughtful frown. I don't know what they all mean, and my excitement at finally sharing my dreams for the space are edged in ban-shee screams. What if they're terrible? What if they're amazing?

What *if, if, if, if*?

Suddenly, I can't take the quiet anymore. He's looked at the whole set of sketches at least twice through, and he still hasn't said a thing.

"Well? Is it—"

"It's like a different place," River says thoughtfully.

My heart's already falling, like it was standing ready to jump at the first sign of criticism. "What, um. What does that mean?"

His eyes flicker up sharply at the strangled sound of my voice. "It means it's transformative. Your ideas are interesting and beautiful, and when we're done, nobody's going to wonder if *Saw* was filmed here."

I laugh, and it ends in a hiccup. "*Really?*"

His brown eyes soften, grow almost tender. He doesn't laugh.

"Really."

And I'm *soaring*.

It's easier to talk after that. In fact, I can't seem to get the words out fast enough. I balance Bowie on the side of my lap, trying to show River different sketches while thinking out loud about how to accomplish them.

"Here, let me," he says, breaking into my frantic monologue about the importance of whimsy when choosing landscaping materials. He holds out both of his big hands for Bowie, and my eyes widen.

"You want to hold Bowie?"

"If that's all right. That way you can use both of your hands, and I'll get some cuddles with my new buddy." He waggles his eyebrows at me and grins, holding his hands out a little higher. I pass Bowie over, my turn to be pleas-antly bewildered. I never liked holding babies before having one. It always felt like trying to balance a hot bag of mashed potatoes so it wouldn't cry and alert everyone to my complete ineptitude to human. But Bowie in my arms feels like the best hug you ever had. Comforting, satisfying, the love pouring into your body from the press of another's skin. I'd hug my little mashed potato bag all day if I could, but it still surprises me when others enjoy it, too.

Bowie takes the handoff in stride. He's been staring at River this whole time anyway.

Do *not* blame you, kid. I'm determined to keep this professional, but it's hard to ignore the way River fills a space. The drive within me to beautify looks at him and sighs in contentment. He leans back in the rocking chair now, his large shoulders spilling out from either side of the chair's frame, and positions Bowie so they're both watching me, alert and attentive.

"Please, continue."

Best audience *ever*. I flush with pleasure and flip to the idea I want most and am least sure is possible. The wraparound window, shamelessly inspired by River's own setup. I tap my finger on the page. "So. Tell it to me straight. Do you think the downstairs structure can support a window like this?" A little mid-century modern, a little Scandinavian, the window would start on the wall facing the lake and wrap around at a clean, frameless angle to the side wall. It'd require a hefty cut out of the cabin's exterior, but the view would be worth it. It would frame in one long panorama the sparkling lake below, the mountains rising in the distance, our meadow, garden, and forest beyond. It would flood the main room with diffused, indirect light, and give early risers a front-row seat to the sunrise.

River pulls his lower lip between his teeth, lightly biting. "What's your budget again?"

"Fifteen thousand, all in."

He tilts his head. "It's theoretically possible, but the structural supports we'd have to put in would eat that budget right up. You'd barely be able to do anything else."

A sigh whooshes out of me. There goes my entire concept for the main room. "I wanted to make the space feel more modern, but I guess— What?"

An idea lights up River's eyes, stopping my disappointment in its tracks.

"What if"—he leans forward, gesturing for my pencil—"we leave the corner intact and frame out the windows using a more modern material, like a matte-black metal casing . . . something like this." He flips to a new page with his free hand and sketches out a series of windows with the same overall footprint of the one I envisioned but broken up into neat partitions with heavy black lines. There are still two massive picture windows on either side of the corner, and he's added a long, thin window flanking each of them. "The big windows would be fixed shut, so that'll save you money, but these two could crank open and let fresh air in."

A thrill flashes through me. I didn't even consider using a cool casing for contrast. Matte-black framing would look *so* good against the buttery pine walls, and it matches my planned aesthetic perfectly. I take the pencil from his hands, and the brush of his fingers sends a different kind of thrill up my spine. His eyes are as excited as I feel, full of that heady buzz of a joint discovery happening in real time. "Could we add some horizontal bars across the thin windows, like this?" I quickly add to his sketch, darkening three thin lines across the flanking windows. "It'd feel like, I don't know, postcards of each individual scene or something." I check his face for a reaction and am rewarded with enthusiastic nodding.

"I've got a great window guy that can whip that up, no problem." He grins at me and bops Bowie on his knee. "This is going to look *so good.*"

I'm grinning back like a fool, feeling something like exhilaration.

Over *some windows? Really?* Killian's voice says in my head.

Really, you asshole. I banish my belittling inner Killian and revel in the moment. River took hold of my vision and affirmed it, built upon it, expanded it. Even better, he saw it, and saw the value in it.

That little seed of hope bursts from its shell and begins to grow.

"Dinner's ready!" Darryl calls from above, and rings an actual *bell*. It's a big old iron thing he mounted on one of the porch beams, and it sounds like the apocalypse. I close my eyes.

"Why'd you want to eat with my batshit family again?"

River smiles. "Other than for the intimidatingly large squash, you mean?" He stretches to standing, Bowie still in his arms, and brushes a lock of Bowie's hair behind his ear, and something inside of me squeezes. "Good food. Better company." He tweaks Bowie's chin, and Bowie *beh-beh-beh*s back, like *yes, it is a very good chin, thank you for noticing.* With his eyes trained on Bowie, River says, "My family used to have Sunday dinners. Always a big affair, people coming and going. I loved how loud it got." A wistful smile spreads across his face, but his voice sounds distant. "I miss it, I guess."

"They don't do them anymore?"

River blinks at me, at my question, then hands Bowie to me suddenly. "Better hit the bathroom and wash up." He gives me a hasty, distracted smile, then ducks into the Airbnb. I almost call him back because, you know, horror toilet, but maybe he wants to check out the interior one more time. After all, we've got work to do.

I press my forehead against Bowie's and let the happiness spill over me again. "It's really happening, Littleman. I'm really doing it."

"I. SAID. DINNAH!!!" Darryl punctuates each word with a gong of the bell.

Lord.

River emerges, and his smile seems truer now. "Shall we?"

Dinner's absolutely delicious. Having River there helps us get a little further down the road from what happened, too. Mama and Darryl still treat me like a deer they're trying not to spook, but River's a happy distraction for us all. The cabin brims with laughter again, mine included, even if I talk a little less and hold Bowie a little more. When it's time to clear the plates, River joins me at the sink. The warm press of his arm against mine as we stand there, washing and drying, is unexpectedly comforting.

He stays late into the evening, after Bowie's bedtime even, poring over each of my sketches with me at the dinner table and working his magic alongside mine. The self-consciousness I usually feel when sharing my ideas is long gone, replaced with that electric sense of rightness when things come together in front of you. We have a natural energy, a give and take that builds and transforms ideas as we go. When we're finally done, I'm almost sad it has to end. I'm exhausted, but my heart feels invigorated, like every inch of it's been worked out, the way I imagine runners must feel after a long, exhilarating race.

I walk him to the door, feeling weirdly on display in front of Mama and Darryl, though there's no need. Mama's deep in a crossword, and Darryl's in his chair, lightly snoring to some Alaska fishing reality show. River pauses in the doorframe, the big, dark night behind him, and smiles. I've only known him for a short time, but already I'm coming to learn the many variations of his smile. There's his good-natured smile, the one he gives everyone for free. His playful smile, a personal favorite, when he's joking. Today I got to see the one that breaks across his face like sunshine when we land on the perfect solution. This smile is different, though. It's earnest and genuine, and it feels like a thank-you. Like the contented weariness that follows a good day.

I give it right back to him.

"Best Sunday dinner I've had in a long time," River says. The words trail happy sparks down my spine.

"Me too." I rest my cheek against the side of the open door. "Hey, shouldn't we exchange numbers? So we can coordinate for the reno?" I quickly add, grateful I have a valid reason to ask for his number.

"I don't know mine. But get Big Daddy to ring that bell, and I'll come running." He grins.

I wait for him to say *just kidding* and pull out his phone, but he doesn't.

"Oh." I laugh a little awkwardly. "Should I . . . give you mine?"

"Nah. I don't use my phone much." River stops to consider. "Not sure where it is, come to think of it. Maybe my truck."

"You don't even text?" I know River's a bit of a hippie, but even hippies have iPhones these days.

"No, ma'am." River shrugs, like he didn't just drop a bomb on me. "Don't believe in it."

"Huh." My mouth's hanging more than a little open. He doesn't *believe* in texting? Is he a time traveler?

Or does he not want to give his number to me?

"Um, okay then. Good night?" I don't mean to make it a question, but everything feels uncertain right now. Maybe he doesn't *believe* in nighttime? I don't know!

"You know where to find me," he says, his eyes sparkling as he tips an imaginary hat my way. "Good night, Hannah."

I watch, stunned, as he walks into the dark mountain night.

CHAPTER ELEVEN

When the chickadees start chattering outside my window, I leap from the bed. I don't even cuss them out! It's taken a few weeks to gather the crew and materials, but today's the big day, and River and his team will be here to start our renovation in . . . I glance at my phone.

Two hours? Ugh. Waking at dawn's truly for the birds.

The cabin is quiet, the purple skies of early morning just starting to lift the shadows inside. Bowie, G-ma, and Big Daddy are all still sleeping, so I take my coffee out to enjoy on the porch swing. The sun's breaking over the curve of mountains, but it hasn't reached our lake yet. Its surface is dark and unbroken.

Movement down by the lake catches my eye, and I gasp out a laugh. I've been trying to catch River doing yoga for weeks now, but I never wake up early enough. I take my mug and prop my elbows on the porch's railing to watch the show. I figure if he doesn't mind Mama spying on him, he won't mind me, either. The pale light paints him in monochrome, and all the golden shades I've come to think of as his aren't yet visible. His lithe body stretches from one pose to the next, fluid and peaceful in the still morning air. It's a good word to describe River—*peaceful*.

Maybe it's because he doesn't constantly doom-scroll on his phone like the rest of America. Psychopath.

The sun finally cascades across the lake, and with it, River. I gasp again, and I don't even feel silly for doing it. The man *glows*. It's like looking at the sun itself. Except, you know, less painful and dangerous for your cornea health. He's doing some kind of one-armed side plank with the other arm stretched to the sky when Mama joins me at the railing.

"God bless that man," she says, sipping her coffee. "*Mmm.* Just how I like it."

I don't know if she's talking about the coffee or River.

"You should ask him out," she says, watching me watch him. "He'd be good for you."

"Mama!" I suddenly sound fifteen again and embarrassed by my mother in the Applebee's. "Please. We are work colleagues." The suggestion alone makes my pulse race.

Mama snorts. "Do you watch all your work colleagues do yoga? Honey, you have a crush."

"I do not have a crush! I have a *baby.*"

"As if that'd matter to a good man!" Mama shakes her head. "I know Killian did a number on you, but you've got to stop counting yourself out. You are smart and funny and cute as a button. Everyone sees it but you."

There she goes again, being supportive. A knot forms in my throat. I've never doubted my mama's love, not for a second. It's the fiercest part of her. But over the years, a distance has grown between us. The more I learned what the world expects of adults, the more I realized how far she was from one. It became hard not to judge her for what she lacked, or what she couldn't give me. When I was old enough to realize my friends didn't get their power turned off every month, or see their ex-stepfathers at the gas station and wonder if they should say hi, I couldn't understand why she wouldn't change and finally grow up. For *me.* But now, it seems like she has, or is trying to, anyway.

"I can't ask him out, Mama. He doesn't text. He lives in a treehouse. He owns seven articles of clothing and considers you his doctor." I heave out a sigh. "Even if I wanted to, which I *don't*, we are operating on different planes of adulthood." What I don't say, but feel throughout every fiber of my being, is that I cannot be the most responsible person in a relationship.

I don't know what I'm doing, and I'm tired of fumbling through life. I've already got Mama, Darryl, and Bowie to take care of. I can't add the quasi-employed, hippie neighbor to my payroll, no matter how highly he scores on the golden sex god scale. Golden sex gods need to retire, too. You telling me River *I-work-when-I-want-to* Aronson has a healthy investment portfolio? I think not.

I sip my coffee, feeling strangely deflated. "Besides, I don't have time to date. I'm only staying until I get the Airbnb up and running."

Mama inhales through her nose, as though me scraping the pieces of my life back together is a personal affront. "And what are you going to do after that?"

I shrug, rotating my coffee mug in slow circles on the railing. "Go back to Atlanta? Find a job? There's nothing for me here, Mama."

She eyes River's perky downward-facing dog pose below and smirks. "I wouldn't say nothing. And you can't leave before your class ends."

"Excuse me, what now?"

"I signed you up for Small Business Owners 101."

"You *what?*" I snap my head to face her. "Why?!"

"Because it'll be good for you," she says. "You need to get out of the cabin for a bit, meet new people, up your game."

"But Mama, I can't . . . I don't want . . ." I'm shaking my head, unable to form the right words. "That class isn't for people like *me!*"

"And why the hell not?" Mama throws her coffee back like a shot. "This is a small business. You're running the show now. We never grow if we don't push ourselves, baby."

I narrow my eyes at her. "You just don't want to handle the taxes."

She narrows her eyes right back. "Do *you* want me to handle the taxes?"

Okay. Fair.

I turn my eyes back sullenly to River's golden form below. "I'll think about it."

"Great." Mama smiles from behind her coffee mug. "It starts this Saturday, and it's nonrefundable."

"Mama!"

≈

At seven thirty sharp, a work truck pulls in front of the cabin.

"They're here!" Big Daddy hollers. He peeps between the blinds and squeals like there's a swimsuit model walking down the road. "Now, that is a *saw*, boy!"

I squeeze a happy, milk-drunk Bowie into his sling and strap him to my back. He loves it in there, peeking over my shoulder like my curious second head. We meet River and his crew out by the road.

"G'morning." River's grin appears over the roof of the truck. It sends flutters through me. "Everybody, this is Hannah."

A woman who looks to be in her forties squints up at me from where she's squatting next to a big bag of . . . wrenches? Let's go with wrenches.

"You Trish's girl?" she asks, rising up and wiping her hands on the seat of her work pants.

"Sure am." I hold my hand out to shake hers.

"I'm Martha." She stares at my open palm.

"Oh, you're, um . . . Sergeant's girl, right?" I finally pull back my hand, but now I don't know what to do with it. Cut it off, maybe?

"I'm his *daughter*." Martha's looking at me like I've made it weird. Sergeant came by the other day to apologize for the *stranger-with-guns-holding-my-baby* incident. He's a nice man, if a little terrifying, and he mentioned his daughter Martha was on River's crew. His other daughter down in Florida has his first grandbaby on the way, and he'd wanted "holding practice" with Bowie, is all. I told him he could come practice his grandpa skills anytime, as long as he consented to a frisk beforehand.

I'm wondering if someone ought to frisk Martha now.

River comes around the truck to join us. He's in a worn pair of jeans I've come to know and respect and a white T-shirt that clings to the curve of his biceps. Not that I'm noticing his arms or anything.

"Martha lays floors," he says by way of introduction. I wonder what he'd say about me if the roles were reversed. *This is Hannah. She makes breast milk.*

"Straight as a fuckin' arrow." Martha hauls up her mysterious bag of wrenches on her shoulder and makes her way down to the Airbnb.

"Good to know." I nod at her retreating back.

River laughs before hoisting up his own bag of tools. "Well, she does."

I lean over to grab some of their gear, and an older dude with curly gray hair in a sleeveless black T-shirt takes the heavier bag before I can. He *definitely* listens to Led Zeppelin.

"Lemme get that, little mama." He straightens and winks at Bowie. "Like yer bandanna, kid."

He pauses for a second like he expects Bowie to respond, then heads down, too.

"That's Gus," River says. "He's my electrician. Smart as hell, though maybe not so much with the babies."

I laugh and glance around for who's next, but there's no one else there.

"Is that everybody?" Seems like a lot of work for a crew of three, but before River can answer, another truck tears up the dirt road. This one's black and has big ass-kickin' energy. At the sight of the flags flapping on the truck's cab, I immediately tense up. Flags on trucks are usually a warning sign of the driver's views on life, views I don't share because I believe in everyone's right to *live* their life in a way that makes them happy.

The truck whips up the road, and the dismay I feel at the conversation I'll have with River about the kind of people I want around my family rumbles just as loud within me. When it pulls off on the side of the road, my mouth actually falls open.

Because one of the flags is a *Pride* flag, and the other proclaims in big capital letters: BLACK LIVES MATTER.

YES! Praise hands!

The door slams, and a man jumps down from the cab, raring to go.

"Hey, buddy!" He marches bow-legged right up to River and grabs him in a big, back-thumping hug. "Thanks for the work, man! Jessica and I appreciate it."

"Without a doubt, Booch. Let me introduce you to the boss." River grins at me. "Booch, Hannah. Booch's my go-to guy. He can do it all."

I shake my head with unexpected delight and hold out my hand. "Booch, it is truly nice to meet you." Unlike Martha, he takes my hand in both of his big, callused ones and shakes it heartily.

"Welcome to Blue Ridge, Hannah!"

And you know what? I *do* feel welcomed. The sun's brighter knowing there are Booches out here.

River's crew wastes no time. First order of business is emptying the cabin and hauling off the furniture. Booch pries the industrial sink out, and soon all that's left of the Airbnb's ghoulish past are the stained concrete floors. Martha's already measuring them to see how many square feet of flooring we'll need.

It's easier to see the space's potential now. River walks the crew through the few structural changes we've decided are worth the splurge. Gus maps out where the wiring is so they can start on the big new windows we designed. They'll make the cuts once we've got a firm ETA on the custom casing. I asked River to pick out the other windows we're adding to match. After seeing his treehouse, I trust his eye as much as my own. Standing beside him while he holds his hands up, describing his ideas to me for where the windows will go, is, not gonna lie . . .

Hot as *fuck*.

This is Mama's fault. She brought up me dating River, and now the lonely, horny side of my brain's latched onto the idea while my inner adult stands by and *tsks* on repeat. To my chagrin, my old sexual fantasy starts playing in my head as I help clear out the kids' room, stealing looks at River completely against my will. This time the role of sexy contractor is played by my *real life* sexy contractor.

Did not see that coming.

When his strong hands steady a box I'm struggling to lift, I can't stop thinking about what they'd feel like steadying my hips and pulling me close.

Insurance! 401(k)s!

The delicious scratch of his cheek bristling against my neck.

A healthy relationship to modern-day technology!!

Cool wood under my warm back, denim crushing between us where hard meets soft.

Oh god, the anti-River mantra is *not* working.

"You okay there, little mama?" Gus hands me a spray bottle full of water. "You lookin' overheated."

I huff out a laugh and mist myself and Bowie, which makes Bowie shriek with delight. "Thanks, Gus." My eyes stray over to River, where he's prying off the splintered baseboard. His old T-shirt barely conceals the ripple of muscles moving across his back. I've never wanted to lick cotton before, but here we are.

I sigh wearily. "Guess I'm just thirsty."

Martha rolls her eyes. "You and half of Blue Ridge." She finishes rolling up a section of the dingy carpet in the kids' room and hauls it off.

The spray bottle slips from my hand. Did she get my—?

Gus chuckles, staring after her, a sparkle in his hazel eyes. "Oh, don't mind Martha. Between you and me, I think she gets tired of fending off questions from River's admirers."

A blush envelops me end to end. I can't see my face, but my chest is the color of ripe tomato. I duck behind the box of vintage toys and books I'm packing. "Um. What?"

"River's hard to find when he wants to be. Martha's pretty good at rootin' him out, though. People find her when they're looking for him. She don't mind a lick when it's for jobs, but when it's for, you know. Other things . . ." Gus shakes his head and laughs. "Whew, boy."

"I don't manage his personal calendar," Martha says, nearly spitting. She's back with the carpet shears and a challenge on her face, like she's daring me to make an inquiry on the spot.

Bowie *mehh-mehs*, then whacks me in the ear. I clear my throat. "Sounds like Bowie needs a break."

I plow past everybody and up the stairs feeling disappointed, though I don't know why. Of course River would have admirers around town. So what if I find him charming and pleasant and dripping with sex appeal? I'm not going to do anything about it. I have a *baby*. I live with my *mama*. I am Hannah Tate, utterly beyond repair, and River Aronson, gorgeous tree-dwelling lost boy that he is, doesn't have what it takes to fix *me*.

While I feed Bowie, I devour three bananas myself. Between the hard labor, embarrassment, and breastfeeding, the hunger's rather desperate. Big Daddy mumbles something about me eating all his *nanners*, then disappears. When he shows up twenty minutes later, he's carrying five bags full of Cuban sandwiches and empanadas from the Rum Cake Lady's stand up the road for everyone.

I legit tear up.

G-ma sets up the picnic table out back for our feast, complete with leftover chicken and cold apple pie, and within seconds of sitting down, Booch's said grace and half a dozen wrappers come crinkling off.

Good *God*. I moan a little as my teeth sink into the crispy Cuban bread, and everybody laughs. River's eyes linger over my face a little longer, and it kindles a different kind of appetite in me.

Despite all my misgivings, I want him to keep looking. I want him to *see me.*

Unless there's chimichurri sauce on my chin. Oh, *shit.* I fumble with a napkin. There is, isn't there.

Bowie, who's been happy on my back all morning, begins to fuss from G-ma's arms. I frown and hold my arms out for him. Yes, child. Please bring me back to reality.

"What is it, Littleman?" His mouth is turned down in a pitiful pout, chin shimmering with drool. "You just ate, you've napped, your butt is fresh, so what's wrong?"

His fussing escalates to crying, with real tears, and my gut twists. His eyes are scared, looking to mine for reassurance, but all he sees is my own growing anxiety. Is there anything worse than not knowing what to do and realizing your mommy doesn't, either?

G-ma's getting just as worked up, buzzing behind my shoulders like a bee and peppering me with questions that have nothing to do with anything.

"Is it his shirt? I got it at the consignment shop, do you think he knows it's not new?"

"Pretty sure he's indifferent on that, Mama."

"Is Big Daddy's hat scaring him?" She snaps at Big Daddy before I have a chance to answer. "Take off your hat, Darryl!"

It's hard to concentrate, what with Bowie wailing and G-ma's frantic interrogation. The ever-present mommy tears prick my eyes. What is *wrong?*

"Does he want some sandwich?" G-ma thrusts a scrap of my Cuban sandwich toward his face, and I bat her hand away. First of all, as if I'd share. Secondly, Bowie's only four months old! He doesn't have any—

"Teeth!" I proclaim, like Sherlock's bedraggled mother. I run my index finger along his gums and earn a furious *wah!* for my efforts. There, in the bottom center, is a puffy red mound with a hint of white poking through. "You're getting your first tooth, baby!"

"That's my grandson!" Big Daddy smacks the table hard enough to shake the ice in the sweet tea pitcher. "You grow them teeth, boy!"

Bowie wails, oblivious to the strange round of praise he's getting from the table.

"Give 'im a chicken bone," Gus says amid the bedlam, his scratchy, low voice rising above the others with the authority of a preacher on Sunday.

A *chicken bone*? I've never seen that advice on Mommy-Insta.

"What you talking about, Gus?" Big Daddy says. When G-ma's not looking, he slips his hat back on real fast.

"It helps their teething. Tastes good, so they'll gnaw on it for hours. Feels good, too, to mash that sore spot against something hard."

My gaze meets River's unintentionally, then I jerk it back to Bowie.

Focus, pervert!!

A shiny drumstick bone sits on my plate. The table's eyes are on me, and it feels like a test. Am I, a city girl, too good for Blue Ridge's folk wisdom?

"It won't . . . break off or splinter in his mouth?"

"Not unless you got a baby piranha on your lap," Gus says.

TBD, honestly.

With a deep breath and the infant CPR training looping in my head, I pick the bone until it's clean, then hand it to Bowie. He stops crying to stare at it. I try to take it back to model gnawing on it, but he bleats at me and shoves it at his own mouth first.

The table watches, fascinated, as Bowie bats the bone at his face, tries to jam it into his nose, and then finally, grasps it between both gums and *goes to town*.

He screeches with joy, and the table erupts into cheers once more.

Booch gives me a thumbs-up, and Martha claps me on the back. I inexplicably feel like a champ. When River catches my gaze again, amusement lighting up his eyes, I'm ready to burst. With happiness, with the weird, primal pride at witnessing your baby's milestones, but also the satisfaction at all we've done this morning. It's been a long time since I've felt like this. Like I'm in the right place, at the right time, doing the right things, with the right people. It's a good feeling. The kind that lifts your heart but weighs you down, too, like dropping an anchor exactly where you want so you can sit back and enjoy the view.

As the table laughs and River clinks his glass of sweet tea against my own in a toast to my child's first incisor, I find myself enjoying the view very much.

Temporarily, that's all. Not forever.

CHAPTER TWELVE

"**H**an-nah!" G-ma sings through the open doorframe to the Airbnb, Bowie in her arms. "It's almost time for cla-ass!"

Really regretting removing the door off the hinges this morning. I blow out a gust of breath, ruffling my sweaty bangs, and reluctantly turn the sander off. "I can't go, Mama. We've got too much to do here."

"What class?" River pushes his safety goggles up on his forehead. His bright eyes and quick smile make my heart flip like a pancake.

"Small Business Owners 101," G-ma says.

"Oh, I took that." River stretches all the way to standing and rests his palms against his lower back.

"You *did*?" G-ma and I say at the same time.

River laughs. "Why so surprised? I own a small business."

"Yes you do, baby, but you only charge people half the time, and your office is a treehouse." G-ma pats his arm.

"So?" River asks in mock indignation. "I defy your capitalist expectations."

"You literally get paid in Sunday dinners." I squint my eyes and rub my chin. "How many biscuits will you earn this quarter?"

He throws his hands up in surrender, unable to stop grinning even as we tease him. The way this man can find a laugh from thin air, pluck joy like it's a peach from the tree, makes my own mood rise to meet his.

"Okay, maybe I didn't pay a lot of attention, but the instructor's great. You'll love her." River's sly smile warms my blood.

But my own smile falters when I look at all the work we have left to do. "I've only sanded one wall, though, and we were hoping to stain them all before the end of the day."

River crouches down in front of where I'm kneeling and, still smiling that dangerous smile, gently takes the sander from my hands. His knees press lightly into my thighs, each point of contact sending trails of sparks up to my—

"Let me earn my biscuits, Ms. Tate."

I'm pretty sure I'd apply to an MBA program if he told me to right now. I pass my tongue across my suddenly parched lips. His eyes track the movement before flicking back up to meet my gaze.

"Okay. If you don't need me here."

"Now, I didn't say that," he murmurs, and the sheer mischief this man gives off makes my whole body alight with prickles.

The next thing I'm fully cognizant of is having to parallel park in Blue Ridge's old-timey downtown. The task shocks my consciousness back into my body, making me swear each time the back tire lurches up the curb. Mama and River, teaming up on me like that? I huff as I finally slam my door and gaze at the charming storefront in the center of Main Street. The bottom floor is a tasting room for Brennan Vineyards, but the class is sadly upstairs, far away from the wine that could convince me to stay.

The urge to run is strong. The vintage hall lamps zing and crackle overhead as I let myself in the door labeled COME ON IN! The room is about two-thirds full, with all manner of people sitting behind long wooden tables organized into neat rows. At the front of the room is an oak-paneled bar with green leather stools, but we won't be sampling wines here today. Someone's dragged a whiteboard in front of it. Scrawled in purple marker is: WELCOME SMALL BUSINESS OWNERS!

The words alone send unease itching up my back. Killian's voice creeps in. *You and money don't mix.*

Jesus, Hannah—did you check the budget?

How can you possibly owe that much?!

I know logically if you're bad at something, you should practice. Learn as much as you can. But the fear around money runs so deep in me, the logical response isn't always in reach.

"Excuse me," someone says from behind, and I realize I'm still hovering in front of the doorway. It's a woman about my age, her short black hair curling around her jaw. "Are you coming or going?"

Two men sitting nearby are discussing depreciation schedules, and I think I might faint.

"Ah, sorry! I'm—"

Going. Definitely going. Running. Getting TF outta—

"I'm coming. Ha!" I push a hand to my mouth and laugh like a total idiot. "I mean, I'm staying. I'm—staying. Yes."

The woman gives me a wry smile and extends her hand. "I'm Zoe Brennan, the instructor."

"I'm—scared." I shake her hand too long, then laugh again. "Shit."

She laughs, too, but it's a sweet, twinkling sound. "Nice to meet you, Scared. Why don't you take a seat up front so you don't bolt?"

I breathe deeply through my nose and nod. "Good idea."

Zoe smiles and ushers me to one of the empty chairs up front.

Class goes better than I expected. Zoe is easy and approachable, and I thank Mama's crystals that it's a young woman teaching instead of the surly, condescending white man full of ear hair my fears had conjured up. She talks about business like it's exciting, which helps me realize that it *is*. All this time, I've been so focused on making our Airbnb habitable that I've somehow divorced that work from what we're trying to accomplish, which is establishing a revenue stream that will support my parents in their golden years. The two aren't mutually exclusive, and the way Zoe presents the strategy behind making small businesses tick makes it feel like a fun puzzle to solve. Not a series of life-or-death decisions I'm doomed to fail. When she asks each person to introduce themselves and share about their small business, my words come out confident and strong. A few others are also starting up rentals, and the room is full of friendly faces. A woman with shiny blond hair even catches my eye and waves, mouthing: *Let's talk after class!*

I stand up when it's over, invigorated.

"So, Scared. How're you feeling?" Zoe pauses by my seat as I gather my things.

"Like I'll be here next week," I say, my smile genuine this time. "This was great."

Zoe nods, tilting her head as she assesses me. "You're new to town, right?"

"What gave it away? My lack of guns, or was it rifles?"

She smiles and taps the rainbow button pinned to my bag. "I know every queer person in a fifty-mile radius."

My eyes widen. "Oh my God. Can we be friends? Or is that an instructor-student conflict?"

Zoe laughs, and the instant kinship I feel with her makes sense. There's something about the queer community that makes me feel at home, whether I'm dating a man or a woman or someone in between. It's like a secret club where the default position is that everyone's welcome. It fucking rocks.

I leave with Zoe's number in my phone and information about her friends' next scheduled hang at a vineyard I've been wanting to try. They call themselves the Queer Mountaineers Who Occasionally Drink Beers, which, adorable. She even tells me to bring Bowie—several of the couples bring their kids because the vineyards surrounding Blue Ridge are family-friendly as a rule.

The sun's shining down, the skies made bluer by the green mountains. Everything feels perfect right now. A new friend, a business class, renovation, built-in babysitters, River . . .

I swallow against my throat. Maybe not River. Crushing on him feels so delicious when we're together, but it's like ogling a sexy swimsuit in the dead of winter on your own personal tundra for one. It's *fantasy*. I need to remember that.

I've just unlocked my car when a hand lightly taps my shoulder.

"Hannah? Hi! I'm Madison!" It's the blond woman from class, who mentioned starting up a rental, too. She says *hi* like it has two syllables, and her smile's sugar sweet.

"Um, hi there," I shake off my feelings and quickly drop my bag inside the car so I can take her outstretched hand. It feels more like a butterfly landing in my fingers than a handshake.

"So where's your cabin rental located? I'm up in Mineral Bluff!"

"We're on Cherry Log Mountain. Mineral Bluff's grea—"

"OOH! Cherry Log! What an ideal area! What street?" This woman's intense. Her blue eyes are jacked wide open, and a thick line of lashes rims each lid. The effect is disconcerting, like a pair of hairy evil eyes staring at me.

"M-Magnolia road." I back toward my car.

"OOH! You're gonna do so well!" She claps and jumps with a little *squee* in my honor.

"Ha, thanks. See you next week?" I say, sincerely hoping I won't, but Madison agrees, waving effusively at me as I pull away. I see her pounce on the next person emerging from class in my rearview mirror.

Well. She's . . . nice?

CHAPTER THIRTEEN

With the new windows in, sunlight streams into the renovated space. The views they provide are nothing short of magical. It's amazing how far the Airbnb has come with three weeks' attention from the crew. There's a small kitchenette with butcher-block counters and a farmhouse sink in the corner, and the bathroom's complete, too, after we wrestled the sleek soaking tub in on Friday. Gus hooked up the vintage schoolhouse lights over the framed mirror, and I've been pinching myself ever since. The clean white lines and matte-black accents look *so good* against the pine walls. The cabin practically glows, from the first touch of morning sun to deep into the evening's grips, lit only by the fire. Standing here in the big, empty space, surrounded by sunlit walls, it feels like I'm submerged in honey.

I slowly revolve on the spot, thinking. I've been trying to come up with a catchy, distinctive name for the cabin since we arrived. It's harder than I thought. Cabins are usually named some variation on the formula of Adjective + Wildlife + Dwelling type. Cozy Bear Cabin. Soaring Eagle Lodge. Ridiculous Lemur Hut. But I want something sweet and memorable that fits the space.

Like . . . honey. Honey. Flies to Honey? Jesus, no.

The Honey Pot? Maybe. Don't want to encourage drugs, though.

The Honey . . . Jar?

Hmmm . . . The Honey Jar. The smile lifts my mouth as I imagine the name printed in a simple sans serif, modern but inviting. Millennials are very sensitive to anything that feels too extra. We either want it so over-the-top kitschy it's part of the experience, or something that doesn't insult our taste. It's part of what makes renting cabins so cringy in the first place for my generation—the animal heads, the tan everything, those curtains that are just a pointless ruffle. All that cringe starts with the formulaic names.

But The Honey Jar . . . that *works*. I'll run it by River when he gets here, see if he agrees. A pubescent rush of hormones curls my insides because today, River's helping me *build the bed*.

I'm trying to be cool about this. When I woke up, I did *not* drink my coffee on the porch during River's morning yoga session. I don't need horny vibes clouding my head while I'm handling power tools. I also didn't wear my super short pair of cutoffs River's eyes kept drifting to the other day, nor did I tie my shirt into a knot to show off the curve of my hips.

I'm wearing my second shortest pair, and this tank top's too tight to tie in a knot, so there.

"Good morning."

I turn to find Killian standing in the doorway. "Oh, hey." I check my watch, frowning. "You're early."

His curious eyes rove around the Airbnb, and my stomach clenches with unease. "You've been busy."

He's not wrong. I didn't negotiate a quick turnaround with River, but the crew's worked with a steadfast devotion that feels unexpectedly personal. It's like Gus, Martha, and Booch want this cabin to be the answer to Mama and Darryl's money problems as much as I do. We start every morning with a pot of coffee and end every day with a pitcher of sweet tea. I work as much as Bowie lets me, not because the crew needs me to, but because it fills me with satisfaction. There hasn't been a lot in my life that I've been able to change this quickly, or this well. It makes the world feel like a fixable place.

Killian's eyes finally settle on me, and he says, slightly bewildered, "It looks . . . great, Hannah."

I release a deep breath. He was *this* close to getting his ass kicked.

"How are your folks paying for it? Did they get a loan, or . . ." His eyes widen. "*Hannah.* Tell me you're not using the child supp—"

"Stop right there." I hold up a hand, the anger rising like a tide within me. "First of all, no. Of *course* not. Second, how dare you ask me that? You don't get to be a dick to me anymore. You'll treat me and my family with respect, or you won't see me at all."

I know I could shut Killian up if I told him about the settlement. How I wiped out my credit card debt, opened up a college savings account for Bowie, and paid off my ratty Corolla all in one month. But I don't want Bob's money to be the thing that finally earns me Killian's respect. He should learn to treat me right because I'm a *person*, and that won't happen if he thinks I'm just a whiny child who dipped into an asshole's fortune.

"Hannah, wait. I'm sorry," Killian says to my back as I stomp toward the door. I look at him over one shoulder, eyes narrowed. I'm not used to Killian apologizing, it's weird. His face is bashful, chin turned down. "Have you ever noticed that you slip into certain routines with people, even when you've sworn you'll stop?"

My mouth screws to the side. I know exactly what he means. A constant loop plays in my head instructing me *not* to bail Mama and Darryl out at the first sign of trouble, *not* to feel like I'm automatically responsible for all their problems, and most of all, *not* to judge them for it. And yet, I spent two hours on the phone yesterday getting Mama out of her ridiculously high cell phone plan when I saw the past due notice laying on her stack of crosswords. Did Mama ask me to do that? No.

Did I hold it against her anyway . . .

I turn all the way around. Still not talking, though. I'm not giving him any more outs.

He scrubs his face with a hand. "I'm trying to be less critical. Jamie calls me out on it."

Jamie. The Fellow Animals guitarist. The one who drove him home from his first visit with Bowie. The one I screeched at.

"Ah. I see." I close my eyes and sigh.

"It's not like that." Killian clears his throat. "It's . . . well. Complicated? Fellow Animals asked me to play with them on a few shows locally. They've been thinking about adding another guitarist to round out the sound, and we get along. At least, not when I'm being too critical. So."

I guess I should be glad he's growing emotionally for *someone*, but Killian ditching the band he co-fronts to play second guitar for Fellow Animals? Sure, Fellow Animals is getting big, but Killian's never been content to stand in the background.

"What about Jeremiah Was a Frog Boy, or whatever?"

He half shrugs, a sullen look washing over his face. "They'll get over it."

My eyebrows rise. Dumping his girlfriend *and* his band in the span of a few months? Killian's showing all the signs of a millennial third-life crisis. Next thing you know, he'll start making his own sourdough bread and switch to an Android phone.

"Well, come on. Bowie's with G-ma."

I lead him around to the side of the cabin, where G-ma's little garden grows. She's doing her morning weeding, and Bowie's sitting beside her, picking up handfuls of dirt and throwing them helpfully at the tomato plants. The way she's praising him, you'd think he just solved the global food crisis.

She's busy cleaning off his teething giraffe (because that's a thing that exists) when I snatch Bowie up and cover his pink cheeks in kisses, his throaty baby laugh dissolving my residual bad feelings. He smells like sun-warmed skin and dirt, and when he smiles at me, not one, but *two* bottom teeth glisten in the sun. It's taken us a little bit of infant ibuprofen and a whole lotta chicken bones to get here, but we've survived. It helps that whenever he pouts, he looks like a bulldog with an underbite.

"Whoa!" Killian takes Bowie from me and holds him in the air. "Who are you, and what have you done with my baby?"

"He ate him." I smile at Bowie batting playfully at his daddy's nose.

Harder, son.

Killian's eyebrows rise as he takes in Bowie's new fangs. He eyes me with polite concern. "Everything still . . . intact?"

"More or less." I nod graciously. "Thank you for your sympathy in this trying time."

G-ma wields a hand trowel at Killian's face. "You trying to leave here with my grandbaby today?"

"Uh, no, ma'am."

For the last few visits, Killian has kept mostly to the yard. We set up a picnic blanket under the sugar maple tree with some toys for Bowie and a fresh bottle in an ice bucket because Bowie's fancy AF. Killian's still too nervous to go out with Bowie on his own, which is fine by me. We're getting better with each visit, but it's still hard on us both. For Killian, he's got to learn how to parent solo, and for me, I've got to let him.

"Good." G-ma yanks a weed with extra vigor, never breaking eye contact with him. The gate squeaks open behind us, and Killian jumps a mile.

"Good morning!" River calls out, his playful voice making my neck prickle with heat. He lopes through the yard and sets a bundle of wood against the cabin steps, Battle-cat waddling behind him. River's shining hair is tied up in a messy bun at the crown of his head, and he's wearing an old V-neck, nearly sheer from use. The contrast between his tawny collarbone and the struggling white shirt makes the breath stutter in my lungs. The fabric's sticking lightly to the place between his pecs, and suddenly, I get the appeal of a wet T-shirt contest.

His warm eyes crinkle with his smile. His gaze flicks from me, to Bowie, then to Killian holding him. Something flashes in River's eyes as his smile cools. It's fierce and a little protective, and it sends a thrill up my arms. Killian clears his throat pointedly, and I realize I have to introduce them. River knows who Killian is after witnessing my meltdown that day, but not the other way around. "River, this is Killian Abbott. He's Bowie's father." And when that doesn't feel like enough, I add, "He's also my ex, from a relationship that is very much over."

There. That's better.

River's smile stretches as Killian's frown blooms. Frankly, I'm fine with that dynamic. I want the record clear on how done I am with Killian for *all* parties involved.

I throw a hand up at the dewy dream that is River on a warm September morning and forcibly remove my gaze from that incredibly lickable spot where his V-neck dips. "Killian, this is River Aronson. He's our neighbor and contractor for the renovation." I briefly consider introducing Battle-cat, too, but he's already transformed into a sleeping floof loaf on one of the rocking chairs.

Killian stares at River and sniffs louder than I thought humanly possible. "Nice to meet you."

If River notices the hostile testosterone signaling, he doesn't show it. "Likewise. Hannah, you ready to get to work?" He gives me another one of those golden smiles. I could be wrong, but the look in his mischievous eyes seems to communicate that all I have to do is say the word, and he'll throw Killian into the lake.

I grin back. "Let's go earn some biscuits."

It took a few sketches and a *lot* of hours on Pinterest, but I'm pumped about the DIY canopy bed I've designed. It'll be the centerpiece of the Airbnb's main space. Since this big room needs to serve as both a living and sleeping area for the parents, the bed has to earn its keep. I want families to walk in and breathe a happy sigh of delight. The kids will have their own whimsical bedroom, woodsy and magical and filled with toys, but I want the parents to feel just as special. After they tuck their kids in, they can close the door and retreat into a place designed just for them. Something grown up but romantic, stylish and comfort forward.

Most importantly, somewhere they can *get it on*. I'm pretty sure if you're inspired to have five-star sex, you're going to leave a five-star review.

"How does the poplar look?" I peek over River's shoulder to see the bundled wood he's set against the porch.

River's eyes brighten. "Completely badass." He leads me over, and I squee with pleasure. I'd asked him to source native wood for the project, and after looking at a dozen options, we finally settled on using the poplar so plentiful in the Blue Ridge Mountains. The long, brindled posts are a silvery brown, textured but not coarse, and will serve as the supports. Thinner, curved branches will create natural arches between the posts, reaching for each other like hands entwining.

"Oh, *hell* yes!" I run my hands down the silky ridged bark of the posts. "It's going to look like something out of a fairy tale!" I stop to smile my gratitude. "They're perfect. Thank you."

He runs one of his big, graceful hands over the back of his neck and gives me that shy little smile, the one that peeks out between his more confident moments.

"Anytime, Hannah."

He still won't take a dime from us for his labor, but if he would, I'd pay him just to say my name. It's a naturally breathy word, *Hannah*, but in his mouth, it sounds like suede feels. Soft, warm, velveteen. Sparks flare in my belly every time he says it. *Hannah*.

Mama's right. I do have a big, sweaty crush on River, but it doesn't change the fact that I live in my parents' guest room with my baby. The breakup with Killian is like an old, ugly bruise on my shin I keep bumping into sharp furniture. It doesn't hurt most of the time, but when life collides with it unexpectedly, the pain can be breathtaking. I don't know when that's going to stop. When I'll finally heal enough that tears won't prick my eyes when a young family of three stands in front of me at the checkout line.

And that's just *me*. Who's to say River would even be interested? Apparently half of Blue Ridge hopes his playful grins are just for them. I know that, I do, but . . . I *have* noticed that his eyes follow me when I leave a room, or linger over my lips when Booch's made me laugh. After years of being nearly invisible to Killian, I feel River's gentle attention like sunlight breaking through the clouds. It's weird because I feel so far away from my prettiest years, when I straightened my hair and wore darling dresses. It's like me and that Hannah got divorced, and she took all the fucks I had to give with her, along with my hair dryer. I'm still figuring out who *this* Hannah is, the one that slides into old shorts and lets her hair run wild every day. The one who has Bowie and no idea what to do with her life.

And for some mysterious reason, the one River seems to like. But just because he checks out my ass and laughs at my jokes doesn't mean he's ready to babyproof his treehouse and rejoin modern society.

"Okay!" River claps his big hands together, looking genuinely happy to be here. "Let's start with the base."

Together, we position the bottom and side rails together. Our shoulders are touching softly when he says, "All right, hold the wood for me."

I clear my throat, a fierce blush starting in my neck, but I take the wood in both hands and breathe deeply.

You will not giggle, Hannah Tate. You will NOT GIGGLE—

"Yeah, just like that." He drags out each word as he pulls on a pair of goggles and drills two neat holes, while I struggle not to tremble from the laughter I'm holding back.

I'm many things, but mature in the face of innuendo is not one of them.

He sits back on his haunches and starts rooting through his toolbox, a little smirk forming on his full lips.

"Hmm. You know what I need? A screw. A nice, long—"

"Oh my *God*, you're doing it on purpose!"

He throws his head back and laughs, and I shove his arm. The muscle beneath his sleeve is hard and warm, and my own laughter hitches at the touch. Yeah, I realize we're acting thirteen years old, and no, there's nothing I can or will do about it. Seeing River laugh is quickly becoming one of my favorite things. It's so joyful, like he's gulping down life with every breath.

"I couldn't help it," he says, still laughing. "You were trying so hard not to lose it."

"We don't have to hammer anything today, do we?" I ask wryly. "Nothing needs to get nailed?"

His eyebrows rise as he huffs out between laughs, "There may need to be some . . . light pounding."

"But the wood's *so hard.*"

"Then we'll just have to bang it out, I guess." He's dabbing at the tears leaking from his gleeful eyes. "Now, give me a screw?"

I eye him with mock consternation.

"Please?" he adds, his laughter finally dying down, his eyes all smoky and dark.

I pull in my bottom lip involuntarily and thrust the literal screw into his waiting hand. He's just joking, but the flush of wanting is stirred within me all the same.

It's a tense game of Twister with power tools as we climb over each other to slide bolts in and screw things tight. It's difficult to ignore the heat of his body next to mine. When it's time to connect the footboard to the base, he lies on his back and slides beneath it.

"Can you hold these pieces flush for me?"

The question's innocent enough, but to do what he's asking, I'd practically need to straddle him. I can't survive that kind of contact with *him*! I scoot as close as I can and lean over his chest awkwardly instead. I glance down at him between my outstretched arms. His cheeks are flushed, mouth parted in concentration on his task. Even with his safety goggles on, beneath me is a damn good look on him.

"Like this?" It comes out breathless, and it's not just because the wood is heavy.

His brown eyes take me in, from my eyes to one of the locks that's escaped from my own messy bun, trailing down my neck like a vine. "Could be better." He gives me a sideways smirk and readjusts my hands for me, bringing me even closer. "There."

The *punk*. Our faces are now inches apart. I could close the distance in an instant, press my lips against that smirk and kiss him until he gasps for breath. Is . . . that what he wants?

"So! What's your deal with technology?" I blurt straight into his face, then wince. *Fuck.* The tension dissolves between us in River's surprised snort.

"My deal?" He gestures with his power drill. "Don't you see this sweet, sweet technology I'm holding right now?"

"You know what I mean. Modern cell phones. The internet. *Real* technology." If I'm going to cockblock myself, might as well lean into it.

He frowns at me as he pets the drill affectionately. "There, there. She didn't mean it."

"Come on, tell me!" I laugh, still breathless hovering over him, but at least I didn't smash my face against his. "Your phone can't even text, you charge it up to listen to your voice mail, like, once a month, and I saw your laptop. It's old enough to go to high school. What's the story there?"

River's laugh slides into his pleasant smile as he positions a bolt into place, then starts the next one. "Oh, it's life story time, is it?"

"If you please."

He groans theatrically, and I hand him the wrench he points to. "My first job after college did a real number on me. I pretty much wanted to chuck everything that had a cord out the window, and when I moved back here, I basically did." He squints, then drills a perfect hole. "Not like the citizens of Blue Ridge expect a fancy website. Martha handles most of our calls, and I can get away with the bare minimum here and still run my business the way I want to."

My mouth quirks to the side. "Fueled by biscuits?"

"With butter, if I'm lucky."

"So what was the job?" I ask, hoping I sound innocent. His old profile flashes in my mind—a River from another era. I want to know what happened to that sweet-faced kid, how he transformed to this sexy, gruff-faced man.

"I was a fraud investigator for an insurance company. Entry-level stuff."

Ahhh, so that's what *Digital Associate* is code for.

"I nosed into good people's privacy, looking for any reason my company could deny their claim." He tightens the nut a little fiercer than necessary. "I was good at it, too, but my bosses were always up my ass, calling me at all hours, texting me, demanding my evenings and weekends and everything I had. I let them trample me for five years before I finally quit and came back home. It took me ages to find myself again, and unplugging from all that *real* technology was a big part of how I got better."

The words resonate within me like the clear strike of a bell. *Fucking Bob* called me day and night. His intrusions soured my free time and robbed me of the ability to relax. But then there's my near constant texting with Kira and Mattie, and how that lifeline keeps me going, keeps me laughing, keeps me from missing them unbearably. I don't think I could give that up.

The footboard secured, River scoots out and sits up, pushing off his goggles. "Regret asking?" He glances at me, as though he's worried I might run off from his unusual bout of seriousness.

"No, no. I can . . . relate." My mouth twists into a half smile. "But you can take my phone from my cold, dead hands. Actually, no." I hold up a finger. "Better leave it in the coffin in case mistakes were made."

River throws his head back and laughs, and my heart lifts from seeing his sunny face restored.

I did that.

"Not me." His laughter subsides, his eyes still twinkling. "I'm all about *this* moment, and what I choose to do with it." His small, shy smile returns. "And who I choose to spend it with. I don't want a phone interrupting that."

I breathe in deeply, as if the feelings he's giving me are air. How does he do this? Make me feel both exhilarated and yet deeply, deeply calm? *Goddamn* this sexy hippie, making me question everything.

"Now, you ready for some drilling?"

The laugh startles me out of my feelings and I roll my eyes, handing him the first set of prepped branches. It's hard, finding the right home for each branch and then affixing them together for the desired effect, but I'm grateful for the quiet, peaceful way we work beside each other. The way he opened up to me and shared real feelings—I'm grateful for that, too. I couldn't set the boundaries he has with the outside world, but I understand a little better why he needed to.

Three hours later, there's a masterpiece waiting for a mattress in our Airbnb. I stand back and wipe the sweat from my brow. I feel anything but casual right now, but I try for a casual tone, anyway. "It's perfect. It's completely perfect."

"It is." River hangs an arm over my shoulders. The feel of his warm, smooth skin against my bare neck makes my stomach flip for the hundredth time today. "And it came from you."

River's shaking his head, his eyes full of quiet appreciation. "You have such good ideas, Hannah, and you work so hard. Hey, you wanna be on my crew?" He jostles my shoulders and brings me a bit closer. My breath hitches. He smiles down at me, but his eyes seem to register something in mine. Does he see the happiness and longing there? The bittersweet triumph of someone finally recognizing my worth that so, so many others denied? Does he see the confusion about what I'm doing here, staring up at him as if I have any right to?

"Hannah," he breathes, my name tumbling softly from his lips. The arm encircling my shoulders brings me closer, his other hand lifting to touch my face. It's a light touch, an exploring one, and yet it sets off an explosion of feelings throughout my body, popping and crackling like fireworks.

I want this so bad, I want *him* so bad, I want to feel this good about myself always. But a vicious, unforeseen wave of loathing crashes through me. A couple months ago, I was ready to marry Killian. I thought I loved him; some dark nights I think I *still* do. And here I am, ready to latch onto the very next guy I meet? One who's even worse at adulting than I am? I have an *infant*. I live with my *mama*. None of that's changed just because the neighbor's hot! Jesus. River can live in the moment, but I can't. This heart's not built for flings; these feelings are already too big and embarrassing and—

"I can't." I pull out of his arms suddenly, miserably. "I'm sorry. I'm just—not ready. For this."

Yet, my mind insists, but I squash it down. As if there's a future where me and the off-the-grid heartbreaker next door makes any sense. Leave it to Hannah Tate, human disaster, to catch feelings for someone so utterly incompatible. Fuck.

River's eyes cloud over, and he drops his hands. "I understand."

God, I hope not.

CHAPTER FOURTEEN

t's been two weeks of early mornings, long days, and late nights, but the Airbnb is *done*. Praise Jesus, Mama's crystals, empanadas, and ibuprofen, it is done. After the almost—whatever that was with River—the only relief I've had has come from working on The Honey Jar. Between taking care of Bowie, going to class, and tricking out the Airbnb, I've had time for little else. This part's been all on me, too. The crew finished up a week or so ago, though they've each stopped by here and there to see my progress. I get the impression that's just how it is now. Martha stops at the cabin for coffee on her morning hikes. Booch swings by after picking up his two cute kids from school. Bella and Edward, five and seven respectively and blissfully unaware of their namesakes, play on the big tire swing Booch hung for us while he drinks Mountain Dew on the dock with Darryl. Gus usually comes by after dusk, so Mama treats him to a beer and a shit-talking game of gin rummy.

And River, well. He's come faithfully to every Sunday dinner, showing up in the afternoon to play with Bowie and making my ovaries scream into the abyss until the food's ready. At the table, he's the perfect guest, raving over Darryl's cooking, laughing at Mama's crazy stories, and clearing the table to wash the dishes before anyone can stop him. He usually lets me dry, though. Standing side by side, my shoulder against his triceps, he smiles down at me *kindly*, as a *friend*, and hands me the clean, wet plates, completely oblivious to how hard he's making it to breathe.

A soft, sad smile creeps up my face as I finish artfully draping a new chunky knit throw over one of the cushy armchairs. River's just . . .

Amazing. He's amazing.

But the embarrassment hits me like a recoil, like it always does. I feel so foolish for having these feelings for him so soon after things with Killian imploded. The mean little voice in my head loves to draw parallels between me now and Mama back then, when I was the little kid trying to remember the name of whatever man was hanging out on our porch that day. I don't want that for Bowie, I *don't*. But there's nothing wrong with having a close family friend, right? That's all River is, a *friend*, which is pretty incredible after I freaked out and practically ran away from his tender touch.

I try to ignore the sinking feeling in my chest. My phone chirrups against the dresser, and before I can register what it means, Mama and Darryl burst through the Airbnb's door like the Kool-Aid Man with Bowie in tow. Darryl pushes his cell phone's screen into my face. "It's the Airbnb people! We got a message from the app!"

"Oh my God." Mama fans herself and Bowie in her arms. "Oh my God!"

"It's from Kira and Mattie!" I take Darryl's phone and scan the automated text with their email. "They're almost here. It's go time, people!"

We invited Kira, Mattie, and June to be our first official guests for the Airbnb's soft opening. Mama, Darryl, and I all agreed it'd only be right to replace the horror of that first weekend here by pampering Kira to the gills.

Plus, her therapist strongly suggested it, so.

Mama thrusts Bowie at me and races back upstairs. When she returns, it's with a tray full of local pastries—apple fritters, apple cider donuts, apple-filled bear claws. It's September in Blue Ridge, Georgia, aka *I hope you like dem apples* season because they're in absolutely everything. Big Daddy turns on the romantic string-bulb lighting that we installed down the stair railing and zigzagged above the Airbnb's porch, even though it's only two p.m. Bowie and I go down the soft opening checklist as I inspect The Honey Jar for the hundredth time. There's wood for the firepit by the lake and propane for the gas firepit by the cabin because "city slickers" deserve s'mores, too. The air is set to the perfect temperature, the toys are temptingly displayed in the kids' room, the towels are fresh and fluffy.

"Am I missing anything, Bowie?" I give him a big smacking kiss on his soft cheek as we head back up, which makes him coo and laugh. I'm way more nervous than I should be. I mean, this is Kira and Mattie, my best friends, not some unknown strangers with murder fetishes staying right beneath my family.

Deep breath. Bowie seems to realize I'm bottoming out and starts swatting my face with his tiny hand, like *snap out of it, woman!*, and I immediately scrunch my eyes closed in self-preservation.

"Gah! No pokey, baby! Not the eyeballs!"

"I don't know. You could rock an eye patch."

"Mattie!" I'd been so busy flitting about, I didn't even hear them pull up. Excitement and that special brand of homesickness you have for people you love rushes over me. It's been a little over a month since I've seen them last, and of course we text constantly, but it's not the same as having them in the same city. I realize how much I've been looking forward to this in one crushing swoop—to seeing them, to showing them all that we've accomplished since the taxidermy shop from hell. I rush forward to give Mattie and baby June a hug, but then Kira sweeps out from behind them with an imperious frown. Her head cranes this way and that, her big movie-star sunglasses sizing up the place.

"Hmm," she says flatly with a sniff. "It doesn't look like the pictures, does it?"

I take a step back, my heart already swimming with hurt. My eyes sweep over the cabin with its baskets of spilling flowers to the brand-new entryway, to the landscaped path down to the Airbnb, its quaint terraced steps ringed with wildflowers, the rolling meadows down to the water, trying to see what Kira sees. Is it . . . bad? After all this work, weeks of renovation and yard work and decorating, I feel so stupid, I feel so . . . Shit, I'm going to *cry.*

"I—"

"You must be the *host*." The way Kira says it, you'd think she's referring to somebody riddled with parasites. "I am Jasmine St. Jermaine, this is my sugar boy, Philippe, and our love child, Guinevere." Kira flings her hand luggage down and sashays toward the path. "No elevator? How *dare* you."

"Um . . ." My eyebrows pinch together, a stray sob escaping even as the smile creeps up my face. "The fuck?" It's only then that I notice how Mattie and June are dressed. Mattie's wearing a white and blue striped shirt, a red jaunty bandanna tied around her throat, and a grimace. Someone's drawn an anchor and a heart flagged with the word *Mommies* on her forearm in Sharpie. Poor June's wearing a beret and looking very confused about it.

Mattie/Philippe sighs grandly, which earns her a reproving *ahem!* from below.

"Coming, milady." Mattie rolls her eyes and grins at me, swooping in to give me a quick kiss on the cheek. "Sorry, I would have warned you, but Madame St. Jermaine stole my phone so I couldn't."

"Oh. Oh, *shit*." Understanding slowly dawns. "She's going to make this soft opening hard on us . . ."

"AND WHERE, PRAY TELL, ARE THE HORS D'OEUVRES?"

I squeeze Bowie and laugh into his little neck.

Jasmine St. Jermaine is one tough customer. She commandeers Big Daddy to carry their luggage down, refers to G-ma only as "Cook," and blithely eats an apple fritter with her feet up on the ottoman while I bring her not one, not two, not even three (which would be within the realm of reasonability), but *seven* types of herbal tea before she declares the first to be good enough. She walks around The Honey Jar, dragging her finger across every surface looking for dust, demands that I come down to inspect a fuzzy on the bedspread that *is definitely bedbugs or herpes* (??), and requires a full demonstration on how to use the air-conditioning remote, which consists of two buttons, a blue one and a red one.

It is . . . an education in patience. She keeps us all on our toes for the better part of two hours, but to our credit, nobody cusses her out.

Not to her face, anyway.

When she "rings" for me à la Airbnb notification for the twentieth time, I'm fully prepared for her to ask for a sensual sponge bath or inquire as to our Austrian masseuse. But instead, Kira's waiting for me at the door.

"What is it, my liege?" I ask warily, bowing low as I was commanded to do earlier.

She folds her arms, eyes me up and down, and says with a cold, disdainful authority:

"Five. Star. Review."

She grins and throws her arms around me.

"Really?!" We hug-jump in a circle on the porch. There are squeals.

"It's amazing! Hannah, it's so beautiful!"

"Gah! You really think so?!" I didn't realize how much I craved her approval until she withheld it for two godforsaken hours, and it makes me sprout happy, relieved tears.

Kira pushes me back to look at me. "Hannah. You are so talented. I am incredibly proud of you." She gestures to the stunning modern windows that frame the perfect September mountain view with its first kiss of yellow and orange among the green of summer. To the round wooden pedestal table I've set up in the corner, with locally made ceramic mugs, and the lake gleaming below. To the black wicker lanterns swagged in a cluster overhead and the creamy curtains striped with thin, black woven thread pushed all the way to the sides, their tassels pooling gently on the floor. Then, with her other hand, she waves at the poplar bed, outfitted in an oaty natural linen piled with pillows of every possible texture, the canopy of branches framing it like a portal to another world. I must not look impressed enough at my own work because she grabs me by the shoulders and shakes me.

"Hannah! It. Is. Everything." She shakes me again for good measure. "Do you know what Philippe's going to do to me later on that bed? Do you?!"

My words stumble over my happy laughter. "I thought the ruse was over!"

Mattie stops on her way in, having just put June down for her nap in the kids' room. Her eyes flick from Kira to me and back to Kira, a deep, weary suspicion settling over her face. "Kira . . . you promised!"

"Oh, you think Philippe and Jasmine are *new*?" Kira arches a wicked eyebrow, ignoring Mattie's grumpy frown completely. "How sweet."

Mattie groans and flops backward onto the couch, smashing a pillow over her face. "Oversharing, Kiki!" comes her muffled voice.

Kira smiles drolly, then tucks a twenty-dollar bill into the rim of my tank top. "Forget what you've learned here today."

CHAPTER FIFTEEN

The Corolla's ignition clears its throat with a sound like grinding metal. I know I should stop, but I'm nothing if not dumbly persistent in the face of failure. I twist the key for the fiftieth time, but the chewing sound abruptly chokes into the dreaded click of death.

"Fuck." Bowie's strapped into his car seat in the back, and we're alone with my dead-ass car. Kira, Mattie, and June already headed out to the apple festival in the Subaru. We couldn't all ride together because of June's massive new car seat. Then, I stupidly shooed G-ma and Big Daddy off, too, so they could go on their bowling date with Sarge. I try calling everyone's cell phones, but the lines don't even ring. They just crackle and hiss, as if our mountain itself answered and said, *You're on your own, asshole.*

"Fuck, fuck, fuck." I rest my forehead on the steering wheel. It's not like Blue Ridge has a ride service. The apple festival is a thirty-minute drive from the cabin, just like everywhere else in Blue Ridge. I try calling again, nothing. Once K&M get to the main road, they'll have reception again, but by that point, they'll be twenty minutes away.

I throw my head back and groan, a deep, guttural anthem of frustration. It makes me feel a little better and now Bowie's laughing, too, so I keep it up, groaning even louder to get all my feelings out. It's got tones, it's got texture, it's getting funky—

A pair of knuckles raps gently on my window, and my primal song ends with a grunt.

River's eyebrows are high, his full mouth shaped by mirth.

"Oh, god." A hot, feverish blush consumes my entire head.

He opens my car door, his soft chuckle now audible. "No, please don't stop."

This is what I get for feeling my feelings. I'm unfollowing every last therapist on Insta.

"Got some bongos up in the treehouse. Should I get them?" He rests the long line of his arms along the open door's frame, his teasing grin eating me up from the inside out. The worn red flannel shirt he's wearing looks softer than kitten fur, and the top few buttons are undone. I nearly choke on my own dry tonsils.

"No bongos necessary. Um, what're you doing here?" The question comes out huskier than I mean it to, but between the mortification at him hearing me and the way he's draped over my open space, normal speech is currently unavailable.

"I heard a . . . well, not a damsel, exactly, but *something* in distress." His shoulders shake with quiet laughter. "Maybe a raccoon?"

I sigh through my nose.

"Or a very angry chipmunk."

"It's my car. It won't start." I slap the wheel for emphasis. Yes, turn the attention to the car.

He nods, eyebrows still high and jolly. "I heard you kill it, you murderer. Where's everybody else?"

"I'm supposed to meet Kira and Mattie at the apple festival, but I can't get ahold of them to let them know that my car . . . died of natural causes."

"The Beckett Orchards Apple Festival?" River scoffs playfully. "Isn't that for *tourists*?"

"I need to go so I can write it up for the Airbnb's guidebook. It's supposed to be a lot of fun." I sniff a little. It's supposed to be a lot of food, if I'm being honest. Caramel apples. Funnel cake. Curly fries.

My stomach grumbles with angst.

River straightens and smacks his hands on the roof of the car. "Well, then. Can't have you missing it. Let's go."

"Really?" The palms of my hands are sweaty against the steering wheel. I'd wanted to invite River. I'd thought about it all last night as I tossed in bed, but I kept hemming and hawing over whether he'd think it was a date, which is unacceptable because it would absolutely *not be a date*. It'd be an excursion into public where I got to sneak covert glances at his collarbone. As friends.

River offers his hand to me in response, gently pulling me up and out of the car. I am so glad Kira heckled me until I changed into a clean pair of black leggings and my favorite oversized camel cardigan. It always makes me feel cozy and cute. It's also the only thing that makes this pearly white tunic-tank modest enough for public.

And I'm not wearing it yet.

We both notice the riotous swell of my breasts fighting to escape my shirt at the same time. His eyes sweep over me, drinking me in, leaving a blaze of heat in their wake. It startles me with its intensity, and the ground shifts beneath my feet. I tip forward on my horny, idiot feet, and for a second, our bodies try to occupy the same space at the same time. He catches me easily, and the press of my skin against his flannel-covered chest sends a shock wave of sensation across my body.

Warm. Hard. Big.

I shiver against him. Surprising everyone, I don't resume my primal grunting.

He cups me by the elbows, righting me before I knock him into the freshly fallen leaves and mount him with a war cry. For an instant, our eyes lock, and a current of electricity flows between us. Then Bowie *mehs* loudly from the car seat, and the spell's broken.

"Sorry," I murmur, a little breathless.

"Anytime," he says, a faint blush coloring his cheeks. *Sweet Jesus*, swooning in progress.

Five minutes later, River's fought and won the battle with Bowie's car seat while I stand to the side and try not to gape at his strong shoulders moving beneath his flannel shirt, or the stretch of dark golden skin exposed when it rides up his back. I've developed a fine appreciation for the sight of River working. He makes everything look easy, even when it's hard and he's never done it before. I don't know if it's the yoga or what, but River approaches life like he already knows he can handle whatever's thrown his way. It's not cockiness or arrogance, it's more like . . . faith.

Faith in *himself.*

It's hot as hell.

He takes Bowie gently from my arms and places him in the car seat, taking his time securing the sun in my solar system safely in, cooing sweet, silly nothings to him the whole time.

I encase myself in cardigan like it's body armor, tying the sweater belt tightly around me like its purpose is to preserve my chastity. Is it weird to be turned on by how a man holds your baby?

It *is*, isn't it.

I swallow roughly as I climb into the front seat next to River.

Maybe I'll hold off on unfollowing all those therapists after all.

≈

"There you are!" Kira proclaims, hustling her way through the crowds milling about the festival. She greets Bowie with a kiss and me with a shiny, red candy apple on a stick. "I knew you'd be hangry, so I got you something sweet." Her eyes finally register River standing beside me, and a surprised little *o* forms on her lips.

"I see you brought your own." She winks at us, and I grab the candy apple from her so I can hide behind it. "Hey, River."

"Hey, Kira. Good to see you." From anyone else, it'd sound like an empty platitude, but real, genuine warmth suffuses his words, and Kira visibly softens in response. It wasn't that long ago he was saving her from a skanky dead snake, and I'm pretty sure it got him in her good graces forever.

"Right back atcha." She pats his arm fondly, and her eyebrows rise. "Oooh, strong . . ." The pat turns into a mild frisking. "Mattie, you gotta come feel this!"

River's crooked, playful smile emerges. "Here, let me flex appropriately for you." He squats, lifting his arms up like an old-timey muscle man.

Mattie appears with June strapped to her chest and gently peels Kira's roaming hands off a very amused River. "Sorry. Kira doesn't know how to menfolk appropriately."

"You say that like it's a verb," River says.

"It is," Kira and Mattie say together, and River laughs again. I stand back, bewildered. I can't think of a single time Kira and Mattie shared a joke with Killian like this. Seeing my best friends laughing and teasing River winds something inside of me, like those pull-back cars that race off into the abyss when you finally let them go.

I take a big, frantic bite of the candy apple.

We amble over to the games area, taking in the sights, sounds, and *mmmm* smells of the festival. I make quick work of the candy apple so I can replace it with a tall cone of curly fries. I'm in *heaven*. Even Bowie gnaws on one for a while, his eyes lighting up in true love.

"His first greasy potato," I say, tearing up.

Kira places a hand on my arm. "It's a special moment."

After I show River *three times* how to work the camera on my phone, he good-naturedly takes our picture to capture this important milestone: Kira, Mattie, and me, all smiling, proud mommies, while Bowie and June squawk with curly fries hanging out of their mouths. They look like little walruses with orange mushy tusks. I'm obsessed.

"Definitely a framer," Mattie says, peering over my shoulder at the picture. When no one's looking, she leans in and whispers, "Is River secretly in his seventies? How does he not know how to operate a phone camera?"

I shrug. "He doesn't have one."

"A phone?!" Mattie hisses, and I shush her quickly.

"No, he's got an ancient flip phone. No camera, no texting, no internet."

"No internet?" Mattie raises one quizzical eyebrow. "How does he anxiety-google weird rashes that show up?"

"I don't think he anxiety-googles at all."

Mattie's mouth falls open, and I nod grimly.

When we get to the petting zoo area, a chorus of peeps greets us.

"They've got chicks! Come on!" Kira's eyes are so bright and happy, it makes me laugh. She takes June on her hip over to the hatchery's chick area, and the rest of us follow, too, entering the dark barn. The hay smell is rich and ticklish in my nose, and the dueling scents of burning firewood and powdered sugar carry on the breeze. I breathe it all in, eyes fluttering closed in happiness. Fall is my happy place. I've always felt like the seasons have personalities. Winter's got mood swings—either cheerful and brimming with nostalgia or moody and hiding under the blankets. Spring's optimistic and eager, a child waiting at the door impatiently to play outside. Summer's that friend that's obsessed with CrossFit—works hard, plays harder, sweats entirely too much. But fall is all things cozy and delicious. It's tables set for feasts, floppy turtleneck sweaters, and piles of crisp red leaves inviting you to jump in. And the best part is that it's always beautiful, whether the skies are blue or a thick, woolen gray.

River leans down over the large wooden crate filled with straw, and I swear to G-ma's crystals, a chick hops straight into his palms. He's no Disney prince, but he *may* be Cinderella.

Kira elbows me, and I remember to breathe like a human.

Or try to, anyway.

He brings the soft, yellow baby up to his chest, and we gather around him like congregants to a cult leader, gently taking turns stroking the chick's downy back.

River's head is ducked low over the baby chick, brushing it softly with his finger. His smile is small and sweet. The image is so charming, it might destroy me.

He leans close, his warm breath fluttering against my ear, and murmurs, "It just pooped in my hand."

A laugh bursts out of me. There are miniature goats, too, which eat leaves out of our hands and stay for ear scratches. One baby goat keeps gently butting June's diapered bottom, like it's trying to round her up to go play. June totters on her feet each time, giggling with joy, her small hands locked in Mattie's as she helps her walk around the yard. Meanwhile, Bowie's eyes are bright and curious as a goat licks his outstretched hand.

"Oh, *shit*. This is all too cute." Kira presses a hand against her heart and takes a ragged breath. "I just started ovulating."

I snort. "Like, on demand?"

She nods, eyes still wide. "Mattie, baby—"

"I don't have any sperm on me, Kiki. You'll just have to wait." Mattie's voice is wry and calm as always, but her face tells a different story. The frown is deep and sad and, more than anything, tired. When Kira makes grabby hands for June, she passes her over and sighs while Kira takes deep, emergency sniffs of June's baby skin, then demands the same of Bowie.

"Hey." I wrap an arm around Mattie as we head toward the hayrides. "You okay?"

She bites both lips and nods. "More or less." The way she accepts my embrace, leaning her head on my shoulder as we walk, fills me with concern. Mattie's the stalwart one, always has been. My eyes flicker over to Kira, but she's too busy bouncing June on one hip and Bowie on the other, neighing like a horse and galloping around to make them squeal. Kira's in her element, full glorious happiness written all over her face, so what the hell's going on?

"Do you want to talk about it?"

Mattie sighs. "It'll be the same old conversation."

"The next baby?"

Mattie nods. "After everything we went through, she's still hell-bent on getting pregnant again. I feel . . ." Mattie frowns, blinks. "I don't know. Like she views me as an obstacle these days. Not her partner."

I breathe in deeply. "Kira's wanted kids as long as I can remember. That kind of dream doesn't go away."

"She almost died, Hannah," Mattie says, the corners of her voice raw.

"I know." I squeeze Mattie a little tighter. "I know."

Mattie straightens and clears her throat. "I'm sorry. I'm not trying to get you in the middle of this. It's something we've got to work through, that's all."

"Okay, Philippe. I'm here if you need me."

Mattie's lips twitch into a halfhearted smile, and she brushes her hair off her forehead. She looks so defeated, and I feel for her. Holding Kira off is like standing in the middle of a rushing river. You're lucky if you keep your balance at all. I watch as Mattie goes to Kira and gives her a long, sweet kiss on her cheek and puts her arm around her. Kira beams back at her, and my heart squeezes. It's funny how two people can love each other so much, and yet be at such fundamental odds.

The afternoon's faded into twilight when we reach the hayrides. The tractor's already humming, and Bowie's mesmerized by the giant, trembling machine. I poke his belly till he laughs.

"Tractors, buddy? Kinda basic."

Kira looks at the line, then at her watch. "I hate to be a killjoy, but I'm worn out. Mattie, are you cool with heading back now?"

Mattie starts to protest, but something unspoken passes between them, and suddenly she's nodding. "Whew, yeah. Me too." Mattie turns and smacks

River on the back, a bit theatrically. "You can take Hannah and Bowie home, right, River?"

Oh. I see how it is.

"Of course, but . . ." River looks uncertainly between me and Mattie. "Do you want to head back now, too, Hannah?" He runs a newly washed and disinfected hand over the hair escaping the low knot at the back of his head, looking strangely out of place for once. For someone so at ease at everything he does, seeing him like this is unbearably endearing. I'm not completely in control of my body when my free hand reaches up and loops through his arm.

"Not yet." The words come out low and silky. River comes willingly to my side, letting me reel him in close.

"Excellent. Philippe? Attend to our love child." Kira proffers June to Mattie, who groans and straps June back into her baby carrier. River raises an eyebrow, and I shake my head, breathing out a small laugh.

"Y'all enjoy the Airbnb. I'll text you later."

"Oh, we *will*—" Kira's saying, and I laugh again as Mattie drags her off.

River's head dips low to look at me, his rich, brown eyes almost black in the lavender evening. My arm shivers against his. Should I take it away? Or should I leave it there, forever, until my body fails me and they have to physically pry me off with a crowbar? Hard to say. I'm saved from this existential crisis by the movement of the line, because now it's our turn to board, and we're forced to part. I feel a weird, buzzing disappointment at having to let him go until the warm press of his hand helps me and Bowie up the steps, and I nearly forget my own name.

We're the last ones in, and a surly preteen boy in a Monster Jam T-shirt closes the gate with a loud bang. We settle in the hay as the first of the stars twinkle through the dusk. River extends an arm behind Bowie and me, letting it rest against the wagon's rim. The tractor rumbles forward, and the wagon jolts in response, bouncing me into the crook of River's arm. He curls around me protectively, automatically, the other arm going to Bowie where he sits cradled in my lap. River's hand rests on top of mine there, and okay, I'm a feminist. I'm bisexual. I kill my own spiders. But the feeling of River's strong arms around me and my baby is nothing I've ever experienced. A powerful but soft reassurance. A promise to protect I can feel. So what if he doesn't have medical insurance, or a retirement plan, or a normal plumbing situation? I feel happy. I feel *safe*.

I lift my chin to face him, dazed from the heat of his body radiating into mine. Is this okay? *Please*, let this be okay. I want it to be okay so, so badly. Maybe if it didn't feel so much like the cycle of Mama's romances I watched unwillingly as a child, I wouldn't feel so scared. But the explosion of a relationship, the despair and fury that followed, then the quick descent into new love, it's all sickeningly familiar. I don't want any part of it, for me or for Bowie.

But this is different. This is *real*. Isn't it?

Why does that feel even scarier?

Lavender skies and gentle mountains frame the strong lines of his face, and I see the same questions, the same pleas, lingering unspoken on his barely parted lips.

Are you ready now?

For a second, I don't breathe. I realize he's been waiting, ever since the moment we almost kissed; he's been giving me the space I needed to get to this moment. This beautiful, perfect moment where *I* get to choose what I want to do, and who I want to be with. This beautiful, perfect moment under the stars that he's chosen, too. His eyes lock onto mine, his thumb brushing languidly against my upper arm. A deep current of understanding flows between us, bare and unvarnished with all the empty lies I've been telling myself since the moment I met him. That I don't want this. That I *shouldn't* want this. That we're too different, and he's too irresponsible. That feeling this pull to him is wrong, that it makes me like Mama, that it's too soon, that he'll hurt me, that it's *anything* but right.

Because it *is* real, whether I'm ready for it or not.

River's arm, still cradling my shoulders, pulls me against him. He leans in and presses his full lips to my temple, his smile warm against my skin, and it all falls away. He breathes in the scent of my hair, and nothing exists beyond the circle of his arms.

Just me,

and Bowie,

and now *him*.

≈

Ever since the hayride, some part of River is always touching some part of me. The large expanse of his hand on my lower back as we walk through the festival, the heat of his arm against mine when we sit to eat funnel cake, the gentle brush of his finger against my nose.

"You're covered in sugar." He smiles fondly as he inspects my face, sweeping the powdered sugar away with his light touch. "Here, here, and here."

So is Bowie, but I barely care. He's long asleep, nestled against my chest in his sling like a little powdered donut, completely unaware of how River's proximity, his touch, are *doing* things to me.

"Want a taste?" The words are spoken low, under my breath, and so flirtatious, I can't believe I said them.

His dark eyes shimmer with heat. "Yes."

With my face still in his hand, he leans in close and hovers an inch from my mouth. I feel the glow of his warmth before his full lips graze against my cheek. The kiss is like a whisper, a secret shared between our bodies. I've never been so happy to be an enthusiastic funnel cake eater in my life. His lips part, and the warm press of his tongue against my skin tastes me, makes me softly gasp.

River stops to search my eyes for reassurance, which he finds. I feel like liquid beneath my clothes, flowing warm and easy. The feeling follows me all the way to his truck, along the country roads under this clear, black night, and up our mountain. He pulls up to our cabin, letting the truck idle.

"Thanks for rescuing us."

His arm rests along the cab's seat, and his fingers wind around one of my curls. "Always."

The words squeeze my heart, because God help me, I believe him.

"Can I take you out Friday night, Hannah Tate?" His eyes glimmer in the dark cab.

Pressure builds in my chest because I can't think of anything I want more, but it feels dangerous, too, like I'm starting something I may never be able to quit. "You know I'm leaving here one day, right?" I blurt out, the easy feeling gone. "I'm only here until I get Mama and Darryl sorted." Until I get *me* sorted, more like it, but I don't need to say it for him to understand.

The finger winding my curl stops, but only for an instant. His face is thoughtful when he says, simply, "You're here now."

"I am," I whisper, unsure why.

"Do you want to spend your here and now with me?"

I blink, but I can't lie anymore. "Yes."

His soft smile returns. "I'll pick you up at seven."

CHAPTER SIXTEEN

Within three days of listing The Honey Jar on Airbnb, we're booked solid through October. The professional pictures I had taken of the space sparkle, and it doesn't hurt that our first guest, a Ms. Jasmine St. Jermaine, wrote a manifesto on the cabin's perfection, the hosts' hospitality, the idyllic views, etc. We barely had time to scrub the place down before our next arrival, a lovely family of three that thankfully did *not* message me for *turndown and turn-me-on service* as Ms. St. Jermaine had. After they left, a kind older couple celebrated their anniversary here. It's been frantic and exhilarating in the best possible way. I relish every glowing review. They're like little love letters to all our hard work. Each one feels like a voice whispering in my ear, *You were right, this is right, everything is good and perfect and right.*

It's been so busy, I've barely had time to see River. He's stopped by here and there to help when we've needed him, giving me looks that melt me like a candle. This morning, I woke up to find a perfect red leaf on our doorstep, with the words *See you tonight, Hannah Tate* etched on it.

I've been swooning ever since.

I smooth down the front of my dress and scrunch at my still damp waves in the mirror. With Mama and Darryl fully fluent in Bowie now, I had more than enough time to get ready for tonight's date. When the thought occurred to me that I could straighten my hair and curl the ends like old times, I immediately dismissed it. This is what I look like now, and I like it. Windswept and soft, flowy and unburdened. As soon as I stopped struggling against my body, everything became easier. Not just with getting ready, but also with . . . *being*. It seems obvious to me now, but before, every pass of my old straightener felt like a rebuke. Like how I am naturally isn't good enough.

I'm done with that.

The dress is new, and I love it. It's a pale smoky blue gossamer thing, with long sleeves and a delicate line of pearl buttons down the front. A few are undone at the top, exposing the soft skin there, and at the bottom, too, letting my legs peek through where the dress ends just below my knees. The brown belt at my waist matches my ankle boots, and I feel like a vintage prairie woman, but hot as fuck.

"Come here, Littleman." I scoop Bowie up from his activity mat and nuzzle my face into his neck. I breathe deep, the scent of his baby skin grounding me to this earth with boulders of love. "Time for a quick milky?"

Bowie happily coos, and I take him to our favorite nursing spot on the porch swing. Another bonus of a button-down dress—easy to pop a boob out. He latches on easily, like we've been doing this for a million years. So funny how that works. Nursing felt like the most difficult thing in the world when we started, and now, it's the easiest. As the milk lets down, I breathe a deep sigh of relief. I don't do yoga like River, but this is how I get my zen. There's nothing better than holding my baby close, feeling his warm, heavy weight in my arms, and letting this simple biological connection link us together.

I run my finger against the soft mound of Bowie's cheek, so consumed in mommy bliss I don't hear the footsteps until they stop a few feet away.

River's tall frame fills the porch, and for a second I gaze at him, lost in feelings. His hair is down, pooling softly against his shoulders. He's wearing a cream-colored Henley that fits him snugly across the chest, the beautiful structure of his collarbones on full display. A taupe-colored cardigan stretches across his shoulders, the sleeves of both it and the Henley rolled up to his forearms. I want to bury my face in them, in him. Oh *God*, I bet he smells like wood again.

For as long as I've been staring at him, he's been staring at me, too, and I realize with a start that I'm still nursing Bowie.

"Oh, sorry, I'll—"

"You look so beautiful, Hannah." His voice, always so ready to laugh, is quiet this time, almost reverent. My heart judders in my chest.

"Thanks. I'll be just a minute." After I discreetly rearrange my prairie dress, I gently carry Bowie inside and hand him over to G-ma. His eyes are already swinging shut as he rests his head on her shoulder, and the small, trusting move twists my heart. Sometimes the love I feel for him is so beautiful, it's almost painful. Big Daddy warns me to keep an eye on the weather as a storm may be coming through, and I warn him and G-ma to text me if Bowie so much as burps funny.

When I rejoin River on the porch, he offers me his hand. Suddenly I'm seventeen again, blushing and overwhelmed with the burst of warmth flooding my body from my crush's touch. He opens the truck's door for me, and though it is *completely* unnecessary, I'm not complaining when he places both hands on my waist and helps me into the cab. His hands burn through the thin fabric of my dress, the imprints he left behind still tingling and warm as I buckle up.

As we head down the dirt road, a white SUV turns onto it, driving slowly up toward our cabin.

"That might be our guests." I lean over to peer out River's window. Sure enough, the SUV rolls to a stop in our guest parking spot. A small woman gets out alone.

I frown because I *know* her. "Hey, can you back up for a second?"

River does as I ask, and I hop out of the cab. "Madison?"

The small, overfriendly blonde from Small Business Owners 101 freezes where she stands, halfway down the landscaped path to our Airbnb. "Oh, Hannah! There you are!" She turns her full-wattage smile on me and climbs back up toward the road.

"What are you doing here?"

"I was looking for you, of course!"

She definitely was not. She puts her hands on her hips and sighs happily. "Let me tell you, this cabin is *adorable*. Can you give me a tour since I'm here?"

I frown even more. "Sorry, no. I'm on my way out, and we're expecting guests any minute."

"You sure about that?" She winks, and my stomach clenches. What the hell does that mean? "Just kidding. Another time, then." She waves me off but makes no move to leave. When it's clear I'm not going to leave until she does, she reluctantly clicks her key to unlock her car. "Y'all have a good time now!"

I get back into River's truck, and we both watch as her shiny white Jeep Grand Cherokee descends the mountain. "That was so weird. What was she doing snooping around our cabin like that?"

"Madison McGee?"

"You know her?"

"A little. She hired us to work on one of her properties once."

"Proper-*ties*?" She'd mentioned a cabin up in Mineral Bluff, but that was it.

"She works for the big property management group in town. Handles cabin rentals for their owner-investors."

"But she said . . ." I trail off, thinking back to how she pounced on the other people from class with rental properties, too. "Well, damn."

"Madison's a shark, no doubt about it." River gives me a sideways smile. "She's probably here scoping out the competition."

I don't like that one bit. I shoot off a quick text to Mama and Darryl to keep an eye out for any squirrelly blondes lurking about. When I look up, River catches my eye, and it reminds me where I am, who I'm with, and what is finally going down. Our first *date*. I slip the phone back in my purse and clear my throat.

"So where are we going?" I sound nervous, even to my own ears. It makes sense, I guess. The last time I went on a date, my entire life fell apart.

Wordlessly, River places his right palm up on the long seat, and after a second, I take it, twining my fingers with his. I may be nervous, but this doesn't feel like a first date. It feels new and yet, like it's always been this way.

Goddammit, I've got it bad.

River seems to sense my unease and squeezes my hand. "We're going to the Ellijay River Vineyards. It's the harvest moon tonight. They do it up right." His soft smile unravels the knot forming inside me with a simple tug, and I squeeze him back.

"Sounds perfect."

His headlights bounce across a small vine-covered gate, nearly swallowed by forest. The woods part like curtains, revealing a dusky valley covered in neat rows of grapevines. At the bottom of the winding dirt road, a red barn's lit up with strands of lights crisscrossed between it and a thin stand of trees. Beyond must be the Ellijay River. I can't see it, but the river's song rushes through our open windows.

He parks in a long row of beat-up trucks and cars. These aren't rentals from the airport, or the luxury vehicles of Atlanta weekenders. The tags are all Fannin or Gilmer counties.

Locals, then.

"I'm not allowed to put this event in our Airbnb's guidebook, am I?" I swing our joined hands playfully as we make our way to the barn.

He smirks at me, then pulls me into his side and wraps an arm around me. "Don't you go giving out all my secrets, Hannah Tate."

All he has to do is say my name, and my body floats into the air, tethered to the ground by him alone. Beneath the lights, people murmur to each other, laughing and sipping wine. A few small tables are scattered about, camping chairs are ringed around an open fire, and a set of rope swings hangs from the limb of a massive tree. There's a small stage area set up, too, the musicians' instruments propped up and ready to go. River leads me to the bar, a few planks of wood balanced across two barrels of wine, where none other than Gus, our heavy metal electrician, stands.

"Gus Claxton!" I announce in delight. "What are you doing behind there?"

"Moonlightin', little mama." He grins, then jabs a finger up at the sky. And there, hanging just above the tree line, is the full moon. It's as round and yellow as an unbroken yolk, like any minute the tops of the trees might pierce it and spill its light across the mountains.

It's *magic*.

Not in your typical black cats and broomsticks sense, but in that way where the impossible suddenly dips within your reach. The air itself feels charged with potential.

"Bartending *and* electrical? Color me impressed. Your shirt's got sleeves and everything!"

I'm treated to one of River's full-throated laughs. "Wait until winter. Gus wears that torn-up Metallica shirt over long johns like a heavy metal sweater vest."

Gus shrugs. "What can I say? Women love the rock 'n' roll." He pours us the house favorite, a rich, ruby Merlot.

"You mean Martha. *Martha* loves the rock 'n' roll." River leans his elbows on the makeshift bar, flashing his teasing smile.

"Martha? And *Gus*?" I swing to face the moppy-haired bartender, searching for the truth in the weathered creases of his face. Gus's dimples appear as he struggles not to grin.

I've seen all I need to know.

"Y'all were vibing right in front of me, and I didn't even pick up on it."

"You were a mite distracted, too, I recall." Gus winks at me and slides our glasses over. "Now, git. Gotta make me some tips if I'm gonna take my woman out for Waffle House later."

Gus shoos us away, and we amble lazily through the vineyards, then down by the river, talking about nothing and everything and always, always laughing. The air is brisk, but I'm not cold. The evening air cools the thin layers of my dress, blowing it against my flushed skin. River's in the middle of describing the newest book he's reading when he's interrupted by a loud *ding!* from my purse.

"Sorry." I fish my phone out. "Gotta make sure Bowie's okay." I scan the notification quickly and frown.

"Is everything all right?"

"It's the guests coming in tonight. They just canceled due to the storm forecast. Kinda late notice for that."

I glance up, and River's peaceful face looks a little strained. He tries to smile. "On call, as always."

I shrug. "You have to be when people depend on you."

For a long, quiet moment, we stare into the dark water tumbling along the rocky bed below, filigreed with the golden light of the harvest moon. I breathe it all in, pulling the magic of this moment deep inside as though I could inhale this perfect place and make it part of me. When I exhale, I push out all my worries and thoughts of the Airbnb, lost revenue, the welcome basket of baked goods we'll end up eating instead. It's easier to do that here, where the sharp smell of seasoned wood burning mixes with the wet, earthy leaves underfoot. I take River's hand in mine and focus on the feel of him, the fresh scent of river rocks, the wine's dark cherry notes on my tongue.

I am here in this moment that I've chosen, and it's a good one.

My eyes flutter open to see River watching me with a knowing smile on his face. I don't need to explain the spell this evening's put me under. It's drifting over us, collecting in eddies and whirling past, tugging at hands and pushing locks of hair aside to whisper its secrets.

We reach the rope swings looking out onto the water. River sits on one, and I settle onto the smooth wooden seat of the other.

I bring the wine to my lips, unable to tear my eyes from River's. The wine is plummy and sweet, and River's eyes trace the movement of my tongue as I lick my lower lip. His gaze brings a heat to my cheeks that the wine carries down my throat. And in this moment, it's all I want. Tonight, this swing, the feel of River's fingers interlaced with mine.

Soft strands of music overlay the sounds of the river, the band jumping straight into a slow, dreamy melody. They know what magic is on everyone's mind here tonight.

"Dance with me." River stands, steps before my idling legs. One thick thigh enters between my two as my swing comes to a rest, the dress sliding up slowly against his leg. My breath hitches as he takes my wine, sets it down with his, and sweeps me up to standing. This time when I fall into him, I let myself stay.

"Here?" It comes out a whisper, and River answers by taking my hand, the other coming to rest on the curve of my lower back. We're dancing in the dark beneath a canopy of leaves, the string lights far enough away they could be fireflies flickering in the fields.

I don't know how we got to this place. How we started with plans and sketches but ended here, where I can't even talk for fear of all the feelings that might pour out. How do people do this, summon the courage to start all over again? I don't want to be hurt in front of Bowie, like Mama was with me. Those long nights of her muffled sobs coming through the thin walls of our apartment did something to me. *Changed* something within me. How many seven-year-olds don't believe in true love?

Everything I saw back then taught me that love has an expiration date. Why should it be any different for me? It's probably why I ignored all the problems with Killian for so long. We had Bowie, we didn't throw things when we fought, and we could keep the lights on. Right there, our relationship was already better than every one of Mama's past marriages. Of course I wanted to lock it down; it was already better than anything I'd expected for myself.

But if we ever loved each other, those feelings have expired, too.

"Hannah." River's voice is low and throaty. "You're shaking."

"I'm just . . . cold." He seems to know I'm lying, his eyes tender as he shifts our stance till my arms wrap around his neck, and his travel down my sides, his hands joining around the small of my back. Does he know how scared I am? It's not fair to River to want the future on the first date. To demand upfront all the devotion and love I'm not sure even exists in real life before I've even lifted my chin for his kiss.

So I do it anyway.

The callused pads of his fingers brush down my cheek, resting beneath my chin, tipping me into his mouth like he wants to drink me up. I must've imagined this kiss a thousand times, his lips on mine in a thousand different variations. A soft kiss goodnight, a hot kiss between the sheets, the sweet, simple kisses that belong to the morning. But none of my fantasies prepared me for this. The kiss envelops me, like warm velvet colliding against bare skin. His full lips are impossibly soft against my own, sliding over me until our lips part, the kiss deepening. I shiver into his chest, and his arms wrap around me tighter, sheltering me from the cool night air, but that's not what's making me feel this way. My nipples peak against the warmth of him, the soft, sweet ache between my legs longing for his pressure, his heat. I tug his lower lip into my mouth, and he groans softly into me, pressing harder like every inch of him wants to feel every inch of me.

I want it, too.

When we finally part, we're both out of breath, but his mouth dives back for more, pressing hungry kisses against the side of my lips, my jaw, scooping me up to reach my neck. His breath is ragged where he crushes his face into my hair, pulling my earlobe between his lips. It's a good thing he's holding me up because my legs turn to water. His hands easily support my weight, cradling my ass to hold me flush against him. His old, faded jeans that always look so soft don't feel soft now. They're barely containing the hard length of him. I want to wrap my legs around his hips, surround him with the soft length of me. Thoughts spark like flint in my head, burning through the miasma of want pervading my entire body.

This is too fast, Hannah, stop! You've got to stop!

A streak of white connects land to sky, the clap of thunder following quick as a gunshot. I let go of River's neck on reflex, and as he releases me, one of my booted feet slams into our wine.

The glasses shatter.

I'm breathless, head reeling. That was more than a first kiss, this is more than a first date, and the feelings exploding in my chest bring hot tears to my eyes. I want this so much it hurts, so much that it's scaring me, but the instinct to run makes me take a wobbly step back.

River's eyes track all of this, the feverish want there slowly receding, replaced by concern. Caution. Fuck, is he scared of me, too? Is he scared I'll tie him down, truss him up so he can never get away?

He should be.

River takes me by the shoulders before I step into the shattered glass, steadying me. I'm so afraid he's going to say something, that he's going to call out my cowardice or worse, try to play this off like it's no big deal.

Maybe it shouldn't be, but it is. It's a *big* fucking deal.

Thunder rumbles again through the thick, angry clouds. The full moon is gone, its magic bled away. The metaphorical midnight hour has struck, and just like Cinderella, I want to flee before the magic that brought me here melts away in front of him, leaving the real me exposed and even more vulnerable than I already am.

River's eyes lift from mine to the skies as the wind picks up, whipping locks of his hair against his neck hard enough to sting.

"Storm's here. Best be getting you home." His hands relax their grip on my arms, and when they slide away, I feel cold.

Cold and alone.

CHAPTER SEVENTEEN

Mama takes one look at my wind-snarled hair, dress freckled with rain, and the absolute panic on my face, and without saying a word, goes to make me a cup of peppermint tea. I collapse in Big Daddy's armchair and take the cup with shaking hands.

"Do you want to talk about it?"

My eyes sink closed. I shake my head. The ride home was torture. I couldn't explain to River why I'd gotten so spooked without devolving into a bawling mess, so I barely spoke at all. The longer I was quiet, the worse I felt about *being* quiet. But what—am I supposed to tell him how terrified I am of becoming Mama? That trying to date as a single mom with a baby at home makes me feel inexplicably shameful, even though I *know* it's just the patriarchy messing with my head?

I can't tell River all that, not without scaring him off, too. The man will give you all of his present, but his future is a moment-by-moment choice for him. Our chemistry may be unreal, but what happens when he stops choosing to spend his minutes with me? What if he never comes down from his treehouse, and I'm left here in the real world, broken and alone? So I sat there in his truck, numb and silent, after the best kiss of my entire life. My *existence*. I was relieved when the rain got so heavy that the dirt roads turned into mud flumes, and River's attention shifted from the statue sitting next to him to getting us home safely. I curled up against the passenger window and lost myself in the thrashing storm, both outside and within.

It's quiet in the cabin except for Big Daddy's soft snores coming from the bedroom and the baby monitor's staticky buzz where it sits between us on the side table. Bowie's stretched out in his crib, Hippo Sucky the Second dangling from his mouth.

"How was Bowie tonight?" If Mama couldn't tell I was upset before, she can now. My throat feels too tight to speak, and the words struggle out.

"Bowie is a perfect baby, everything he does is perfection, and we had a glorious evening together," Mama says matter-of-factly as she sips her own tea. "Also, he pooped on Darryl's hand in the bathtub, and I laughed so hard, I thought Jesus was coming to take me home."

I hiccup a little into my tea. "Incredible."

"I took some video at the end. Mostly just Darryl cursing up a storm and scrubbing off his watch."

"Oh my God, send it to me *now.*"

"Done," Mama says, and smiles. She's gotten pretty good with her phone after approximately 1,000 hours of tutelage. Lightning flashes over our lake, briefly illuminating the darkness. "This is some storm."

Though I can't see a thing, I still squint out the window at River's patch of woods. I wonder what he's thinking right now. Is he replaying the kiss in his head, remembering the feel of our bodies locked tight against each other? Or is he puzzling over why the woman who so clearly wants to jump his bones turned into a human ice cube?

Thunder crashes against the mountains, its echo strange and metallic on the howling winds.

I hope he's safe in that treehouse.

Mama shrugs. "We get these storms a lot this time of year. Spring, too. You'll see."

The words tighten my throat all over again. *Will* I see? Will we still be here, living in the guest bedroom of my parents' cabin? I raise the tea to my lips and let it burn me so I can feel something other than this unrelenting anxiety.

Gradually, my heart stops racing. There's something about our quiet inside while the rain pounds outside that brings its own special magic to the dark living room, sitting next to my mother.

"I was scared," I say without context, but she knows what I mean anyway.

"It's scary, putting yourself out there again."

The words coat the raw parts of me. Amazing how far a simple validation of a person's feelings can go. I nod into my tea. "How did you . . ." I'm not sure how to finish that. *How did you try and fail only to try and fail all over again? And again?* Was she brave, or stupid, or just lonely? It's surprising, but I've never considered what it must've been like for Mama to make that choice to begin with.

"I am an incredibly optimistic person." Mama raises a finger. "Also horny."

I sigh, too winded from this evening to be grossed out. "Sounds right."

She chuckles, rocking in her recliner.

"I know it was hard on you, baby girl. Seeing all my failures come and go through our door. But if you think that's gonna happen to you, you're wrong."

"It's already happening to me, Mama."

She shakes her head. "You're smarter now than I ever was. You've got savings. You've got family. You're so, so talented, and you're finally realizing it." She reaches over and tucks a curl behind my ear, then wipes the tear rolling down my cheek away with her thumb. "What I'm trying to tell you is that you've got a safe platform to jump from, baby. You can afford to take a risk with River, if that's what your heart wants. We'll be here to catch you."

My throat's aching so hard, I only nod and let her fuss over me the way I always wanted her to. It's a bittersweet feeling, getting a mother now when I needed her then. But tonight, the only person in the world who could walk me back from this ledge of doubt is her.

And I'll be damned if she isn't doing it.

"Is he worth the bother?" Mama asks softly, still brushing my hair off my face.

It takes a millisecond for the satin press of his lips sliding down my neck to envelop me all over again. The hard planes of his body, taut and alert against mine. The heartbreakingly tender look in his eyes when he saw Bowie in my arms on the porch.

Mama watches my face, then smiles. "Then I think you have your answer, baby." She stands up, stretches her back, and takes the baby monitor. "I'll be on Bowie duty tonight. There are bottles in the fridge. Stay out here as long as you need."

She kisses the top of my head and leaves me sitting in the darkness. Her quiet snores soon join Big Daddy's as I sip my tea, letting her words swirl through me.

Thunder crashes again, flinging itself against our back door.

Or were those knocks?

River?

I throw the door open and find him drenched on the porch. Lightning flares, silhouetting his broad shoulders, the tilt of his bowed head. Rain streams down his arms in winding rivulets to his already saturated jeans.

"River! Are you all right?"

His eyes are woeful when he looks up to face me. "The storm took off half my roof. I'm so sorry to bother you, Hannah, I swear I'm not trying—"

I grab the front of his rain-slicked shirt, warm from his furnacing skin, and bring his lush mouth down to mine. The kiss is brief but has us both reeling.

"Sorry about your roof," I whisper, close enough to feel his breath.

"I'm not," he whispers back, then dips down for another. It's slow and hypnotic, not from lack of passion but from the overwhelming intensity of it. It's the two of us against a flood, holding it back with our hands alone.

I want to let go. This time, I'm going to.

His fingers fan out across my ribs, burning through my dress. I arch my back, bringing my hips to his, and a low, predatory sound rumbles from his throat. His grip slides down and tightens, holding me against him. When I pull my mouth away, we're both breathless. The hands I'd coiled around his neck grasp his face, bringing his gaze down to mine.

"You're not going to hurt me." It's a command. It's a statement. It better be the goddamn truth. I run my thumb over his parted lips, then dip inside. "You're not allowed to. Understand?"

He moans against me in his mouth, eyes fluttering closed. When they open again, his dark eyes smolder with hunger. His tongue caresses my thumb as he kisses, then bites down my palm. "Yes, Hannah," he whispers into my flesh.

"Come on." I take him by the hand and lead him back into the rain again. If this is a mistake, it's a mistake I choose.

Drops sting our skin, cold air bites our wet flesh, and it feels like I'm a part of this storm now, too, raging and needful, as we take the terraced path down as fast as we can. I reach the door first, fumbling with the knob when River's body surrounds mine, warm and wet against my shivering back. One hand hits the wood above my head while the other dives into the wet tangle of curls sticking to my neck, pushing them roughly aside, and then his mouth is on me again, kissing, biting, eating me alive as the zipper of my dress plunges down. A gasp escapes my lips as his body pushes into mine, my nipples contracting tightly as they meet the cold glass pane of the door. Every part of me is on fire, burning, aching. Like two binary stars orbiting each other for what feels like millennia, we're so close now that the crash of him into me, me into him, is inevitable. And even though I might not survive it, though this fire may burn us both out bright, absolutely nothing can stop it now.

His kisses slide down my bare shoulder he's yanked exposed, and I spin within the confines of his arms to face him. I wrest his chin upward to my open, panting mouth. The hand freeing me from my dress wastes no time in grabbing my thigh, hoisting it against his hip, nearly lifting me off my feet. There are so very many clothes between us, and I want to burn them all away. To ash, to nothing.

Maybe we will.

Through wizardry or sheer will, the door shudders open behind me, and my free leg bounces upward to wrap around him completely. Now it's his turn to focus while I kiss a burning trail down his neck, the cords of muscle taut in my mouth, beneath my licking tongue. He tastes like rain and sweat and *River*, and I want all of him, now, on me, against me, *in* me. He groans as he kicks the door all the way open, swaggers inside with his hands cupped beneath my ass, fingers digging deep into my flesh.

He pauses before the fireplace, the merry fire built for our late-arriving guests still smoldering in the grate, and I pull his silky wet hair hard enough to expose his throat.

"Take me to the bed." My command is urgent, fierce, ending in a moan as he centers me against the rigid column rebelling against his jeans. *"Now."*

"Yes, Hannah." His voice is dangerous and low, full of promise of all the things he's about to do to me and *fuck*. I'm never going to be okay again, am I?

He surrenders me to the bed, wrenching off the wet dress still sucking against my skin as he does. I'm down to my bra and truly wrecked panties, which are even wetter than my dress. He stands between my shivering knees at the edge of the bed, his eyes roving over every inch of me like he's a marauder and I'm about to get pillaged. I always felt self-conscious when Killian looked at me, like he was cataloging every silvery stretch mark, every flaw, and patting himself on the back for accepting me into his bed anyway. That's probably not fair, but that's what living under his microscopic judgment did to me. I was so aware of everything wrong with me that I never celebrated everything that's right. But beneath River's hungry gaze, I feel delicious and sultry and powerful.

More than anything, I feel wanted.

"Take off your shirt." The demand rises up from that new place within me, where I know my value and power, and the man I'm about to ravish does, too.

"Yes, Hannah." The shirt comes off in a quick upward sweep of motion, revealing his broad shoulders, his smooth chest the color of a copper penny in the light of the fire. A thin sheen of dark hair curls down his lean torso. I want to bury my face in it. I want to pull him down, feel his heaviness atop me, luxuriate in the warmth thrumming off his hard body.

But before I can do any of that, he sinks to his knees on the floor before me. His strong hands wrap around my hips and tug me forward, putting me just where he wants me. The kisses begin on the inside of my knees, getting wetter and more aggressive as they slide up my inner thighs. My muscles clench in anticipation, aching for release already. The scratch of his stubble on my sensitive skin sends chills all the way to the roots of my hair, and I take fistfuls of sheets in both hands. But when he places his luscious mouth against the wettest part of my panties and breathes deeply in, the need rises within me with a fury. Either oblivious or unconcerned with my torment, he runs the pad of his index finger from the start of my split slowly down, the pressure maddeningly light against my drenched panties. I buck against his hand, seriously about to cuss him out, when he grabs the panties and yanks them off completely.

About fucking time.

His brown eyes are like pools of black when he looks up, meeting my desperate gaze.

"Can I make you come now, Hannah?"

Oh my God, you fucking better, but all that comes out is a low moan. He runs the bridge of his nose against my clit in a long, languid sweep. My hands grope downward until they find his soft, damp hair between my legs, the ends tickling my trembling thighs. I run my fingers through it, clutching tight when his tongue finally meets my flesh. I cry out, I can't help it. I'm strung so tightly now that everything he does reverberates through me. He slides a hand up until his palm is pressed flat against me, and the pressure feels so good, I grind into it. His fingers part into a V, framing my clit between them, and slowly, rhythmically, he drives his palm forward while his mouth envelops my clit.

Fuck, fuck, *fuck*! The hard heel of his hand meets my ache where it begins, his tongue flicking and circling until my hips heave against him, my hands pushing his head down and in, keeping him prisoner until the first wave of orgasm crashes over me. The moan rips out of me, his name and a long string of expletives that has him chuckling against me while the orgasm jolts my limbs, my brain, my everything. It's all gone haywire, and I lie there, glitching in the sheets until he rises over me again. His smile is somehow satisfied and hungrier than ever as I lie there prone before him.

"River Aronson, if you don't take those jeans off right now, I swear to God." I prop myself on my elbows and give him my best *I mean business* look, but he's not chuckling now.

"Are you sure you want to do this?" His eyes are concerned again, and I know he's remembering how I all but ran away from him earlier. I can't explain to him the fear I felt in that moment, looking down at the abyss of feelings I already have for him and being too scared to jump. All I know is that I'm all in. I've never wanted anyone or anything as much as I want him right now, and even if it's stupid and doomed to hurt, I'm not playing it safe anymore.

"Yes." I sit up, and he inhales a sharp, ragged breath when my face comes level with his hips. I look up at him as I undo the button of his jeans, drag the zipper down slow. "But I told you to take these off."

I breathe against the black cotton of his underwear. They're stretched tight over the rock-hard length of him, and the sight of it makes me ache all over again. He groans as I gently drag his clothes off, kissing the soft skin beneath the waistband as I go, until his thick, smooth cock springs free. I grasp him at the base, feeling his pulse hammer through my fingers, and squeeze. This touch is more for me than him. I like the unforgiving feel of his desire, how his cock fills my hand, overflows from my grip. The weight of him, the taut skin. It feels like silk when it enters my mouth, first the head, then a little more until his fingers dig into my hair. I can tell he wants to thrust into my mouth, wants to fill me up, but he's holding back, barely. What a gentleman.

If only he knew how much I'd like it, too. Just thinking of the heavy feel of his hand on the back of my head, guiding me forward, insistent, makes me clench until I'm newly slick. It brings to mind this thing Kat, one of our straight friends in college, used to say. She always knew if she really liked a guy if "his dick tasted good." It floored Kira, who couldn't conceive of such a thing, and it made me howl with laughter at the time. If you're not into it, blow jobs can be a lip-chafing chore, especially to completion. But right now, as I run my tongue up his hard shaft until he moans, entering my mouth once more, I finally get what Kat was talking about.

Because River tastes *good*.

"Hannah," River says, his fingers still meshed in my hair. "Hannah, please."

My eyes are wicked when I turn up to him again, releasing him just enough to say, "Yes?"

"I need to be inside you." His eyes are glazed with firelight, his words just as hot. He wraps his hand around his wet cock, strokes it once as if he can't help himself, and groans again. "Now, Hannah."

There's no use in denying the urgency in his voice, or the tightening in my belly it causes. I almost mourn the sound of the condom wrapper coming off. It's probably just hormones, but I want River's skin on my skin, the flush heat of his cock burning me up from the inside out. I want him to fill me, then fill me again. I want to wring him dry.

These intense biological impulses would be alarming, if it wasn't all so goddamn hot.

River's knees push between mine, stretching me out to accommodate him, before falling forward onto his palms, hovering over me. The plump crown of his dick is pressing into me, and I want him so bad it feels like a medical emergency. He dips forward and nips at the swell of my breasts, sliding his tongue beneath the bra's rim to caress my painfully erect nipples. He pulls my bra roughly down, lifting a breast from its cup. And when he draws me into his mouth, he plunges inside. We both cry out, me with my hands in his hair, him with my breast in his mouth, and he plunges again, and again. It takes only the slightest touch from my finger, and I'm coming again, clenching and releasing around the unbelievable hardness he's driving into me. The feel of my nipple in his mouth, his cock relentlessly squeezing through my wetness, my legs wrapped around his hips, his hair in my hands, all of it together turns into one tingling explosion, and the orgasm breaks me apart beneath him.

It's everything I thought it would be, but it's also nothing I could ever imagine. I've never felt this wanted, this appreciated. With River, sex has transformed from its usual self-conscious bumbling event into an exaltation of me. *Me!* Hannah the disaster no more. I feel like a goddess in his arms. With his heady, addictive attention lavished upon me, my orgasms reach new heights. It's like he's unlocked my body's potential, torn down the walls no one's ever bothered to climb, all because he wants to.

He wants *me.*

I arch beneath him, and the tilt of my hips and the friction it causes destroys whatever willpower River has left. One strong arm slides beneath the curve of my back and lifts, rocking me up and forward onto his cock. With his arms cradling my back, his thighs spread wide to support us both, he thrusts up into me, penetrating me deeper than I've ever felt. I weigh nothing in his arms, and I love the way he's controlling us both, bringing me down hard against him again and again. He's looking at me with such awe, such fierce desire, his lips parted and panting, that I cup his face in my hands. I want to memorize this moment. The beauty of him, the safety I feel, the power I have. He's pulsing inside of me, so close now, and when I press his face to my breasts, his broken groan vibrates into my flesh. River's entire body goes rigid, and for one instant, stills, before he explodes into me. His arms hooked behind my back drive me down by the shoulders onto him in a big, last crash before pulling me into him, locking around me, in the best goddamn hug of my life.

He holds me like that, our bodies still joined and heaving for breath, my head nestled into the crook of his neck, until the fever of our fucking ebbs and slows, replaced by a deep, sleepy contentment. When I wake up later in the cocoon of his arms, snuggled in the bed that we built, my heart flutters with sweet, vulnerable happiness. As I nod back off, I can't help wondering what else we could build together.

A life?

A home?

A family.

CHAPTER EIGHTEEN

Tyrannical Infant Support Group

6:22 AM

Hannah

OH MY GOD

Kira

!!! OH MY GOD?? RLY?

Hannah

YES!!

Kira

OH MY GOD!!!!!!!

Mattie

You guys. What the actual fuck is wrong with you?

Hannah

Mattie

It's 6 fucking a.m.

Kira

I FUCKING KNEW IT!

Hannah

HIS ARMS ARE WRAPPED AROUND ME RIGHT NOW!

Mattie

You're speaking in goddamn TONGUES.

Kira

I can smell a fuck match a mile away. NEVER doubt me again!

Mattie

Wait. Does this mean . . .

Hannah

That I just had the best sex of my entire life? Yes. Also "smell" and "fuck match" is too visceral for the morning, Kiki.

Kira

Tell that to your stanky pheromones!

Mattie

This conversation is upsetting me. But not the part about you and River playing Pin the Tail on the Donkey. That's great, Hannah.

Hannah

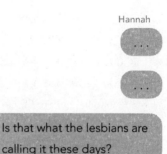

Is that what the lesbians are calling it these days?

Kira

I think Mattie's regressing.

Mattie

It's 6 a.m., and y'all are blowing up my phone. That's as hetero-supportive as I can be right now.

Hannah

You're doing great, Matts.

Kira

Seriously, babe. River's legit. I'm really happy you're getting flappy.

Mattie

SIRI, MUTE THIS TEXT CHAIN NOW

Hannah

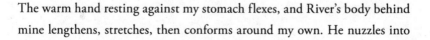

The warm hand resting against my stomach flexes, and River's body behind mine lengthens, stretches, then conforms around my own. He nuzzles into my neck, practically purring into my hair. His breath against my ear sets my stomach afloat.

"Good morning," I whisper, curling into him. The touch feels luxurious. After holding someone else all day, I crave being held like this. It feels so good to be the one being cared for.

His throat rumbles in response, but then he lifts his head, squints an eye open at the phone in my hand. "Is Bowie okay?"

"Yeah. Everything's fine." I quickly put the phone on the nightstand, facedown. I don't want him to know I was giddily texting my best friends in our sexual afterglow. "Just checking in on the state of the world. Making sure the United States is still intact, that kind of thing."

River frowns as if I've said something wrong. "Before you've even gotten out of bed?"

Ah, now I get it. This is a *boo, technology!* thing. I twist in his arms and cuddle up to him. "Maybe I don't intend to get out of bed. Think of that?"

River's lips twirl into his usual grin, and he brings me with him as he rolls onto his back. I'm spread out on top of him like a starfish, the weight of me resting completely on him. I sigh happily into his chest. I didn't realize how much effort it took holding back my feelings for him until I let them crash out of me. It's like finally letting a two-hundred-pound dog off its leash, and now it's barreling through the woods off-trail, jumping on people and coating everything in exuberant slobber.

"I can get behind that." His eyes twinkle as his big palms slide around my ass.

"Well, you're already *underneath* me, so . . ." I let the words trail off into his laughing mouth as I kiss him deeply, morning breath be damned.

My phone buzzes angrily from the nightstand. I want to ignore it, but it's almost seven, Bowie's usual wake-up time, and my breasts are so full, they'll probably start leaking soon. I break off the kiss. "Sorry, I need to check that."

The delight recedes from his eyes, but he nods, the smile turning patient as I reach for my phone.

Mama

Wake up, it's boob o'clock!

Unless you want me to give him another bottle?

I sit up quickly, straddling River's lap in the process. The feel of his bare morning erection against me makes me groan as I bang out a frantic, utterly typo'ed *Nnerp, no wafit! Be rigfht sup!*

"It's Bowie, I gotta go." I lean over him again, aware of how easy it'd be for him to slip inside me. It makes me ache with want.

"I am—"

kiss

"utterly bereft"

groan

"fucking *verklempt*"

pant

"to leave you right now."

The delight is back in his eyes, as is that hunger, and I know he's hurting as bad as I am to postpone this. "You can stay all weekend while you fix your roof. We don't have guests until Tuesday. See you later?"

River nods, his Adam's apple bobbing in his throat.

I want to lick it. Maybe tonight.

My dress is still damp as I slide it over my head, bid my reluctant farewell to River, and race up the path.

Ten minutes later, I'm drinking my morning coffee while Bowie revenge-nurses on the porch swing. He's glowering up at me from around my engorged breast, like each bottle he got overnight is a separate grudge that I shall atone for.

"Sorry, Littleman. Mommy needed to get her some." I stroke his soft, curly hair, the love physically pouring out of me.

Mama settles next to me on the swing, looking smug. I'm beyond grateful for getting the night off, but the undereye circles she's sporting today tell me how last night went down. It's easy to forget that she's getting older, the way she dances while she cooks and attacks the weeds in her garden like they're sent from the Antichrist. But getting up three times a night for a half hour each is enough to bring anybody low, even spry grannies like G-ma. Guilt pools in my stomach.

"Sorry, Mama. I shouldn't have—"

"Hush," she says, but not unkindly. "If you never say the word *should* again, it'll be too soon."

We drink our coffee quietly.

With the weekend's guests canceled, the morning moves slower than usual. Peekaboo with Bowie, clapping as he bangs on the tiny keyboard Mama got him, making him spinach pancakes and watching him not eat them. It's all glorious. When it's naptime, I switch to classwork. Today's my turn to give my "How It Started, How It's Going" presentation on The Honey Jar, but in a strange turn of personality, I'm not nervous at all. As I flip through the slide deck I prepared, I feel undeniably, incredibly proud. I'm loading up Big Daddy's truck with my laptop to leave for class when River sprints over from his roof repair to give me a bouquet of kisses all over my face, my neck, the hollow behind my ears. If he presses me up against the truck's door, pinning me there with the hardness between his hips for a brief, gasping makeout session, only a squirrel or two sees.

"Later," I promise with one final kiss goodbye. His gaze is dark and hot, and I know he'll hold me to it.

Thoughts of last night carry me dreamily down the mountain and all the way downtown. I take my seat in the front next to Ms. Betty, a hyper-religious old lady who sells herbs and tinctures and insists it's not witchcraft. Madison tries to catch my eye, but I let her wave at the side of my head. I don't know what to make of her reconnaissance mission, but I don't like it.

"Thank you, Frank." Zoe claps her hands together after the first presentation ends, looking slightly disturbed. "It's safe to say we all know a lot more about deer processing now."

"Speak for yourself," Ms. Betty mutters under her breath. Frank shoots her a sniffy look as he gathers his photographs into a neat stack of gore and takes his seat.

"Hannah? The floor is yours." Zoe gestures to the front of the room. I blow out a small breath, hook up my laptop, and start the presentation.

"Hello, I'm Hannah Tate, and I'm the manager and host of The Honey Jar, a cabin rental on Cherry Log Mountain." My face flushes with satisfaction as the words leave my mouth, and the presentation picks up speed from there. From the sympathetic murmurs through the "before" pictures to my explanations for how we prioritized our small renovation budget, the class listens attentively. I feel amazing, in charge, powerful.

"Modern design elements, like the large picture windows and black accents, set The Honey Jar apart from the crowded cabin rental market in the Blue Ridge area. By making its appearance appeal directly to the young Atlanta professionals demographic, we signal our cabin will provide the type of getaway experience they expect, but don't usually get, in the mountains."

"You're catering to the liberals?" Frank scrunches up his face, and I point to him.

"Exactly, Frank!" I click through pictures of the renovated cabin, from the cheery exterior with our rainbow flag flapping proudly to the bidet attachment on the toilet seat. "But young professionals aren't our only focus—

small families are, too. Airbnb's platform currently has no way for cabins to self-identify as family-friendly with explicit criteria to match that designation. Sure, you can indicate you have a crib, but what about toys for small children? Outdoor play equipment? Life vests for little ones?" Madison's typing so loudly on her laptop it's almost distracting, but I'm heartened to see the rest of the room nodding along thoughtfully. "We have all those things and more, and we advertise it on our listing front and center. If parents see that we're well-equipped for small kids, that's less to pack and less stress once they're here." I smile at the room. "Plus, those little kids are our guests, too. Their happiness and needs shouldn't be an afterthought."

"You identified underserved demographics in your market and built your business model to accommodate them," Zoe says, nodding in appreciation. "That's how you do it, folks. How are your bookings?"

"We've got a few empty weekdays here and there, but otherwise, we're booked through December, and our five-star rating is holding strong."

The class bursts into applause. I am a sexy Steve Jobs. An ethical Martha Stewart. A single Olsen twin. The fact is, we *are* kicking ass. Even my nastiest, most doubtful internal voices can't say shit. At this rate, we'll recoup the initial investment way earlier than expected, and everything after will go straight into helping my family afford groceries and medical care. The idea warms me from the inside out.

I'm still floating on a sea of good feelings on the way out to the truck when a voice clears behind me. "Hannah! There you are!"

Madison. I press my eyes closed and sigh. Now that I know about her sharky business behavior, her sweet southern lilt feels downright ominous. "What is it, Madison?"

She steps closer, invading my space until I have to take a step back. "Your presentation was inspired. You've got a real keen eye for the hospitality business. Have you ever considered going into property management?"

I blink. "Can't say that I have."

She looks both ways, then slips me her card. There it is, her name and title: BUSINESS DEVELOPMENT OFFICER, BEAUTY OF BLUE RIDGE RENTAL MANAGEMENT COMPANY. "I'll be honest. At first, I was going to pitch our services to manage your property, but after seeing what you've accomplished, I want to recruit you for our team. You could help us repackage our struggling rentals, make them something your young professionals would go crazy for!" Her big blue eyes take on a manic sheen.

"I *knew* you were up to something." Zoe appears behind Madison, then steps around her to join my side. "You're in my class to poach!"

Madison throws her small hands in the air and giggles a little. "Caught me! Hannah, you have my card. Think about my offer, 'kay? Byeee!" With that, she spins on her heeled boots and marches up Main Street toward her offices.

"You're *not* welcome back!" Zoe yells after her. Without turning around, Madison thrusts her delicate middle finger up and sashays on her way.

We look at each other, eyebrows raised, and laugh.

"That was the most unsettling job offer I've ever received."

"That was . . ." Zoe shakes her head and laughs again. "Kinda fun? Blue Ridge doesn't have nearly enough scandal for my taste." She throws her arm around my shoulders conspiratorially, and I'm grateful she came along when she did. "Queer Mountaineers are meeting up at Angry Bear Brewery today. Wanna come?"

"I thought y'all met up at vineyards?"

"We're the Queer Mountaineers Who *Occasionally* Drink Beer, remember?" Zoe winks at me.

After some mild hemming and hawing, I clear it with Mama and walk with Zoe to the brewery up the street. Zoe's a bit like Kira in that it's very hard to say no to her, and you'd never want to, anyway. I've wanted to join one of the Queer Mountaineers' weekly hangs, and besides, it's a beautiful day to spend a little time in downtown Blue Ridge. The leaves are starting to change, and the smells of fresh fudge carry on the crisp breeze. When we enter the brewery, Zoe's friends send up a whoop, arms raised in celebration.

"When did this start?" I whisper as we approach the boisterous table.

"Oh, hours ago." Zoe grins. "Come on, I'll introduce you to everyone."

First around the table is Maeve, a short woman with red hair streaming out from under a UGA baseball hat, and her partner Gloria, who's still wearing her cleats and a pair of long, dirt-streaked socks. When she catches me looking at them, she says, "Yeah. We're softball lesbians. You?"

"I'm more of a drama club bisexual," I respond, a bit startled. The table busts out laughing.

"Oooh, just Zoe's type!" says Teddy, the handsome older white man wearing top-to-bottom slinky athleisure. He grins at Zoe, who turns a charming shade of fuchsia.

"I apologize for them. They will not rest until they see me happily coupled up." Zoe swings a warning finger at Teddy's face. "I'll cut you off if you keep embarrassing me." Teddy grabs his pint glass and holds it to his chest.

"Stop, Teddy, you know our Zoe's a sensitive soul," Diego, Teddy's partner, reprimands him gently. He leans over the high top and puts his round, softly bearded face in his hands. "But since he brought it up, are you seeing anyone?" He smiles cattily at me, and now I'm blushing harder than Zoe.

"I—maybe?" The table laughs more, and Tristan, the youngest of the crew, points a black-painted fingernail at me.

"That means yes. Who are they?" He fixes his smoky-rimmed eyes on me, and I *know* things with River just began, I *do*, but I've missed this—hanging out with friends, laughing over stupid stuff, feeling included.

I smile into my pint glass and let go. "River Aronson."

To my horror, the whooping begins again.

"Sorry, Zoe, that's gotta hurt!" Teddy booms.

I turn, wide-eyed, to her. He's not her ex, is he? But she's laughing, too. When she sees my terrified face, she waves *no no no* with her hands.

"He's my cousin," she finally manages to say. "He's like a big brother to me!"

"Ohhhhhhhh." A smile breaks out across my face. So *that's* why River said I'd like the instructor—they're related! "Wait. That means you can give me the full River scoop, then!"

"The long, sordid history!" Teddy exclaims. "Yes, tell her!"

"What, like how he fosters old, asshole cats for my rescue?" Maeve says, eyebrow arched.

Aww, Battle-cat. Heart eyes.

"He's a great shortstop," Gloria says simply. "Sucks at pitching."

"I was thinking more like how he's a giant man-child, but sure, we can paint the full picture." Teddy huffs and crosses his arms. "I mean, when was the last time he went to a dentist?"

"You're just miffed because you *are* the dentist." Diego smiles at him indulgently.

"Exactly! He should declare his loyalties." Teddy holds his finger in the air. "So help me, if he goes to that twisted sadist down in Jasper, I'll—"

"River's a free spirit, that's all," Zoe says to me, still laughing.

"It's more than that, and you know it," Teddy says, fully indignant. "He doesn't want to grow up! He tried it when he moved to Atlanta, but he regressed, baby! He's impossible to get ahold of, he only shows up half the time once you *do* manage to invite him out. He lives in a treehouse, for Thor's sake!"

The table's laughing, but the words unsettle me all the same. Diego must notice, because he reaches out and pats my arm.

"Don't worry. Maybe you're the woman who can make our River grow up."

Teddy goes on, counting on his fingers all the ways River's failing at adulthood. What's worse is how many I identify with, too. I once ate Jimmy Dean breakfast sandwiches for dinner for an entire month because I was too overwhelmed to decide on anything else. I set an alarm each week to remind me to open mail, and if I don't have enough Skittles to bribe myself to do it, it doesn't get done. I *also* avoid the dentist, though I'm not telling Teddy that. This whole conversation's making my skin itch.

"River may approach adulthood unconventionally," Zoe says, raising her voice over the laughter, "but he's loyal and loving and open-minded, which is a damn miracle considering who his mama is."

The mood sombers at that, with little nods and murmurs of agreement. Zoe sees the confusion on my face and a shadow of sadness passes over her own. "When my own mother passed young, River's mother, my Aunt Bri, stepped in to help my dad with me. She didn't have a daughter of her own, and my father was really struggling at the time. It's because of her I went to prom and wore my hair long, the way she liked it." Zoe runs her hand absently over the back of her bob. "Even tried a boyfriend." She raises her eyebrows and her glass to the table. "And you see how well that turned out."

When the hoots and whistles around the table subside, Zoe shrugs. "It's a small town. Eventually Aunt Bri and Uncle Russell found out I was dating a woman. They disowned me, but River stood up for me, tried to get them to change their minds." She pauses to take a deep breath. "Well, they didn't, and he was so, so upset. River's an idealist, you know, and when the world doesn't live up to his expectations, he doesn't know how to handle it. They don't talk much anymore, and we're each other's family now." She smiles, but it's as bittersweet as the truth. You can't take family for granted, but that goes both ways, doesn't it? You can't know who'll love you no matter what.

Something squeezes deep inside of me for Zoe, who lost her mother, then her second mother. And River . . . He chose to love instead of hate, and in so doing, lost his family, too. I touch Zoe's hand.

"Thanks for telling me."

The conversation meanders to happier topics, and I can't remember the last time I laughed like this. When it's time to say my goodbyes, the table takes turns hugging me and making me promise to bring Bowie next time, and another piece of my life in Blue Ridge slots into place. Friends.

I drive home, happy and wistful, thinking of the people who love me no matter what, feeling lucky and proud and quiet for those who don't have the same blessings I do.

Though I'm not screwing around; I'm making an appointment with Teddy *tomorrow*.

CHAPTER NINETEEN

River's truck thrums along the curving mountain road, with enough dips and turns to make Bowie squeal with delight from his car seat. River smiles from the side of his mouth each time, and I wonder if he took this extra hilly route to Amicalola Falls on purpose. It makes me like him even more. Frankly, I'm not even sure *like* is the right word. It's like describing the World Series as a ball toss in your backyard. *Smitten* feels more accurate. *Enamored.* The having of complete and never-ending thirst.

He catches me ogling him, and his smile grows. "Can't believe I let a tourist talk me into this."

"*I* can't believe *you* haven't been to Amicalola Falls before! It's the tallest waterfall in Georgia."

River lifts a shoulder, his face gathered in merry lines. "Tallest you know about. Us locals have our own waterfalls." He glances over at me, his playful smirk downright dangerous. "Maybe I'll take you sometime."

Pleasure heats up my neck, curling behind my ears. He turns on my fucking *ears* now? Jesus.

"Can I put it in the guidebook?"

"Strictly off the record, Ms. Tate."

I want my name in this man's mouth forever.

He rests his arm on the back of the seat, and his strong fingers push gently through the mass of wavy hair until they find my neck. He runs the tip of his callused finger along the sensitive skin, and my body shivers in response. He massages the muscles there, slipping a finger beneath my collar. "This is a family hike, goddammit," I murmur.

He laughs, but I can hear the want stretching outward in his voice, too. "My apologies."

My skin still burns from his touch as I twine my fingers with his. What a weekend. I know he can't live in our Airbnb forever but having River within grabbing distance is now my preferred status quo. I shift in the seat, deliciously sore from last night. I didn't want to put Mama on Bowie duty twice in a row, so River set up the tricked-out travel crib in the kids' room, and we turned on the sound machine *real* high. Drinking coffee on the porch swing beside each other while Bowie nursed this morning was unexpectedly tender. And when River opted to come on our hike instead of working on his roof, I cheered aloud. I don't want him out of my sight.

Mama and Darryl follow behind since there's too many of us to fit in one vehicle. We're headed to Amicalola Falls State Park to hike the Appalachian Trail approach. I'm surprised they wanted to come, to be honest. While the hike to the top of the falls is only a mile long, it's labeled as "strenuous" and "moderate" and "probably a bad idea" due to the approximately one million steps up the long snaking staircase that climbs alongside the falls. Mama *pshaw*'ed me, though, saying they could handle anything for one mile. Darryl looked skeptical, but he knows better than to contradict Mama when she's got a hair up her ass. She's making up for lost time, I guess, because we never went on hikes in the wilderness when I was growing up. Closest we got was Walmart on Black Friday.

We hit a spot with reception, and my phone buzzes in my pocket. Mostly junk, but there's an angry red notice email from Gilmer County's Planning & Zoning Department. "Huh." I skim over it, my heart picking up a beat. "Apparently, we didn't file the right permit before beginning construction on the cabin. Do you know what that's about?"

"We didn't file for a permit at all," River says, a bit sheepish. "They never find out when it's minor renovations. Who ratted you out?"

"I don't know." I turn to face him, anxiety bubbling up. "I thought the contractor handles the permitting."

"You needed the reno done fast, and the permit would've held y'all up for months." River makes sympathetic eyes at me. "What do they want?"

"We have to file one retroactively. There's a fine." I'm trying not to get upset, but I wish River would have told me this. I *hate* being in trouble, even more so when it's because of someone else's bad decision.

"I'll pay it," River says quickly. "It's my fault."

"No, you worked for free as it is. It's not that much, anyway." I swallow, a confused mash of feelings pulsing through me. I know River does things his own way, but I trusted him. I didn't realize I needed to look over his shoulder, too.

He squeezes my hand and apologizes, and I put my phone and all the responsibilities it shoves in my face away. He's right, after all; we *did* need the reno done quickly, and it's just a little slap on the wrist. I have no clue who could have outed us to the Planning & Zoning department, though. It's unsettling, but I push it all away because it's Sunday. Monday Hannah can figure this out.

Poor bitch.

"There it is." I point to the stone arch that marks the beginning of the Appalachian Trail approach. I pause to take pictures for the Airbnb's guidebook. This trail is iconic, a must for hikers visiting the area. *Hey, you! Can't do the Appalachian Trail? Why not approach it?*

It's a misty Sunday afternoon, but the thick white skies make it feel like morning. The air is damp and chilly against my cheeks, and after five minutes outside, it's already turned Bowie's into shiny red apples. His eyes are their very bluest right now, happily tracking every snapping twig, every bird call, as we make our way into the gilded woods. Copper leaves at our feet, green brush at our knees, slender gray trunks of yellow-capped trees overhead, red and gold reflecting off water in the distance. It's a bedrock of color. A Grand Canyon told in leaves and wood, with loose, impressionist strokes.

I can't stop taking pictures. Me with Bowie on my back grinning. Big Daddy kicking a pile of leaves at G-ma. G-ma cussing Big Daddy out. River laughing at it all. My heart buoys in my chest, happiness cascading through me like the tumbling water. It feels almost too perfect. A family hike before Sunday dinner surrounded by autumnal glory? In *my* life? GTFO.

It's less perfect after climbing the first "flight" of stairs. We're 125 steps in with several hundred to go, and my thighs already feel like taffy in the stretching machine. It's worth the sweat, though. Amicalola Falls stretches up, up, up before us, so tall we can't take it all in at once. River whistles at the view from the first landing.

"Damn. You tourists got it right for once."

"Told you!" My grin melts as he wraps his arms around me and Bowie both and kisses the top of my head. The embrace fills me up from the outside in. This doesn't feel like it began Friday evening, beneath the full moon.

It just feels right.

"Got-*damn*, I want a cigarette," Big Daddy says, fully panting as he pulls himself onto the landing by the rail. He hobbles slowly over to us, sweat darkening the front of his shirt. "I love you more, though, little buddy." He tickles Bowie's neck until Bowie giggles, and Big Daddy starts coughing.

"Those cigarettes are the reason you're panting like a dog," G-ma says, a little out of breath herself. Her eyes are sparkling, though, her color flushed and wonderfully alive. "Hannah and Bowie moving in with us is the best thing that ever happened to you."

"Second best," he says, then plants a big, sloppy kiss on G-ma's cheek. She swats him away, laughing and yelling at him to get his old sweaty mustache off her. I snap a quick picture of them, then G-ma snatches my phone and orders River and me to stand with the falls at our back, all together. It's a little embarrassing. We've only been on one real date, and my mother's already shouting at us to say cheese. But if River feels uncomfortable at all, he doesn't show it. He brings me to his chest, and we all smile for Mama.

Well, Bowie blows a big raspberry into my ear and cackles, but five-month-olds can get away with that shit.

As we resume this rude stairway to heaven, Mama and Darryl fall behind again but shoo us on so they can take their time. I don't blame them. River offered to wear Bowie in the carrier at the first landing, and by the second landing, I caved and let him. Even without hauling Bowie's hefty ass, I'm winded and fully sweating now, grateful for the chilly fall air.

The wooden bridge that crosses the falls' crest is within sight when a loud wheezing sound from behind us stops me short. I tug River's sleeve.

"Do you hear that?"

River frowns. "Is that—Darryl?"

We both peer down the stairs. The wheezing comes again, along with Mama's urgent voice, drifting up.

"We'd better go check on them." I don't like how Mama sounded just now. River nods, his eyes registering my concern, and we take the stairs down as fast as we safely can.

A few dozen steps below, Darryl's sitting with his back propped up against the railing. His ruddy skin is an unnatural shade of gray, and Mama's standing over him fanning him with his Braves hat.

"Darryl! What happened?" I rush to his side, but Mama holds her hand up to stop me.

"Nothing except a lifetime of smoking. Big Daddy's out of breath, that's all."

Darryl looks worse than that, though. His hand is draped across his chest, and he winces with each breath in. He tries to smile at me. "Your mama's trying to kill me. Like a damn drill sergeant in my ear."

Mama's got her arms crossed, her lips set in a thin, resolute line. I recognize the expression immediately. You don't get sick in Mama's presence. You get cured.

Or else.

"Drink more water," she orders, and thrusts a bottle at his mouth. He complies, but splutters, spraying water down the front of his shirt.

"Now she's tryin' to drown me!"

"Okay, that's it. River, give Bowie back to Hannah. You and me are gonna help Big Daddy get back to the car."

The way down goes faster, even with Mama and River struggling beneath Darryl's arms. The forest is still as beautiful as it was, but the mist rising off the water feels ominous now. A slip risk, a hazard. On the way home, I feel every bump in the road. I notice every twist. The mountains aren't an easy place to grow old, and yet this is where Mama and Darryl have chosen to do exactly that. What if River and I hadn't been there to help? What would Mama have done on her own?

I can't rest easy until we have Darryl in his chair with his feet propped up. Mama's declared no Sunday dinner tonight as our primary chef needs to rest. His color's returning, but there's an age there I hadn't noticed before. Mama and Darryl aren't young. I know this logically, but it still sends a spike of anxiety through my stomach. Today more than ever before, I felt like we were a unit, a real family. People who depend on me that I can depend on, too. But seeing Darryl gray and wheezing and unable to walk on his own felt like a once sturdy chair wobbling beneath me, threatening to spill me onto the ground.

As I walk River to the door, my phone dings loudly from my pocket. "God*dammit,*" I growl at the screen. "Another cancelation!"

River runs his warm palms up my arms, then puts on a smile that's meant to make me feel brave, I think. "Don't worry, it happens."

"Does it, though?" That's two in the same week, and already my brain's whizzing through the financial recalculations for the month's expenses. "It seems . . . strange."

River presses a kiss to my forehead, pushing some of the bad feelings away to make room for the small swell of happiness it brings. "I'll be next door if you need me. Gonna try to get some work done before the light goes."

I nod, fully exhausted by the hike, the stairs, the worry, and the five-month-old baby that wakes up three times a night. I rest my cheek against his chest and sag into the hug. "Mmm. Text me when you're coming over," I murmur into his broad chest.

"Neither I nor my ancient phone do that. Remember?" He tips my chin up to smile. "But I'm in hollering distance."

"Right. Sure." I smile back at him weakly. "I'll see you when I see you, I guess."

His eyes sparkle, and then he's gone.

≈

The next two weeks pass in a blur of frustrating calls to the permit office, guest prep, sweet kisses, and mind-blowing sex whenever I can sneak over to River's treehouse. I even like climbing the ladder now, which has to be the strangest Pavlovian response ever. I haven't seen him since Wednesday, though, and it's eating me alive. It's not like I can text him. What did people even do before phones? Just think about each other all the damn time? I've been doing that plenty. A particular favorite is the memory of his hands sliding down my ribs, cupping my breasts, his thumbs drifting slowly down the tops of my nipples. *Mmm.*

I try to banish my *I'm horny* face as I stand in line at Das Kaffee Haus to order my new fall favorite, a Black Forest latte, but it doesn't work because I'm also horny for this drink. Espresso, chocolate, cherry, frothed *almond* milk? Get in me. Caffeinated reinforcements are necessary today. I've been running nonstop since six a.m., first with business tasks like reordering the fancy biodegradable K-Cups and sending out emails to local businesses for potential partnerships, then with hard physical labor after last night's guests checked out, all while taking care of Bowie. It's been so busy lately, my only break came when *another* set of guests canceled last-minute. It's extremely frustrating when they cancel that late because there's no way the cabin will get rebooked, and premium price autumn days when Blue Ridge is at its most glorious are flushed away. Maybe when we're more established, we can implement a strict cancelation policy, but that's a real turn-off to customers. For now, we're stuck taking it on the chin.

Ding! I sigh, then check the Airbnb notification on my phone as I take a seat at one of the small tables. When I don't have a rag in my hand, I'm on the Airbnb app, answering guests' questions and helping to troubleshoot. It's probably because we're new, but The Honey Jar gets what feels like a dozen inquiries a day. Do we have black-out shades in the kids' room? *Yes.* What kinds of fishing lures do we provide? *The alluring kind?* Can I bring my pack of Great Pyrenees? *Aww, adorable! No.*

I get it. Booking a newer rental with only a few reviews is a little nerve-racking, even if they're glowing. The fact is, until we get Superhost status, we've got to be on our best behavior. Reviews on these vacation rental sites are everything. All it takes is one nasty diatribe to tank your rating, and your listing will get pushed so far down you'll be lucky if people ever see it again.

I'm still blowing on my latte when the shop door jingles open, and in walks Killian with our son beaming front and center in his carrier. When Killian sees me, he waves with a big, genuine smile. "Look, buddy! There's Mommy!"

"Hey, boys!" I know I just saw Bowie less than an hour ago but seeing his face light up when he spots me rushes me with joy. I start to reach for him but then stop. This is Killian's time, and he gets precious little of it.

"What's on the Daddy-Bowie agenda today?" He was too afraid to go out alone like this with Bowie at first, but after a few months, Killian's finally gotten the hang of things. He gives Bowie bottles like a pro, changes even the foulest diapers with a big, doting grin, and can soothe Bowie almost as well as Big Daddy can. He's in a solid fourth place for Bowie's favorite adults, and that's not nothing.

"Littleman and I are taking in the sights today. We might visit the choo-choo train, maybe taste our first fudge . . ." Killian wiggles his eyebrows.

"You *wouldn't*." I narrow my eyes and play along in the role of the finger-wagging mother.

He laughs, and that makes Bowie laugh, too, and I can't help it, my heart squeezes. I will never not want Bowie to have the family I dreamed of for him. Even if it's impossible.

"Maybe I'll drop a chunk of it in his milk bottle, who knows." He kisses Bowie on one of his big, velvety cheeks, and Bowie coos. "Baby's first chocolate milk? Mmm!"

Killian glances back at me, his gaze still soft. "You could join us, if you're free."

My calendar app dings on cue, and I pull out my phone and scan the reminders. "Can't. I have to pick up some swag for the cabin, and then it's time for class."

"Class?" Killian raises an eyebrow, and my shoulders tense in anticipation of his bullshit. If he makes fun of me, I swear to G-ma's crystals, he'll regret it.

"Small Business Owners 101." I lift my chin, daring him to say something. "We're going over QuickBooks today, so I can't miss it."

Now both Killian's eyebrows rise in legit surprise. "Hannah, that's—that's *incredible*. You're learning QuickBooks? Be still, my heart!" He presses a hand to his chest and laughs, but he's not making fun of me. He looks—proud?

My cheeks flush, and I hate myself for it. I don't need Killian's approval, not anymore, but I'd be lying if I said it didn't soothe a spot that's ached for years.

"Yeah." I smile, but my guard's up. This confident, boss-bitch version of Hannah Tate is still being forged, and I refuse to let Killian tear it down. "Maybe I'll do my own taxes this year and everything."

I absolutely will *not* do my own taxes, you can't make me, but he doesn't need to know that.

Killian looks at me, his icy blue eyes flickering across me like I'm a map he doesn't recognize, marking each change. My clean, untamed hair, the circles under my eyes nearly gone, the fact I'm wearing clothes with a real waistband. It's just a pair of jeans and my favorite cardigan, but I look good. I *feel* good.

Killian's mouth opens, but whatever he wants to say, he seems to think better of it. "You—you look really happy, Hannah." His face crumples into a bittersweet almost-smile. "I forgot what that looks like."

"Amazing what seven hours of sleep a night will do for a woman." I take a long sip from my cup. "Having G-ma and Big Daddy to help with Bowie makes a big difference." I'm not trying to rub in what an absentee father he was before, but I also won't pretend it never happened, either. I'm tired of protecting the feelings of people who never cared about protecting mine.

"That's really good to hear." Killian readjusts a strap of Bowie's carrier. "I didn't know what to expect when you moved out here. Spitting lessons and camouflage onesies, or something."

"Hey." I point a finger at him. "You never know when your baby may need to disappear into the brush."

Killian snorts a little. After a beat of silence, he asks, "Can I sit down? For just a second. I need to ask you something."

It's still weird to me that he thinks he needs to ask, but I nod and clock how nervous he looks. What's he about to say?

"These weekend visits, two hours here and there, they're not enough."

My pulse picks up. I knew this would come eventually. The talk. How we're going to split time with Bowie. My fingers tighten around my cup hard enough to hurt. I've been able to put it off because of breastfeeding, but Bowie's almost six months old now. I've got a pumped stash of milk large enough for Killian to take him for an overnight back to Atlanta and then some, but it's not the logistics making my heart hammer in my chest. Being away from Bowie for an entire twenty-four hours? Tears involuntarily well in my eyes, everything in my biology screaming *DANGER DANGER DANGER!*

I take a shaky breath in. "I—know." Because even though I hate it, I *do* know. I don't understand how Killian bears being apart from Bowie as much as he is. There's an invisible tether between me and Bowie that physically pains me when it stretches too far. "What do you want to do?"

Killian pushes one of Bowie's wispy blond curls behind his ear. "I haven't taken any vacation time this year, and I realized it's because I don't want to *go* on vacation. Not without Bowie."

This is worse than I thought. Atlanta's one thing, but a vacation? Where the fuck does he think he's taking Bowie?!

"I was thinking, maybe the three of us could go somewhere? As a family?" Killian's forehead crinkles into worried rows. "You can call all the shots, if you want. Where we go, how long, when. I can take off whenever's best for you. And I'll—I'll pay for everything." He takes a deep breath in. "What do you think?"

I'm pretty sure my mouth's hanging open. "Um . . . together?"

"As friends, of course. We can have separate bedrooms and everything. I just . . ." He pauses, pressing his cheek against Bowie's. "I need more time with him, Hannah."

I nod slowly, not in acceptance, but as confirmation that yes, I am still here on this mortal plane of existence, bearing witness to this extraordinarily weird moment. A vacation? With Killian?

And he's *paying?*

"I'll . . . think about it. Give me a bit to mull it over, okay?" My calendar dings again, this time with the second warning, which means: *Seriously, Hannah, move your ass.* "I've gotta go."

"Yeah, sure. Whatever you need." Killian tries to smile, but the weight of how much he wants this is too firmly entrenched on his face. As I kiss Bowie goodbye and head out the door, my heart aches for him. Unlike Killian, I know *exactly* how much he's missing, and it's a lot. Too much to be summed up in our Bowie catch-up texts, or our video calls. Our son changes every day. Keeping up with him is like trying to track the sun's journey across the sky. The movements are too slow to catch looking straight on, but every time you turn away, it climbs higher and higher, until before you know it, it's slipping beyond the horizon, out of your reach, the day gone.

Killian did me dirty, but I don't want that for him. A vacation together with my ex, though? What would River think? Would he get all jealous and chest-beaty and try to kick Killian's ass? Or would he be weirded out that I brought it up, as if I needed his blessing? As if we're more than . . . whatever we are.

I run my hands down my face as I stare into the bustle of downtown Blue Ridge. *"Fuck."*

I'm gonna have to have this conversation with him face-to-face, aren't I.

CHAPTER TWENTY

The moon is high in the cold night air, but the lake's too restless to catch its reflection. I've stood long enough by the water's edge to differentiate between the stripe of black mountains and the forest beneath it.

The grass here's so soft, his steps sound like whispers. River's hands rove up my arms, and he leans in, a tall and welcome warmth against my back. He presses his lips to my jaw.

"Hello there."

My eyes slide closed as his smooth kiss trails across my neck, sending warm currents through my breasts and down my stomach. Sweet Jesus, it's been ten seconds, and I'm ready to jump him in the grass.

"You got my note."

"I found it propped against my door earlier." He turns me around to face him gently, his eyes sparkling in the firelight. "My security guard let you up the ladder?"

I *mmm* a little as he kisses the side of my mouth, my ear. "Battle-cat is powerless in the face of kitty tuna snacks."

He chuckles into my hair, and my hips rock toward him involuntarily. If I don't spit it out now, someone's gonna end up straddling a lap, and that someone is me.

"I need to talk to you about something."

He leans back, extricating himself just enough to peer down at me. "Yes?"

"I—I missed you this week." My voice is breathless with the truth of it. "We were so busy, I barely got to see you, and I kept wishing I could talk to you." I watch his face closely for any sign of unease at my confession. Over the past few weeks, I've collected snips of intel about River. From the Queer Mountaineers, from Gus, even a little something from Martha. Apparently, he's a bit of an emotional vagabond, never in any relationship for too long. Gus told me he does what he wants when he wants, and when certain people no longer fit into those wants, he doesn't pretend otherwise. If that's already happening to me, part of me hopes to see it now. If he's not as smitten as I am, let me find out quick before I absolutely lose my mind over him.

It may be too late for that, as it is.

But there's no unease or discomfort. If anything, his eyes grow more tender. He runs the cool back of his hand against my cheek. "I missed you, too."

My heart bobs like a buoy, giddy and relieved. I reach for the small, wrapped present I left on the chair by the fire. "Here. I got you something."

"A gift?" River's eyebrows lift as he takes it from me slowly. "It's book-shaped." His mouth begins to curve.

"Not a book." I push it into his hands, smiling before he's even got the paper off. "Just open it."

"It's a . . ." River pauses, then holds the box upside down, frowning. Then turns it back the other way. "What is it?"

"It's a new phone, silly!" I slide the box open and hand him the burner phone I bought downtown after class let out. "It's nothing fancy, but it's from this decade at least. This way I can text you when I go out of town."

He's quiet for a long minute, still staring at the phone I thrust into his hand.

I take a deep breath, feeling terrified as I even utter the words. "Or . . . call. We could call each other, too. While I'm away."

Whew. There. If he doesn't know I like him already, he should now. I talk on the phone for *no one*.

"You got me a phone?" His brow is furrowed, looking at the hunk of plastic and metal as though it's stealing his identity on the spot.

"Just a burner phone; your minutes card should work on this one, too. I'm going up to Asheville for a long weekend. With Bowie. And Killian." I'm aware I'm rambling, but River's perturbed expression isn't going away, and my brain thinks the solution to this is words, and lots of them. "It's as friends. Or parents, I guess. Parent friends? He misses Bowie so badly, and I can't stand to be away from Bowie for more than a few hours at this point, so when he suggested it, I thought, why not try this conscious co-parenting crap out?" I pause to catch my breath. River still hasn't looked up.

"Does that—bother you? I mean, are you okay with it? I know we're not, you know, but I don't know, could you say something?"

River's head jerks up at that. "No, no, it doesn't bother me. He's family. If you want to go, you should go." He's still frowning, though. "I don't need a new phone, though, Hannah."

"I thought maybe, now that we're doing all this . . . this"—I gesture between us, like that makes any more sense than my rambling—"that maybe you could use one so we could stay in touch. You don't have to give your number out to anybody else. It could be just for me, and only while I'm away."

My face is on fire, the embarrassment hotter than the actual flames licking the rim of the firepit. He's letting the silence stretch out between us, making things more and more awkward, and this is why I don't like face-to-face communication!

"You're what, thirty-two? A little old for your girlfriend to be passing you notes when she wants to meet up." I force out a laugh, then nearly swallow my own tongue. *Girlfriend?! You really called yourself his girlfriend now?!* "I know how you feel about being on call, but I'm trying to have an adult relationship here."

It sounds snarkier than I mean it to but come on. I was expecting the fact I'm going on a vacation with my ex-boyfriend to be the main topic of discussion, not the phone I bought him on a whim. All through class, I mulled over the weekend away with Killian and Bowie, and a strange sort of resolve emerged. Bowie doesn't have the family life I wanted for him, but that doesn't mean he can't have parents who happily spend time together with their son. In the beginning the idea of co-parenting with Killian was enough to make me punch a wall, but after the disappointment and anger wore down, all that's left is a desire to salvage what I can for Bowie. When I saw that a cabin rental I've been following for inspiration had a last-minute cancelation for later this week, the deal was done. I texted Killian and told him my terms: Asheville, three days max, separate bedrooms, just friends, and absolutely *no fighting*. He'd texted back immediately, so happy and grateful that when I found a smear of chocolate under Bowie's chin later, I didn't say anything. Killian doesn't get these precious firsts with Bowie, but even as much as he's missing, he isn't trying to take Bowie away to have more. I appreciate that.

So, let him have first chocolate. Let him have an Asheville weekend. I can spare that much.

But the whole careful explanation I'd prepared for River is wasted because all he's worried about is *the phone*? I'm not corporate America, I just want to flirt with my . . . person over text like the rest of my generation. Is that really too much to ask?

He looks up finally, slides the phone back into the box, and shoves it in his back pocket. "Adult relationship, got it." The tender look in his eyes is gone, replaced with weary resignation.

It makes me feel like shit.

"I'm sorry. I just want to talk to you." I run my hand down his arm, giving him a conciliatory squeeze. "Please turn it on, okay? While I'm gone? If you still hate it, you never have to use it again."

"Sure, Hannah." He rubs his hand over the back of his neck and tries to smile, but it seems to take a lot of effort. He throws the bucket of lake water

I had ready on the fire, dousing the last of the remaining embers. When it's fully dead, he holds out his hand to me. "I'll walk you back."

I take it reluctantly, unhappy with how our lakeside rendezvous is ending. I didn't even get to straddle him. The silence between us is the kind where anything you say will make things worse, and you're not sure why. I hate it. My only comfort is when he swoops down for a soft kiss at my door and brushes a lock of hair from my cheek.

"Come find me when you get back, okay?"

I nod, feeling as snuffed out and abandoned as the fire below.

≈

The week passes, and I don't see River once. I'm trying not to take it personally, but it *feels* personal. Every time I walk by his empty parking spot, or call up to his dark treehouse, his absence feels like retaliation. My eyes trail up the road, but his truck isn't there today, either. I wish I could kiss him goodbye.

Would he even let me?

"Call when you get in, baby. And once on the way, too." Mama thrusts Bowie's loaded diaper bag into my arms, bringing me back to the present with an *oof.*

"I will *not.*" I roll my eyes. "I'll text."

"Are you sure you've got everything?" Mama doesn't even register my words. She's too busy buzzing around Killian's Accord, tossing an assortment of Bowie's top one hundred favorite toys into the back seat and storing a cooler full of snacks in the floorboard.

"There's food in Asheville, you know." I raise an eyebrow at the bag of beef jerky she shoves in the side of the car door. What *is* it with them and beef jerky?

"You've gotta keep up your milk supply," she says as she straightens before shooting Killian a nasty look. "Lord knows whether he'll feed you."

"I am right here, Trish," Killian says, with a timid wave. "I will feed Hannah as often as she wants, I promise."

"Five square meals a day?" Mama says, still glowering.

"With water and everything." Killian smiles sweetly.

"I'm not a hamster, y'all." I frown at the both of them but stop to watch Darryl as he bends over and slaps something on the underside of Killian's car. "What the hell are you doing, Big Daddy?"

"GPS tracker," he growls under his breath. "Gonna keep my eye on him."

I raise both my hands. "Y'all are officially too much. We'll be back in three days. Now chill!" I tuck Bowie into his car seat, give him Hippo Sucky the Second, and tweak his nose.

Mama and Darryl are still standing there, pinched faces over crossed arms, as we pull out onto the road. Killian keeps checking the rearview mirror until they fade out of sight.

"What are the odds Darryl's gonna tail me to Asheville?"

"Significant." I shake my head, and Killian snorts.

"Well, I think it's awesome."

I turn to him, legitimately surprised. "You do?"

Killian side-eyes me and smiles. "Every kid should be so lucky to have grandparents that care that much."

I *tsk*. "When you wake up with Big Daddy hovering over your bed tonight, I'll accept your retraction."

The drive from Blue Ridge to Asheville is a little over two and a half hours and absolutely spectacular. Killian drives slow around the good turns so I can take pictures with my phone, and he even pulls over when we reach the Nantahala River Gorge so I can grab some brochures for whitewater rafting for our guests. The forest walls rise so high on either side of the narrow country highway, with the river rushing first to our right, then to our left, it feels like we're riding along the valley's floor, racing the river itself. With the windows half down, the smell of fresh green and hoarse hawk calls fill the car. We don't need to talk, the benefit of having known each other for years coming into play with the easy silence.

When my service comes back, my phone lights up with Airbnb notifications. I quickly tap open the app to see several messages from the guests arriving later this week.

"What the hell is this?" I mutter out loud without thinking.

"What?" Killian asks, but he doesn't take his eyes off the road. "Anything wrong?"

"No, it's just . . . a list of demands?" I scroll through a never-ending message with all the incoming guests' requirements. "Sheets must be washed in unscented detergent, fresh lilac flowers preferred, two gallons of unsweetened tea to be left in refrigerator, severe allergies to coconut and furniture polish, *what?* What even *is* this?"

Killian laughs. "Yikes. Sounds like you've got some high-maintenance guests coming in." His face turns serious for a second. "They're not my parents, are they?"

I laugh a little. "No, their profile says they're new to Airbnb. No reviews."

"They must not know Airbnb doesn't work like that," Killian says. "Why don't you email them and tell them?"

"What, that we aren't going to do any of that? They've already booked, which means they could leave a nasty review if we can't accommodate their requests." Unease bubbles in my stomach. These are the kind of guests who have zero problem with leaving a scathing review if everything isn't exactly to their liking. "Do lilacs even bloom in October? The *fuck.*"

Killian's face turns thoughtful. "When do they check in?"

"This Saturday, the day after we get back," I murmur, my brain whirring. That means Mama and Darryl are going to have to do both the quick flip from the last guests *and* the brunt of preparation for these people by themselves, which makes my stomach churn more. When I booked this last-minute trip, it was because the current guests would already be settled, and

Mama and Darryl assured me they could handle the flip for the next set coming in. But guests like this?

"Well, we'll leave early that day so you have plenty of time to help. How's that?" Killian glances at me before taking the last turn toward our cabin rental.

My eyes widen in surprise. "That'd be—great. You sure you're okay with cutting the last day short?"

Killian half shrugs as he pulls onto the long winding dirt driveway. "Well, if this is going to be a thing we do, it has to work for you as much as it does for me. I don't want to interfere with your new business."

I sit back, words temporarily robbed from my mouth. It's not that it's a crazy thing to ask for, or to offer. It's just Killian, being considerate . . . being respectful, even.

To *me*.

Kinda glad Big Daddy put the tracker on the car because I'm not sure *what's* going on.

"Damn, Hannah." Killian closes the door behind us as we enter The Blackbird's Nest, his eyes roaming upward over the exposed beams, the cozy furniture, taking it all in. "This place is incredible."

"Right?" I breathe a sigh of happiness with just a touch of envy. The Blackbird's Nest is my absolute ideal. Unlike the log cabins that populate these mountains almost more than the deer, this cabin is in the Nordic style. The wide wooden boards of its exterior are painted a smoky black, while everything inside is in shades of cream and taupe. It's perched on the side of a mountain, and its many paned windows overlook Asheville below and more mountains beyond. It's so hygge, I could happily close the doors and winter here without ever wanting to leave.

Not with Killian, I mean. Just in general.

I flop onto the plush couch and reach for Bowie, who's still in Killian's arms. He's squirming in that way that means he's hungry and two seconds from letting you know. Relief floods my veins as the milk begins to flow, and I yawn, nuzzling into Bowie while he nurses. The place smells clean and cottony, with just a hint of spice. Chai, maybe? It's delicious. Killian turns on the gas fireplace with a remote, which *classy,* and ambles around the cabin, admiring as he goes.

"They have a framed list of recommendations up here," he says, peering closer to read it. "It's broken out by date nights, family nights, single and looking nights . . . Huh. Awesome."

"Take a picture of it for me? My phone's on the coffee table."

Killian nods, giving me a sideways grin. "Reconnaissance mission? I like it."

"Damn right," I say, yawning again. "This place has a 4.99 rating with over four hundred reviews. Whatever they're doing, I want to know."

Killian eyes me, then the darkening skies outside. "You tired? We could order in tonight, take it easy if you want."

My head perks up at that. "I thought you wanted to go to that vineyard for dinner."

Again, Killian shrugs and sets my bottle of water down next to me. "I'm here to spend time with Bowie more than seeing Asheville and wearing his mommy out. Thai sound good?"

"Mmm," I say in response, mouth already watering. "Yes."

He gets on his phone, and in a few minutes, announces it's done and that it'll be here in thirty minutes.

"But you didn't ask me what I wanted!"

Killian snorts. "Hannah, you have never in your life wanted anything other than Penang curry, extra vegetables, with mango sticky rice for dessert."

"Unless there's—"

"Khao soi," he finishes for me, smiling.

My eyebrows lift. "Okay. You clearly know what you're doing."

When Bowie finishes, Killian takes him from me. "I'll get this guy a fresh diaper. You should go investigate the competition before you pass out on that couch."

Am I in the *Twilight Zone*? I never watched that show, so you tell me. I *am* eager to explore the cabin, though. I've already seen its big features from the listing, of course, but it's the touches I'm here to study. Zoe's always telling us in class that anticipating your customer's needs and wants before they even crystallize in their heads is the key to making impressions that last, and The Blackbird's Nest does just that. In addition to the framed recommendations in the area, there's also a bookshelf filled with local gifts and souvenirs for sale on the honor system, along with a freaking *scanner* thing so you can pay with your credit card. I pick up a handmade candle and smell.

"Oh yeah." My eyes flutter closed. "This is the cabin smell!" I flip it over and read the bottom. "'Sarah's Coconut Candles, made in Asheville.' *Ha!* It is chai!" I grab it and a set of cute bear-shaped soaps, and my credit card's out and swiped in less than a minute. What an amazing idea. Generate more income, support local business and artists, give the joy of boutique artisanal shopping right from the cabin itself. I snap a few pictures of the setup. These people are pros.

I steal a few more of their ideas, too, like their "concierge service," where you can order a massage or have a private chef come to the cabin to prepare a meal for you. For a tidy sum, the hosts will even give you a vineyard or brewery tour of Asheville curated to your tastes. I think of Darryl carting drunk people around in his truck and laugh. Not all of these ideas are doable for The Honey Jar, but it's good to dream, right?

≈

By the next afternoon, I'm seriously considering ordering the in-home massage myself. We spent the morning hiking a small portion of the Mountains-to-Sea trail, which was gorgeous, but worked my ass in such a way I will not soon forget. Killian was in charge of Bowie in the carrier, and even though it made it harder for him, he wore Bowie in front so he had the best views. It was painfully cute, watching Killian hold each of Bowie's little hands in his, telling him all about different trees and snake species and God knows what else.

"Hey, you know he's asleep, right?" I'd nudged Killian in the ribs at one point, interrupting a long monologue on the creation of the Appalachian Trail. I'd forgotten how much Killian loves reading nonfiction and watching documentaries, and how he's always so full of information.

"Oh yeah . . . sure I did." Killian grins at me sheepishly. It was all so different from our actual past and yet, so uncannily like the future I'd always dreamed of for us that it left me feeling confused and quiet for the rest of the hike.

Now, we're sitting outside on a sunny fall afternoon, warmer than it has any right to be in late October, at a brewery The Blackbird's Nest recommended. It is, of course, perfect. The service is great, the food is on point, and we each order a flight of tiny beers in those little wooden paddles so we can try everything they have.

When Bowie decides he's ready for his own drink, Killian shields me while I get him settled to nurse.

"So, how's Fellow Animals?" I say, taking a small sip of a rich, chocolaty stout. "Played any shows lately?"

Killian's happiness fades just a bit, but it's noticeable. "Um, here and there. The band's recording new material, so we play local shows to test out some of the newer songs. Opening up for other indie bands, stuff like that." He takes a longer than normal drink from his pilsner.

"Oh. Does that mean you're in studio, too? How do you work that in with your job?"

He winces into his glass. "Yeah, no. I'm not really *in the band* in the band. You know, still on probation."

I take another sip, this time from a hazy IPA. *Mmm.* "That's a long probation."

He sighs and nods. "Jamie isn't sure I 'add enough' to their existing dynamic." He air quotes the words, and I wince, too. Isn't Jamie his girl-friend? That's gotta sting.

"You could come into town next time we play, though." His face lights up a little. "Bring Bowie, and—"

Killian cuts off mid-sentence, perhaps noticing the death stare I'm level-ing his way.

"Okay, no." He clears his throat. "That makes sense."

I've almost finished the hazy IPA when an old white golfer dude stops by our table and sneers down at me. "Get that out of your hand. That's bad for the baby."

Killian's to his feet before I can even tell the guy to fuck off. "Who the hell do you think you are talking to someone you don't know that way? Leave before I get you kicked out."

My mouth drops open. Then, as if that wasn't badass enough, Killian yells after the scarlet-faced golfer, "Oh, and alcohol doesn't pass into breast milk! It's SCIENCE!"

The tables around us erupt into applause at Killian's heroic moment, but all I can do is stare. Who is this man? And where was he the last three and a half years of my life?

≈

After showers and playtime and a nice long nap, Killian drives us to down-town Asheville. It's chillier now, and I had fun dressing Bowie. He looks like a little lumberjack in his plaid hat with earflaps. I dressed up, too, in what I think of as the millennial-lady-in-fall uniform: dark skinny jeans, suede ankle boots, a long camel coat with a cozy plaid scarf. Killian has kept his word—he's been a total gentleman, never making me feel like anything more than a friend and Bowie's mommy, but he sucked in a breath when he saw me leave my room. I thought he'd pretend not to notice that I'm fine as hell, but to my surprise, he didn't.

"You look lovely, Hannah." His blue eyes twinkled in that infuriating way they do, and something in me flip-flopped on reflex.

I've been cool ever since. After what Killian put me through, it's amazing we've gotten to this point, but I'm not about to jeopardize what I have with River, no matter how good Killian's behavior's been this trip.

It sure would help if River texted me back, though. I try him again, but he hasn't responded to anything I've sent so far. Not even the cute picture of Bowie in his earflaps. Disappointment twinges inside of me, and I stash my phone away and try to focus on beautiful Asheville in the evening.

"Those guests bothering you again?" Killian asks, seeing the look on my face. He navigates the stroller deftly over the cobblestone sidewalk.

"No. I was texting a friend."

"A friend?" Killian says, his voice carefully neutral.

"Yeah." I try to match his tone. "River. My carpenter."

My carpenter. If only that were true.

Killian looks thoughtful for a second, then the recognition washes over his face and dismay follows. "Oh. Is he . . . are you . . ."

I shrug, desperately not wanting to have this conversation. Killian has always made me feel insecure, and right now, I need zero help in that department. I have no clue what River and I are, and if it all blows over because of the freaking phone, the last thing I want is for Killian to know.

"It's getting late," I say instead. "Should we head back home?"

Home. It's obviously a slipup, The Blackbird's Nest is not our beautiful black cabin in the woods, but it feels true in a way that strangles my chest.

"Sure," Killian says, his voice quiet. "This way." His hand hovers over the small of my back as he guides me to turn down the next street to the car. We almost bump into an older couple window-shopping outside a cute home decor store. The woman breaks into a knowing smile when she sees us and tugs on her husband's arm.

"Look, James, a young family. It hasn't been so long ago that that was us."

"Feels like yesterday." He kisses his wife's temple, then smiles kindly at us as they pass. We smile back and nod politely, but Killian's hand disappears. We don't talk the rest of the way back, their words hitting us both harder than they could have realized. Why couldn't it have been like this from the beginning? Sweet weekends in Asheville. Hikes and breweries and taking turns making Bowie laugh. It's everything I wanted for so long but was made to feel I didn't deserve. Why do I deserve it now? Because I started an Airbnb? Shower more often? *Why?*

Later, I fall asleep with the same questions tumbling through my mind on repeat, and when I wake up to the sound of Bowie snuffling, Killian's already there. He leans over the travel crib, gently picks up our son, and cradles him to his chest, unaware that I'm awake. He rocks from foot to foot with him, patting his back just the way he likes, until Bowie nods off, milk fully forgotten.

My throat tightens. *Why now, Killian?*

And why not then?

CHAPTER TWENTY-ONE

M H K

Tyrannical Infant Support Group

10:03 AM

Mattie

So Killian was NOT an asshole on the trip?

Hannah

 For the tenth time, yes.
That's what I'm saying.

Kira

Wait, he WAS an asshole? I'm confused.

Hannah

No! AHHH! He was nice and
helpful and considerate.

Mattie

Sounds fake.

Kira

Maybe he's jealous of the carpenter. 🤠

Hannah

He . . . doesn't know about River.

Mattie

HANNAH.

Why the fuck not??

Hannah

What's there to say? I'm screwing
my parents' neighbor?

Kira

Don't do that. You know it's already way more than that.

Hannah

Then why didn't he text me back?
I bought him a PHONE!

Mattie

Didn't he tell you he doesn't believe in texting?

Hannah

Yes, but that was with his old corporate
overlords, which I get, but not me!

WHY IS HE AFRAID OF TEXTING ME?!!

Mattie

Wow . . . I feel attacked.

Kira

Maybe that's how River feels.

Hannah

GROANS FOREVER

Kira

If you told someone you don't eat meat by choice, and they bought you a big, raw steak, you're telling me you wouldn't feel some kind of way?

Hannah

. . .

. . .

But why doesn't he want to talk to me?

Kira

Go ask him.

Except don't. Say something else. Then have more sex. Get this Killian trip out of your head.

Hannah

AUDIBLY GROANING FOR ALL TIME

I have to give it to Mama and Darryl, they've done a great job getting The Honey Jar ready for our "fancy guests." When Killian dropped Bowie and I off this morning, I feared the worst, but Mama was on the ball. The previous guests had just checked out, but she already had all the beds stripped and was mid-mop when I came down to help.

"Hannah! Thank God you're back early. Darryl and I don't have half the things checked off the fancy guests' list yet." Mama pauses to fan herself with her own shirt. "Can we charge them extra for all this?"

"Already on it." I smile. It was Killian's idea, actually, and it's a good one. Later that day, I messaged the fancy guests back and let them know we'd be happy to accommodate their requests as part of our optional "concierge services," for a fee. They grumbled but sent the extra payment. I didn't see any way around it, though. We tallied up the cost of everything they wanted, and it would have run us over half our profit from their stay easily, not to mention the extra effort during an already busy week. This way, we bring in extra revenue, and they get fresh lilacs in October.

Seriously, WTF.

Mama thrusts the list into my hand. "Can you see to the rest? Darryl and I can handle the cleaning if you do the errands, but you'll need to take Bowie with you."

"Sure, Mama." I scan the list and die a little. There are at least fifteen items left. "Come on, Bo-seph." I hoist him higher on my hip. "More car time, yaaaaay."

I'm about to tuck Bowie into his car seat when I see River's truck parked out front. He told me to come find him when I got back, but . . . what does the ghosting/no texting mean? Does he still want to see me? *Ugh!* I am determined not to worry about what another man may or may not be thinking, that is *not* how I operate now, goddammit. I shut the door with my hip, and together Bowie and I march through River's woods down the path to his treehouse.

"Rapunzel, Rapunzel, let down your hair," I call up to his open window. When he sticks his head out and grins, the anxiety melts, just a bit.

But the annoyance is still there. I asked him for one thing. Why couldn't he do it for me?

He climbs down the ladder and is on his feet before me in less than a minute. "I'm so glad to see you." He cups my cheek with one hand and leans in for a sweet, simple kiss, then turns and gives Bowie one on his forehead before I can even breathe out a hello. "You're back early. Everything go okay?"

"Yeah, it went great, actually." I frown, confused despite myself. He seems legitimately happy to see me, which is what I wanted, right? But he's also acting like he didn't ignore my texts for the last three days, too, which means . . . what?

"I tried texting you. Did you turn on the new phone?" I'm trying not to interrogate him like a jealous girlfriend, but I'm *also* trying not to date another man who won't treat me the way I deserve.

"Oh, you texted? I left the phone in my truck so I'd have it while I was at work, but . . ." He rubs a hand down his face, thinking. "The battery might have died, huh."

I raise an eyebrow. "They do that, yes. Did you charge it?"

He scrunches up his forehead, grimacing, and he looks so comical, the annoyance is starting to melt away, too. "Maybe . . . not? Sorry!" He pulls me closer. "But you're back now, and we can talk all you want. I'm not doing anything today."

It's my turn to grimace. "Well, I am. I have a list of errands a mile long for the guests coming in tomorrow."

He plucks the list from my hand and throws his arm around me, turning us toward the road. "Let's see what we're up against, then."

My eyes widen. "You're coming with me? To do *errands*?"

He smiles mischievously. "I'll even drive, Ms. Tate."

Well, then. I didn't think procuring flax milk, men's slippers (size fifteen??), the latest edition of *Martha Stewart Living,* Charmin Extra Strong toilet paper, a cool mist humidifier, Pepto Bismol but *only* in pill form, and nose hair clippers could possibly be fun, but River's turned the afternoon's workload into a bizarre scavenger hunt with a senior citizen theme. It's helped to have a local's assistance, too, as he swept me through obscure dollar stores and discount shops until we found the giant slippers. That wasn't even the hardest item, though. Finding unsweet tea sold by the gallon in Georgia? Come *on*.

"Okay, what's next?" River claps his hands while we stand in the checkout line. Bowie laughs at him from the buggy, so he does it again and again until it devolves into a game of peekaboo. I smile and pull out the accursed list.

"There's only one item left." I throw my head up and groan. "Fresh lilac flowers. Where are we going to find those?"

River's mouth twists to the side. "Does it have to be lilacs?"

"Yes. It's apparently their 'signature flower,' whatever that means."

River's thoughtful as I pay and he helps the cashier bag the groceries, then he straightens. River's already tall, but when he stands his full height, it's like standing next to a tree. "I know where we can go."

"For lilacs?" I turn to stare at him. "Where?"

"I don't know about lilacs, but if anywhere has them, they do. Come on."

The ride out to River's mysterious flower source is as beautiful as they come. Mountains slope on either side of the small two-lane road cutting through the valley. The land's all cultivated out here, the rolling farms showing off the smooth curves of earth. When the road ends, we reach a farm that spans across the valley.

"This is it," River says simply.

He's been quiet on the ride over, his jovial mood softened by something serious. I'm not sure what to make of it, but this place obviously has meaning to him. He sparkles a little every time I gasp at how beautiful it is. He parks the truck on the side of the road by a big, sprawling farmhouse, and leans into the back to unbuckle Bowie from his car seat.

"Are you sure we can park here?" It doesn't seem like a spot. It doesn't seem very *public,* either.

"It's fine. Come on, I'll take you to the greenhouse."

With Bowie cradled in one arm like a football, he leads me by the hand toward a big glass greenhouse the size of a barn. A man bent over at the waist out front is shoveling fertilizer from a big pile into buckets, but he stops, eyes widening when he sees River.

"Hey there, Jack," River says. "Is the boss in?"

"No, she's out with the sheep right now. Should I get her?"

River shakes his head. "No, better not. I'll be in and out."

"All right, River. Good to see you." Jack looks bewildered as we walk by but doesn't say more.

"You too, man."

I scrunch my eyebrows at him as he lets me into the greenhouse with a familiarity that seems out of place. "Did you work here?"

River huffs out a laugh. "Only every day of my young life. Flowering plants are back on the left." He starts to lead me there when a woman's voice clears behind us.

"River?"

I watch as his back noticeably stiffens, but he doesn't let go of my hand. He turns around, an easy smile plastered to his face. It's totally unlike his normal one. It's not real at all.

"Hey, Mom."

≈

The woman standing before us is almost as tall as River. *His mother,* I mentally correct. *River's mother.* The one who disowned Zoe. The one *he* disowned. Holy shit, this is awkward.

I realize my mouth's hanging open, so I close it and swallow. River and his mother seem to be in a staring contest, and when I realize he's not going to introduce me, I war with my southern manners and the intense desire to hide.

The manners win.

"Um, hi, I'm Hannah, and this is Bowie—"

"Is he your son?" Her voice is sharp as a knife as she addresses River, and *oops*, my mouth's dropped open again.

Emotions roil under the surface of his tight, twitching jaw. "No."

The word falls like an anvil between us, creating distance. I hate it, but it seems to be the right answer to her. Her shoulders visibly relax, and she turns to me. "I'm sorry." She says the words stiffly, as though they took great difficulty. "I haven't seen or heard from my son in five years. I wouldn't *know* if I had a grandchild. You'll have to excuse my mistake."

"Oh! I . . . understand," I mumble, but she's already back to staring at River. She looks so much like him. But instead of happiness and the imprint of a smile, her face is lined with sadness and anger. Her hair's a lighter shade of blond, more summer wheat than his deep honey, and her skin's a paler complexion, too, but the strong nose, the full mouth . . . it's like she spat him out.

"Do you have any lilacs in stock?" River asks, and the question is so weird, so terribly out of place, I actually cringe. But his mother breathes deeply through her nose and marches toward the flower section.

She shows us to the potted lilacs, which *wow*, I cannot believe they have, and when I offer to pay, she waves me off like I've said the dumbest thing ever. The air inside the greenhouse is warm enough to make me sweat, but the tension between them is ice cold. When we exit, I take a deep, steadying breath, glad to be free of the stifling air.

We've almost reached the truck when the spell of silence finally breaks. "Wait a minute," River's mom shouts. "Wait one goddamn *minute*."

Oh, boy.

"You haven't come home in five years, but you came here for flowers?" Her dark, stony eyes shine with fierce tears. "For *lilacs*?"

River finishes buckling Bowie into his car seat and straightens, his jaw tight and ready to spring. "Not gonna do this with you, Mama."

"Why, you worried that your unwed mommy girlfriend will learn what you did?" She spits the words out like fireballs, her neck arching behind each one. Her face is rife with judgment. "How you're so selfish, you broke all our hearts?"

"You broke Zoe's first." River's mouth twists into a grim line. "Then you broke mine."

His words bounce off her, visibly unabsorbed. Her chest is heaving now, and she levels her finger right at his face. "You threw your family away!"

A kick of white-hot defensive energy springs inside of me, and I step in front of River. "Excuse me, hi? Unwed mommy here!" I wave so passive-aggressively, it's just aggressive. "I don't know you, and you sure *as hell* don't know me, but I know Zoe, and the fact that *you* threw *her* away because she's gay, after you stepped in as a mother for her? Makes you a *villain*."

Scary-Mama's nostrils flare so wide, I think she really may spit fire, but I can't stop now. "Family isn't conditional. *Love* isn't conditional. And when it is, the problem is with your conditions. Not the people who can't meet them." I think of every tender look Bowie's given me, every look of trust and need and ask for comfort. For this woman to see all that, and then turn her back on it for some petty, small-minded bullshit?

It makes me want to *scream*.

"River stood up for Zoe because it was the right thing to do. It was on you to make it right after that. The fact that you haven't means *you're* the one who threw your family away. Not River."

I take River's hand in mine and watch him meet his mother's gaze once more. He grips me tight. "I'm gonna take my girlfriend home now. Bye, Mama."

Girlfriend. The word only makes me feel more protective over him.

"Thank you for the lilacs," I say, still hopelessly southern as I wrench the door to the truck open. "It was *not* nice to meet you!"

"Fine! Run off to your treehouse, keep hiding from your family! You disappear when anyone wants anything from you, always have!" His mother's face is contorted in anger and confusion, but despair, too. Unrelenting despair. For an instant, I grieve for this woman and the hurt her hands have caused.

But I also understand why River turns the ignition and takes us away.

As the fields pass us by, River says quietly, "So you know about Zoe."

"Yeah, she told me. You want to talk about it?" I run a hand across his shoulders and squeeze the back of his neck gently. His eyes are snared on the dirt road ahead, but the small touch brings a deep, trembling breath out of him.

"Well, you may have gathered this, but that was my mother."

"You don't say. Is this your family farm?"

He nods once, the clouded valley surrounding us now feeling like enemy territory.

"So. You took me to your family farm, which you have not been to for five years, and faced your estranged mother for some lilacs?"

His jaw flexes like he's weighing how much he wants to say, then he glances at me and smiles. It's his sad smile, I realize, a new one for me. It makes my heart ache. "I wanted to show you my home. Or where it used to be, at least."

"I'm so sorry." I gently brush a lock of hair behind his ear, and he takes my hand, kisses my palm. It's shocking, really. River's always felt so alone to me, so untethered to anything but himself. Like a lone wildflower that takes root where it pleases. To think he comes from this massive place tilts my entire understanding of him on its side.

We're quiet the rest of the way back, the lilacs intrusively fragrant in my lap. Zoe's right, he *is* an idealist, and it strikes me now how hard that must be. To live despite society's expectations of him, to carve away the rotten parts of his life so that love can thrive, to walk away from the people who've hurt him. I've never been able to do any of that. It puts everything in context for me, from his devoted yoga practice to his love for Mama and Darryl. They may be ridiculous half the time, but they've never judged me or anyone else, not for a minute. At my lowest—jobless, broke, no place to stay, with a tiny baby in tow—they welcomed me home with joy. They've been a lot of things to me over the years: irresponsible, neglectful, undependable in their own right, but they've *always* been on my side.

And River doesn't have that. When he chose Zoe, his parents didn't choose him back. I can't comprehend such a thing. I can't comprehend letting *anything* stand in the way of loving my son. It feels like a violation of nature itself. I reach back and check on Bowie, still sleeping snugly in his car seat, and take his little hand in mine. It's warm and soft and wraps instinctively around my finger.

When River parks out in front of the cabin, the first thing I do is hug him tightly. "I'm coming over later," I whisper into his neck, not a question. He nods and holds me back, just as tight.

I work as quickly as I can to prepare for the fancy guests, feed Bowie, then beg off for the evening.

I can't climb the ladder fast enough.

CHAPTER TWENTY-TWO

'm out of breath when I reach the top, but River's there waiting. He pulls me up, and his mouth is on me before I can say his name. The kisses are slow and molten against my skin, the tender nip of teeth leaves me gasping. He gathers me in his arms, pulling me by the small of my back until I'm pressed flush against him. He holds me like I'm something precious. God help me, but I'm starting to believe him.

His lips travel down my jaw, my neck, as one arm lifts me, dragging me upward slowly until I feel every inch of him between my legs. His other hand dives into my loose hair, bringing my face back up to his, his mouth finding mine and the moan building there. He kisses me as though he's searching for all he's lost.

Does he know I'll give him anything he wants?

In his arms like this, I am captive, boneless, at his command. He carries me through the door, never breaking our kiss. He sets me on top of the low bookshelf in his living room and drops to his knees. His warm hands settle on the insides of my knees and gently push until my thighs spread open wide. My fingers plunge into his hair, warm and soft, and when he pushes my dress up to my waist, exposing my dark, wet panties to his hungry gaze, it's all I can do not to pull his head into me. He presses his open mouth against where I ache and kisses me slowly through the fabric, and every hair on my body stands erect. I do pull him in then, crushing him into me, the pressure and pain making me cry out in relief. He groans, his patience wavering, and yanks my panties to the side. His tongue leaves a burn of pleasure up to my clit, which he tastes slowly, rolling the plump, hard nub between his lips until I cry out his name and rock into his face.

I can't get him close enough, it's torture. Wherever his mouth isn't aches with want. A hard knuckle slides against me, making me whimper until he pushes a finger inside, giving me something to clench around. The fierce rub of his tongue brooks no argument, no holding back. He devours me, and I offer up every part of myself to be consumed, grinding against him until I come, thrusting into his mouth. He rises before the aftershocks of pleasure are done electrifying my body and lifts me off the bookshelf, setting me down and spinning me until I'm facing the wall. I lean into it gratefully, my legs weak from the desire pulsing down the length of them. He presses into my ass, and I want him so badly, it hurts.

His hands climb over me, prowling, until he grabs the bottom of my dress and rips it over my head. I shimmy out of my underwear and unclasp my bra, while he throws off his shirt, unbuttons his jeans, and kicks them off. The clash of our naked bodies against each other makes him groan again. He covers my back with kisses, his lips swollen from making me come. One hand is wrapped around my left breast, the other between my front, slick and urgent.

"I need you, Hannah."

All I manage out is a whimpered *please.*

The hand stroking me disappears, and a condom wrapper rips. He sucks in a sharp intake of breath, then he's there, pushing between my legs. I gasp with pleasure as he drives into me, relishing the thick smoothness of his cock filling me up where before there was only desperate wanting. My hands stay planted on the wall, but his are wrapped around me, one arm below my breasts, the other across my hips. He brings me up as he thrusts into me, and it's enough to make me shout with relief. Our bodies joined like this makes me feel powerful, like together we can conquer the damage done by our pasts and build a future we both deserve.

"I want to see your face," he rasps into my ear, his breath hot and close. When he pulls away and spins me around, I throw my arms around his neck, the chills his words worked on my body still visible in my prickled skin. "You're so beautiful, Hannah," he murmurs, eyes dilated and shining. He slides his hands beneath my ass and picks me up, kissing me like he'll never stop. He lays me on his bed, his eyes starlit and dreamy as his gaze roves over my prone body. I pull him by the hand until he's beside me, then roll him onto his back. I straddle his lap, enjoying his ragged breathing when I slowly, slowly take him in. I throw my head back and moan as my muscles stretch around him, tightening as soon as they give, until our bodies are fully joined. The hard press of his hands against my ass, urging me forward, up and down, is almost too much. With each rock of my hips, he pushes deeper, the rhythm of pleasure hypnotic. The windows around his bed are open, and the cold night air licks my nipples, makes my hair stand on end, dries our sweat before it can form. His thumb finds my clit, and he pinches lightly. When he slides one warm palm over my right breast I come all over again, my cries swallowed by the thick forest surrounding us. His own fill the air, his hands locking around my hips, thrusting inside me so completely, I collapse against his chest. When he comes, I feel it. And again, against all my better judgment, I wish there was nothing between us. That when he exploded with pleasure, I'd drip with it.

Is this what raw attraction feels like? Everything animal in my body wants him, wants to claim him for my own. The way he's wrapping his arms around me, holding me so tight I can barely move, tells me he feels the same way. And even though he's the one holding me, I whisper into his chest, "I've got you. I've got you."

He presses kisses into my hair and holds me like he'll never let me go.

God, I hope he doesn't.

We lay like that for some time, taking comfort in the rise and fall of each other's chests.

"River." My voice comes out little more than a whisper. "I like you so much. It's scary."

He *mmms* against me. "I'm crazy about you, Hannah. Crazy. You and Bowie."

The words fill me to the brim. I run my fingers down his chest. "But why? How'd we get so lucky?"

"You both make this world better by being in it." He brushes the hair gently off my neck. "And you're incredibly hot."

I laugh, and he squeezes me tighter. "I'm serious!" he says, laughing, too. "Don't laugh."

"But I'm such a mess, River. I don't have a job, I live with my parents. I'm an unwed mother," I add, unable to hold back my smirk. "I'm actively lactating."

He laughs again. "Hannah Cleopatra Tate—"

"You know my—"

"*Yes,* I know your middle name. The way your mama yells for you? The whole mountain knows." He turns on his side to face me. "You listen here, Ms. Tate: you are not a mess. You rescued your parents from certain doom with that Airbnb. You have vision and taste. You're smart as hell, and you're always ready to learn more. I've never had a client work alongside me the way you did. And this part may sound strange, but bear with me, okay?" He smiles, running his finger across my lips, studying them intently as they part beneath his touch. "I fell for you the first time I saw how you were with Bowie."

"Really? Why?"

He smiles sadly. "The way you love him is so full. Knowing there are people out there like you, loving their kids like that . . . It's beautiful."

I caress his cheek, silver in the moonlight, understanding flowing through me. "You are safe with me."

"I know." His eyes shine, and he pulls the covers up until they cocoon my cold shoulders. "Maybe I'm biased, but I think you'd excel at any job you chose, and if you don't want to live with Trish and Darryl forever, you don't have to. You'll figure something out." He pulls me in for a long, slow kiss.

"And as for the unwed mother thing, well, thank god you didn't marry that guy because you belong with me." He kisses me again, deeper, and if he notices the tears seeping into my hair, he doesn't say so.

"And the lactating breasts?" I whisper when we come up for air. "What about them?"

"Hannah, your breasts could shoot lasers, and I'd still do this." He swoops down, kissing my nipples until they're vicious points again. "And this." He runs his tongue across one, closing his mouth over it and pulling it gently until I moan.

"Okay, point made," I say, breathless as he climbs fully on top of me. "But you can make it some more, if you want."

Much later, when the moon's risen above the sleepy mountains, River helps me down the ladder and walks me home. It's so dark, but I feel the warmth of his hand in mine. He makes me feel safe, too. I want him to know it.

"River, I—"

"Hannah, *stop*. Be quiet." His voice is low and serious, and I freeze. He raises a finger and points. About thirty yards ahead of us is a big, black shape, moving through the brush. I almost can't see it, but the sound of breaking twigs and rustling leaves helps me locate it in the darkness. A sour, musky odor floats on the still air.

"Oh no," I whisper, my heart thundering in my chest. "Is that a *bear*?"

"Yes," he breathes. "We're going to back up and head toward the road. We'll be okay."

"What the hell!" I gasp when we finally step foot safely inside our dark cabin, everyone else long in bed. "Don't bears hibernate? It's almost November!"

"The black bears here don't hibernate," River says, bringing me in for a hug. He kisses the top of my forehead and grins. "My little scaredy tourist."

"Being afraid of bears is justified!" I peer around his shoulder out the window, as if the bear followed us up onto the porch. "Is it safe for you to walk home right now?"

"I'll be fine."

"How will I know you got back safely?"

"You'll hear the screaming if I don't?"

"River!" I bang a fist on his chest, but he swoops in for another kiss before I can chastise him further.

"Made it this long in the mountains, didn't I? Now, you get to bed. The fancy guests are coming in tomorrow."

I sigh deeply. They might be scarier than the bear.

CHAPTER TWENTY-THREE

It takes most of the morning, but we get the Airbnb in perfect shape for the fancy guests. Their names are Bruce and Lolly McFaherty, which Darryl insists must be pronounced *McFarty*.

"I'm of Irish heritage, I should know," he says as he artfully folds a towel into a swan. When did he learn that?

"You are not." I side-eye him and his swan and arrange the goddamn lilacs on the pedestal table. "You told me your family came from the swamp."

"Before the swamp. My great-great-great-great-great granddaddy was brought over from Ireland for one of them debtor's colonies, which is where he met my great-great-great-great-great grandma." He bats his eyelashes and gives me a smug smile. "Being broke runs in my family. Ain't my fault."

Mama looks up from the floor where she's playing with Bowie. "Hannah, you're gonna be late for your class."

"I know, but I'd feel better if I could be here to greet the Mc—guests when they arrive." The back-and-forth messaging with Lolly has me rattled. She keeps asking for *more* things or informing me of more things they "absolutely can*not* stand," and it sends us scrambling each time. When I couldn't report on the exact fiber content of our sheets, I thought for one blissful minute she might cancel.

Never did have good luck.

The app dings on my phone. "It's them. They're arriving in three minutes! Make haste!" Turns out, I morph into an addled servant from a BBC period drama when I'm nervous.

Mama grabs Bowie and his toys. "You doing the last once-over?"

"We got it, you go on now," Darryl says. Together we zoom through each room and take stock—the bathroom looks great, complete with fluffy towels and the new bear soaps I bought in the dish, the kitchen area has their strawberry oolong tea and a tin of chicory coffee, and the kids' room is adorable, even though they're not bringing any.

"Dining and bedroom areas are satisfactory, boss," Darryl says with a salute. We exit the cabin and position ourselves outside right as a car that could better be described as a land-faring boat scrapes into the guest spot.

Barely.

A man with wiry, gray hair and a lemon-puckered mouth jumps out of the passenger's seat and slams the door. A Mr. Bruce McFaherty squints at me and Darryl. "The listing said there was parking for guests," he declares loudly, as though there clearly isn't.

Kill me now.

The other door slams, and Lolly appears, a twitchy, little thing with big glasses and a *Jurassic Park* sweatshirt. She's got to be thirty years younger than the man at least, younger than me even, and judging by how baggy her jeans are, we're not even in the same generation.

Maybe I misunderstood. Maybe Lolly is his daughter? But she sidles around the boat she's somehow navigated up the mountain and burrows her fingers into Bruce's. He smiles down at her, licks his crusty old-man lips, and I can't. I am *revolted*.

"Uhhh," my mouth starts without me, but there are no words.

Darryl nudges me hard in the ribs, and I blink rapidly, trying to remember why we're standing here, witnessing these atrocities.

"Um, hello there," I squeak. "Welcome to The Honey Jar."

Oh *god,* Bruce's nipples are visible through the coral pink sweater he's wearing. "You must be the McF—"

Farty. Farty! *FARTY!!*

"Bruce! And Lolly. So nice to meet you." I laugh nervously.

Bruce immediately frowns at me. "It's Mr. and Mrs. McFaherty. You must be the housekeeper." He glances up at Darryl, who is at least a foot taller. "Aren't you a little old to be a bellboy? Bags are back there."

"Oh, *hell*—"

"Right this way," I cut over Darryl before he has a chance to lay him out. "Mr., um, McFarty."

"It's McFarty, girl!"

I swear that's how it sounds when he spits it at the back of my head as I lead them down the path. If there's some subtle Irish distinction, I don't hear it.

I· try to turn things around during the tour of the Airbnb, but Lolly *umms* dramatically almost as soon as we enter the door.

"Is that . . . *fluid* on the floor?" She pushes her glasses up her nose and hides a little behind Bruce. "Big yikes."

Shit, it *is*. It's Bowie's drool from where he was playing with Mama. Darryl must have missed it during our once-over. "Oh! That's just a little—mopping fluid. Sorry about that." I wipe it up fast, hoping to God they didn't see the half-digested cheerio bits.

"All natural, I hope," Lolly says, a challenge in her nasal tone. Maybe they're meant for each other, after all.

"Couldn't get more natural." When I straighten back up, my ear brushes against something soft, then scrapes against something strangely hard. I glance up. It's Bruce. It's Bruce's chest. My hand shoots to my stinging ear. The *horror*.

It was Bruce's *nipple*.

My mouth gapes open, and I have to tear my eyes back to his face. Why'd he get so close to me? Why is he *still* standing so close to me?

"Umm . . ." Lolly steps between us, nostrils flaring. "Are you sexually objectifying my husband?"

"God, no!" I blink and take two, three, four steps back, just to be safe. "I mean, sorry, of course not, that was an accident, Mrs.—"

They both stare at me, daring me.

"Mc—"

Glaring intensifies.

"Farty?"

"Mc*Farty!*"

At that moment, Darryl drops all seven of their bags at the threshold, wheezing. "From the clan McFarty?"

"Yes, actually," Bruce says.

"That's how *I* said it!" Everyone looks at me, and I raise my hands in surrender. "Sorry, sorry. Please let me know if you need anything. Thanks! Bye!" I grab Darryl by the sleeve and haul him up the path before either of us can do more damage.

The app pings before I reach the top. I face the heavens and groan.

"Jasmine St. Jermaine didn't prepare me for this shit," Darryl says, rubbing his back. He stops to squint at me. "Did that man think you were comin' on to him?"

When I nod miserably, Darryl presses a hand to his chest and practically howls. "Nipples McFarty? My heart. I can't take it."

"Shut up, bellboy."

"Go on to your class. G-ma and I will handle all the requests that come in. Probably best they don't see your face for a while."

I hate that he's right, but I take the out and *flee.*

≈

"Every business hinges on one critical component, no matter what you sell or do," Zoe says, strolling in front of the class. "Anyone know what it is?"

Ms. Betty raises her hand and smiles beatifically. "Serving the Lord."

Zoe, to her own eternal heavenly credit, nods appreciatively. "Sure, that's one opinion. Anything else?"

"Keeping only *one* set of books." Timmy glances around the room, points to his prison tats. "Learned that the hard way."

The room murmurs in agreement, plus one *Praise the Lord!* from Ms. Betty.

"What do you think it is, Hannah?" Zoe stops in front of me and smiles. She knows I'll know the answer—I'm her most diligent student. Doesn't make me feel any better, though.

"Customer service." I lower my head into my hands.

"That's right! How you treat your customers or clients is the make-or-break factor for your livelihood. One bad review can cause a ripple effect, hurting your business for years to come."

I whimper.

"Is there something wrong, Hannah?" Zoe frowns. "Are you having customer service issues?"

I look up from my hands. "You could say that."

Zoe hops up on a bar stool at the front and sits, swinging her legs. "Class, we're going to have a customer service case study. Let's help Hannah troubleshoot what's going on."

The last thing I want to do is talk about it, but as I'm spilling the tea over the incessant requests, the impossible questions, the McFartys and their nasty comments, I start to feel better. There's something therapeutic about the gasps of dismay and cursing on my behalf from my fellow classmates. Even Zoe's shocked at how rough we've got it, and she manages her family's vineyard and has plenty of customer horror stories herself.

Ms. Betty shakes her head. "I'mma pray for those assholes."

Everybody's laughing now, even me. "And y'all, their last name is *McFarty!* They're allergic to *everything!* Furniture polish, MDF particleboard, plastic wrap, a specific type of lightbulb—no, I'm serious! Coconuts—"

Coconuts.

I suck in a throatful of air and nearly choke. "Oh, god! They're allergic to coconut!"

"They can't have piña coladas?" Frank asks.

"Or Thai curry," old Mr. Jones says from the back. "Now that is sad."

I stare at Zoe. "The bear soaps in the bathroom. They're made with coconut oil! I didn't even think about it!"

Zoe's laugh disappears. "Call your folks now. You've got to get those soaps out of the bathroom before they use them."

"Shit!" I shoot off a succession of emergency *help me!!!* texts to Mama, Darryl, and even River.

No one replies.

I'm still cursing as I tear up our dirt road twenty minutes later. Mama finally answered her phone and told me one bit of good news—the McFartys must've headed out because their car is gone. I can sneak in, get the soaps, and be out before they know it. God, I hope they're the gross kind of people who don't wash their hands.

I rap quickly on the door. When no one answers, I give the Universe a spiritual high five and let myself in with my spare key. It's extremely inappropriate for a host to enter a rented Airbnb without permission or the guests present, but something tells me that Bruce and Lolly won't just leave a bad review if they find out my mistake.

They'll get us kicked off the platform.

I dart toward the bathroom, but my foot catches on the wheel of one of their suitcases. The lid flies open. It's *full* of books. Not like novels you read, but veritable *tomes*. Dusty encyclopedias, an old phonebook. I glance over my shoulder at the door, but there are no shadows on the porch. I'm still alone. Mama and Darryl are on lookout, promising to stomp repeatedly if they see the car on its way back so I can get out undetected. Even Sarge is watching the road for me.

This is so, so wrong, but the suitcase next to it's already half unzipped, too, so I inch it a little farther along. Just to take a peek.

And *it's* full of bags of flour! No wonder Darryl was complaining about carrying their bags. They must weigh a ton each. What the hell is going on?

I start to check the third bag, but the sound of a doorknob turning freezes me in place. My eyes flick to the entrance, fury and panic rising in my chest.

Mama! You had one job!

But there's nobody there. The bathroom door swings open behind me instead, and I whirl around.

Oh *god,* I wish I hadn't.

Bruce McFaherty, of the McFaherty clan, is standing there, nude as the day is long. It's epic. It's horrible. My traitorous eyeballs immediately lock on the orange dinner plates he has for nipples, and I gag a little into my hand.

Bruce, on the other hand, looks *triumphant.*

"I KNEW IT!" he crows. He puts his hands on his hips and juts his business in my general direction. "You want it, and you want it bad!"

I'm *dead.*

"Well, missy! You can't have it!" He gestures at his business again with a giant *schwing,* which I refuse to look at. "Now, get out of my cabin before I call the authorities on your peeping ass!"

Upstairs, Mama and Darryl are stomping like crazy, but it's too late. Everything is ruined, and I'm probably going to get arrested. I nearly barrel Lolly McFarty over as I reach the top of the path.

"Ummmm," she begins, but I don't wait for her to finish pushing her glasses up her nose. I run inside our cabin, slam the door, and lock it.

"Fuck!" I screech. Mama and Darryl are staring at me, eyes wide and a little frightened.

"Hannah, baby, wh—"

"He was still there, Mama! He was IN THE BATHROOM!" The tears are streaming down my face. "You told me he was gone, but he wasn't!"

Mama's face goes pink. "Oh *no.*"

"I saw his old man d-d-dong!" I'm sobbing out the words. "He's gonna get me arrested!"

Mama's jaw tightens. "The hell he is! Calm down, Hannah. We're gonna figure this out."

"*Who is,* Mama?! *Who's* going to figure it out?" I drag a hand across my snotty nose. "You? *Darryl?*" I laugh, a bitter, despairing sound, and shake my head. "We're doomed."

"Hey, now," Darryl begins, but I don't let him finish. My head feels like it's about to explode, so I let the hot, toxic steam pour from my mouth instead.

"This always happens! I try to do something right for you, I try to *protect you,* but I end up screwing everything up, too, because you *never taught me how to do anything!*" I wrap my arms around myself, trying to squeeze the feeling of rich, lurid failure out of me. "We're all fuckups, and now this is fucked up, too."

"Hannah," Mama says, her voice hard as stone. "You're upset, but this is not the end of the world. Go lie down. Bowie's napping, too. We'll deal with the guests. You're taking too much on yourself, like usual."

Oho. That's rich. Mama put too much on me my whole life, and now she's complaining about it like it was my *choice?* I wipe my eyes furiously and go to my room just like she said to, which adds to the whole vicious irony of it all because it's taken her *how many years* to actually start mothering me?

I collapse into my bed and let the tears soak the pillow. River hasn't responded to any of my texts, and I'm alone in my despair. I can't do this, and the worst part is, for a minute there, I thought I could. I thought I was kicking ass, saving the goddamn day. But now the truth's come to spit in my face and remind me who I really am. Hannah Tate, human disaster, broken beyond repair. Why did I ever think I could run my own business? Mama and Darryl may be the reason I'm thrown into jail for crusty-dick voyeurism, but I'm the one who left the poison soaps in the bathroom.

I roll over and groan. I didn't even get them out. Maybe the McFartys will die a tropical histamine death before they can report me to the police. Will it be accidental manslaughter or third-degree murder? I don't know, I'll text Kira later. If I'm lucky, I'll be out in time for Bowie to be a surly teenager who blames me for everything.

As he should.

Cycle complete.

CHAPTER TWENTY-FOUR

Lolly
October 2024

GREAT IF YOU LIKE OLD PERVERTS. Not trying to kink-shame, but from the moment we arrived, this middle-aged housekeeper could not keep her eyes off my husband. Yeah, he's hot, lady, but get your own daddy? SMH. When she high-key stroked his chest during our tour, that was officially too much. Or so I thought. While I was out, she entered our Airbnb with her own key (!!!), cornered him while he was showering (!!!), and tried to seduce him!!! We almost called the police, but I'm no Karen for kinky-olds who can't get their own action. Anyway, avoid at all costs. The beds are weirdly flat, they nickel-and-dimed us for, like, every single request, and the whole place smelled like wood. Ugh. 0 stars, do not recommend.

≈

BACK OFF, BITCH

These texts are
Attorney-Client Privileged

Kira

Good morning!

Hannah

Is it? Is it a good morning?

Kira

Well . . . no. I heard back from Airbnb's resolution department about the McFartys' claims.

Hannah

Gulp. What did they say?

Kira

They won't take down the review.

Hannah

😭 OMG, did you tell them we're getting harassed b/c of it?? We had to block the Airbnb's calendar because all the new bookings are from pervert enthusiasts.

Kira

I told them that, but plus side: they're not
suspending or banning your account yet.

Hannah

Yet?

Kira

Not until they finish the investigation. But Hannah,
it doesn't look good. Even if they rule you're not the
"Pervert Host Upstairs" as the McFartys claim, you
still entered the Airbnb without permission while
it was occupied and caught the guest naked.

Hannah

Doesn't the fact that they stayed the night
ANYWAY mean they couldn't have been that
upset? And what about the books inside
their suitcases? And the bags of flour?

Kira

You do realize that telling Airbnb you know what was inside
their closed suitcases makes you look even worse?

Hannah

Ugh, yeah. But it's so weird! They were all
up in each other's business in front of us,
but the next day, I found the wife's stuff in
the kids' room. She'd slept on one of the
bunkbeds! WHAT DOES IT MEAN??

Kira

🫢 Maybe she was mad because she thought he was flirting back?

Hannah

GROAN. Make it make sense.

Kira

I can't, babe, but we'll figure this out, like we always do. Love you.

Hannah

Sigh. Love you back.

I slide into my boots and grab my coat before slipping quietly out the door into the cold, bleak morning. Maybe the bitter wind whipping down the mountain will blow my malaise away, though nothing else has. The whole world seems gray and brittle, cracking beneath my feet. And like so many other times in the weeks since McFartgate, I make my way to River's treehouse, seeking the comfort I can't produce for myself.

His truck's not there. That's been happening more and more often. I settle beneath his tree, draw my knees to my chest, and breathe. Is he avoiding me? The epic and ongoing crash and burn of the Airbnb has all but consumed me. I've tried talking to River about it over our late-night conversations by the fire, but I can tell he doesn't understand. I present all the evidence of my bad decisions, of each wrong turn I took, and how it all amounts to an incompetence I've been born into and can't seem to shake, but his answer's always infuriatingly the same: *You're wrong, Hannah. None of that really matters, Hannah. It'll be okay, Hannah.*

But with our fledgling business already shuttered, the income stream my family needs dried up, and me, still living in the cramped guest room of my parents' cabin with my son and no idea of what to do with my life, haven't I proved that I'm right? That it *does* matter?

It won't be okay.

≈

Killian

> Goooooood morning! Leaving ATL now. Excited to spend Thanksgiving with my family. 🤍 Big Daddy's not going to poison my mashed potatoes, is he? 👀

I blink at the words. It shouldn't be a surprise anymore, but no matter how many sweet, friendly texts he sends, I can't acclimate to Killian's about-face. It's the Killian from the early days of my pregnancy, the one who cried the first time he felt Bowie kick. To jump back to that way of being now feels like a dream I forgot about coming true. I don't know what to do with it.

I text back:

> Me too. 😊

That feels safe. And then, because it's true:

> I cannot vouch for the safety of your mashed potatoes. Eat at your own risk.

Bowie stirs in his crib in the winter morning sunshine. I watch as he *mehs* a bit, then scooches his knees beneath him, and wobbles up to sitting.

His arms waver, like a tightrope walker getting his balance. The smile that breaks across his face when he finds it is nothing short of pure joy. It makes me feel better, in a way. It's easy to take for granted all you know when you forget you started with sitting up.

It also makes me feel daunted on his behalf, though, because dude. If you think sitting up is hard, wait until you have to figure out what to do with your life.

He grabs hold of the bars of his crib and hauls himself up to standing, tall enough now that his head peers over the top rail. He happily *blehs!* at me watching, completely delighted with himself and his accomplishments.

"Good morning, Littleman." I lift him over the crib and into bed, covering his giggling face with kisses. I raise him high over my chest like an airplane and zoom him around until his joy is catching. I swear I *feel* my dopamine levels rise hearing him laugh, warming beneath his loving big-eyed gaze. The older Bowie gets, the more I feel the profound love and trust he has in me.

I hope I don't let him down.

Outside, the forest is covered in a sheen of brittle ice, but inside the cabin is warm and humid as G-ma and Big Daddy hustle about the kitchen. The smell of salty butter and rich pumpkin pie permeates the air, and the turkey's just gone in, though Big Daddy started brining it last night. For my part, I made the sweet potato casserole, which requires both crushed pineapple *and* miniature marshmallows, and no, I will not be taking any questions at this time.

Later, Killian knocks at the door and, even though it's unlocked, waits for me to let him in.

"Hey," I say, smiling as I open the door. A sharp wind immediately cuts into me, making me shudder. "Come in."

Killian's cheeks are rosy as he shrugs off his charcoal gray peacoat.

"Hey." He runs a hand down my arm affectionately and leans in for a quick kiss on my cheek. Out of the corner of my eye, I see Darryl scowling from the kitchen, a large steel pan in his hand.

"Who's letting all the cold air in?" he yells, staring straight at Killian. "Oh. It's you."

"Happy Thanksgiving, Big Daddy," Killian says gamely. "Thank you for having me."

Big Daddy's frowning so hard, it's almost comical. "Hannah made us invite you. Don't mess it up."

Killian exhales, his eyes meeting mine. "I'll be on my best behavior."

Sorry, I mouth, cringing. Big Daddy's not lying—I did force them to invite him. But after our idyllic family vacation in Asheville, it feels wrong to envision our holidays without him. He's a part of Bowie's life, and that means he's a part of all our lives, too.

And G-ma and Big Daddy absolutely can't stand it. They were even more pissed when I told them not to invite River. It's not that I don't want him here, *I do.* But he'd be an extra piece to a puzzle, throwing off the whole day. I don't know how to be *Hannah and River* while also being *Hannah, Bowie, and Killian.* Everything's felt so hard lately. I don't want this day to be hard, too.

Killian gives me a brave smile and asks, "Where's Bowie?"

"Outfit change." I hitch a thumb over my shoulder. "G-ma declared the Thanksgiving outfit I picked out wasn't 'festive' enough."

Killian's eyebrows rise. "That's concerning."

I nod enthusiastically. "Mm-hmm."

"Hold onto yer booties, people, because *here comes the tur-kaaaay!*" G-ma singsongs as she comes out holding my precious only child dressed in a fuzzy brown zipper-suit resplendent with a felt feather tail, bug-eyed hood, and most disturbing of all, a flappy *chin-wattle.* It hangs from Bowie's neck like a red, rubbery scrotum, which on my baby's face is so wrong, a desperate sob of laughter escapes me.

My hand flies up to my mouth. "Mama. *Noooooooo*. No!"

Mama sniffs at me. "And why not? He likes it! Look." She turns to Bowie and runs her finger up and down the wattle. "Gobble-gobble-gobble!"

Bowie cackles.

"Fine." I sigh, and reach for him. The wattle slaps me in the face, which feels insulting. "I don't know what's wrong with what *I* put him in—"

"Oh, please. Like a bowtie covered in pies is any more dignified."

"It was a bow-pie, Mama. A *bow-pie!*"

Killian snorts, and Mama's eyes dart to him for the first time, narrowing. "Oh. It's you."

"That seems to be the consensus." Killian smiles grimly.

Mama breezes past us both. "Well, don't get in the way. We've got a lot of cooking to do."

At first, our family visit's a little awkward. It's hard to recreate the magic we had in Asheville in full view of G-ma and Big Daddy, who seem hell-bent on sniping at Killian every chance they get. But the cabin smells incredible, and with the bitter wind whistling through the nooks, Killian helps build a fire that adds cozy holiday vibes. Bowie's making us laugh, scooting around on his belly like some kind of turkey-lizard, and I'm actually coming around to Mama's way of thinking about festive attire. Sitting on the big plush rug before the crackling logs, playing with Bowie and Killian while G-ma and Big Daddy make a veritable *feast,* soothes the places within me the last few weeks have grated raw.

The only person missing is River. Maybe he's already at Zoe's for Thanksgiving. Zoe and her dad are hosting at their vineyard for the Queer Mountaineers and asked him to come, too. I snap a picture of Bowie in his turkey regalia and text it to him, though he never responds. He always has some excuse when I bring it up—he left his phone in his truck, Sarge borrowed it, the battery died, he forgot his password. So I don't bring it up. River is so present when we're together, fully engaged and attentive. But when we're apart, he's just as absent. I don't know where he is, where he goes, what his schedule is, and often, when I'm going to see him again. Half the time, he doesn't seem to live at his treehouse, and even Battle-cat is gone. Where does he go? And though his mother's words that day at the greenhouse made me feel so defensive of him, I hate that they've started to make sense, too.

You disappear when anyone wants anything from you, always have!

"Oh my God, OH MY GOD! Hannah!" Killian's excited voice rings like a bell. "Bowie's crawling!"

I gasp, then clap my hands and squeal because *he is!* "Bowie-boy, that's it! You're doing it, baby!"

Bowie looks up at me with a huge, open-mouthed grin, and happy tears spring to my eyes. He moves forward another step, then another toward me, his turkey tail fanning out proudly behind him. I laugh with joy as his wattle wags beneath his chin, so hilariously obscene, and quickly flip to video to capture this historic moment.

G-ma throws a pot of boiled potatoes down with a splash and comes running, Big Daddy right behind her. "My grandbaby's crawling?!"

"Yes, he is! Look at him *go!*" Big Daddy slaps his thighs and hoots like Bowie's his favorite Nascar driver instead of a baby inching forward across a slippery wooden floor. But on the video rolling on my phone screen, amid all the joy and hollering and Bowie's triumphant bleating, Killian's face is wrenched with pain.

I glance up, surprised. "Killian, you okay?" I guess the words break whatever last bit of control he has, because tears start streaming down his cheeks. He stands up quickly.

"I'm—sorry, I need a moment." With an anguished look at Bowie, now bouncing on Big Daddy's knee and giggling under G-ma's kisses, he slips out the door and into the cold.

I frown. "I'm gonna check on him," I say, but G-ma and Big Daddy have been transported to Proud Grandparent Planet and are unable to process anything else. I grab a shawl and wrap it around me tightly before following him out onto the porch. He's staring at the lake and its reflection of the dark gray monoliths of the Appalachian Mountains, his hands gripping the porch railing, his back shaking.

"Killian, what's wrong?" I hesitate for a second but place my hand on his back. It's freezing out here, and he's trembling with cold and misery both.

"I'm so proud of him," Killian says between bursts of breath. "I never get to see him, and I'm so proud of him."

The words strike fear in my heart, even as pity floods through me. "Oh, Killian."

He spins around to face me, his normally composed face a ruin of tears. "I messed up so bad, Hannah. I'm missing out on his life. I just happened to see that milestone today. Had I been late, or uninvited like your parents wanted, I'd have missed it, like I'm missing everything else." His voice breaks, and he looks so tortured, I pull him into my arms and hug him close.

"You're not missing everything. You're still his daddy. He loves you." I don't know what else to say, what platitudes I could offer that would comfort him right now. Because the truth is, he's right. He did mess up, and he's been paying for it with all the moments of his son's life he doesn't get to share. As hurt as I was by Killian, I only feel sorrow for him now. Nothing is worth time lost with the ones you love. Nothing.

Killian pushes me back to look at me, his eyes so blue against the reddened whites that they almost seem new to me. "Hannah, please come home. I know you've got a life here, but please, I'm begging you, come home."

I suck in a sharp breath, but before I can say anything, Killian continues. "I will support you this time, Hannah, I swear. You can keep running your parents' cabin, take the time for yourself to figure out what you want to do next, whatever you need." He swallows, takes my hands in his, and holds them against his chest. "I underestimated you, Hannah, and I will never do it again. I know now I was part of what was holding you back. Me, and that awful job I kept pushing you toward, all of our son's needs falling on you while I was out playing shows. I just—" He stops, screws his eyes tight, and shakes his head, as if he could take back all my lonely nights by condemning his behavior now. "I was overwhelmed and so, so selfish. I will be sorry for the rest of my life for ruining what we had."

"Wait, are you—" I try to speak around the block of unidentifiable *feelings* lodged in my throat. "Talking about *us,* too?"

His grip around my hands tightens, and he pulls me closer. "Well, I'm definitely not talking about conscious co-parenting." He frees one hand, wipes a tear from my cheek so tenderly, more begin to fall. "I'm an asshole for taking this long to realize it, Hannah, but watching you blossom out here in the mountains has made me see how amazing you are. You're kind and generous, which I already knew, but you're so *creative,* too. Your parents' cabin looks incredible, and the business you're running is thoughtful and smart."

He can't know how those last words sting after I spent the last few weeks tanking everything. Would he still think all those nice things if he knew what an idiot I've been? How long would it take for it all to revert to his default opinion of me—*Hannah Tate, human disaster?*

"There's nothing more beautiful in the world than seeing our son in your arms." He dips low, runs the bridge of his nose across my cheek. "I want to see you together every day for the rest of my life. Please, Hannah," he whispers into my ear, making my cold skin shiver. "I love you."

And I'm . . . speechless. All his fleeting glances caught when I wasn't looking, the way his eyes lingered over my hair, the new, easier smile I have from living in the mountains, the sweet check-in texts, Asheville. I guess those things should have pointed me to this conclusion, but it's hard to shake the fact I was never enough for him before. Why now?

"What about the band?" I finally muster. "What about touring and Jamie and recording the new album?" *What about all the things that kept you away from us and made my life hell?*

"Oh," he exhales. "They kicked me out weeks ago. Right after Asheville. I missed a gig to go on our trip, and Jamie, well . . ." He shrugs. "That made it easy for her to finally give me the boot." The look of sadness that crosses his face is undeniable, and for a second, the gravity of the loss.

My forehead knits together. Is that why he's suddenly throwing his lot back in with mine? When his dreams crumble, there I am, waiting for him to leave it all behind and come dad it up?

When Killian drops to his knee in front of me, my heart's beating so hard, my chest physically hurts. The moment has the quality of a dream, not because it's ideal, but because I'm trapped in the heavy, surreal machinations of it. Like nothing that happens needs to make sense to get to where the dream is determined to go, and I'm along for the ride.

"Hannah, I'm a mess without you and Bowie," he says without one drop of irony. "I should have asked you this before I gave you so many reasons to say no, but—"

"What the *hell* you doing, boy?" Big Daddy's voice booms through the open door. "I know you ain't trying to propose!" He stands there, straight-up menacing, with a dirty dish towel over one shoulder, still wielding his pan.

"Darryl, this is none of your business." I pull my hands from Killian's gently and hold one up to stop him.

"The hell it ain't!" Darryl says, his face so red, it looks like it might pop. "That boy abandoned you and Bowie, and that makes him the biggest son of a bitch I ever met! And you're gonna give him a chance to do it all over again? Hell no!"

"Darryl." I can barely get the name out of my mouth, I'm so mad. Why does he think he has any say in this at all? "You need to back up."

He points the pan at Killian, who hastily stands. "Get your shit and leave."

"Darryl!" I yell, furious. "Killian's staying because he's Bowie's daddy, and this is Thanks*fucking*giving. My son's lost enough, he's not going to lose this, too!"

"What are y'all fussing about?" Mama says, appearing with Turkey-Bowie on her hip through the screen door. They both look concerned.

"What about River, Hannah?" Darryl spits. "You gonna dog him now this asshole wants you back?"

"I'm not dogging anybody!" I press my hands against my temples. "I was just *standing here* when you came out swinging!"

"Wait a minute," Mama says, her face growing stormy. "You mean to tell me *this boy* thinks you'll take him back after what he's done? I didn't raise you to be stupid!" Her voice is venomous, and Bowie starts to cry uncertainly.

"No, you didn't raise me at all!" I snap back. I reach for Bowie, but she doesn't budge.

Her lips thin into a grim line. "Do not even think about going with him, Hannah, or I'll—"

"You'll what? Drop out of my life again? Been there before, I'll survive." I finally manage to snatch Bowie out of her arms and press his cheek against my shoulder, needing his comfort as much as he needs mine. "There, there, baby. Shhh, it's all right."

"River?" Killian shakes his head slowly like he's waking up from the dream, too. "So you *are* dating the neighbor. Since when?"

"Since she had enough of your bullshit," River says. Our heads collectively swivel to see him standing there on the porch, because *of course,* a bouquet of flowers in one hand and a platter of freshly baked biscuits in the other. My mouth waters in full denial of my life imploding. River's face is pulled into a deep frown as he surveys the scene, his eyes resting on mine last. "You didn't tell him about us?"

"I—I didn't know you were coming!" I say instead, which is *not* the right thing to say, but my brain is fully fritzing out. I didn't ask for this proposal, I didn't ask for *any of* this, and I'm so tired and hungry, I just want to *eat biscuits.* "I never know when you're coming. I never know where you are *at all,* or what you're doing, or when I'm going to see you again. So yeah, I didn't tell my ex that I'm screwing my neighbor who, despite living next door, still manages to ghost me!" The tears are running down my cheeks, having never really stopped, and I'm just so angry at all of them. Killian for ruining Thanksgiving with his declarations of love that are five months too late, Darryl for butting his country ass into my business, Mama for thinking she knows best when she definitely does not, and River for being yet *another* man who won't make room for me and Bowie in his life.

They can all suck it.

Darryl folds his arms over his chest, still gripping his pan. "*I* invited him."

After I asked him not to, after calmly explaining how that'd be too stressful for me. Great. So glad nobody gives a shit about how I feel.

Killian turns his back to all of them, puts his hands on my arms, and looks me deep in the eyes. "Hannah, I don't care about any of that. I love you, and I want us to be a family again under one roof. You *know* that's best for Bowie. Please, come home with me." The words are calculated for a direct hit, and they land. He knows how important it is to me that Bowie have the stable family I never did.

But he knew it back then, too. And he still dumped me.

"I—don't—I—" I stammer, feeling the pull of everyone else's expectations for what I should do like ropes yanking me in opposite directions. What do *I* want? What's best for me?

Beyond Killian's shoulder, I can see River watching me with the same intensity. His face is a torrent of emotions I don't know how to name, but anger's one of them, and hurt's definitely another.

Well, I'm angry and hurt, too. Let him see it.

I turn back to Killian. "I don't know. I'll think about it."

"How could you even think about leaving?" Darryl says, his eyes burning red, tears beginning to well there. I'm not sure I've ever seen him cry. "What are you looking for that's better than what you got here?"

"What I've always been looking for." I sweep past Mama and Darryl both and throw open the door, tired of the bitter cold, tired of being so hungry, tired of everyone expecting me to subsist on the scraps of love they offer me.

"A goddamn family."

CHAPTER TWENTY-FIVE

flop and roll on my bed late into the night, but a comfortable position doesn't exist when your stomach feels like a water balloon filled to bursting. I groan a little into my pillow. Who am I kidding? There's no water in there. Only sweet potato casserole and despair.

It turns out rage-eating a Thanksgiving feast from the floor of your cramped bedroom isn't the best for digestion. Pretty sure Mama hid the Tums out of pure spite, too. I wish the fight had ended outside on the porch, but it didn't. With every scoop of strange casserole onto my plate, Mama and Darryl told me how dumb I am, how naive, how *insert adjective you wish your mother would never call you* here for even considering taking Killian back, which only made me angrier.

They only stopped berating me when I announced Bowie and I were moving out. *Announced* is the wrong word. *Bellowed*? *Bellowed* works. I've had enough of this tiny room and more than enough of them trying to parent me. I need *out*.

When Mama tried to give me that ultimatum . . . I pull a deep breath in to steady the sobs before they come rushing back. I don't want to wake Bowie, who was as amped up as I was and took forever to fall asleep. Is that how it's always going to be with her? She'll only be there for me on her own terms, and if I don't take care of her, or do as she says, or love who she wants me to, she'll disappear again? Before I moved out here, she and Darryl visited us in Atlanta twice. Once right after Bowie was born, and for an afternoon two months later. It wasn't surprising at the time, but I was hurt all the same. Unlike my dreams of Killian changing, I was never under any delusion

Mama might transform into the perfect grandmother. She'd given me no reason to believe it was possible. So is it any wonder I blinked every time she brought me a cup of tea, or rocked Bowie to sleep so I could get some rest? Just when I started to believe she'd *really* changed, that she was going to be here for me from here on out, she threatens to take it all away again? I squeeze my eyes shut against the stinging tears, the muscles behind them aching.

Maybe that's why I can imagine taking Killian back. I've been abandoned in one way or another my whole life.

The click of the front door opening, followed by the soft close, breaks through my thoughts. My phone on its charging stand says it's two a.m. Who the hell is up? It's freezing outside, the first snow of the year lightly falling. I crack the window open and smell it—cigarette smoke.

Darryl, *goddammit!* My fingers clench into fists. The moment I say I'm moving out, he picks up the cigarettes again? I start to slam the window shut so I can go out there and cuss him out, when heavy, erratic steps shuffle by.

That's not Darryl. He smokes on the *back* porch, with his elbows propped on the railing so he can stare out at the lake. Another smell seeps through the open window—this one pungent and sour, like dirt and concentrated urine. Alarm bells ring through my head.

Bear. There's a bear on the porch. It releases a deep, huffing growl.

"Darryl!" I scream. I run for the door. Mama rushes out of her room in her robe, and we nearly collide.

"What is it?" she asks, eyes wide. "What's wrong?"

Darryl's surprised yell answers her, a loud, gasping, choking sound. The crash outside shakes the floors of the cabin.

"Bear!"

Mama grabs her walking stick and races out the front door, like she's ready to engage in woman-to-bear combat. I follow her, but more slowly. What if it's still out there? What has it done to Darryl? What was that crash?! My heart is beating so hard it hurts, blood slamming through my temples.

"Darryl!" Mama cries, and runs toward his dark shape lying prone on the porch. A cold, sick feeling pierces my stomach. He's not moving.

"Turn on the floodlights!" Mama orders me, and I realize I'm standing there frozen, so terrified I'm not even breathing. "Get your phone. Call 911!"

I flip on the floodlights and scan the porch in all directions. The small gate's swinging open. The bear's gone, but its tracks in the snow remain. Our trash cans are toppled over, their contents spilled across the porch. The lights blare unforgivingly onto Darryl's face. His skin is a dull gray, his mouth stretched into an open grimace. He's still not moving. Mama throws herself to the ground next to him.

Phone. *Phone!* My fingers fumble over my cell phone, the face recognition failing to work with my pinched, panting face. I finally unlock it and dial. The operator answers on the first ring.

"911, what's your emergency?"

"There—there was a bear. My stepdad, I don't know, he's on the ground, he's—"

"He's had a heart attack," Mama says, her voice iron. Her small frame's working like a piston over Darryl, taking his pulse, listening to his chest, checking his pupils. "We need an ambulance right now!"

A heart attack. I stumble through giving the information to the operator, momentarily forgetting our address only to shriek it into the mouthpiece a half second later. There's a pause before the operator addresses me.

"Ma'am, can you get your stepfather into your car?"

"What?" The question doesn't register until the operator repeats it.

"It's going to take at least an hour to get an ambulance up that mountain in this snow, maybe longer. You need to get him into your car and drive him before the roads get impassable. Every second matters, ma'am."

Move Darryl? He weighs over two fifty, easy. "I—I don't know if we can."

"That's right, asshole," Mama announces over Darryl's choking breaths. "Don't you even *think* about quitting on me right now."

His chest rises and falls in an unnatural stuttering motion, but his eyes are open, and he's staring up at Mama.

"We'll try," I say, my voice small and unsure.

"Get him to chew an aspirin. I'm dispatching EMTs to your location now, but if you can get him in the car, don't wait for help, go straight to the hospital."

The line disconnects, and I feel like a failure.

"You're gonna be fine, Darryl," Mama says, more a command than a statement. "Just breathe through it. You lived through one of these before, and you're gonna do it again! Breathe in, that's right!"

Darryl whimpers. "It—hurts, baby." He sounds as though someone's strangling him.

Mama's head whips up. "How long till the ambulance gets here?"

"Operator says an hour at least. We've got to move him ourselves to the car and drive him. Every second matters." The words flow out of me in one long run-on sentence, like a child's guilty confession.

Mama's mouth tightens. "Well, come on."

We shove an aspirin in Darryl's mouth, but he's barely conscious enough to chew. It reminds me of the time he got piss-drunk on tequila at the bowling alley, and Mama had to fish a half-eaten wing out of his mouth. We each pull one of his arms over our shoulders and try to heave him into a sitting position. He cries out once before his body slumps over in Mama's arms.

"Goddammit, he's fallen unconscious!" Mama heaves against his unwieldy chest, weighing her down like an anchor. "We've got to lay him back down."

It takes all our combined strength to lay Darryl on his back without cracking his skull against the wooden boards. Mama promptly leans over and starts smacking the shit out of him.

"Darryl, wake up! You're giving yourself brain damage!" When his eyes flutter open before rolling back shut, she smacks him again. "*Goddammit, Darryl!* I'm not playing around!"

His skin is still gray, but Mama's abuse is pinking his cheeks. Despite the snow coming down, a thin sheen of sweat coats his face, making him look waxy and unreal. When Mama listens to his pulse again, she shakes her head.

"It's weak and thready. We've got to try to get him in the car again."

"But how?"

"Call River. We can't lift him by ourselves."

"Um, okay. Right." I bring up his number, but fear is already sluicing through my veins. Please let him answer. Please let him be there. Please, please, *please*.

It doesn't even ring.

"The number you have dialed is an invalid number. The line has either been disconnected or not activated and is unregistered on this network."

I scream in frustration. "His phone's not fucking set up! Fuck!"

"Go see if his truck's there. Run, Hannah!"

Just then, Bowie begins to wail from inside. I sob, stumble to a stop, and double back to get him.

"Leave him, Hannah! He's safe inside!"

"But—" Bowie's screaming, his little voice shrill with fear. He's scared. I'm scared. I don't know what to do.

"You can't take Bowie with you into the woods. It's snowing, and the bear may be out there still. Bowie's safe inside. He may not know it, but he's safe. Go, NOW!"

The words burn a trail down my back. Mama's eyes bore into mine, and I know in this minute, it's either Bowie's comfort or Darryl's life. So I go, my child's screams audible through the walls. They unravel what little composure I have left, and I leave a string of sobs in my wake. I run into the snowy night, into the fucking dark, pelting up the loose gravel of our road to River's. My nerves are on high alert, every dark shrub sending jolts of terror through my body. When I get to the dugout parking spot in front of River's woods, I almost pass it by because it's so dark.

His truck's not there.

"Fuck!" I scream into the night. "Fuck!"

Darryl's body's trying to die, and all that's standing between him and the end is me and Mama and her fierce commands. The night is silent except for my shaking breath, no sirens in the distance, no crunch of wheels coming. It feels like the world's ceased to exist beyond our small piece of mountain, leaving us alone with our tragedy already set in motion.

Who will stop it?

I try the next two cabins, hammering at doors of people I don't know. Nobody answers, and I remember they're all rentals, empty and dark. I turn back and pant down the mountain, terrified at returning empty-handed, terrified at what I might find, what may have already happened.

I try Martha next, and after six rings, she answers.

"What."

"Martha? I'm so sorry to call you like this, but do you know where River is? Can you—"

"You call me at two in the goddamn morning looking for your boyfriend—"

"Martha, *listen!* Darryl's had a heart attack! We can't lift him by ourselves to get him to the car. I can't find River. The ambulance won't be here for an hour, and I'm—I'm so scared!"

Martha's silent for a beat. "Gus and me are on our way." The line clicks, and I'm alone on the snowy road again.

I exhale a sob. When I think about the tears in Darryl's eyes when I told him that I was taking Bowie and moving out, a wave of nausea sweeps over me. I trip, fall, skin my hands against the rocks, pick myself up again, and keep running.

I hear Mama's tearful voice before I even reach our gate. She sounds scared, and that's scarier than everything put together. No matter what happened when I was a kid, no matter what colors the bills turned, or how little food we had to eat, or what crazy ex was beating down our door, Mama was never afraid.

But she is now.

I kick the trash out of the way, clearing a path to where she sits hunched over him. His eyes are still open, but they're glassy, and he's not responding to her anymore.

"Where's River?" she asks, her voice trembling. I know she hates the weakness showing through.

I swallow. "Martha and Gus are coming."

"We just have to wait, then." She combs through Darryl's hair softly with her fingers, whispering to him, while I finally go in to Bowie. It's quiet when I enter the cabin, and I find him sleeping again, puffy-faced and his eyelashes still wet. He's thrown everything out of his crib, and it takes me a minute to find the big, fuzzy blanket he loves. I wrap it around his little body and take him back outside, into the cold, snowy night. It feels like a vigil, one for someone we all love. Bowie should be there, too.

Martha and Gus arrive on foot ten minutes later. Thank goodness they were at Sergeant's. It takes all four of us the better part of twenty minutes to move Darryl out to the road. He's halfway in the car when the fire station EMTs arrive. The red flashing lights of their ambulance bounce off the dark mountain and slide across our faces. Everything's covered in cotton, or so it seems. The snow is thick and unrelenting, the ambulance's tracks already faint divots in the white. The EMTs slide Darryl onto the body board, strap his unmoving body into place. He's awake, but not present. The paramedic, an older man with a softly lined face, informs us this is normal when the heart is struggling to pump enough blood to where it needs to go. All I know is that it isn't normal at all. It isn't normal to see the gap between Darryl's teeth surrounded by anything other than a smile. It isn't normal to see his face wrung out and slack. I used to think that Darryl was permanently sunburned, all red, freckled skin scorched from long days spent fishing, but that's gone, too.

The heart attack's left him a pale, chalky gray, and I realize now that it was his blood coursing through him, his life force, that gave him that flush.

Please, God. Let it come back.

Mama's transformed, too. From demanding medical warrior to meek watcher-on, she hangs back. I put my arm around her—she's still in her robe—and hold her. She feels as gone from this place as Darryl. Darryl, who was her knight in shining armor. The man who stayed, who made her laugh, who loved her the way she'd always wanted.

Is he going to leave now, too?

I let my arm drop, bring it back to Bowie. He's stayed asleep this whole time, which I'm grateful for. I couldn't have handled his happy shrieking when the ambulance's siren came wailing up the mountain, its flashing lights headed for our family's disaster this time.

Mama climbs into the ambulance and sits beside Darryl on the stretcher. I hover at the open back doors while the paramedics rush to start the ECG that will tell them what we already know—that he's suffered a terrible heart attack. That he's suffering still.

"You and Bowie stay here," Mama says to Darryl's face instead of mine. "I'll text you updates."

"Okay, Mama," I whisper.

The doors close, and I watch my family descend the mountain.

≈

I don't sleep. How can I? I sit in the old velveteen rocker and hold Bowie in my arms, letting his sweetly sleeping body anchor me to this dark, dark night. If he wakes up, I want the first thing he senses to be my skin against his. I want him to know I am here, that I'm sorry for leaving him to cry, so sorry for everything that's happened. His weight on my chest is a comfort, but it makes me think of the weight pressing down against Darryl's, his trapped, breathless voice trying to escape his own body to reach us.

Mama's texts are frequent, but clinical. She's narrating every procedure, every test, his reactions to the clot-busting drugs they finally give him, the first time he passes urine. Everything except the words we yelled at each other, just hours ago. Those sit on my chest, too, heavy and unrelenting. What a fucked-up day. I woke excited for a holiday of eating food with my family, and now I'm counting what family I have left.

The text comes as the sun begins its creep across the sleepy white mountains:

Mama

Darryl's in stable condition.

The exhale rushes out of me, and in its wake, a wave of exhaustion. I finally lay Bowie down in his crib, as if the text from Mama is permission to rest, and sleep takes me almost immediately.

It ends all too quick.

The strike of a shovel clangs outside my window, waking me up.

I groan, running my hands over my gritty, swollen eyes. It's painful to rouse after so little sleep. Bowie must be beyond tired, because the loud, repetitive bangs and scrapes have no effect on him. I prop myself up on an elbow and peer out the snow-spattered window. A strong back leans over, the flash of yellow plastic swings, and a scoop of snow flies toward the ditch.

River.

An avalanche of feelings crashes through me. Confusion, affection, happiness. Then, like whiplash, regret and panic and a thick, bubbling anger that sends me scrambling out of bed. I drag on my boots and put on my big coat right over my flannel nightgown and stomp outside onto the godforsaken porch where I spent half the night. It still reeks of trash and bear piss, and the stench pulls me back into the horror of watching Darryl struggle to live. We had to sit there, not knowing whether those minutes would later be painted over with relief or become a time revisited in our worst dreams. A low place we'd return to, again and again, unwilling but dragged back all the same.

Seeing River here and now when I needed him there and then sends fire crackling through me. Maybe it's not fair, but it *feels* like River's fault. If he'd been someone I could count on, Darryl would've gotten the help he so desperately needed faster. Because the fact is, Darryl is stable, but he hasn't woken up. The prolonged lack of oxygenated blood to his brain has likely done lasting damage, the extent of which we'll learn over the next few days, maybe weeks. Because when we needed help, River was unreachable.

The way he likes it.

River hauls up another shovel-load of snow from around the truck, tosses it in the ditch. The trash crinkles around my boots as I wrench open the front gate, and he finally realizes I'm there.

I didn't know it could hurt so much to look at a man. His tan cheeks are red with effort, his honey-golden hair vivid against the snowy forest behind him. He's wearing one of those plaid shirts lined with wool, and it hugs the broad line of his shoulders. Ever the Urban Outfitters model, and without an ounce of effort. He wipes a gloved hand across his sweating brow, his chest rising and falling from the exercise. There's a path shoveled from his place to here, maybe even enough for a car to get through. It's so considerate, it makes me want to scream. Because that's his way, isn't it? He's here for me when he wants to be, but it doesn't make up for the times he isn't.

His usually joyful face is all tight, restrained lines. Ah, so he's angry, too. This is fury-shoveling. When I'm pissed, I usually rant to Mattie and Kira while binge-watching period dramas, but hey man, you do you. Knowing he's angry with me wrenches me open, and a bitter, incredulous laugh flies out. I'm both terrified of losing him and beyond caring if I do. I've lost everything else—the Airbnb, my new confidence, the love and acceptance of my wayward parents, the dream of giving Bowie the stable childhood I didn't have. Why not complete the set?

"I called you last night." My words come out biting like junkyard dogs. "You never set the phone up."

River's jaw stiffens. "I told you before. My time is my own, and I don't do phones."

"That's right. You don't do anything you don't want to do." I fold my arms over my chest. "You live life on your own terms, right? Who you want, what you want, when you want. Never compromise your values!"

"What are you *talking* about?"

Honestly? I don't know. All I know is that I'm furious, exhausted, and utterly terrified. The words about Darryl won't come. Maybe it feels easier to fight about everything else, because those things don't have a person I love hanging in the balance. "The PHONE!"

River huffs out a disbelieving laugh. "So I don't use a cell phone, and that makes me a villain? Tell me how that works."

"*No!* It makes you *another* man who won't make room in his life for me." I take a step forward, into the snow. "It makes you *another* person who thinks they can be there for me when they want, and I'll lap it up no questions asked because I don't have anyone else!"

His eyebrows shoot up. "You sure about that, Hannah? What about that marriage proposal I got to see yesterday? The one you're *thinking about?*" His cheeks have gone crimson now. "If something happened in Asheville, and you want to be with that smug banker asshole, tell me, Hannah. Don't lead me on."

I blink, my mouth falling open. "*Me,* lead *you* on?" I yank my coat around me tighter. Had I known I'd be dealing with this bullshit, I'd have worn pants. "Nothing happened in Asheville, and that proposal was as big a surprise to me as everybody else, not that it really matters to you."

"Of course it matters to me!" River tosses the shovel down and grasps his temples with both palms, like *I'm* the one who's mysterious and incomprehensible.

"Oh sure, it matters to you *right now*," I spit out. "What about when I'm out of your direct line of sight, River? If a Hannah calls in the forest and River's not around to hear, does she even make a sound?!"

"For Christ's sake, could you speak plainly right now?"

"When you're with me, it feels real. Like you—" I swallow around the growing lump in my throat. "Love me."

I want him to say, *I do, Hannah! Of course I do!* But things never work out the way I want. He just stands there, staring at me like I accused him of witchcraft.

"It's so good, and then, you disappear. I can't find you. You're not at home. You stop coming around. Here one minute, gone the next. Where *were* you last night?"

River flexes his jaw. "I have other places I stay. Other land."

"You *what?* Where?!" An angry laugh peals out of me, and I slap my forehead. "No, no, don't tell me. Wouldn't want to ruin your hiding places."

"I wasn't hiding."

"What else should I call it? In that moment, you were *not* choosing me? Does that jive better with your philosophy? All these boundaries you made to protect yourself—the phone, the disappearing, choosing yourself over everybody else—they keep me out, too, River." My eyes are full of burning tears, and I'm so goddamn tired of it. "No matter how you spin it, you only want this relationship when you feel like it. Do you know how that makes me feel? Like an idiot, River. Like I've once again mistaken another man's bullshit for love. So maybe don't lead *me* on, asshole."

He shifts from foot to foot. "I know you've been hurt before, but do *not* compare me to Killian. Just don't."

"Why not? I was an afterthought to him, too." I'm so furious to be here again. Just like Mama, after all. "But at least Killian's trying to change, and he's an adult with a residence and a phone I can call when I need him!"

"Is that what this is about?" River drags a hand down his face. "I'm not *adult* enough for you?"

"I don't know," I say, hating the mocking tone in my voice and yet. unable to hold it back. "How many treehouses do you have, River? Are girls allowed in all of them?"

The look he gives me is stone-cold. "You told my mother that love isn't conditional, but you've been trying to change me since we met—the digs about my phone, my home, the way I run my business."

I rear back, the words hitting like a slap to my face. "I'm not trying to change you, I'm trying to *be with* you, but you're determined to shut me out!"

He laughs incredulously into the air. "No, you look at me like another person to fix, just like Trish and Darryl. Well, I'm not broken, Hannah, and neither are they."

He's so wrong, my entire being rejects his words. Wanting someone to be there for you isn't asking them to change. It's asking them to love you. He turns his back to me, and I cry out, "Yeah, why listen to a word of criticism when you can just leave?" The tears are streaming down my face, and I fling a hand at his truck. "Maybe I should follow your lead and run away, too. Go back to Atlanta and get a real job instead of fucking around at my parents' house like a kid with the boy next door."

He spins back around. "See? Right there! You're always saying this place is temporary, and you don't know what you're doing with your life here. How's that supposed to make *me* feel, Hannah? How am I supposed to depend on *you* if I don't know where you're going to be tomorrow?"

"*Woooow*, welcome to the club! Feels shitty, doesn't it."

For a second, River looks shocked. Whether it's from admitting he worries about me staying in Blue Ridge, or that his precious living-in-the-present philosophy doesn't feel so good when he's on the receiving end, I don't know. He throws his hands in the air. "It's *different!*"

"Different how?"

"Because you keep reaching for what you don't want! You think there's only one right way to live your life, and this isn't it." River gestures wildly at the snowy white forest around us. "Have you considered that maybe your idea of adulthood doesn't come easy to you because it's not supposed to come to you at all? That maybe your idea of adulthood *sucks?*"

"Says the man whose retirement plan is to go off the grid." I laugh weakly. "Please, give me more life advice. What carrier pigeon gets the best service out here?"

"Enough with the fucking phone!" River finally yells. "Why's it so important to you?!"

"Because I needed you, and you weren't there!" I yell back, his words freeing me of any restraints I had. Let the whole mountain hear what's happened. "Darryl had a heart attack last night. He almost died! We needed your help to get him to the hospital, but you hadn't set up your *fucking phone!* You weren't at your *goddamn treehouse!* You were *hiding from me,* just like you hide from anything that's not perfect enough for your precious worldview, and Darryl almost died because of it!" A sob chokes out of me as the news hits him.

"What?" He takes an uncertain step back, then another. Fleeing from me already. "Is he—"

"He's alive, thanks to Martha and Gus and the Gilmer County EMTs." I shake my head, then shake it some more. I can't stop saying *no* to all of this. *No, no, no.* "Your mother's an asshole, but she was right about one thing."

His face is stricken, and he swallows once. "Hannah, I—"

"You disappear when anyone wants anything from you, even me." I stick my chin out, shaking in the cold that's permeating my bones. "Well, maybe you should go ahead and disappear now. It's what you want, isn't it?"

River's shoulders collapse, defeated. "If that's how you feel, maybe I should."

Feel? Who can feel anything? I am as hollow as a dead tree, empty and broken and ready to collapse. When he turns around and leaves, this time I let him.

CHAPTER TWENTY-SIX

K **H** **M**

Tyrannical Infant Support Group

Kira

How's our big guy?

Hannah

About to see him for the first time. 🥺

Mattie

We love you, Hannah. We're rooting for all of you.

Hannah

♥♥♥

Kira

♡♡♡

"He's awake if you want to go inside." The soft voice at my shoulder makes me jump. It's his nurse, I think. Her name tag reads SUSANNE WHIPPLE, R.N. CARDIO UNIT. She's looking at me knowingly over her tablet, like she's seen lots of nervous family members hovering outside the rooms of loved ones, too scared to go in and let their realities be altered forever. Her eyes are warm and kind, and everything about her looks soft—her worn green scrubs, her long brown hair streaked with gray.

"Thank you"—or that's what I intend to say, but all that comes out is a sob. Mama didn't say much in her last text, only that he's awake. I don't know what to expect. Will he still be Darryl, with his gap-toothed grin and smart-ass remarks?

Or will he be different? Less somehow? The thought terrifies me.

Without hesitation, Susanne the nurse wraps her arms around me and Bowie and brings us in for a hug. This is definitely not in her job description, but you can tell she doesn't feel that way. She pats my back in the way good mothers know how to, with uncomplicated support and patience.

"Bless your heart. It was a scary night for you all. Your mother told me everything." The hug feels so bracing, so comforting, I find myself wishing *this* woman was my mother, and then feeling even worse for thinking such a thing. It isn't Mama's fault that things are so terrible right now.

"Thank you," I manage to say this time, my words muffled into her shoulder. "This is a great hug." She laughs, releasing me and gesturing for the door.

"Go on in. It'll all be okay, one way or the other."

She opens the door for me before I can stall any longer, and I step lightly into the room, hovering in the doorway like the sound of my feet against the floor might hurt Darryl worse.

"Git your ass in here," Darryl says, his voice raspy but wonderfully *him*, and I huff out a laugh, wiping my tears away with the back of my free hand. Bowie thinks it's a game and starts smacking my face with his own tiny palms, which yeah. I guess I deserve.

Mama's passed out cold in one of those hospital recliners that are more pressboard than chair, her slack mouth emitting a light snore. Darryl sees me eyeing her. "She slept through them taking out my catheter and putting it back in damn sideways, and if my hollering didn't wake her then, nothing will." He lifts a finger toward the defibrillator machine hanging on the wall beside him. He can't lift it very far, not with the mass of IV needles and tubes hanging out of him. "Gonna have to shock her ass awake. Heh, heh."

I smile as I settle Bowie and myself into the chair beside his bed, grateful for his dumb jokes, grateful for this moment he's giving me to collect myself before whatever's about to be said. He's the one lying in a hospital bed, but he's worried about me. How does that work?

"Did you miss me, Littleman? Hmmm?" Darryl manages to tweak Bowie's knee, and Bowie lets out a delighted yelp. Darryl's mischievous smile stretches across his pallid face, and the relief I feel can't be put into words. He's still him, and he's still here. Thank God, Jesus, and G-ma's crystals, because he's still here.

Suddenly, I fall apart.

"Aww, Hannah, I'm okay," Darryl says, his forehead stitched with worry. "Don't cry like that."

"You're the only one who—who ever stayed. And then you almost left us, after all." I can barely get the words out. All the times I watched Mama cry, watched her rage, witnessed the months of depression that followed each departing man, come flooding back. I was never sad to see those men leave, I never wanted them to stay in the first place. But Darryl was different. He stayed and loved my mama, and by doing so, he'd patched a hole in our family that had existed since I was born. I never realized how much comfort that gave me until I saw him lying there, gray and glassy and gone. How could Mama go on without him?

How could our family?

"Hannah, you listen to me now." He takes my hand in both of his big ones. "I can't promise I won't die one day, but know that I will never, ever choose to leave you and your mama."

"Darryl, I—"

"Big Daddy, if you please, ma'am." His voice is hoarse, but gentle.

"Big Daddy." I turn my face up and smile at the ceiling. "I'm so, so sorry."

He shakes his head slowly. "No, I was out of line, the way I was treating Killian. He's a low-down son of a bitch for doing you like he did, and I'll never forgive him for that. But without him, we wouldn't have Bowie, and then where would I be?" Big Daddy's voice trails off as he takes Bowie's small, socked foot in his hand and squeezes. Bowie *bah-bah-bahs* at him like he's agreeing, like *yes, old man, you live for these drool-kisses.*

"Probably lying in a grave instead of this bed because of those damn cigarettes." His mouth trembles as his gaze meets mine. "I owe you both for giving this old bastard a reason to get up in the morning, Hannah. These been the best damn days of my life, and I know your mama feels the same way."

"Why, Big Daddy. I didn't know you loved getting pooped on and watching grown-ass women have their hearts broken so much." I try to laugh off his words, but the sound chokes in my throat.

"I'm serious, Hannah. There are whole years you spent on this earth I didn't get to witness or be a part of. I hate that. I'll always be an add-on to you. But Bowie won't see me that way, not if I have anything to do about it. I'll be a part of his life from the time it started, a good part. Someone who makes him feel safe and loved, like I wish I could have made you feel when you were little." He takes my hand again. His skin is rough and thick from long days working outside, but his touch is tender. I never knew he felt like an add-on. But then, I think of all the times I've told him to back off, to stay in his lane, to quit trying to father me, and it's not so hard to imagine.

"I ain't always been the best stepdaddy, but I'll do my damnedest to be the best Big Daddy. If y'all let me. Just—don't move back to Atlanta." His hazel eyes are bloodshot and a little desperate. The monitors tracking his heart rate pick up and beep in warning, and my own pulse quickens.

"Okay, calm down right now. We're not going anywhere." I summon up a sad smile even as my heart sinks, because it's true. How can we possibly move out now? Mama and Darryl need me more than ever. They need Bowie even more.

Big Daddy sniffs back tears, and the cannula giving him oxygen's nearly sucked up into his nose. "Aww, damn. I'm filling this thing with boogers. Susanne!" he hollers. His voice may be hoarse, but it still carries.

"You know they've got buttons for that." I root around for the nurse call button, but he's already hollering again. A minute later, the door opens, and Susanne sticks her head in.

"What—you need to urinate again? I'm telling you, they got the catheter in right this time." When she sees us both red-faced and wet-eyed, she smiles kindly. "Nothing like a near-death experience to bring family back together. Does that mean you're staying put? You're not gonna marry that boy, are you?"

Damn, Big Daddy. How much did he tell her? Then I realize he's waiting for me to answer, too.

"Um, yes to staying put." My eyes flicker between Big Daddy and the nurse who may be a part of my family now? Unclear. "No to marrying Killian." I hadn't realized I'd made up my mind until I said it, but it never could have been yes. To Killian's credit, I think he was right all those months ago when he dumped me over Taiwanese sausages. We were never meant to be married, but that doesn't mean we can't be a family. When you think about it, it's kind of weird that in your average nuclear family, two people are boning each other. In our little family, it'll just be *family*, with feelings ranging from bare tolerance to affectionate love. I like that.

"Oh yes!" Susanne claps her hands together. "So have you patched it up with your fine-ass neighbor, then?"

I raise an eyebrow at Big Daddy.

"Don't look at me! That was your mama's ed-it-torial-i-zation."

I hold Bowie a little closer. "No. We had a big fight this morning, actually."

Big Daddy's face falls. "Damn. I should've never invited him yesterday. You told me not to, but I screwed it all up, didn't I. *Dammit!*"

"Uh-uh-uh." Susanne wags her finger at him as she finishes hooking up the new, booger-free cannula. "No stressing about it now. You let the young people handle their business. It'll all work out."

I wish I could be so sure. River's haunted, miserable eyes, the way he collapsed inward . . . I left that fight feeling like something broke between us. You could almost hear it snap.

≈

When I get home, there's a letter waiting on our doorstep.

It's from him. I put Bowie down when we enter the lonely cabin, so quiet without Mama and Darryl and the ever-present warble of the TV. He scoots off and starts playing with one of those baby noise tables, so it's with trembling hands, crashing cymbals, and sad trombone noises that I sit down to read River's letter.

> Dear Hannah,
> I'm taking your advice and disappearing for a while. I'm taking a job up in Murphy that'll last until after the new year and staying up that way for the duration. You'll probably think I'm just hiding again, and perhaps you're right. I'm sorry it didn't work out between us, but maybe it's better this way. I can't change into the adult you want, but for the record, I'm sorry my boundaries kept you out. I only ever wanted you in.
> I hope you find where you're meant to be. Give Darryl and Trish my love.
>
>   -R

I sit back in the chair, breathless, stung, crushed.

≈

It's been two weeks since my heart was broken and Big Daddy's got fixed. After a successful stent procedure, they released him from the hospital. He's been telling all his visitors the doctors filled his heart with tiny balloons, then proudly proclaiming, "Science!"

Martha, Gus, and Sergeant come visit every day, but Booch and his wife have stopped by with the kids, too. Their noise opens the place up, makes it feel less like a sick house and more like the happy cabin we all miss. There are always plenty of errands to do now that Mama's a full-time nurse again, tending to Darryl while he regains his strength and administering the literal briefcase of drugs he's on. Between Bowie and helping run the household, I feel so used up, I almost don't think about River every waking second of the day.

Almost.

I wanted to drop out of Small Business Owners 101, but Mama and Darryl forbade it. Mama started in with that cross tone she gets. "Just because your first business was—"

"Shut down for being a pervert," I interrupt.

"—*unsuccessful* doesn't mean your next one will be—"

"Shut down for being a pervert."

"Exactly," Big Daddy says from beneath a pile of blankets in his armchair. "You'll be a better pervert from now on."

So I've agreed to keep going. After class, Zoe and I decide to have a glass of wine at her vineyard. It's understandably slow in the wintertime, and we have the tasting room to ourselves. It's just us today, and I'm grateful. I love the Queer Mountaineers, but I don't feel like facing their sympathetic faces yet.

"It finally happened," I admit from behind the rim of my wineglass. "We're done."

"Airbnb deactivated your account?"

I nod. "Plus a forever ban from the platform."

"Damn," Zoe says, shaking her head. "All because you saw some old dong you didn't want to see."

"I know!" I take another swallow. "They should be paying *me* for pain and suffering. The whole thing's so weird. You know I tried to look them up? I couldn't find the McFahertys of Atlanta anywhere."

"That *is* weird." Zoe rolls the wine on her tongue, thinking. "And they had no other reviews on their Airbnb profile, right?"

"Nope."

"Well, it's time you list the cabin on another vacation rental site. Airbnb isn't the only fish in the sea."

"I know." I look down into my wine. "But what if someone connects us to the bad review? It was up for a month before Airbnb deactivated our listing, and there's a whole Reddit post about it. What if I have to disclose the reason why I was banned to another site?"

What if it's just another failure, waiting to happen?

Zoe shrugs. "You won't find out unless you try."

"I know." Doesn't make it easier, though.

After a few minutes, Zoe asks carefully, "So. Heard from River?"

"No." I close my eyes and sigh. "That's been deactivated, too. Have you?"

After a second, Zoe nods. "He stopped by the vineyard before heading up to Murphy. He's really torn up, Hannah."

I swirl the wine in my glass. "Then why'd he leave?"

"When we were growing up, River was never alone," Zoe says, staring out the huge glass windows at the gray rows of wintered vines. "Always surrounded by friends and family, always laughing. But that Atlanta job took that away from him, and then after the blowup with his parents, that changed him for good. River just . . . disappeared. That's how he coped, I guess. He resurfaced in town a few months later, but he was different by then.

Still quick to laugh, still kind, but you couldn't pin him down. Not for work, not for hanging out, not for anything."

"He chooses what he wants, when he wants, and who he wants it with. Minute by minute, that's all you get." My eyes cast downward, lost in the swallow of red wine at the bottom of my glass. "My minutes ran out, I guess."

"That's not why he left, Hannah," Zoe says, and throws back the rest of her wine. "River believes love shouldn't be conditional on changing anything about yourself. That's why he stood up for me to his parents. They were only willing to love a version of me that conformed to their views. Based on what he told me you said to his mama, which, bra*vo* by the way"— she stops to fist-bump me—"he thought you felt the same way." She winces. "At first."

"I thought I did, too. At first." When River accused me of putting conditions on my love that day standing in the snow, I couldn't believe it. But his words kept finding me in the odd moments of the days that followed. While I sat in the waiting room during Darryl's stent procedure, fuming over how Mama shared with the entire ICU that I was suffering from stress-induced constipation. When the first thing Darryl did when we got home was order KFC delivery. When I struggled to get out of bed because my entire self-esteem was vanquished by an *Airbnb*. It took those moments for me to finally recognize the truth in what he said. To realize that at some point, my ability to love and accept others, and *especially* myself, without resentment or judgment, was severely damaged.

But not beyond repair.

The truth is, I would have changed River. Not the hundred versions of his smile, or his ability to see how things could be and turn them into reality. But I would've wished him into the financially stable, responsible adult I always dreamed would fix me. These months in Blue Ridge have changed me, though, are changing me still. They've challenged my old ideas of who I *should* be and what I *should* look like and who I *should* be with. They've shown me how all those *shoulds* kept me from seeing what I really have. They kept me from seeing what I *didn't* have, too. With my old job. With Killian.

"I know now I wouldn't change a thing about River," I say, relieved that it's finally true. "But asking someone to take down the fences they've built to protect themselves isn't asking them to change. It's asking them to be vulnerable and trust again after others have hurt them. And I think River's too scared to do that."

Zoe bites her lip, thinking, then pours herself a new glass. "You're one wise bitch, Hannah Tate."

I laugh sadly and *cheers* to that. If I am, it's too little, too late, and the ashes of my life are proof. I just need to forgive myself now and move on.

My phone buzzes on the counter, and an involuntary chill sweeps over me. No matter how well the doctors say Darryl's doing, part of me is still waiting for disaster to strike. But it's not from Mama.

BACK OFF, BITCH

These texts are
Attorney-Client Privileged

Kira

Hannah.

Hannah, I need you. 💔💔💔

Can you please come right now?

Hannah

!!! On my way!!!

CHAPTER TWENTY-SEVEN

Kira's asked for help exactly three times in the twelve years we've been friends. The first time, when she wanted to teach that racist girl to stop stealing her soy milk. I supplied the condiments. The second time, the night before her bar exam. She was suddenly convinced she'd forgotten all eleventy billion rules of civil procedure, and I drove two hours to spend the night with her in her hotel room after an epic round of flash cards for Skittles. She of course completely annihilated the exam with a near perfect score, and I now have an uncanny knowledge of personal jurisdiction. The third time was when she was too nervous to approach the lanky, gender-fluid Timothée Chalamet lookalike perusing the premade guacamoles at Trader Joe's and asked me to instead. It was a strange place to pick up your future wife, ten minutes before closing on a humid Tuesday night. But Mattie took my bumbling introduction in stride and met Kira's interested glances with her own. When the three of us chatted in the parking lot until the employees turned the lights off, she gamely followed us to Kira's apartment for our bad-reality-TV-and-snack night. We totally could've murdered her.

And I still might, depending on what she's done. I tried calling Kira on the way back to the cabin to make sure she was okay, but she was crying too hard to understand much. So I packed an overnight bag for Bowie and myself, made sure Mama and Darryl had something to eat for dinner, and headed for Atlanta. I don't know what's going on, but Kira said Mattie's left, and that she needs me. That's enough.

When Kira answers the door, her eyes are bloodshot and swollen, and she's wearing a fuzzy yellow robe that's as short as it is wide.

"You look like Easter candy personified." I tilt my head to the side. "Like a Peep."

Kira sniffs and gestures us in. "Mattie calls it my sexy Pikachu robe." She tries to smile, but it wavers too much to stick the landing. "I think we've got some Peeps left over from June's Easter basket. You want?"

"Easter? Kira, they've gotta be eight months old."

Kira shrugs. "You want any or not?"

I blow out a breath. "Bring the whole basket."

Kira takes Bowie from me while I make us two cups of tea. Their tea collection is truly witch-level, and after a minute, I choose a lovely matcha green varietal. Caffeinated AF, of course. We've got a long night of soul-retching ahead of us.

I settle next to her on her cozy couch like I've done so many times before. Only this time, we're both emotionally wrecked and have giant babies latched to our breasts.

"I ordered us our favorite," she says, checking her phone with her free hand. "It'll be here in twenty minutes."

"Boneless teriyaki wings with blue cheese dressing and old bay fries?" My eyes round. Pulling out our college midnight munchies food? This is serious.

Kira nods. "A pound each."

"Geez, Kira. At eight forty-seven p.m.? We're gonna have so much indigestion."

Kira's head dips low. "I deserve it."

I reach over to June's Easter basket, pull out a rock-hard Peep, and wait for Kira to begin. Mattie and Kira fight from time to time, but it's usually small stuff. Kira working too much, Mattie scorching the stainless-steel pans. Whether Mattie *really* needs VIP passes to see Tegan and Sara. But Mattie's never left, even when Kira admitted she doesn't care for Taylor Swift, and that was a big one.

Kira exhales in pure sadness and turns to June, running her index finger across her little face. Down the scoop of her nose, around the shell of each baby ear. "Hannah, things are awful." She sounds miserable and defeated, which are two words I don't associate with Kira. She's a sunshiny badass and always has been.

"What happened?"

Kira reaches over June to pluck a file folder sitting on the side table and hands it to me. "Mattie found this."

I use Bowie's forehead to prop the folder open. The milk must be good tonight, because he doesn't mind. He cares a little more when a brochure slides out and bops him on the nose, but I snatch it out of the way. It's a brochure for the sperm bank Kira used before. Behind it are copies of several signed consent and waiver forms, along with a hand-scribbled note for an appointment at a women's fertility clinic.

"Is this . . . an insemination appointment?"

Kira winces and nods, and I hand back the folder.

"But it's for Monday . . . *Kira.* That's two days from now!" My stomach sinks as the facts fall in place. "You were going to get inseminated without talking to Mattie first?"

Kira's face crumples. "I'm so tired of the stalemate, you know? I want another baby, but Mattie doesn't feel comfortable with getting pregnant herself, which I *completely* understand. But she also doesn't feel comfortable with me getting pregnant after my minor pregnancy scares with June, and—"

"Kira." I hold a hand up to stop her. "You almost died. I know you want to have another baby, but don't downplay what happened." It was one of the scariest days of my life, and it was absolutely traumatic for Mattie, but Kira always tries to pretend that it wasn't as serious as it really was. I don't know if it's out of denial or fear or sheer stubbornness, or maybe all three.

Kira had been struggling with steadily rising blood pressure throughout the last trimester of her pregnancy, but her doctor kept brushing it off. Usually, he'd use it as an excuse to get on to Kira about her weight, or whether she was eating too much sugar, which honestly pissed me off so much it raised *my* blood pressure. Her doctor dismissed her sharp increase in headaches and worsening vision. It was all stress and sugar, she was told over and over again. It took Kira getting so dizzy at a pretrial conference that she slammed into the judge's bench and had a seizure on the floor for her doctor to take it seriously. Mattie got the call at work that Kira had been hospitalized and was scheduled for immediate induction at thirty-five weeks. It was preeclampsia, made far more severe due to her symptoms being ignored for so long. Both Kira's and the baby's lives were at stake.

Now, Mattie has always had reservoirs of chill that Kira and I can only dream of. But that day, she was on fire. They wouldn't let her see Kira because she wasn't "family," and then wouldn't talk to her because she was "out of control." When I showed up winded and four months pregnant myself with a copy of their marriage certificate, Mattie was beyond furious. She wasn't capable of speaking. She was breathing so hard, I heard it down the hall before I got to the waiting room. I channeled Kira's calmest, most convincing tone to intervene on Mattie's behalf, explaining to the bigot receptionist behind the desk that yes, Mattie and Kira are legally married, and that refusing Mattie's right to be at her wife's side would bring a world of trouble down on her head.

That bitch let Mattie go back.

Kira would have been so proud of me, but she was too busy suffering from runaway blood pressure and being prepared for an emergency C-section. All because her doctor didn't listen to her.

Wouldn't listen to her.

The C-section went as well as it could, what with Kira's blood pressure jumping all over the place, but the preeclampsia didn't stop after June was safely delivered. It morphed into postpartum eclampsia, and Kira had three more seizures before she was finally discharged from the hospital, weeks after she was first admitted. She was ill for a long time afterward, too, and I stayed over more nights than not. Partly because she needed me, but partly because I needed her. To *see* her and make sure she was okay. Because of that ignorant doctor, June spent her first weeks on this earth in a neonatal care unit, and my best friend almost died.

So yeah, I get Mattie's perspective on Kira getting pregnant a second time. It was terrifying, and now Kira wants to go through all that again?

"I'm not downplaying it," Kira says, grabbing a handful of old jellybeans and shoving them all into her mouth at once. "I just don't want to live my life in fear over it anymore. I want another baby, Hannah."

At least, that's what I think she said.

"I know." I lean over and hold out my free hand to hers, and she takes it. "But you realize why Mattie's so scared, right? She almost lost you and June in one blow."

"Yeah. I don't think she's ever gotten over it," Kira says, taking her hand away to wipe a tear from her eye. "But doesn't *she* realize this is my body and my life? That I want this more than I want to be safe? Besides, it's not a guarantee I'll develop preeclampsia again. There's a very good chance I won't."

I take a deep breath, weighing my words carefully. I care about Mattie deeply, but Kira is my ride or die best friend. They understand how hard it is for me when they argue, so they usually don't bring me into it. But right now, they both really need my support, and here I am, stuck in the middle of what could be a life-or-death decision. "I think Mattie does understand that it's your body, and that you get to make decisions about what it will or won't do. But, Kira, your life is entwined with hers now. When you act like it's not, like it's only your decision to put your life at risk, it negates that. She's your partner, but making this decision behind her back shows that you don't really view her that way." I swallow, feeling utterly out on a limb. "That's probably why she's so upset."

The tears spill freely down Kira's cheeks, dropping onto June's tight curls. "I don't know what to do, Hannah."

"Cancel the appointment. For now," I add, when Kira's jaw clicks shut. "Call Mattie and schedule a sit-down. You're the best lawyer in the world, Kira. If you can't negotiate a solution that appeases you both, it doesn't exist."

After a long minute, Kira finally nods. "But I don't have to like this. I get to be impatient and demanding and as manipulative as it takes." She glares at me, as if I'm officially Babygate Referee, and I'm two seconds from making a bad call.

"I'll allow it."

We sit in silence for a while as our sweet babies doze off against us. When Bowie's good and fully conked out, I place him gently in their travel crib, and June goes into her crib, too. Then it's just us, me and Kira in our jammies and two pounds of sticky wings waiting for us on the kitchen table. I stop her there in the hallway outside of June's room and wrap my arms around her. For someone so strong, she feels small in my embrace. "I love you, Kiki, and so does Mattie."

"Love you, too." We sway there for a minute, a mass of fluff and flannel and feelings until the siren smell of the wings pulls us inexorably to the kitchen.

"Your turn," Kira says as she dunks the first teriyaki wing into the blue cheese dressing. "Have you talked to Killian yet?"

"No." I look sheepishly down at my wings. "Been putting that off, God knows why."

Kira smiles sympathetically. "It's the end of an era. Those can be hard, even when they're for the best. What about . . . Any other developments?"

I shake my head slowly, dousing my sadness with sauce. "Not since the letter." I pause, double-dipping because Kira got me my own cup.

"You could try talking to him."

"Even if I could find him, which, doubtful, what would I say? Slip a note into his treehouse, asking, *Do you like-like me? Check Yes or No.* Tell him I'm okay with whatever scraps he'll give me?" I close my eyes and breathe deeply through my nose. "I'm just like Mama, after all."

"What's so wrong with that?" Kira demands before licking her thumb clean. "Trish is one of my favorite people. She's hilarious and deeply kind, and I freaking love all the weird stuff she's bought me over the years." Kira gestures at the shelves behind her, either referring to the porcelain set of Scooby Doo figurines or the Barack and Michelle Obama bobbleheads, both acquired during the height of Mama's eBay addiction.

"I thought—I don't know." I stuff a particularly salty fry in my mouth and chew it wistfully. "I'm really trying to let go of all my preconceived ideas about who I should be, but I thought I'd have reached Adult Island by now."

"That sounds like a bad dating show," Kira says, then half a beat later, "I wish it existed."

We *cheers* our water bottles to that, and then Kira looks at me soberly over our decimated boxes of food.

"Look, I say this with love, but you really need to stop expecting your life to match some boring ideal you made up when you were little. Other kids were dreaming of growing up to be unicorn doctors and living on the moon, and meanwhile you were, what—picturing a mom and dad in matching pinstripe suits? A weekly allowance if you did all your chores, trips to see Grandma, strict bedtimes and savings accounts?"

"Healthy dinners on the table," I add. "Regular dentist appointments."

"A matching beige living room set."

I nod resolutely. "So much beige."

Kira reaches for my hand again, and it's a testament to our love for each other, because our hands are ferociously sticky, and no one even makes a face.

"I know your childhood wasn't really a childhood, and realizing your dream of becoming a responsible, beige-loving adult became a moral imperative to you for Bowie's sake, but, Hannah, I think you're missing the point."

She squeezes my hand, as though she's willing me enough strength to hear what she's saying. "It wasn't your mama's undone taxes, or job insecurity, or even her unsuccessful string of romances that made you feel so scared and unhappy growing up. It's because she wasn't there for you. When you needed her to kiss your ouchies or make you a damn peanut butter sandwich or fill out your financial aid forms, she just wasn't there."

Kira's lovely face blurs in my wet eyes, and all I can do is squeeze her hand back because my throat is too swollen to speak.

"You are there for Bowie. You will *always* be there for Bowie, and I guarantee that's all that boy will ever care about. Not your job and definitely not how much of an 'adult' you are." Kira lifts our joined hands and brings them down on the table for emphasis. "He can handle whatever else happens because you *are there* for him."

She smiles at me, tears shining in her eyes now, too.

"You can buy whatever color furniture you want."

≈

When the morning comes, I have a wicked sodium hangover and an intense need to shower off the teriyaki. As I close the bathroom door, a true parental luxury, I leave Kira chasing Bowie and June around her ottoman on all fours, cackling maniacally. My heart twinges for her and her dreams of a big family. She'd be getting loaded with sperm tomorrow, had I not convinced her to cancel the appointment. After the shower, I pull out my phone and tap out a quick text.

Hannah

Hey, Matts. You there?

Mattie

Yes.

Hannah

Where are you? When are you coming home?

Mattie

I mean, I'm literally here. I'm in my car parked three houses down. Been here since yesterday.

Hannah

What?? Like a stakeout?? Is this Law & Order?

Mattie

If by stakeout, you mean so confused you cannot figure out what to do with your corporeal form, so you just sit in proximity to the people you love the most and cry a lot, then yes.

Hannah

Aww, Matts. Come inside. Y'all need to talk to each other.

Mattie

I can't give her what she wants, Hannah. It's either shut up and let another terrifying pregnancy happen, or face her unending wrath. There's no viable option.

Hannah

Living in your car is not a viable option, either. Besides, you don't know that until you talk to her.

Mattie

You know, with all these food delivery apps, it's not as inconvenient as you'd think. Bathroom's tricky, tho.

Hannah

Mattie. She canceled the appointment. Come inside.

Mattie

. . .

Okay. Tell her I'm coming in, but I need fifteen minutes of amnesty before the talking begins.

I *really* have to go to the bathroom.

I stay long enough to usher Mattie to the bathroom as promised, because let's face it—Kira's not above withholding access to amenities to get what she wants. Kira walks me to the door and gives me and Bowie a long, long hug.

"Thank you for being here," she whispers into my shoulder.

"Thank you for being you."

"Are you heading back home?" Kira asks when she finally releases me.

My mouth bunches to the side. "No. Not yet."

Kira squeezes my arm. "Text me after you talk to Killian."

"Love you."

"Love you, too."

The ride to Killian's from Kira's is short and a well-worn path for me, having made this trip so many times before. Killian was delighted when I asked if we could stop by. He hasn't seen Bowie since Thanksgiving. I didn't think it was a good idea for him to visit while Darryl's recovering, considering the stress it might cause. Killian's been understanding, though, and he hasn't brought up the proposal once. I'm grateful for the space he implicitly knew I needed, and for how good he's gotten at considering my needs at all. So much has changed since I found that ring in his boot, and yet, here we are, still trying to answer the Big Question. So weird how that works.

When he opens the front door, the first thing he does is hug me.

"I'm so sorry, Hannah."

The apology feels all-encompassing, like it's for Darryl and the hardships we're facing, for his small part in that day, and for his larger part in everything else.

"Thanks." I smile sadly as he releases me, then moves aside to let us in. I'm pleasantly surprised to see he's decorated the place a little. He's hung his favorite album covers on the walls and set up his vinyl collection in the living room. His guitars are all out, too, along with his practice amp, and a new stool for playing. There's some incredibly tacky rope lighting he's run along the ceiling, but I keep my mouth shut. I like that he's figuring out how to make this place a home.

"You got a tree!" My eyes light up at the small, skinny tree in the corner of the living room. Artificial because that's how Killian rolls, but I won't hold it against him. It's surrounded by presents for Bowie already, which is alarming since December's barely begun. I look at him, eyebrows raised.

He laughs and shrugs one shoulder. "I got a little carried away."

He holds his arms out, and Bowie goes to him gladly. It thaws me from the inside out. It really has been such a hard few weeks. Even before the heart attack and the ongoing hostilities with Mama, the McFartys, my fuckup, the loss of our Airbnb and business and the confidence they'd given me . . .

River. My eyes squeeze close. *River.*

The visit with Killian is nice, though. Bowie scoots around like lightning on the rug while Killian lies down and lets him crawl over him, and their laughter fills the cracks in my mood, smoothing them over so I can function again.

When Bowie decides it's boob o'clock, Killian starts to leave the room, but I tug on his shirt. "No, stay."

"Okay." He settles beside me. When he offers me his hand, I take it and hold it tight.

"We can't get married, Killian."

He takes a deep breath in, then deflates. After a long, quiet minute, he says, "I thought you might say that."

"I always thought Bowie having two parents in a stable home was best for him, but I don't think that's true anymore." The words come out slow and unsure. It feels so wrong to negate what I've believed for so long to Killian, out loud, in the place I wanted to be our *home*.

But these words feel true.

"What matters is that Bowie has people who love him, who are there for him, whether or not they love each other."

"But I love you," Killian insists, his fingers gripping mine tightly. The tears welling in his crystal blue eyes make my heart hurt. "I know I missed my chance to prove that to you, but I do, Hannah."

"I love you, too, Killian." I smile through my tears. "You're the father of my baby, and when you're not being a dick, one of my closest friends. But it's not the kind of love that makes a happy marriage. I think we both know that."

I rise to leave, shifting Bowie's sleeping body to lie against my shoulder. The tears are streaming down Killian's face now, and I hate it for him, for all of us, really. But I can't make something true when it's not.

"See you next week, Daddy?" I run my hand across his shoulder, and he covers my hand with his, squeezes it.

After a long, halting breath, he looks up at me.

"Yeah. See you next week."

CHAPTER TWENTY-EIGHT

I t's past dark as my old Corolla trawls its way up the mountain. Driving at night when we first moved here used to scare me. Now, I navigate to the cabin like a bird drawn to its nest by powers of recognition it doesn't even register. I hate that it feels like home, but also a trap I can't escape.

I want my own life. I want a place to live that conforms to my needs. I want, for once in my life, to be the main ingredient in the recipe, with everything else there to support *me*, to bring out *my* flavor. My stomach growls as I pull into my spot along the road. Really should have eaten dinner before leaving.

When I open the door, the cabin's quiet except for the low rumble of the fire in the hearth. Mama looks up from her crosswords chair.

"I ordered Chinese after Darryl tucked in," she says by way of greeting. "Don't tell him. Can't have it because of the sodium." She stands and stretches with her palms pressed flat against her back. "Got you your favorite."

It takes me a minute to realize what Mama thinks that is. "Sesame chicken?"

Mama flaps a tired hand at me. "That's the one."

The corners of my mouth quirk up. I haven't eaten sesame chicken since I was in high school. It's mall Chinese cuisine at its finest, but a minute in the microwave later, and the sticky, sweet smell has my mouth watering. Mama joins me at the table, and we watch in silence as Bowie crawls around in the baby corral at our feet, getting the last wiggles out for the day.

"How's Kiki doing?" Her voice is cautious with me, always so cautious these days.

"Mattie came back, so better, but . . ." I pause to stuff a bite of sweet fried chicken in my mouth. "They've got a lot to talk about before things get right again."

Just like we do.

Mama sips at a mug of chamomile tea, the faint smell of honey surrounding her like a tiny spot of summer in the middle of all this cold. I think she's been waiting for me to bring up our fight, and for some reason, I keep refusing to. Maybe I've been hoping my feelings would change—that I'd realize I don't want to move out, that I'm happy here just as things are. But that's not true. Everything else I said in anger—that she didn't raise me, that I'd survive if she left me again—those words *are* true, and I'm not taking them back. There is one thing left to say, though.

"I told Killian no."

Mama *mmms* over the rim of her cup. I wait for her to *Praise Jesus!* and pull out her crystals to kiss or something. She takes another sip, unexpectedly solemn.

"Well?"

"Hannah, you've already proven you're a thousand times smarter than I ever was." She sighs, her cheeks sagging. The outline of her smile is still there, though, the imprint of happier times. "Only a fool would've taken that boy back." When the lines gather, her smile is rueful. "A fool like me. And thank God for everybody here, you're no fool."

"You didn't think so on Thanksgiving." The memory of being called stupid by my own mother still hurts.

"I was scared you'd make the same decision I did when I was your age." She mulls over her tea for a long moment. "There was a time when all I wanted was a man. Any man. I was so desperate, I let any old bastard with half a heart into my life."

I raise an eyebrow.

She sees it and reconsiders. "*Our* lives. When I saw that boy on the ground and you really considering it, after all he did to you? It broke my heart seeing you live under the same damn delusions I did."

I push back from the table. "I don't just *want a man*, Mama. First of all, I'm bisexual, and second of all, what I want more than anything is—"

"To give Bowie a family, yeah, I know," Mama finishes for me. "Don't you see how they're the same?"

"No," I huff out.

"I watched you pine over that fairy tale of a family ever since you got pregnant. Even when Killian stayed out all day and night and left you alone with that baby, even when he criticized you. You took those punches because your fairy tale needed a warm body, and there he was. Just because you did it for Bowie instead of yourself doesn't change the bottom line, Hannah." Mama's smile turns into a grimace. "Settling for assholes is the family legacy."

I let the front legs of my chair rest slowly on the floor, unaware that I've been teetering this whole time. By trying so hard to be different than Mama, to give Bowie the family I never had growing up, I'd ended up repeating her same mistakes?

"Ain't that a motherfucker," I whisper. I never clocked that Mama's dogged pursuit of a partner was fueled by the same desperation I've felt about giving Bowie the perfect family. It helps me see some of her actions through different eyes.

Some.

Bowie lets out a sleepy *meh!* and raises his arms to be picked up. When I hoist him into my arms, he settles happily into the crook of my elbow for his good-night milk-snack. We fit together so naturally, it's instinct to us both. For me to hold, for him to be held.

But that's not true for every parent and every child.

"Why, Mama?" I breathe out, running my fingertip across his pale brow. "Why are you here for Bowie?" My exhausted eyes water on command, like troops reporting for duty. "But weren't there for me then?"

Mama's gaze breaks away reluctantly from Bowie to meet mine. She lowers her mug. "People learn how to live and love on their own timelines. Some people are born knowing what to do, and others take sixty years to figure it out."

I blink against the sting, but I've always known these would be the tears that hurt most. I push a lock of Bowie's blond, curly hair off his forehead, the sight of his face my safe space. "So I was shit out of luck. That's all you have to say?"

Mama's voice softens. "You are such an easy person to love, Hannah. You expect so little, and you give so much. You have always been the easiest part of my life. So I turned my attention to other, more difficult things. The unpaid bills. The asshole boyfriends. The loneliness that pummeled me from the moment you closed your eyes until you woke up again." Mama breathes deeply in. "I took advantage of how easy you made it for me, Hannah. I'm sorry, and I'll never do that to you again."

The tears slowly wend their way down my cheeks, and I let them. It's hard to grieve a childhood you didn't have, a mother who wasn't there, the feeling of safety that never came. Those empty apartments are written into my genetic code, shaping all my thoughts and decisions in ways I don't see until someone points them out to me.

"That's why you've got to move out."

My head jerks up. "*Now?* What about Darryl? How will y'all—"

"Get by?" Mama chuckles. "I can manage driving his old cantankerous ass around, and after this big a scare, he won't touch a cigarette again, I'll see to that."

"But"—I shake my head, the image of Darryl's gray, slack face flooding back—"what if something happens again?"

"You're so used to getting us out of trouble you don't know how to let us be. But I'm in a different time in my life, Hannah, and so is Darryl. We don't need you to take care of us anymore." Mama reaches out, strokes my hand. "And no offense, honey, but you mostly ran up and down the road screaming your head off."

Okay, fair.

"Look around us, baby." Mama gestures at the glowing logs in the fireplace, the windows fogged with steam. You can't see it for the dark, but the white forest is beyond, and the mountains rising and falling beneath our feet. "This place is magical. It is beyond my wildest dreams to be here, now, with my wonderful goofball husband, my talented and compassionate daughter, and my perfect, perfect grandson. I always believed things would work out for us, Hannah, and they did. They really did."

Her fingers squeeze around mine. "It's time for you to put your own needs first. And believe you me, we'll be there to support you every step of the way."

Her words don't change the past, they can't. But they do change the present, and I think, the future, too. The heaviness that settled over me the night of Darryl's heart attack begins to lift. I'm *not* trapped here. I don't think I ever was.

"I do have one request of you, though."

"It's not your taxes, is it?"

Mama's eyebrows rise. "Okay, two requests. But the first one's the most important. Try to stay in hollering distance. It's selfish, yes, but putting that aside, the mountains suit you, baby girl. I don't want you going back to Atlanta and working for some asshole when you could be here, working with us assholes." She smiles wearily. "We may not be the family you wanted for Bowie, but we will do our best for as long as we have left."

I wipe the last of my tears away and laugh a little.

"Okay. I'll think about it. But seriously, hire a tax professional, my *god*."

~

A deep sigh rattles out of me as I open the door to the Artist's Studio, a ridiculously cute store in downtown Blue Ridge. I got the call earlier that the wooden sign I custom-ordered for The Honey Jar was finally done, and I'll be damned if this isn't the weirdest walk of shame I've ever experienced.

"Hannah!" Kai, the petite Japanese owner of the shop, waves at me from behind the counter. She's one of those hopelessly cool people who can wear overalls without it looking like farmer cosplay. "The sign turned out so great, you're going to *love* it." She reaches for a package under the counter and lays it out before me.

I summon a smile and take a deep breath in, willing this not to hurt. I fold back the tissue paper, and the art is *exactly* as I pictured it. A honey jar in vivid tones of amber, with two dippers crossed at the bottom, outlined in black. The name, written in the beautiful, modern sans serif I'd imagined. Below the dippers is etched EST. 2024.

The irony is almost suffocating.

"Aww, what's wrong? Don't you like it?" Kai asks, mistaking my hitched breath. I quickly swipe at my eyes and laugh. "No, no, it's beautiful, Kai. I love it."

"Ooooh, that is *too cute,* Kai!" A voice like metal scraping across teeth bounces off my side.

"Madison." I utter her name like a curse as she leans over the counter on her elbows.

"Too bad it's useless since you've already gotten kicked off Airbnb." Madison smiles sweetly, but it looks more like a snake preparing to strike.

"Oh my God, I didn't know!" Kai says, legit horrified. "I'm so sorry, Hannah. If you don't want the—"

"I want it." I pull it quickly to my chest. "Thank you. How much do I owe you, Kai?"

"You know, Hannah, my offer still stands," Madison says as I hand over my pointless new business credit card. "Not the job offer, of course, we can't hire perverts, but we do specialize in turning around disaster rentals. You've still got my card?"

"I threw it away."

She reaches for a new one, but I hold my hand up to stop her. "Oops, I've thrown that one away, too."

She huffs out a laugh, but it doesn't sound nice. "I see. Well, the McFahertys are tough customers. Too bad they got the best of you."

My blood pressure spikes. "How'd you know their last name? It wasn't on the review."

"Oh, I think you know." Madison winks, and I want to punch her right in the eyelash extensions. "The rental community loves to gossip. Better luck next time! Bye, ladies!" With that, she prances out the door on the tips of her heeled boots.

She was involved. Oh my GOD, she set me up somehow!

"That woman is a sociopath," Kai says. She offers me a lollipop in consolation, and I rip the wrapper off with my teeth.

"She's going *down*."

When I get into my car, I fire off a litany of texts to Zoe, explaining all my suspicions.

P H

An Extremely Professional
Teacher-Pupil Relationship Text Chain

For studying purposes, only

Professor Zoe

THAT BITCH!!

Hannah

RIGHT?! But how do we prove it?

Professor Zoe

We've got to link her to your cabin's
sabotage somehow.

Hannah

I think she knows the McFahertys.
Maybe if I could find them, I could
figure out the link between them.

Professor Zoe

I . . . might know someone who could help.

Hannah

You've got a guy?

Professor Zoe

I've got a guy. Maybe.

Hannah

That's weirdly hot.

Professor Zoe

riiiiiiiiiight? 😉

Let me talk to him. I'll update you if he can help us out.

Hannah

!!!!Thank you!!!!

CHAPTER TWENTY-NINE

A week passes, but Zoe's guy isn't taking jobs anymore, and my own attempts at investigative research have all panned. The McFahertys, their ridiculous demands, the suitcases full of flour . . . It was all a setup, and I remain *convinced* Madison is at the center of it all. She's simply too bleached to be trusted.

Mama comes up and rubs my shoulders while I sit hunched over my laptop at the table. "Baby, why don't you call it a night? Come watch *The Nightmare Before Christmas*. I've got it all cued up and ready to go. We'll keep the volume low and won't disturb Bowie a lick. I'll even make hot chocolate." She gives me a big pleading smile, and I sigh, letting her close my laptop.

"That does sound good," I admit. I scrub my face with my hands, then stand and stretch. Three vertebrae pop in succession.

"Maybe it's time to give up the goose, baby." Mama reaches into the cabinet for the mini marshmallows. "I'm always up for an internet obsession, but this one doesn't seem fun at all."

"It'll be fun when I catch her." I take the mug of hot chocolate gratefully and ease into a recliner.

"Oh! That reminds me, you got a piece of mail." She places a holly green envelope in my hand.

"How on earth did that make you think of mail?" I mutter while I carefully open it. Might be a glitter bomb from Madison. I would *not* put it past her.

A short letter falls out, along with two golden tickets. My pulse picks up involuntarily when I see the handwriting.

Dear Hannah,

You probably want to throw this out unread, but please, we need to talk. Meet me on board the Blue Ridge Santa Train tomorrow at 5 p.m., and I'll tell you everything. I've included tickets for both you and Bowie.

—R

I turn the envelope over, but there's no stamp or address on the front. Just my name. I spin on Mama. "Did River drop this off today?"

"River?" She shrugs too theatrically for my liking. "I haven't the foggiest idea what you're talking about." She snatches up the tickets and *oohs*. "The Santa Train! You wanted to take Bowie, right?"

I raise a suspicious eyebrow. "Yes, but they were all sold out."

"Well, ain't that providence!" She stacks the tickets neatly on the table by the door, avoiding eye contact. "It's supposed to be fun. Everybody dresses up, the children go in their pajamas, and you can get your picture taken with Santa on board! Isn't that precious? Ms. Claus even reads *The Night Before Christmas!*"

"You're pushing this awfully hard, Mama." I cross my arms. "What do you know?"

"I just think you should go and hear him out, baby." She sprinkles a few extra marshmallows into my mug of hot chocolate and gives me her Cheshire cat grin. "Good thing I already washed Bowie's gingerbread pajamas. You should wear that pretty red sweater. The one with the big cow neck."

"*Cowl* neck."

"That's the one!" She settles into her own recliner, smug as fuck, and starts the movie. I sit back, dazed. What does River need to tell me that has to happen on the Santa Train? This doesn't sound like an *I'm so sorry, please take me back* letter.

What the *hell* is going on?

≈

The cold December wind bites at my nose, and I burrow further into my cow neck. *Cowl* neck, dammit. Bowie's all gaping-mouthed wonder at the loud hisses and clangs of the steam engine as we prepare to board, and for better or worse, I'm happy we're here. Santa's helpers are *everywhere.* The Blue Ridge Santa Train is a big community event, and I recognize several of my friends dressed as various Christmas characters. Kai's checking tickets, old Ms. Betty from class is giving out hot chocolates, and Booch is dressed like an old-timey conductor helping passengers find the right car to enter. No wonder there aren't any tickets left. Half the town is here.

"Hey, drama kid!" I haven't fully turned around before Diego envelops me in a big hug. Teddy's with him, too, dressed as an ornery gnome, his white beard ending at his belt buckle. "Season's greetings, miss!"

I snort, then press my hand to my mouth to stop. It fits him too well. "Is everyone I know working this event?"

"All the local businesses send a volunteer." Diego wags his eyebrows at me. They've been painted green. "Maybe next year you can volunteer, too?"

I smile. "Yeah. Maybe I will."

"Ahem!" Teddy bows to me, and it takes me a second to notice the red velvet pillow he's proffering and the small envelope on top. "Well, take it, wench!"

"All right, all right." I laugh and pluck the envelope with my free hand. "But can you please tell me what this is about?"

"How should I know? Ask the man-child, I'm just the delivery gnome." Teddy rolls his eyes, but he looks pleased, too.

"You better read that." Diego grins. "River's bartered a dental appointment for this delivery."

I smirk, a little charmed despite myself. I've been both dreading and absolutely *dying* to come today. I can't wait to see him, and yet, River's note was all business, no apologies, no nothing. I don't think I can handle being friends, and if that's what this is about, it will crush me. He's given me no reason to hope for more, and yet . . . here I am, wearing my best red lipstick.

I wait until after Teddy and Diego kiss me goodbye to open the letter, fingers trembling.

> Dear Hannah,
> If you're reading this, that means you came! I promise you, this will be worth it. You'll be boarding Car #4. At exactly 5:35 p.m., enter the line to take pictures with Santa in Car #1. I'll meet you there and explain everything.
>
>   -R

The mystery deepens. I frown down at the letter and read it again, but then it's our turn to board, and a giant abominable snowman holds out a furry paw to help me and Bowie climb up.

"Timmy, is that you?" I peer within the open mouth of the furry suit and find my tatted ex-con classmate grinning back. "It is!"

"Hey there, Miss Hannah. You have a merry Christmas now."

"You too, Timmy."

We take our seats, and Bowie's immediately delighted when Rudolph prances by and lets him touch his blinking nose. I hold Bowie a little closer as I laugh with him. I can handle this, *I can*. Despite my nerves, the festive atmosphere pulls me into its magic. The starry-eyed kids in their matching pajamas, the parents sharing sentimental glances over their heads. I take a sip of the special hot chocolate Ms. Betty slipped me and nearly cough it all over Bowie's head. It's *loaded* with peppermint schnapps. The train whistle blows three short bursts, the drive wheels rumble into motion, and we're tugged into the dark, snowy night.

As the minutes click closer to our 5:35 rendezvous, neither the Christmas caroling nor the schnapps dulls the anxiety gripping me. My neck is hot beneath my heavy sweater, and I wish for the hundredth time since setting foot aboard this train that I knew what River is up to.

At 5:25, I can wait no longer. I spring to my feet with Bowie, startling the Grinch passing out candy canes in the aisle. "Sorry!" I squeeze past and head toward Car #1. There, Santa's triple-wide holiday throne is still empty, and I'm first in the line for pictures. I look around for River, but my heart sinks.

He's not here.

I breathe deeply through my nose. He wouldn't go to the dentist for nothing. He'll show, *he will.*

From behind me, a loud handbell begins to ring. "Right this way for pictures with Santa!" The voice makes my stomach tighten.

Madison. Then she appears, and sweet Jesus, she's dressed as a sexy Mrs. Claus. Her red ruffled petticoat barely covers her ass, and she's wearing red patent leather stripper heels. I'm all for embracing sexuality, but that outfit topped with a gray curly wig and half-moon spectacles is going to confuse a generation of children. I whip around and pray she didn't see me, too.

"Ho, ho, ho!" Santa bellows as he appears in front of his throne, waving to the children waiting their turn. He's a little skinny for a Santa, which is weirdly disappointing.

"Time to make some holiday magic," a bored, nasal voice announces at the door to Car #1 from behind me. It brings a chill down my spine. Why do I know that voice? A yeti in a Christmas scarf removes the velvet rope from the line and gestures me and Bowie onto the dais. I scan the car quickly, then my watch: 5:32. River's still not here.

I actually have to go forward with this?

I climb the steps to the dais, and with extreme misgivings, hand Bowie over to Santa. Bowie's lip is trembling, and it's clear he's one second away from imploding with tears. The yeti takes one look at him and orders me to be in the picture, too.

"Do I have to?" I don't want to sit on this man's *lap*.

"We're on a schedule, people," the nasal voice announces. I'm positive it belongs to a woman with a clipboard and an earpiece. "Is there a problem?"

"No, no problem." I laugh uncertainly and take my place. The yuck feels bone-deep, but hesitating's just delaying the inevitable. Santa takes Bowie on one knee, and I miserably take my place above Santa's other leg, hovering over it like a dirty toilet. A dry, crusty hand finds my waist and brings me down, hard, onto his lap. The hand tightens, and I slide toward Santa's corpus, shoulder colliding with his chest.

And then I feel it.

Like a marble.

No, like a thumbtack.

NO. Like a marble impaled by a . . . nail?

NO! I gasp and recoil.

Like a *nipple*. It's currently corkscrewing into my shoulder.

I peel off Santa's crusty hand. "Get off me!"

The parents in line begin to murmur nervously as I grab Bowie from his arms. A few phones slip out.

"What is it *now*?" The clipboard woman bustles to the front of the line, and I get my first look at her. My eyes widen.

"You!"

The long brown hair, the big round glasses. It's Lolly McFaherty behind that clipboard, staring at my outraged face with an *Oh, fuck!* expression. Her name tag reads STEPHANIE CLAYTON, MGR. FESTIVE ENTERTAINMENT.

"Big yikes," Lolly says, slowly raising the clipboard up until it hides most of her face.

And just like that, it *allllll* comes together. Because I already know who this diamond nipple belongs to.

I swing around and yank his fake beard off.

"McFarty! Or is your real name *Santa*?"

The crowd appropriately gasps, though they can't be following what's really going on.

"You've got it all wrong!" His pink, scrubby face is filled with fear. "Can we go somewhere and talk about this privately?"

"Sure," I reply. "Right after I leave my review."

"Wha—"

"THIS SANTA IS A PERVERT! HE EXPOSED HIS OLD MAN DONG TO ME, AND HIS NIPPLES ARE LIKE ICEBERGS!" I yell out into the crowds. "*ZERO STARS!*"

"I *knew* it!" I swivel to see River pushing through the crowded car, his face blazing with victory. A bright green tunic stretches over his broad shoulders, his candy-cane striped tights outline every ripple of leg muscle, the silky plaid Scotty cap complete with red pom-pom sits jauntily on his golden head.

I have never wanted to fuck him more.

"You're here." I feel like crying and laughing and running for him, all at the same time.

"You're early." A hesitant, hopeful smile peeks out, but then he raises his finger into the air. "Hannah Tate, is this the man who posed as the guest named Bruce McFaherty and subsequently got your cabin thrown off the Airbnb platform?"

No. Now. *Now* I've never wanted to fuck River more.

"Yes!" I cry, and the crowd takes turns gaping at me and Santa.

River turns back to Bruce McFaherty, righteous fury narrowing his eyes. "Gerald Broder, director of the Blairsville Community Theater, do you confess to aiding and abetting Madison McGee and Beauty of Blue Ridge Rental Co. in an ongoing conspiracy to run independently operated cabin rentals out of business?"

The crowd explodes in shock.

"Beauty of Blue Ridge's crooked?"

"But Madison runs my cabin rental!"

"Mommy, is Santa going to jail?"

"I—I," Santa stutters, then stands and *runs*. He barrels through the crowd, which parts like hair to let him through.

For an instant, River stares in disbelief as Santa dashes away before he, too, launches after him, his candy-cane tights a blur of motion. "Stop that Santa!" he bellows.

"Where the hell they think they going?" someone's grandpa says. "Don't they know this train's moving?"

I hoist Bowie up higher on my hip and take off after them, too. It's hard running on a train, especially holding a tiny human. Every bump sends us careening, but we're not alone. Strong hands steady us, joining our pursuit as we race through the cars after a furious elf and a terrified Santa. Kai, Diego, and Teddy are right behind me, then Gus and Martha join, too. All the people I've come to know and love, and even more that I haven't met yet, are leaving their seats to watch this very unorthodox Christmas spectacle.

A loud commotion sounds from up ahead, and I crash into Car #4 in time to see Gloria and Maeve, dressed like nutcrackers if nutcrackers also played softball, block Santa's path with a cross of their bats-turned-candy-cane spears. River flies through the air in a flash of green, tackling Santa in a great big *OOF*.

"What in the world is going on, River Aronson?!" Madison stands up from her story-time station and tip-taps forward on her stripper heels, hands on her hips, looking stern as hell in her spectacles.

River's too busy wrestling Santa to answer, though, until finally he mounts him and jabs his finger into Santa's chest. "CONFESS, SANTA!"

"OKAY, OKAY, I CONFESS!" Gerald, aka McFarty, aka Santa, screeches. "Now get offa me!"

River's face breaks into a bloodthirsty grin, and okay, *now*, for real, I've never wanted to fuck him more.

He drags Santa up by his white fur collar and levels his gaze at Mrs. Claus now. "Your gig is up, Madison. I've linked you to the targeting and sabotage of over twenty-two cabin rentals in Blue Ridge, and I'm sure there's more."

"What are you talking about?" But her words are more a whisper of fear than a question.

"It's easy—your MO's always the same. You offer management services, and if turned down, you use a series of fake alias accounts to book up dates, then cancel at the last minute to deprive the cabin of rental income. I've linked them all to your IP address. If that doesn't scare the owners into your arms, you sic the worst guests imaginable on them, which is where Gerald here comes in." River shakes him by the collar. "But you're not content with tanking their rating. You plant evidence that gets them kicked off the platform. You've faked bed bugs, black mold, and now, sexual harassment."

Madison's crimson lips drop open just as mine do. I knew she was involved, but I didn't realize it went *this* far. The spying, the cancelations that started shortly after, the job offer that, once I spurned it, triggered an all-out blitz on me and our cabin. I bet she was the one who ratted us out to the permit office, too. It was all *this* little bitch!

The train churns to a halt. Conductor Booch's coming through the train, yelling that we've arrived at the North Pole, and to please exit in an orderly fashion to get our complimentary Christmas bells. He stops dead when he sees half the train stuffed into Car #4, voices getting louder and angrier as more townspeople realize that they, too, have been duped into giving their cabin rental business to Madison, whose cut is so large, it's predatory.

"Well, hell," Booch mutters, eyes wide.

"Alert the authorities, Conductor," River says. "These people are wanted for questioning for criminal conspiracy, racketeering, and fraud."

I'm pretty sure none of that is true, at least not yet, but it's so endearing I want to grab River by the candy cane and kiss him anyway.

Timmy, the abominable snowman, appears holding Stephanie by the arm. "This one was hiding in the toilets, River."

"Thank you, Timmy," River says. "Please escort her, Gerald, and Madison off the train. The Blue Ridge PD can take it from here."

The crowds disperse in a frenzy of fast-paced gossip until Car #4 is empty except for River, Bowie, and me. River readjusts his Scotty cap, which fell off during the tussle with Santa, and clears his throat awkwardly.

"Thanks for coming. I . . . wasn't sure you would." His warm, brown eyes are strangely timid as he meets mine.

I hiccup out a laugh. "And miss the most exciting Christmas exposé this town's ever seen? Not for the world."

His smile is small and bashful. "Yeah. I wanted it to be public so that more people would come forward, and I also needed you to identify Gerald to confirm my theory. Win-win."

I shake my head. "That was incredible, River. But how'd you find the McFartys? How did you know?"

"The key was Madison. You suspected her all along, I just had to connect the dots." River shrugs, but his smile grows. "I was a fraud investigator, remember? Turns out my old laptop still boots up, and so does that side of my brain."

My mouth hangs open. "*You're* Zoe's guy? But that means . . . you got online? For *me*?"

River's eyes grow wistful. "Hannah, I'd do anything for you. I'm so sorry it took me ruining everything to figure that out."

"But your philosophy—"

"—is a fancy way of walling myself off from people who've hurt me." River takes a small step forward. "You told me that, but I didn't want to hear it. I thought you wanted me to change, to fall in line, just like my parents did, and my old bosses, too. It took me losing you to realize that *love* makes us change. It makes us tear down our walls and change our minds. I realized that when I missed you so bad, I finally set up that new phone. I read every text you sent, laughed at every picture. When I finished, I went back and read them again and again. Then I called Zoe." He snorts a little. "She didn't believe it was me at first. She told me everything you told her, about how you felt, how I was too scared to be vulnerable, and it finally got through my thick skull." He swallows. "You understood me before I did."

I blink, a tear rolling down my cheek. "But what about now? Are we—"

He reaches out his hand and leaves it hanging in the air, a question.

One I can't wait to answer. I clasp his hand and pull him to me. His head dips low, pressing his forehead against mine. His other arm wraps around me and Bowie both, and we stand there like that, the feelings running through us like current. Hot, sparking, blissfully alive.

"I should have asked you this a long time ago." He presses his soft, full lips to my forehead in a whisper of a kiss, and my insides levitate toward it, like leaves to sunlight. "But can I get them digits, Hannah Tate?"

I burst out laughing, until his hungry mouth covers mine, as though this kiss has to make up for every day we've spent apart. Bowie gurgles in pleasant confusion between us, batting River's face with his hands and *bleh-bleh-bleh*'ing like, *Welcome back, bro. Hurt my mom again, and I'll end you.*

We break apart, grinning at each other, the happy tears in my eyes reflected in his. He runs his hand down the side of my face, and I lean into it.

"Hannah, I'm so sorry that I wasn't there for you when you needed me. I swear I'll never create distance between us again. But"—his brow furrows—"I'm never going to be like Killian. That's not who I am. But if you want *me*, I'm yours."

"Oh, River." I bring his hand to my mouth and kiss his strong knuckles. "I don't want anyone else. But you've got to start going to the dentist."

River groans to the ceiling, and I laugh from within his arms.

When we finally disembark, flashing blue lights illuminate the snowy Christmas village. It's not every day you see Santa, Mrs. Claus, and a Gen Z'er pushed into the back of the same police car. I'm not sure how to feel about Gerald and Stephanie getting arrested, too. They were just people doing a job, but they *did* try to ruin my life. I pause by the open window of the police car where Santa's sad mug peeks out, a feeling of charity and goodish-will sweeping through me.

"You should really get those nipples checked out, Gerald." I frown at him. "They're not right."

Then, because I've always wanted to, I slap the top of the police car and say, "That's all, boys. Take them away."

CHAPTER THIRTY

The warm touch trails from my shoulder down the curve of my waist before gently hooking around my hip. "Your alarm's going off, Ms. Tate."

"Mmm," I grumble without opening my eyes, but I can't stop the smile from forming. "Digital or human?"

"Digital," River says, and I can hear the returning smile in his voice. He pulls me by the hip until I'm pressed flush against him. He's *delightfully* hard. "May I throw it against the wall for you?"

"But then how will I get your bizarre texts?"

He rolls onto his back in the bed we made, taking me with him, and I finally open my eyes. He's smirking at me, his messy hair lying in a halo around his gorgeous face. "I'm new to this texting thing, okay? Cut me some slack."

"I'll do no such thing." I press my hands against his shoulders, arching my back until I'm up, straddling his hips, fitting perfectly against him. The pleasure radiates from where we connect, warm and aching. I lean over to the side table to turn my alarm off without leaving my perch, and because I abuse power when given too much, I fake a gasp. "Oh, look at the time! Sorry, handsome, you gotta scat."

And because he knows my tricks by now, he clenches his jaw and readjusts until we're a mere nudge away from having a *fantastic* morning. "Are you sure, beautiful?"

I tilt my head. "Hmmm, make it fast. But not too fast." I grin at him wickedly until his push slides my mouth into a moan.

God*damn*, I love my life now.

Twenty minutes and a pair of mind-shattering orgasms later, I pant against his chest, "Okay, but for real. You gotta git. Your cousin'll be here in an hour."

He raises his fist into the air. "Fie you, Zoe!" His arms pull me into a final kiss, and when our lips part, he whispers against me, "I'm going to miss this place. Having you in my bed every night and morning."

I smile sadly. "Me too. But it's for the good of the republic."

It took Kira less than forty-eight hours to contact the Airbnb Resolution Center, present the police reports documenting the McFartys' confessions, and get The Honey Jar listing reactivated and back in business. Mama danced for a full five minutes when we got the good news, which is saying something since there was no music playing. With the horrendous review scrubbed from the internet and our good names restored, the bookings have been rolling in, and today's our first day back. We're so busy, we're doing same-day flips for the next six weeks.

But as happy as that makes me, I'm sad to lose the little home River and I have made down here. Not for the first time, the thought of asking River to move in with me and Bowie somewhere crosses my mind, but the idea makes me skittish. I don't want River to think I'm asking for too many changes too fast. It's been a lesson in patience and negotiation as we've carefully worked through his boundaries, which ones will stay (his occasional need for alone time) and which ones will go (his secrecy about those needs). It's hard not to be greedy when it comes to River, but I'm trying.

By the time Zoe arrives, River's cleared out, I've cleaned the place, and Bowie's had breakfast. I greet her at the door with a giant box of decorations, brimming with holiday enthusiasm. Zoe is a fantastic helper. Not only does she have a great eye for decorating, she's also an amazing photographer. We plump, fluff, smooth, hang, tack, and arrange until the cabin is so freaking hygge, Zoe has to wrestle me away. I just want to read my romance novels by the fire, surrounded by luxurious fabrics in shades of ivory and taupe, black buffalo plaid, and pillows, pillows, *pillows*. I groan gutturally as Zoe forces me off the downy couch so she can take pictures of *The Honey Jar, Generic Holiday Edition* for the website.

"It's beautiful," I whisper, thumbing a pretend tear from my eye. The fire is blazing, the scent of fir is heavy in the air, and the treat socks are stuffed and hung neatly in a row. Zoe joins me by the door and slings an arm over my shoulders.

"And a very, merry Plaidmas to us all," she says solemnly, and I thwack her with a pillow right in the face. Buffalo plaid, of course.

My phone buzzes in my pocket, but I don't recognize the numbers that flash across the screen.

"Hello?"

"Hannah, s'that you?" The voice on the other end is fuzzy and cracked, but I can't tell if it's the reception or just him.

"Sergeant?" I laugh, a little startled. "Everything okay, sir?"

"Got somethin' to discuss with you. Can you swing by later?"

I raise my eyebrows at Zoe. "Sure. I'll stop by this afternoon."

The line disconnects, and my hand drops to my side. What the hell could Sergeant want to discuss with *me*?

≈

"Knock, knock," I call, rapping loud enough against the door so that Sarge won't mistake me for an intruder, which would likely be fatal. "It's Hannah, Sarge."

The front door swings open, and I'm shocked to see that his winter robe, a flannel affair lined with white sherpa wool, is nowhere to be seen. Instead, Sarge is wearing a worn plaid cowboy shirt with pearlescent snap buttons that I instantly covet and a tie covered with fish that I do not.

"Sarge! What's the occasion? You're all dressed up." I follow him into the homey cabin. I've never been inside before. The walls are the same honey pine of our cabin, but there's a lofted floor above where he's hung copper pots and iron pans of all sizes along the ledge, like a very dangerous beaded curtain into his kitchen.

Huh. I think Sarge's a foodie.

"This here's a business meeting, and I always dress for business." Sarge clears his throat and straightens his tie. *Sarge* looks *nervous*?

"Well, you look very nice, and your cabin is lovely," I say truthfully. It *is* lovely, even if it's covered by mounted guns on every surface. I'd probably have been terrified to come in when I first met Sarge, but now I know him to be a loving, eccentric gun fanatic who I will never have a political conversation with, ever. "Thank you for inviting me in."

Sarge gestures to a pair of wooden rocking chairs in front of his fireplace. "Please, have a seat. Would you like a cup of tea? I have Darjeeling or Lady Grey."

Sarge *is* a foodie.

"Lady Grey, please, with honey if you've got it."

"Fresh from the hive. I'll be back in a jiff. Make yourself comfortable."

When he returns, my outsides are happily toasty, and now it's up to the Lady Grey to finish the job. It's a bright, cold day, and the forest is a sparkling white limned in dark gray. I love this mountain no matter the season.

Sarge clears his throat again and sets his china cup down in a dainty floral saucer. "As you may recall, my daughter in Florida is pregnant."

"Martha told me she's due any day now, right?"

"That's right." Sarge sits back in his rocker with a contemplative frown. "I've enjoyed watching Trish and Darryl become grandparents. They make it look like fun."

"Yes, sir." I take another sip, still clueless why we're having this conversation.

"I've decided to try my hand at it," Sarge says. "Being a grandpa, that is. That's why I called you here."

"You want more baby-holding practice?"

"I want to sell you my cabin."

I do an honest-to-goodness spit-take. "You *what?*"

Sarge offers me a napkin so I can wipe my sloppy chin. "Martha doesn't want it, and I don't want it to go to some stranger, or worse"—he stops to scowl—"one of those rental company investors. I want it to go to somebody good, who loves this mountain like it deserves. I like thinking of you and Bowie living here, and maybe a beau, if it comes to that." He gives me a small, sly smile.

I place my cup and saucer down before I spill my tea. "Sarge, that is incredibly kind, but I don't have that kind of money." The settlement money's been spoken for—stashed, invested, and tucked out of my reach.

"I know," Sarge says. "But I also know you're good for it. I was thinking a small down payment, enough to buy my one-way ticket down to Florida, and then monthly installments for the next few years. Like rent, but to own." Sarge then pulls a folded piece of paper out of his shirt pocket and slides it across the side table to me. "That's my offer. You don't have to tell me—"

I glance at the paper and screech. "YES!" I jump from the rocking chair, waving the unfolded paper around like a golden ticket. *"ABSOLUTELY YES!"* I stop suddenly and fold my arms. "Counteroffer: if you throw in that shirt you're wearing, you can stay at The Honey Jar for free whenever you come visit, too." I hold my hand out to shake. "What do you say?"

Sarge frowns down at his epic cowboy shirt, then stands and shakes my hand. "You've got yourself a deal, Ms. Tate."

"Damn, Sarge, you don't have to take it off *now!*"

CHAPTER THIRTY-ONE

December has got to be the fastest month of the year. It's like the earth steps on the gas pedal just to screw with parents. Between the Airbnb and scrambling to buy presents and working out the details with Sarge and shopping for our big Christmas Eve dinner tonight, it feels like I've barely sat down for the last month.

I check my phone. River's coming over when he gets done with his carpentry project, around three. Killian will be here by five, and Kira, Mattie, and June are arriving shortly thereafter. After Thanks-God-for-not-killing-Darryl-giving, I'm understandably traumatized by the idea of mixing my parents, River, and Killian in a holiday feast environment, but Kira and Mattie have sworn to escort Killian to a safe house if needed. Mama and Darryl have also promised to be on their best behavior, and I have to hope that my family can actually family in peace.

A tiny reindeer crawls between my ankles lightning fast, nearly upsetting me and the hot apple pie I've just pulled from the oven. It unleashes a manic giggle.

"Watch out, reindeer on the loose!" Big Daddy calls belatedly as Bowie zips through the kitchen danger zone in his furry reindeer onesie-suit. G-ma scoops him up, and he giggles again, pure mischief, and I realize the family resemblance immediately.

"He sounds just like you!" I whirl on Big Daddy, hands on my hips. "You're a bad influence!"

"You just now figurin' that out?" Big Daddy laughs, the similarity between his and Bowie's glee uncanny. "I thought you were s'posed to be the smart one, too." He smacks the arm of his recliner. "C'mere, you little squirt!"

Bowie giggles and hides behind G-ma's frizzy ponytail. She sets him down at Big Daddy's feet, where he watches rapt as Big Daddy uses his remote control to make the new Lionel train and its string of merry red cars go round and round the tree on its tracks. He lets Bowie press the buttons, and the train whistles, chugs, and herky-jerks forward and backward. Bowie howls with delight, and so does Big Daddy.

I shake my head, smiling.

"Mayday, mayday!" G-ma calls from behind me. "I need cleanup on Aisle Three!"

Boy, does she ever. With our resident chef Big Daddy consigned to his chair, still too weak to stand up for more than a handful of minutes, the task of creating a magical Christmas feast has fallen to Mama. Don't get me wrong, her food is delicious, but that handy-dandy feat where you clean up as you go? Yeah. No.

I pop my knuckles, crack my neck, and reach for a rag when a pair of warm arms wraps around my waist from behind and a lush mouth covers my neck in kisses. Happiness floods my body.

"Hey, handsome." I *mmm* as River nuzzles into me. "You know what would be *really* hot?"

"Getting a rag and going to town on this kitchen?"

"You get me, babe."

He grins and gets to work beside me.

Killian arrives to the party thirty minutes early, but Mama doesn't chew him out for this transgression. To her credit, she gives him a big hug and welcomes him inside.

And promptly puts him to work building a fire.

Kira, Mattie, and June arrive thirty minutes late, which in Mama's book is right on time. There are hugs and squeals and even a few tears as Kira squeezes Big Daddy's neck extra hard.

"You asshole," she says, laughing and crying. "You scared the hell out of us."

"I ain't going nowhere, Kiki, I promise." His voice is gruff as he lets her go and wipes his own tears away. He doesn't talk about it much, but his near brush with death shook him up like a bottle of his beloved Mountain Dew. His doctors told us he's lucky to be alive, and the weight of that knowledge is both a gift and a responsibility he feels keenly.

The evening runs pretty smoothly, though I burn the biscuits and Mama spikes the cranberry holiday punch with vodka instead of champagne. Everybody's smiles are loose and easy, and the laughter comes and comes and comes. Even Killian's having a good time, and nobody tries to stab him. When we gather around the tree to do the night-before tradition of one gift each, Killian surprises me by raising his hand to go first.

"Bowie and I've got a gift for you, Hannah." He pulls a small, velvet box from his pocket.

Mama's smile falters, and Big Daddy takes a long, deep breath. My own eyes widen in horror, and I feel River tense beside me. *No, no, no, no, no, no, no.*

"Killian, we *talked*—"

"This is not a proposal, everyone! Please, calm down!" Killian raises his hands like a referee crying *Safe!*

The room exhales in unison.

"At least, not that kind."

"What in the *hell*—" Big Daddy begins, but G-ma shushes him.

"Hannah Cleopatra Tate," Killian says, proffering the box to me. "Mother of our beautiful child, and all-around wonderful human being, will you please do me the honor of being *my family*?"

He opens the box, and there it is. A necklace made from the rose gold engagement ring, its pink shimmery diamond hanging from the end of a delicate chain. The same one I found in the closet all those months ago, the same one I threw at his face, the same one he presumably tried to propose to me with a month ago.

This diamond's really been around.

"You were right—we have no business being married—but you're also right that we can still give our child a beautiful family life. I promise to always be there for you and Bowie, to give you the respect you deserve, provide the support you need, and give Bowie all the love in my heart." He pushes the box into my trembling hand. "I know we're family no matter what, Hannah, but when I first saw this ring, I knew it should be yours. It's beautiful and special and different, just like you. So, here. Please take it and know that I'm sorry for what I put you through before, and I'm grateful for all that you've given me since."

Damn, now I'm crying. I laugh a little, wiping the tears from my eyes, and take the box. When I glance up at River, he's beaming down at me.

I turn back to Killian as River helps put the necklace on me. "I accept your apologies and your proposal."

"To conscious co-parenting!" Mattie hollers, holding her punch cup up to cheers.

"To conscious co-parenting," the room echoes back with the merry clink of plastic cups.

G-ma smiles and brings Killian in for a big hug. "Welcome to the family officially, son." She does not miss the opportunity to hiss a threat into his ear that momentarily wipes the smile off his face before releasing him back into the festivities. He laughs a little, swallows, and accepts the backslaps of Big Daddy and Mattie, and also a face-slap from Bowie, who's happy to get in on the action.

"My turn," Mattie says, and turns to Kira. She grasps each of Kira's hands in her own and pulls them to her mouth, kissing them softly. "To my lovely, perfect wife, I want to give you everything in this world, even though I don't always know how."

Kira's breath hitches, her eyes full of a scared, delicate hope. Whatever's coming is a true surprise.

Mattie puts a brochure tied in a big red bow into Kira's outstretched hands.

"It's for an OB/GYN practice?" Kira's eyebrows flick together, then up at Mattie. "What's this about?"

"I did some research," Mattie says, then laughs nervously. "Okay, a *lot* of research. I looked at every OB/GYN practice in Atlanta until I found a practice run by Black women that specializes in providing the very best maternity and postpartum care to other Black women." She folds her hand over Kira's. "I cannot lie to you. The thought of you getting pregnant again makes me nervous as hell. But I'm never going to be a person who stands in your way, Kira. If this is what you want to do, it's what I want to do, too."

Kira's eyes are brimming now, but she laughs. "You're gonna make me drive all the way to Buckhead for these women?"

Mattie smiles ruefully. "Our first appointment is next week."

Kira covers her mouth with her hand. "I'll be ovulating!"

Big Daddy frowns. "This is gettin' intense."

"Already got the sperm from June's donor on lock, ready to blast," Mattie says. "All you've got to do is say the word."

"Okay, now." Big Daddy pulls his collar off his neck. "Y'all trying to give me another heart attack?"

"Semen!" Kira yells. "A thousand times semen!"

I'm laughing so hard I tip over and nearly get run over by the train. G-ma pulls the fir needles out of my hair as congratulations and hugs are shared all around. My heart feels so full for my two best friends. There's so much love there, it feels like something you can reach out and touch. Love and trust and yes, fear, but there's faith, too. And hope.

After that, we watch the babies "open" their night-before gifts. River's made a beautiful wooden train for Bowie and a carved dragon with working joints and wings for June. That he thought of June, too, earns him a spot in the Mattie-Kira Good Guys Hall of Fame.

But he still can't compete with the super deluxe Harry & David's Royal Pear Collection mega basket membership I bought them.

Amid all the revelry, I rest my back against G-ma's chair, letting my head lean against her knee. She brushes the hair off my face and tucks it behind my ear, like she did when I was a child. I'm overwhelmed in the best possible way, and her soft, unhurried touch brings me comfort, like it always did. I watch as Killian snuggles sleepy Reindeer Bowie in his arms, kissing his forehead while Bowie's eyes flutter unwillingly closed. Parents, *amirite*?

"Hannah, I have something for you, too." River brings his fist to his mouth and rumbles his throat, and it strikes me how nervous he looks. He hands me a piece of paper full of addresses.

"What's this?" I ask slowly, reading over each entry. Beside each address is a description of the house on that property. Mostly treehouses, but some tiny homes as well. I look up with an eyebrow raised. "There's a *yurt*?"

River's face cracks into a jittery smile. "Those are all my properties. I was thinking of putting them up for rent, and I hear treehouses do well on Airbnb. Maybe you're up for expanding your business?"

My mouth opens, and no sound comes out at first. "But, River, your place next door is on here, too."

"We could find a place together, somewhere that works for all of us, if you're ready." He takes my hand, his eyes searching mine. "I love you, Hannah Tate. I don't care that it's fast, I only care that it's real. I don't want to spend another minute of my life without you."

"That's funny," I say thickly, happy tears running down my cheeks. "Because I got you something, too."

The fear of blowing it, of rushing things, of making stupid, immature decisions that ruin everything kicks me like a reflex. But those are old Hannah's fears, and I'm not bringing them with me into this new era of my family's life. Hard pass. New Hannah trusts herself and what she wants.

And I want River. I want his big, goofy grin and joyful heart and incredible way of finding delight. I want his body wrapped around mine at the beginning and end of every day. I want my name on his lips, and my child in his arms. Maybe it's too soon, and maybe it's just like Mama, but I'm okay with that. I'm a lot like her, after all. How did she put it that night on the porch, when she explained how she found the strength to start over?

I'm an incredibly optimistic person, and also horny. I snort involuntarily, and River smiles back at me, confused. It takes me a minute to shift around enough to reach my pocket, but I find the key and pull it out. I dangle it until River reaches for it uncertainly, and I place it in his outstretched palm.

"I bought Sergeant's cabin, and I'm gonna need a contractor." I can't fight the joy rising on my face, relieved of the secret at last. "*And* the man I love."

"You *what now*?!" Mama shrieks, the first to react. "Praise Jesus! I'm never taking these crystals off again!" Mama rushes me, hugging me from the side, while Darryl just says, "Dayum!" over and over again, grinning like a fool, until he comes over and embraces us from the other side.

I can't take my eyes off River's, though. It's like watching the sunrise's first beams breaking over the lake, so heartbreakingly beautiful that for an instant, you grasp the tiniest bit of the infinite joy and beauty of this universe in your hand, and you wrap your fingers around it as tight as you can.

Mama and Darryl let me go, and I run my palm down the rough, warm skin of his jaw. He gathers me in his arms and tucks me beneath his chin. "So I've got the job?" he whispers into my hair.

"You're hired," I murmur back. "But I'm telling you now, I can only pay you in Pop-Tarts."

He throws his head back and laughs, and that feeling of home washes over me again. Somehow, I know I won't be leaving it ever again.

The room erupts in joyous yelping. G-ma's kissing Big Daddy, Mattie's kissing Kira, and June is blowing spit bubbles into Bowie's sleeping face, which is close enough. Killian gives me a high five and reaches over to shake River's hand. Cups are filled with more of G-ma's dangerous punch, and Big Daddy starts bellowing a raunchy version of "The Twelve Days of Christmas."

My heart is full.

ACKNOWLEDGMENTS

Y'all. These acknowledgments could be as long as the novel itself. I've got to thank all the people who cared, who chose to believe in me, even if just for a moment, instead of adding to the roaring symphony of *No!!* we all hear every day when we dare try something new. There's been so many over the years. How can I possibly list them all?

I can't. I tried, but I can't. Please check my website www.laurapiperlee .com for the complete unhinged version of my acknowledgments. Chances are, if you feel slighted after reading this, your due is over there. Here's the ultra-abridged version, though.

Thank you to all the writers and friends who've given me and my writing their time, love, and attention: the Mermaid Writing Group, Pitch Wars, ES Luken, Lindsay Hess, Dora Figueiredo, Lily Knoerzer, Kim Colyar, Elise Bungo, Kat Hinkel, Jennifer Camiccia, Marith Zoli, Molly Kasperek, Tom Torre, Ann Fraistat, Jahnisa Tate, Adam Gaylord, Joanna Visser Adjoian, Stephanie Heck, Rachel Lynn Solomon, Annette Christie, Jenny Howe, Camille Kellogg, Courtney Kae, Suzanne Park, Kerry Rea, Alexa Martin, and Jeff Zentner. I'm so, so lucky to know you. The world feels less lonely knowing you're in it.

To my agent, Carrie Pestritto, thank you for taking a chance on me and my wacky novels. You're a complete badass and a wonderful friend, and I want all the best things in the world for you. To my editor, Laura Schreiber, thank you for making my dreams come true. You're a true kindred spirit, a brilliant editor, and you like my jokes, which basically makes you perfect. I am so ecstatic to be working with you. To my critique partner, Leigh Mar, your sharp intuition, writing genius, and all-around brilliance is a big part of why I'm here. Thank you for all that you give me, and for being such an awesome friend, too.

To my team at Union Square and beyond, including Stefanie Chin, Jenny Lu, Daniel Denning, Elke Villa, Elena Blanco, Chris Vaccari, Jo Obarowski, Lindsay Herman, Amanda Englander, Vi-An Nguyen, Amber Williams, and Diane João, thank you for your hard work and support in making Hannah Tate something special. I feel so lucky to have y'all in my corner.

To my mom, Susanne, and my stepdad, Rick, I've always felt loved. That is the biggest thing anyone can give another person, and you gave it to me. Thank you for being my inspiration and for hawking my book at family funerals. I hope Honey Bear Hollow, your real-life Airbnb in Blue Ridge, gets a ton of business from this book, which is basically a novel-length commercial for y'all. You're welcome! To Christy, Guy, and the rest of my family, thank you for being such interesting people and for loving me so much. If I'm weird and funny, it's because of you. To Amy especially, thank you for being so supportive and screaming about my book to the target demographic. I love you all.

To my son, Leo, who might've been named Bowie if your daddy had gotten his way, this book is a keepsake of those first months with you. I don't want to forget a single moment spent being your mom. I love you more than anything. To my partner, Mark, this entire acknowledgments section could be about you, and I still wouldn't have enough space to acknowledge all that you've done and continue to do for me. Your support and belief in me has always been so rock solid. I wanted this for myself, so you did, too. Thank you for loving me. Thank you for being there.

Lastly, thank you, reader. You're holding a tiny piece of my heart in your hands. Thanks for spending time with it, and by proxy, me. I hope you enjoyed it.